Above All Women

The Story of the Virgin Mary

Above All Women

The Story of the Virgin Mary

Patricia Pfeiffer

WinePress Publishing
MUKILTEO, WA 98275

DEDICATION

To those I promised, and especially to my mother,

Effie Usher DeMars, who taught me to love literature.

AUTHOR'S NOTES

When I began teaching a class on the life of Jesus Christ, I had no intention of writing a book, but Mary came to life between the lines of scripture and insisted I write her story.

It was with prayer that I wrote about those days when Jesus of Nazareth walked this earth, and about his mother. Perhaps there is something new under the sun: a picture of Mary, the mother of Jesus, as a very human woman.

Where the Bible speaks, I have taken the Bible literally. Where it is silent, I used extensive research, common sense and imagination. There are no facts about Mary, except those in the Bible. I have included a list of scriptures where Mary is present, one of prophecy concerning her, and others where she may have been present. I encourage you to read them.

Since Bible scholars have disagreed for centuries as to the exact chronology of Jesus' life, I chose to follow Johnston M. Cheney's The Greatest Story.

Because of the similarity of names in the Bible, I have taken the liberty of changing some of those which would confuse the reader. John the Baptist I call Touchon John, to distinguish him from John the beloved disciple. Salome's son, James, is now Thunder James to distinguish him from Jesus' brother. City names and geographical places are called by the names used in that day rather than the modern ones: hence Kapher Nahum for Capernaum and Lake Gennesaret for the Sea of Galilee.

My purpose has been to acquaint readers with a Mary whose life will provide encouragement and direction in times just as troubled as those of her day.

I want to thank all the relatives and friends who encouraged me, my family who managed when I was grinding grain in Nazareth instead of frying hamburger, and my writer friends who never let me give up. Special thanks go to Kathy Callaway, without whom Mary would never have come out of the shadows.

CHARACTERS BY GROUPS

Mary's Family
+   MARY - The Virgin, mother of Jesus the Messiah
+   Eli - Mary's father in Nazareth
+   Anna - Mary's mother
+   Salome - Mary's older sister
+   Zebedee - Salome's husband in Kapher Nahum
+* Thunder James - older son of Zebedee and Salome, apostle
+* John - younger son of Zebedee and Salome, apostle
    Ancilla - Mary's younger sister, wife of Matthias of Cana
+   Elisabeth - cousin of Anna, wife of Zacharias
+   Zacharias - husband of Elisabeth, priest in Temple
+   John (Touchon John) - son of Zacharias and Elisabeth
      (John the Baptist and cousin of Jesus)
    Misheal - cousin of Anna, a former Essene

Joseph's family
+   Joseph - husband of Mary, the Virgin
+   Jacob - Joseph's father (deceased)
    Aaron - Joseph's uncle in Nazareth, brother of Jacob
    Huldah - Aaron's wife
+   Clopas - Joseph's oldest brother in Gabara
+   Rebecca - Clopas wife (the other Mary of the Bible)
+* three sons of Clopas and Rebecca: Thaddaeus, James the Less,
    Simon Zelotes (authorities do not agree on this), apostles
+   Matthias - Joseph's older brother, later apostle, husband of
      (1) Iris in Cana
      (2) Ancilla in Nazareth
+   Chuza - adopted son of Matthias
+   Joanna - daughter of Matthias and Iris

Family of Mary and Joseph
+   JESUS EMMANUEL - Jesus the Messiah, son of Mary and Son of
      God
~   Helen and Julia - twin daughters
+   Joses - oldest son of Mary and Joseph
    Drucilla - wife of Joses
    Joachin - oldest son of Joses and Drucilla
    Josiah - second son of Joses and Drucilla
    Jacob - third son of Joses and Drucilla
+   James - second son of Mary and Joseph
+   Jude - third son of Mary and Joseph
+   Simon - fourth son of Mary and Joseph
~   Elishaba - twin sister of Simon

People of Galilee
>   Ezekias - leader of Zealots, historical person
>   Ezra - next door neighbor of Eli and Anna
>   Sarah - Ezra's wife and friend of Anna
>   Jobab - Eli's head shepherd
>   Malchus - publican in Kapher Nahum
> + Magdalene - Mary of Magdala, Sherah's granddaughter
>   Sherah - harlot of Magdala

People of Kapher Nahum
> +* Andrew - brother of Cephas, apostle
> +* Cephas - Peter, brother of Andrew, apostle

Other Characters
> + Simeon - prophet in the Temple
> + Anna   - prophetess in the Temple
> + Pharisees - followers of a strict religious order
> + Herodians - followers of Herod Antipas
> + Scribes, rabbis, priests, lawyers, the Jews - religious leaders
> + Simon the Pharisee - of Magdala
> + Saul - called Paul after his conversion, later apostle

Disciples of Jesus the Messiah (^ mentioned in story)
> + ^John, ^James, ^Andrew, ^Cephas/Peter, ^Levi Matthew, ^Judas of
>   Kerioth, ^Simon Zelotes, ^Thaddeus,
>   ^James the Less, Thomas, Bartholemew, and Philip / later
> ^Matthias and ^Paul

Rulers of Israel at the time of Jesus the Messiah
> + Herod (The Great) - ruler of all Israel, 37 B.C. to 4 A.D.
> + Herod Archaelaus - son of Herod the Great, ruler of Judea Idumea
>   and Samaria after Herod, 4 A.D.- 6 A.D. deposed
> + Herod Antipas - son of Herod the Great, ruler of Galilee and Perea
>   after Herod, 4 - 39 A.D.
> + Herod Agrippa I - King of Israel from 43 A.D.
> + Herod Philip - son of Herod the Great, ruler of land northeast of
>   Sea of Galilee, 4 - 34 A.C.
>   Caesar Augustus - Roman emperor until 14 A.D.
>   Tiberias Caesar - Roman emperor after 14 A.D.
>   Pontius Pilate - Procurator of Judea 26-36 A.D.

* Apostles
+ Mentioned in the Bible
~ Mentioned, but not named

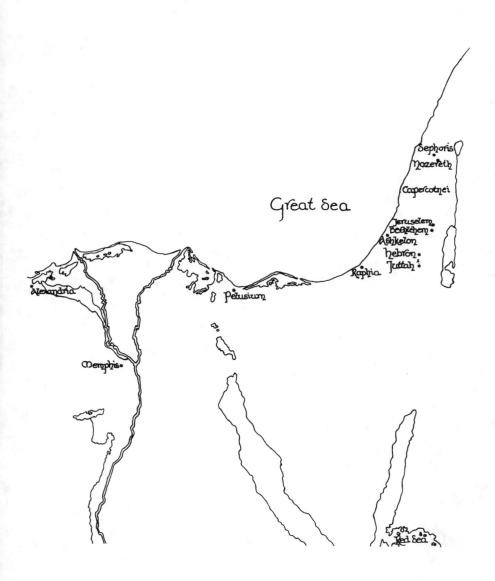

Great Sea

Sephoris
Nazereth
Capercotnei
Jeruselem
Bethlehem
Ashkelon
hebron
Juttah
Raphia
Pelusium
Alexandria
Memphis
Red Sea

PROLOGUE

Almost as an echo I hear the tramp of boots that fateful day in Nazareth, but this time it is on pavement here in Jerusalem. I see leather thongs pressing into swollen flesh, see ugly hair on thick calves as Herod's soldiers march past the house—peering into windows, courtyards, doors. I wish it were today that they might find me—that I might be with you, my Son.

The stamping halts. Spear handles clatter on stone. The leader inspects the corner building for a number, stares at the window where I hide behind a film of beaten parchment.

Blood pounds in my ears. I don't breathe. Is it now?

Although my hair has silvered, your words come back to me. I hear your voice as I prepared to take my first faltering steps in your kingdom, hear you telling me not to fear, that you are with me.

Keep looking, soldier. You cannot touch me until my time is come.

CHAPTER 1

Nestled among its drought-scarred hills, the village of Nazareth awoke to unexpected sleet, but six-year-old Mary woke to the familiar knot in her stomach. Whether it was from hunger or today's spectacle, she could not have told, for famine ruled Galilee. Every person whose legs would hold up a starving body lined the cobbled street that led to the square. Her family stood with neighbors in a narrow lane, hollow eyes straining to catch a glimpse of King Herod with his promised grain.

Mary huddled close to her mother while cold shivered her bony legs protruding from a cloak which only reached her knees. Her father, Eli, occasionally flopped two empty sacks slung over his shoulder, while mumbling discontent with his neighbors.

Eight months pregnant with the hoped-for son, Mary's mother, Anna, tried to pull her cloak more firmly around her stomach and squeezed Mary's shoulders. Salome, her sister older by six years, peered over her head up the Way of Cana.

"I hear something. Listen." She pinched Mary's arm. Mary stretched on tiptoe. Hoofbeats drummed on stone, nearer, nearer. People beyond them cheered:

"Herod! Herod! Herod!"

A trumpet blast ripped through the rain. People strained forward to see if it were really true—that grain was actually coming—grain for bread and for planting— King Herod himself bringing hope to starving Galilee.

"Herod! Herod! Herod!"

Mary grasped her mother's cloak tightly in her fingers. Wheels rumbled across the cobblestones. People backed one another against the wall behind them, making room for the cavalcade to pass. Trumpeters in scarlet lifted golden horns and blared a warning. Next she saw soldiers, three abreast, their lance points stabbing the sky.

Two prancing black horses pulled the king's ebony chariot, the first horses Mary had ever seen. She stared at their bulging eyes, arched necks, straining muscles. The driver, as dark as the horses, held them in check with silver harness.

Mary's big gray eyes widened more when she saw the king. Bracing himself with one hand, Herod languidly waved white fingers from a slit in a purple robe. Blond curls escaped from under a golden crown and wreathed a puffy face. He studied the people through half-lidded eyes. Mary glanced at her mother. "He looks evil." Her mother's hand closed sharply over her mouth.

After the king came soldiers tramping on huge legs, their leather boots slapping the cobbles.

Anna swayed. Mary snatched her mother's cloak, but it pulled through her fingers. A huge foot kicked her mother's stomach as she fell.

Eli grabbed his wife away before the wheels reached her. A wailing Salome covered her face with her hands, but Mary only stared at her mother. Then her eyes narrowed as she heard Herod snicker. Eli knelt beside his wife, along with their neighbor, Sarah.

Now the rain came down in sheets. Past them ten teams of mules pulled carts heavy-laden with grain, one after the other, the drivers swirling whips over their heads. The crowd surged after the last wagon, leaving Mary's family alone in the street with only Sarah. Salome wailed.

Eli wiped a trickle of water from his wife's cheekbone. Sarah said, "Hush, Salome," and held her fingers to Anna's temple. Salome stopped moaning and put an arm around her sister's waist.

"Is she—dead?" Mary could barely get the words past her lips.

"No," said Sarah and put a cheek close to Anna's face. She nodded her head. "She's breathing, but I doubt the babe will live. Here, Salome, give me your cloak." She covered Anna and stuffed her own cloak under Anna's feet. "A bit of color's coming to her cheeks." She poked Eli with a scrawny forefinger. "See?" Anna moved her head ever so slightly.

A dark-haired stranger in a black cloak slipped from an alley to stand beside them.

"Go get your grain," he said and nodded his head toward the crowd disappearing down the street.

Eli took a step, then hesitated.

"Go! Or you'll have nothing to feed your family. I'll carry her to your house."

Eli looked toward the grain wagons, then at his daughters. "Girls, go with your mother and Sarah."

The stranger lifted Anna's inert form and followed Sarah and Salome.

Mary darted into the first alley. She tripped and fell into the muddy water running down the cobblestones. She just laid there, tears rolling down her cheeks. Finally, she brushed them aside with the back of her hand and stood up. *Mother's going to die—and…I'm hungry.* Tears flowed afresh. From the square came distant shouts. While Mary sobbed, the rain fell steadily. Overhead a crow flapped across the sky.

A hand touched her shoulder. Mary drew into herself until she saw the hand belonged to a boy a few years older than herself. Soft brown eyes looked seriously into Mary's gray ones.

"Here, let me clean your face." He pulled a cloth from his pocket and wiped away the tears and dirt. "Are you hurt?"

"No." Mary swiped a sleeve across her nose. "Herod's soldier kicked my mother—in the stomach! And she might die—and my brother; he's not born yet." She pressed her lips tightly and swallowed sobs.

"My father and brothers hate what Herod does," the boy said. "They'll find that soldier." Suddenly he scrambled up the wall, looked about, then dropped back to the ground. He spoke close to her ear. "We are of the Cananeans."

"Oh!" Mary had heard her father and next-door neighbor, Ezra, talk of those men who risked their lives to free Israel from Roman rule. "I didn't know they came to Nazareth."

"We're everywhere we're needed." The boy nodded with importance. "That was my father who carried your

18

mother home. My family follows Ezekias. Do you know who he is?"

"No."

"Ezekias is our leader. Now you'd better see about your mother. Come, I'll go with you."

Mary smoothed her dripping hair behind her ears, wiped her nose on her cloak sleeve and led the way.

"What's your name?" he asked.

"Mary. My mother is from Nathan of the tribe of Judah." He pursed his lips and nodded. "Mary means stubborn." She felt she could confide in this boy. "And Mother says sometimes I am that way." His smile warmed her. "What are you called?"

"Joseph," he said. "Son of Solomon of the tribe of Judah." Mary turned quickly to look at him with new respect. He squared his shoulders. "I have the legal right through my ancestry to be King of Israel—after my brothers, of course, but none of us can be until our land is free. It will be soon, and then you won't have to be hungry or cry anymore."

"That's as may be," Mary said. She was always hungry.

She led him down a tunnel of streets and alleys toward her home. The rain, now turned to mist, dripped from the branches of olive and fig trees hidden in court-yards behind protecting walls.

CHAPTER 2

At her father's gate, Joseph squeezed her hand hard, then ran down the street. Mary felt a blush. She pushed the gate open and slipped inside the family courtyard. Halfway across it Salome sat beside the outdoor fire hole, feeding twigs into a small fire. Beyond stood the white-washed hut with stone steps leading to the shelter on the roof where she and Salome slept. An olive tree dripped water onto a stone bench beside the house.

The grinding trough was empty. Her father had not returned.

"Is Mother…?"

"She's inside with Sarah," Salome said. "The baby is coming, but not soon. Where have you been?"

Mary ignored the question and ran to the low door. She touched her fingertips to the mazuzah beside it and peered inside. Her mother lay on a bedmat. Sarah smiled at Mary.

"Your mother is doing well." Mary knelt and touched her mother's cold fingers. Anna made an effort to smile.

*

Outside Mary spread a mat on the ground beside the fire. Her sister wiped the grinding trough and pestle rock with her skirt.

"Father will be here soon with Herod's barley," Salome said. "Then we'll have bread. Bread, Mary, think of that."

"Herod laughed. Did you hear him?"

"He's insane, you know," Salome said in a lowered voice. "No one in the palace is safe from being poisoned, even his own children. I heard Father say so." Mary shivered and looked toward the gate.

"Don't be afraid. He'll never come to Nazareth again. He only came now to make us think he's a great king."

They huddled together, reaching their toes toward the fire. Mary saw again the way the soldier's boot had kicked her mother. She wished someone would kill him, but her father's words from the scriptures chided her. 'Lo, vengeance is mine: I will repay, saith the Lord...thou shalt not kill.'

Was my anger a sin? Mary looked into the sky. *Have I sinned, El Shaddai?* Mary listened, but God did not answer.

"Salome!" She dug her elbow into her sister's ribs, hoping Salome would not push her away as she usually did, because Salome was twelve and she was only six.

Salome opened sleepy eyes, her face blank. Mary nudged her again, then spoke quietly so the women inside could not hear.

"I hate Herod. Is that a sin? Should I tell Father?"

"No. Not now. When we are not so poor Father will

sacrifice a lamb for all of us at the Temple in Jerusalem."
She put an arm around Mary and patted her knee. "For
now, just think of your sin as already on the lamb's head—
and gone from you. That's the teaching of Moses, Mary.
Do you understand?" Mary nodded, leaned her head
against Salome's shoulder and waited her father's return.

Soon Eli came, carrying two sacks of grain. "Here,
daughters, we'll eat again." He rolled the sacks down
from his shoulders beside the fire hole.

Salome's fingers tore at the lacings and knots. She
dropped to her knees, poured a handful into the stone
grinding trough and pushed the stone furiously across
the barley kernels.

Eli paused to touch the mazuzah, then stooped to
enter.

"The baby is coming some time this night," Sarah
said, preparing to leave now that Eli had come. "Anna's
sleeping. Do not wake her." Sarah paused in the doorway. "When the baby comes, knock on my wall."

Later, as her father downed his last gulp of soup, he
said, "Drink slowly, Mary, your stomach is not used to
such a feast." He went inside with a cup for Anna. After
eating, the girls picked up waterpots and followed the
winding lanes to the spring outside Nazareth.

Night came as the girls finished a second cup of
broth and a thin barley cake. They climbed the steps to
the open shelter on the roof and crawled under their bed
rugs. Immediately Salome slept but not Mary. Through
the open sides of the shelter, she watched stars appear
and disappear among drifting clouds.

Some time in the night Mary awakened to hear her mother moaning and Sarah comforting her in the room below.

Hours later, Anna's scream woke both girls. Salome bolted upright.

"The baby's coming!" Quickly they crawled from the bed to peer over the low wall surrounding the roof.

They looked down to see their father praying. "God of our Fathers," he said, "Abraham, Isaac, Jacob, spare her life."

Never timid of her father as Mary was, Salome asked, "Is Mother all right?"

"Warm the gruel," he said. "She'll need food when this is done."

The girls sped down the stone steps. Mary blew on the fire and pushed twigs under the pot. Eli sat on the bench, shoulders hunched. Above him a hint of morning breeze stirred the leaves while he went on whispering prayers. Inside Sarah fought for Anna's life and the baby's, encouraging, speaking firmly, refusing to let her friend give up.

Another hour passed while clouds chased each other across a star-pricked sky. Inside the house Sarah's voice soothed Anna.

"There now," said Sarah, "one more time. It will be over in just a little while."

"Come, Eli. We have a baby girl."

Eli knelt beside his wife and lifted her fingers to his lips, then glanced at the tiny baby. His face contorted.

24

"Its legs are broken!" he cried. "The soldier did this thing." His face darkened with rage. "May God do unto him and more so as he deserves."

"No," Sarah said calmly. "These little legs are twisted from lack of nourishment. Sarah began rubbing salt briskly on the tiny blue form. It mewed feebly. "Feel not so badly, Eli. You have a live child—and a wife, for which you must never cease to thank a merciful God."

Eli strode across the courtyard, slamming the gate behind him. After Sarah cleaned Anna and the baby, she called the girls inside. They stood looking down at their mother, beads of sweat glistening on her ash-gray skin. She lifted her hand in a feeble greeting.

"See what a beautiful sister you have," said Sarah as she began winding strips of linen around the baby.

It looks more like a dead monkey I saw in the market at Festival. Mary looked at her mother, whose eyes were now closed although a tear trickled down one cheek.

Salome moved closer. "She's crippled?"

"Yes, my child," said Sarah, winding bands of clean linen around the baby, making a tight cocoon. "I doubt her legs will ever be straight. Probably she won't ever walk." Now she held the bundle against her chest and gently massaged the baby's back until its crying ceased.

Mary wished Sarah would let her hold the baby, let her massage the legs. "Did the soldier cause it?" she asked, scowling much as did her father.

"It's more likely your mother didn't get enough food." Sarah laid the baby in the crook of Anna's arm, smoothing Anna's hair from her forehead. The weary eyes half opened.

"Anna," Sarah said softly but firmly. "You must eat as much as you can to give this baby some strength."

Anna nodded and squeezed the baby closer. Sarah looked at Salome. "You must see that she eats." Salome brought a cup of warm soup for Anna, who tried to smile and took a few sips.

Then Sarah put the baby in Mary's arms. The girl gently fingered the linen where the legs would be. The baby opened one eye, her look seemed to scold Mary.

"She looked at me! I want to name her. May I?"

"We'll ask your father," her mother answered.

"You can't name her for eight days." Salome's sharp voice broke Mary's reverie. "Not 'til Naming Day or the demons will hear it and take her away."

Mary had forgotten. Silently, she looked down at the baby. *I'll call you Ancilla because it sounds like a princess. And Mara, bitter.*

CHAPTER 3

Eli stooped to enter the hut with a nod of dismissal to his daughters. They hurried into the courtyard and sat beside the firehole, listening intently. "Cousin Zebedee in Kapher Nahum—down by the sea. He's a fisherman there…has a whole fleet of boats. Makes trip often."

"I will be gone two days," their father said when he came outside. "Sarah will help you with your mother. Cook grain sparingly. We have no promise of more, and crops may fail again." He took an oak staff leaning against the wall and left them.

Two days later in shimmering afternoon sunlight, Eli returned.

"Anna, we have good news," he said to his wife, who sat under the olive tree. He leaned his staff against the house and sat down heavily beside her.

"Mary," he beckoned with a forefinger. Mary stood before him, her hands clasped behind her back, a tiny worm of worry niggling inside, like it always did whenever her father spoke directly to her.

"You know that Nazareth is not in God's favor and Herod's grain will not last the summer. It will help our family if we have one less mouth to feed. You are to go to your mother's cousin, Elisabeth, in Juttah."

Mary bit a knuckle.

Anna put an arm around Mary and drew her to herself. "You will like Elisabeth, Mary. She is a kind person, but has no children of her own."

"When do I...go?" Mary managed to ask.

"Next week," her father answered. "Zebedee will come by on one of his deliveries and take you."

Anna turned Mary toward the door, "Let us go inside." Once out of her father's sight, Mary sobbed soundlessly on her mother's soft stomach.

"I do...not...want...to leave you and baby."

"I know." Mary thought her mother looked sad and would be as lonely as she, but Anna would have Ancilla. "We must do what we must do and be cheerful about it."

"I will try to," Mary said as she wiped tears. She looked about the familiar hut—at the firehole, at the three clay lamps setting on their protruding stones, at the cedar chest which she knew held mysteries and riches she'd never seen.

"Why doesn't Salome go?" she asked.

"Salome is needed here," her mother said, picking up baby Ancilla.

Anna watched from the bench as both Salome and Mary ran to the gate at the sound of hooves. Salome opened it to a laughing man much taller and darker than Eli.

"Ah, hah, little cousins." His voice filled the courtyard.

"This bit of a girl with hair to her knees must be Mary and this beautiful girl must be Salome."

Mary blushed, but Salome thanked him prettily.

"Zebedee, so soon? I thought it would be another week," said Anna.

"Got an order from Memphis. I'll go by way of Samaria. It's shorter."

Zebedee's great, calloused hand rubbed Mary's head. "I'll set you on my lead donkey right beside me and hope I don't pay export tax on you when I pass through villages." A great jolly laugh made Salome smile at him, showing off pearly teeth against red lips.

"Do you go now, or do you spend the night?" Anna asked.

"I will go as soon as Mary is ready. I have six men and laden camels in the square."

Mary followed her mother inside the hut, and Salome stepped closer to Zebedee. "Let me give you a drink of water," she said with her most glowing smile, the one that never failed with her father. "Here is some of Nazareth's famous clear water." She poured it from a skin bag into a mug.

"Thank you, cousin." Zebedee tilted her chin up and turned her face a bit. "How old are you, child? Twelve? I must speak to your father about you."

Salome did not blush or dip her head. Instead she held his eyes with hers. "I will be proud—if Father agrees."

"He'll agree," Zebedee said and drained the mug.

Anna and Mary stepped from the doorway, Mary holding all she possessed wrapped in her cloak.

"She has so little, Zebedee," Anna said, "only an extra undergarment and tunic. She doesn't even have other sandals. The times have been so hard."

"Do not let that worry you. Elisabeth will take pleasure in dressing the child." He held the gate open. "Tell Eli I am sorry to miss him."

Anna gave her daughter a hug. Mary waved at Salome and followed this loud-voiced stranger down the street, away from all she knew. Her tears blurred the familiar lane as they walked toward the square.

I wonder how long I'll be gone? But I shall see the Temple, where God lives, and Bethlehem, where the great King David was born. And I am David's descendant. I could be king if I were a boy—and of Solomon's line, like Joseph.

Then Mary's heart lightened and she gave a little skip. She looked up at Zebedee and shyly took his hand.

They came at last to Jerusalem by the Way of Ephrath on the west. The city lay spread below them with Mount Olivet lifting its face to the sun on the east side. Mary wanted to stop, but the donkey toiled along so slowly that she could ask Zebedee about each building.

"There's the Temple, girl, behind those walls. I don't suppose Eli ever brought you here. Look at it."

"So much gold!"

"There's more gold on that roof than Solomon ever owned, and Herod's leveling the mountain at Gilgal, cutting white marble to make it larger."

Mary swept her arms in an arc, pointing to splendid buildings and listened as Zebedee told her what they were. To the north of the temple wall rose the new

Roman fort of gray sandstone, higher than all other buildings except for the most holy part of the Temple.

"What's that palace below us with all the water?" Mary looked back over her shoulder as the donkey and camels trudged on. She pointed to the splendor of fountains and three watch towers thrusting into the sky. "It's more splendid than the Temple."

"King Herod's, but don't let anyone hear you compare it to the Temple. One thing both Herod and Augustus do is provide work. See over there is the stadium and the amphitheater—and the high priest's palace."

The donkey never varied its pace—away from Nazareth.

"I usually stop there, Little Mary, and sell my special pickled fish to Annas the High Priest, but this load is for Egypt." Mary knew now about Zebedee's special dried and pickled fish. She'd smelt them all this distance.

Mary wished they could have stopped, wished her mother could have seen the splendor with her. She wiped away tears with her forefinger and glanced at Zebedee to see if he had noticed.

In the hill country to the south, Mary forgot Jerusalem. Chrysanthemums turned whole hillsides into Oriental carpets, yellow with patches of red pheasant's eye and poppies, pink cyclamen and hollyhocks, purple sea lavender and blue cornflowers. Spring bathed the air in fragrance. Greenfinches sang as though to burst their throats, but Mary's throat felt dry the nearer they came to Juttah. But first they must pass through Bethlehem.

"That's King David's village, Mary." Zebedee pointed ahead.

She looked at the massive stone caravansary outside the gate, across the hillside to flocks of sacrificial sheep, white spots in the distance. She wrinkled her nose as the warm breeze brought the musty-sweet odor of sheep.

Zebedee paid the goods tax at the gates to Bethlehem and Hebron.

The road wound among the hills through olive and fig groves and into sleepy, peaceful Juttah, lying off the king's highroad to the east. The village had only one main street and no walls. Zebedee left the camel train and led the donkey to the last house standing before a field with a forest at its back.

He knocked on the gate. Mary listened to doves admiring each other—and waited.

CHAPTER 4

"Child, you're the image of your mother." Elisabeth's eyes, gray pools of sadness, lighted at the sight of this dusty skeleton of a girl. She knelt to take Mary in her arms.

"Can you stay a bit?" she asked, rising to speak with Zebedee, but keeping an arm around Mary's shoulders.

"No, I've sent my caravan on toward Askelon and must catch up with it." He reached down to pat Mary's tangled hair. "Take good care of this mite. I'll expect her to be fat as a pigeon when I come back. We've had a good journey, eh, Mary?"

Mary hugged him fiercely. "Oh, I love you." Then, appalled at what she'd said, dropped her arms and hid her face on her chest.

"Hear that, Elisabeth? A beautiful lady loves me and she'll always have first place in my heart." He laughed loud enough to make the donkey take a step. "Give my best to Zacharias, and I'll take Mary home in a few years." He turned the donkey toward the road.

With both hands on Mary's shoulders, Elisabeth looked her up and down. "You're all ribs and eyes. Come inside and we'll have cold pomegranate juice, but first we'll wash. Looks like you've collected all the dust in Israel."

Mary drank pomegranate juice from a silver mug. Elisabeth showed her the fruit and Mary marveled at the seeds.

"How do you get juice from this?" she asked.

"By crushing it, Mary. That is how most good comes from people, too—only after they are crushed."

Mary asked no more questions because she hadn't understood.

Zacharias came home as Elisabeth was preparing the evening meal. He greeted Mary and said he was glad she was with them. *He's older than Abraham*, thought Mary.

Zacharias' home had three rooms, two for sleeping and the large one they were in. The walls were smooth and white washed. Green cushions lay about on a raised platform to one side. In the corner a box held scrolls.

Elisabeth stirred vegetables into a stew bubbling over a fire hole. But Mary couldn't keep her eyes from a low table with three stools around it. She ran her fingers over the smooth oak finish as she laid out wooden spoons.

"Mary, you may shape the loaves. It doesn't matter if they don't look as round as your mother's. Just mold the dough and I'll show you how to feed them into the oven in the courtyard."

While Mary patted the dough, she thought how happy she would be with Elisabeth. At home only Salome or her mother formed bread loaves.

Outside at the oven, Mary watched Elisabeth draw out the bread with a wooden paddle. "I'll teach you many things, Mary," she was saying. "I've never had a little girl." She turned the bread into a basket and let Mary carry it to the table.

The three washed in the ritual way and sat down to the meal. Zacharias said a short prayer of thanksgiving, not like her father's long ones over two or three spoonfuls of food.

"Eat slowly," Elisabeth said, "but all you want. There'll be more tomorrow." She turned to Zacharias. "We must put some fat on Mary's bones." The aged man nodded his head and reached for butter.

It took a few weeks for Mary to feel comfortable with Zacharias. She realized he spoke little because his mind dwelt on deep studies of the scriptures and with the coming of the Messiah. Any question of the Holy One brought a rush of words, however.

Time went quickly, happy times for Mary, except for the empty place in her heart when she thought of her family—and her baby sister. Here she felt she was someone special. As Mary grew, Elisabeth showed her how to sew strong seams in new tunics. The old lady taught her how to crush pomegranates, how to dry figs and dates into cakes. They took long, slow walks in the field and forest behind the house where Elisabeth showed her which plants to pick for dyes and herbals—chamomile and lobelia for poultices, skullcap and wormwood for pain.

Daily Mary went to the village well for water. Only once Elisabeth told Mary of her longing for a son, of how women mocked her for being barren, showed her their sons and grandsons, not realizing the pain they gave her.

"But, Mary, we must accept God's will for our lives, even when we do not understand it." Mary always listened to both Elisabeth and Zacharias and tried to remember all they said to her, for their words seemed to hold great wisdom.

One warm afternoon, with doves cooing outside the window, Zacharias turned to Elisabeth. "Why didn't Eli teach the scriptures to his children?"

"He probably thought all girls needed to know was how to care for their families." Zacharias frowned and opened a scroll.

"Nonsense. What of Deborah, one of Israel's greatest judges? What of Abigail, who saved her household? Come, child, let me teach you." The aged man and the little girl sat cross-legged on the cushions while Elisabeth worked about the house.

He began her lessons with the five books of Moses, with creation and man's disobedience, of the flood to destroy a sinful mankind. He taught her from the prophets and the psalms. Zacharias encouraged Mary to ask questions and to meditate on what she learned, to wonder about it, to ponder.

One day Mary asked what it was like before Adam and Eve disobeyed God.

"Perfect understanding and companionship," he replied. "They were friends, before Adam disobeyed and God had to punish the sin. He is a holy God and must judge it. Only shed blood takes away sin, Mary." He closed his eyes a moment before continuing, his white beard rising and falling on his chest with each breath. "That is why we offer our sacrifices in the Temple."

"Yes, yes," Mary answered. "That is what Father will do for my sin."

The old priest put down the scroll and looked at her with twinkling eyes. "What sin do *you* have?"

"I...I wanted someone to kill the soldier, the one who kicked my mother when Herod came to Nazareth, but Salome said that was sin and Father would offer a sacrifice for me in the Temple."

"True, but always remember that God is a loving god."

During the four years of her stay, Zacharias led her down the path of Israel's history, taking extra time when Mary showed more interest. Sometimes, he told her of his priesthood. He was of the tribe of Levi and when younger ministered in the Temple, but Elisabeth interrupted then.

"His turn has never come to serve in the Holy Place," she said quietly. Again Mary noted the sadness in Elisabeth's eyes. "It was his greatest dream to serve there, behind the curtain, lighting the candles, or the incense, setting out the sacrificial bread."

"What curtain is that?" Mary asked.

"The heavy woven one before the Holy of Holies.

Mary sighed, "Because I am a girl, I'll never see it, will I?"

"You'll see the outer curtain only once, when you dedicate your first-born son."

"Well, first I'll have to have a husband," said ever-practical Mary. "I suppose Father will find someone in Nazareth, but he may not be rich enough to sacrifice in the Temple." She sighed.

"We'll hope for better than that," Elisabeth said. "Seventy years give wise eyes. I truly believe all deeply desired wishes come true at last."

Mary smiled, thinking of Joseph.

On another day, Zacharias continuing Israel's history, told her of Deborah, the judge who led Israel's armies to victory on the Kishon. He watched her puzzle it through, then beam.

"When God couldn't find a man, he used a woman, didn't he?"

"Yes," he laughed, his white beard shaking. "There was another time he used a woman. Did you ever hear of Esther?"

"Oh, yes, every Purim, at the Feast of Esther. I like the stories of the beautiful queen who saved our people."

"Why do you like them?"

"We get gifts—except I never got any. We were too poor. But we went to the synagogue and heard the story and shouted at wicked Haman and sighed for poor Mordecai and acted frightened and clasped our hearts for Esther."

Mary turned serious eyes to Zacharias. "The year before I came we had nothing to feast with except a bigger bowl of barley."

Zacharias unclasped another scroll. "That is behind you now. Crops are improving in Galilee. What other feast do you like?"

"The Feast of Lights. We burned *three* candles that night, instead of just one."

Of all Zacharias' stories, she liked the ones of David best, partly because he was her ancestor and partly because he rose from a humble shepherd to be Israel's greatest king. She had cried when he suffered, made tight fists as Saul's soldiers searched the cave to kill him.

Twice a year Zebedee had stopped in Juttah, bringing news of the family and each time the little stone of hurt would come back to Mary's heart as he walked away. Next time, maybe she could go home.

Then the time came. They walked to the King's highway that led to Hebron and joined Zebedee's camel string. This time she walked beside him.

She learned her mother was well, but not strong—Salome grew more beautiful each day—crops were better, people were no longer starving.

"Baby Ancilla?" Mary's asked.

"Walks now she's four, but with difficulty. If her legs were as strong as her tongue, Herod would tremble. Everyone spoils her," he said, but he said it kindly.

"And I will, too." *And maybe I'll see Joseph again,* but she didn't say that out loud, instead she asked how many days it would take to reach home.

Maybe, just maybe, she would see Joseph again.

CHAPTER 5

Anna had not recovered her strength after Ancilla's birth. Her lips, often outlined with a bluish tinge, made no complaint, however. Instead, with a short little laugh, which seemed to be cut off before it had finished its scale, she encouraged her crippled daughter as she pushed one foot ahead and dragged the other up to meet it. Anna taught the child to accept her lameness without self-pity. If a neighbor made some oblique reference about it having been better if the child had not lived, the laugh would turn to icy scorn.

"She is the joy of my life," Anna would say, "a gift from God." Her eyes would soften each time she looked at Ancilla, unlike Eli, who avoided looking at the misshapen legs, but denied the child no request.

Had Ancilla's legs been straight, she would have been tall for her age, for in spite of the twist, her frame was strong. She inherited her mother's sense of humor and her father's stiff assurance that his thoughts were the only right ones, as though the very act of living at her birth had given her strength. She had neither Salome's outward beauty nor Mary's quiet spirit.

*

Mary sat on a one legged stool behind the house with a new goat, Baba. She pushed her head into the curve of the goat's sleek hip and pulled on the fat teats, skillfully hitting the earthen bowl below with a creamy stream of milk.

"Now that I'm home there are just two things I want more than anything else." The goat turned her head with understanding eyes. "I want Ancilla's legs to be straight—and mother to be strong again."

Then Mary drifted away on her daydream, seeing herself as tall and beautiful as Salome, not the spindly-legged, big-toothed ten-year-old she was. In her dreams a boy with caring eyes came again. She imagined him with his brothers, daggers hidden in their belts, hiding behind rocks, watching for Galilee's enemies.

When Baba flapped her ears and took a step, Mary stopped musing. "Stand still." Then she heard footsteps coming around the house.

Salome looked down at her sister with royal condescension, with the blood of queens flowing in her veins.

"I'll tell *you* first," she said. "I'm to be married."

Mary stopped milking. "Who has Father found?" she asked in a teasing voice, "some old man who needs a cook?"

"And *you'll* marry Malchus," Salome said.

She knows how much I dislike him; serves me right. She listened again to Salome.

"It's Zebedee," Salome said with a happy little laugh. "He owns a whole fleet of fishing ships, and I shall be wealthy." With this she swept out the gate.

Mary wished Salome hadn't mentioned Malchus. Mary pulled Baba's teat a little too hard, as she wished she could have pulled Salome's hair, making the goat flap her great ears.

At the end of Salome's betrothal year, her mother opened the wedding chest holding the rich bridal garments of her mother's family, garments too precious to sell even when the family was starving. Mary and Ancilla stood beside Salome as their mother lifted the lid of the sandalwood chest, breathing in the scent of lavender. Carefully Anna had drawn out the heavy linen dress, dark blue and embroidered in pearls and gold thread. When Salome held the gossamer veil to her face, Mary thought even Queen Bathsheba could not have been as beautiful as she. Mary watched the coins around Salome's face dance and tinkle. Someday she would wear them, too.

Zebedee came from Kapher Nahum, dressed like a prince, bringing gifts and the feast with him. Never had Nazareth seen such abundance, for Zebedee was rich and he must supply food for three days of feasting, the bridegroom's responsibility. They had Zebedee's own special pickled fish from Lake Gennesaret, salty and tickling to the tongue, and sweet saccharum cane from far-off India, as well as gifts of tiny brass bells, which the bridegroom's helpers threw to the people who followed the procession. It trailed back a half mile behind Zebedee as he led Salome away from her father to his city on the shore of Lake Gennesaret.

*

Mary's childhood went with Salome. She took her sister's place grinding grain, cooking, carding and spinning the wool from Eli's flocks, sewing and cleaning, and of course, carrying water from the well outside the village, the responsibility of every girl. It was always a slow walk as Ancilla took a step, pulled her crippled leg to meet it and took another step. That daily trip to the well gave the village girls time to talk with each other and a chance to watch shepherd boys and their sheep.

At eleven Mary worked as hard as many grown girls, taking on the tasks too exhausting for Anna or Ancilla, gathering weeds for the fire on the hills outside the village, milking and caring for the goat, and especially pushing the heavy stone across the grain in the grinding trough. Mary's only rest was the sabbath and festivals.

She worked, as did everyone, daylight to dark, six days a week, with rest only on the sabbath. But festivals! Ah, she dreamed of them, of the feasts, the dancing, the laughter, even the ones which were most holy were days of feasting and rejoicing.

"When you've finished bringing in the thistles for fire, you may go to the square," her mother called to Mary early on the first day of the Festival of Booths. "But always remember why we keep this day—not just for dancing and feasting."

Mary clapped her hands against her cheeks. *Go alone, to the Festival.*

"Why are we rejoicing?" Anna asked. "Why do we build a booth of branches in our courtyard and sleep in it this week of Booths? Do you know your lessons?"

"Yes, Mother," she answered, standing straight and speaking as primly as if the leader of the synagogue were asking. "We remember the time our people were slaves in Egypt and wandered homeless in the wilderness."

Anna nodded approval as she took the wool carder from its hook. Mary sped through twisting lanes, up onto the hills above Nazareth. In her haste she stuffed dry thorns and thistles into her bag heedless of pierced flesh. *To the square! Mother trusts me to go to the square.*

An hour later Mary returned breathless, stacked the fuel out of Baba's reach and furiously ground enough grain for the evening meal. She splashed water on her face and swung her hands in the air to stop the sting from thorn pricks.

"Why aren't you coming, Mother?"

"Neither Ancilla nor I have the strength for dancing," her mother said as Mary pulled on a clean tunic. "We'll stay here and sew a dress for Ancie's doll." Anna slipped two leptons into Mary's hand. She hid the coins in her tunic girdle.

"Don't spend it all for sweets." Anna said, and smiled her blessing upon Mary's day. Her daughter knew from the twinkle in her mother's eye that she could spend it as freely as she wished.

"I'll bring something home for both of you," she said.

Her mother's voice followed her out the gate. "Be home before the first star—mind!"

CHAPTER 6

Mary hurried to the market. She heard the music at the entrance, paused to soak in the scene, hiding it in her mind to enjoy again and again in her dreams. Most of the people in Nazareth filled the square. Timbrels beat rhythms for flying feet in a double circle of dancers: excited children, occasional shy-eyed lovers, chattering adults.

Booths lined the area, with dyed goatskins draped over poles, skins in a rainbow of green, muted blue, every shade of tan and russet. Flute players sat on a raised platform and piped haunting melodies, pulsing notes that captured the spirits. In sing-song voices peddlers hawked foods, leather goods, musty-sweet perfume, fine Egyptian cotton. Mary's eyes feasted on sweets, pastries, fruit, and curious wares from distant lands: brass bells, red sandals, alabaster bottles, doves in reed cages, girdles of snakeskin, cloaks of camel hair or striped wool, and great counters of brass bowls, cups and jars. She searched for her friends, Deborah and Rachel.

Mary walked alone from booth to booth, clutching the coins in her hand, hoping she would meet the girls. Odors assailed her: onions frying over charcoal, the acrid smell of leather, tantalizing musks, the sweat of warm bodies. Clowns, jugglers and acrobats fascinated her. A dog walked on his hind feet and barked a tune, a bear sat up and grinned at her. Sticky-mouthed children ran about freely. She saw her father once or twice but carefully avoided him. This was her day as a grown girl, not a child.

Mary finally found a pink alabaster pot for her mother that fit in the palm of her hand and a white coral necklace for Ancilla. Thrusting them deep into the pocket of her tunic, she noticed her friends Deborah and Rachel among the dancers. With a skip she joined the double ring whirling past each other, hands calloused from work, parchment skin of the old, warm hands of children, the smooth palms of youth holding fingers a second before releasing them, all chanting the joyous festival songs of Galilee.

"It is good to give thanks to the LORD,
and to sing praises to your name,
Oh, Most High.
With the lute and harp,
with resounding music on the lyre.
For thou, Oh, Lord has made me glad.
I will sing for joy at the works of the LORD."

Mary passed Deborah and Rachel, her face flushed, eyes sparkling, the first time she'd danced without Salome being with her, hand over hand around the circle.

A damp hand took hers and it did not let go. Malchus, a bully she'd grown up with, stepped beside her. She tried to jerk away, but his fingers tightened. "I've caught a little bird," he smirked and swept her along with the dancers, then pulled her from the circle.

"Let me go!"

"Oh, no, my little dove." Mary felt a little dart of apprehension. His voice was smooth as new-pressed oil. "I've been studying in Jerusalem," he said as the dancers whirled past them. "Did you know that?"

She twisted to free herself.

"I think I'll take you away with me when I leave this village," he said with a smirk. "I'm going to be a clerk for Levi at King Herod's custom booth in Kapher Nahum."

With all her strength, she kicked his shin, jerked her hand away, and ran through the crowd.

Malchus didn't follow. She looked at her red fingers, then at the dancers. There he was across the square holding Deborah's hand and leering down at *her.*

An hour later Mary and Deborah stood to the side and watched him dance with Rachel.

"Look at her," Deborah said, "She's *smiling.* Silly sheep."

"She should know better."

"He's going to be a tax collector like his father." Deborah's mouth aped her elders when they spoke of these hated officials.

"A publican! I don't trust him," Mary said. "I hope he goes to Kapher Nahum soon." She turned to touch the soft gauze of shawls on the next booth, much finer than either girl could ever dream of wearing. "Let's dance again."

They rejoined the circle and let beating drums and wailing flutes bring back the excitement.

*

The sun dropped below the western hills, and once again the festival captivated Mary. A little girl stepped in front of her. Mary tried to avoid stepping on the child and turned her ankle. She yelped, limped from the circle and hopped between two booths.

"Mary?" The voice was not Malchus'. A head of black curls and a grinning face appeared from behind one booth. "You are Mary, aren't you, the girl I met when Herod was here?"

"Joseph?" Like a flower opening to the sun, a smile bloomed on Mary's face. She hopped a step closer. Birds squawked and fluttered behind a curtain.

"What's wrong," Joseph asked, concern replacing his questioning smile.

"Twisted my ankle." Mary looked up into his face and saw him as she remembered from six years before, the same kind, smiling eyes, the black curls hanging over his ears. She took a step closer to better see him in the failing light, balancing on the toe of the offending foot.

The young man wore a russet cloak with a rawhide pack slung across his back. Big, bony hands held a staff of oak. Could this tall young man really be the boy she had dreamed of so often?

Is he remembering where he found me? Her blush could have fired the curtains beside her. The corners of his eyes crinkled as though he were thinking the same.

"I've looked for you every time I've been in Nazareth since then. I've always wondered if your mother was injured."

"Well, not her, but the baby came too soon, with twisted legs." Grim lines took the place of her smile;

Joseph's vanished. She held a tent pole for balance and rubbed her ankle.

"We've never been able to find the man, not knowing which soldier he might be."

"No, I don't suppose you could." Mary looked over her shoulder, then whispered, "Are you still...a Cananean?" She swallowed the word.

"Yes," his knuckles tightened on his staff, "I go with my brothers, Matthias and Clopas, and do what I can for the cause. But let's not think of that today." Before she could question further, he looked up at the sky. "Shouldn't you be home?" Mary glanced in consternation at three stars sparkling in the east.

"Oh, yes, I must." She took a step, only to have her ankle buckle. "Owh!" Joseph caught her arm.

"Here, climb on my back and I'll carry you home."

He stooped down.

"No! I couldn't. My father would scold."

"He'll not know, and you can't walk." His eyes danced with laughter and gave her confidence. "Put your arms around my neck. Here we go!"

The roughness of his cloak tickled her legs. She wanted to rest her head in his dark curls; instead, she held it as rigidly as a conquering general. *He looked for me, every time.* Mary felt as though she were floating; tinkling bells rang in her ears.

Footsteps echoed behind them. Joseph turned his head and moved faster. He slowed his pace only as they entered the dark corridor of the street that led to her house. He put her down at her gate as gently as a basket of eggs.

"Thank you." She squeezed his hand and watched

him disappear down the street, silent as a shadow.

Footsteps came up behind her as she limped through the gate. Her father closed and locked it with a foot-long wooden key. Mary thought quickly, knowing she must weigh each question he asked.

"It's late! Where have you been?" her father said, hanging the key on its peg.

"In the square, with Deborah and Rachel. I twisted my ankle." She wondered why those truthful words made her feel guilty.

Both parents railed. They warned her of the dangers of night air and of strangers in the dark. *Mother won't trust me again, but it was worth it. I saw Joseph.* They wrapped the ankle so tightly tears came to her eyes.

Later in the shelter on the roof, she pulled the bed rug over her shoulders beside Ancilla and watched stars winking beyond the barrier. Before she could begin a new dream, Ancilla poked her in the ribs.

"I saw you," she whispered so low their parents could not hear.

"Saw me?"

"Yes, I saw you riding on a man's back. I heard you talking, too."

"You won't tell?" Mary knew Ancilla would not sleep until the secret was hers, so Mary told her sister how Joseph had helped her the day she was born. But she didn't tell her that he was of the Cananeans. Mary fell asleep dreaming of the feel of his hands as he carried her home.

A cold wind blew in from the sea the next morning.

Anna rubbed Ancilla's legs with balsam oil, which gave little comfort. The girl sat beside a smoky fire, wrapped in heavy wool, uncomplaining, sorting horse beans. Mary ground barley.

Poor little Ancilla. She hurts in damp weather. I wish the Prophet Elisha were still here and could heal her like he did the little boy.

Two weeks later, under a gray blanket of clouds, Mary started on her daily trip to the well, balancing the clay pot on her head and carrying a water bag on her hip. She left early so she would not have to wait for shepherds to finish watering their sheep. The street lay deserted for once. Ancilla's legs had hurt too badly to go with Mary and she would have to hurry home; there'd be no loitering to talk with the girls.

A voice startled her. "I've been waiting for you." Malchus stepped out of an alley. Mary stepped ahead quickly, but he blocked her way. "I can see your gate from the top of that wall." He waved behind him. "I want you to take this note to Rachel."

"Take it yourself," said Mary and tried to move ahead. He held out his arm and blocked her way.

"I need a little help."

"You won't get any from me. Get out of my path."

"Not so fast. I saw you leave the market on festival day." His lips smiled, but not his eyes. "Your father would be upset, wouldn't he, if he learned how you got home?" He thrust a folded parchment into her hand. "See Rachel gets this." He strode away.

Mary stared blankly at it and angrily tucked it into

her girdle. *I should never have tried to deceive father. Mother will listen. I'll tell her about my ankle. About Joseph bringing me home, but I won't tell her everything.*

Mary hurried home from the well, fearing her father might be there before her. But fortune favored, and Mary told her mother the story: that a stranger had helped her home when she had twisted an ankle, and that Malchus had seen them. Ancilla sat quietly shelling peas, glancing sideways under lowered lids.

"He wants me to give this note to Rachel." Mary looked into her mother's worried eyes. "I don't think I should do that. Should I?"

Anna sighed and reached for the note. "Give it to me." Pinched between her finger and thumb, Mary handed it to her. Her mother read it, shrugged, and sighed again. "You say the lad who helped you didn't come from Nazareth?"

"I think he said Gabara."

"You know that you should have found your father." Anna pressed her temple and closed her eyes. "But what's done is done." She looked up, her voice decisive. "Probably no one else saw you. You can throw this message in the fire and no one will be the wiser, but let this be a lesson to you. Your sins will find you out, Mary."

"I knew you would help "Mary hugged her mother tightly, something the family seldom did. Anna held her daughter for a moment, then crossed the room to the grinding stone.

"There's no need to worry your father with this," she said as she dragged the stone across the grain.

Mary dropped the parchment into the fire and watched the flame.

CHAPTER 7

Mary's slender fingers automatically pulled the strands of wool through the spines on the boards, her dreams no longer those of a child, but of a girl fourteen, ready for a husband. As her body had gone through the mysterious change from child to woman, so her dreams had shifted from Joseph killing the soldier to those of his coming with a casket of jewels as her bride-price. She imagined him loving her as Solomon loved the Shulamite—tenderly, thinking her the most beautiful woman in Israel.

While gathering fire weeds on the hills, Mary imagined herself wearing a robe of purple velvet with a crown of gold, studded with rubies and emeralds. She saw herself ordering servants and slaves kindly but firmly. Joseph would sit upon an ivory throne, the very throne King Solomon sat upon when the Queen of Sheba visited him.

She wasn't the only one who thought of the Cananeans. One evening from inside the house, the women listened to Mary's father and their neighbor, Ezra, fight a battle of words about them. The wall between the two houses separated them as surely as their philosophies.

"Did you hear, Eli?" His neighbor was leaning both elbows on the stone wall. "The Cananeans struck down a whole Roman squad in the Valley of the Doves above Magdala."

"Any Romans killed?" Eli asked.

"Oh, one or two," said Ezra, and now his voice rose. "but they won't give up until Israel is free."

"Hear me, Ezra. Rome will fall in God's own time." Eli stabbed with his finger toward his friend's face. "Not until we turn to God in true repentance—will we ever be free—in spite of these revolutionaries. You've read the prophets."

"Are you saying that the Cananeans are not doing God's will?" his friend challenged him, his face reddening with each word.

"That's what I'm saying." Her father's voice, shrill in its agitation, rose higher. "God will judge those hot-heads." Ezra's lips quivered to retort. "Their only reward will be a felon's death—a cross."

"I doubt Ezekias thinks so." Ezra's face flushed redder.

In the pause that followed, Mary stopped pulling the carder halfway through a stroke, wondering if Joseph would die. She hadn't thought of that. She listened again.

"You know Aaron over on the Street of the Sandal Makers?" Eli asked, his frown deepening. "I think he's one of them." Ezra waved the thought away as he would an insect.

"I know Aaron well." Ezra's flush faded. "No, he's not a Cananean, but he is head of the family now his brother Jacob died fighting. His sons take Jacob's place leading the Cananeans in Gabara and Cana. Even the lad, Joseph. Aaron talks down an empty well as far as convincing his nephews to tend to their work and leave politics to Herod." He shrugged his shoulders as if to indicate he was thankful the responsibility of those nephews was Aaron's and not his.

In the gathering darkness Mary pulled the wool firmly across the teeth, oblivious to all but her thoughts of Joseph. How sad for him, with his father dead. *I wish I could tell him I'm sorry.* But she had heard what she hoped to hear: Joseph was still alive—still among the Cananeans. She listened with half an ear while her father and Ezra talked of King Herod, how he'd just killed a son to keep him from his throne.

"God will judge him," Eli said.

"We'll wait and see," said Ezra. "Now for bed." He reached out a hand to shake Eli's and both men went inside their houses.

Mary realized that her father would never consent to her marrying Joseph, a Cananean—if Joseph ever asked.

In the month Adar, on a day when showers and sunshine took turns, Mary and her mother ground pomegranate rinds and boiled them in an iron pot in the courtyard. Mary dipped strands of wool up and down in the blue-black water while Anna hung them on the olive branches to dry. Mary's arms, to the elbows, looked like those of a Nubian slave as she lifted the new-spun wool from the dye and handed it to her mother.

Ancilla hobbled inside the gate. She stood behind

her mother, facing Mary, and jerked her head toward the street. Mary nodded.

"I'll leave you to finish, Mother," she said as she hung the last strand to dry and washed her arms to a smoky gray. "I've just time to go for water."

"I'm going with you," Ancilla said. "I just saw a stranger. Out there." She waved toward the street. Mary laughed and hoisted the water jar onto her head.

"Is that so odd, to see a stranger walking down a street?" Mary asked as Ancilla picked up the leather water bag she usually carried.

"He might be a Cananean." Ancilla grinned as she saw Mary's eye widen. Anna untangled the strands of wool to catch the sun and smiled at her youngest.

"Best go along to protect her, Ancilla."

Mary pushed open the gate, and her sister shuffled after her.

"He's tall with curly black hair and he said his name is Joseph," Ancilla said. "He said he'd give me a sweet if I could get you to meet him down the street without any-one knowing."

Mary's heart beat faster. *Can it be? Can it be Joseph?*

The sun glinted off puddles in the street, and Mary's heart thumped with each cobblestone step. They turned a corner and there he stood in the recess of a wall. Feeling suddenly a bit dizzy, Mary's hands steadied the jug on her head. She looked up into Joseph's laughing eyes, then at Ancilla, who was beaming triumphantly. Joseph stepped forward and put his hand on Ancilla's head.

"Stand around the corner in the street and sing if

you see anyone." She went stealthy as a mousing cat.

Mary looked up at Joseph's sun-browned face, heavy dark brows shading the brown eyes she remembered. Suddenly she felt shy.

"You're beautiful," he said quietly. Mary felt the crimson on her cheeks.

"Oh, no," she blurted, "That's Salome!"

"Yes, you're right." He teased. "You're too short. Eyes too gray." She turned to go, but he pulled her back. "Mary," he said, "I had to see you! Your face is with me when I should be looking for the enemy, trying to sleep or laying stones. Always your eyes are looking at me."

Mary searched his face trying to fathom all he was saying—and not saying.

"Mary, the LORD is telling me—" he swallowed and a patch of color burned on each cheek, "—is telling me to take you for my wife."

Mary's mouth went dry, but her thoughts were a torrent. *He wants to marry me. Marry me! But what about Father?*

Now he held out her gray-dyed arms and pretended to frown. "I don't know if I want you, though, if your arms are rotting. You look like you're dying." She pulled back.

"I was dyeing," she blurted out.

"That's what I said." They both covered their mouths with their hands, trying not to laugh out loud, then her laugh died.

"Father will say no! You're a Cananean, and he says they are not of God." Worry lines puckered Mary's forehead. Joseph frowned and waited for more. She set the pot on the ground. "Father will want to know what you do for work."

"I'm building a stadium for Herod—in Sepphoris."

"And he'll want to know where we'll live."

"I'll find a place," Joseph answered.

"And Father will ask what you can give for a bride-price? Oh, he'll never consent."

"I'll settle these matters. They are not your worry."

"This is all wrong. You should be talking to Father, not me." She looked up into Joseph's face. He took her hands in his and gently rubbed her fingers with his callused ones. Neither spoke for a moment. When he did, his eyes showed genuine concern, two short lines dividing his black brows. Mary could not read his thoughts, could only wait—wait for the end of all her dreams. When he finally spoke, it was not of marriage.

"How can he say we are not of Him? When we would free Israel for God. Your father's got no love for his country."

"He has the scriptures on his side. I've heard him telling Ezra, next door."

Suddenly Ancilla's voice sang out, "When I survey my en-e-mies—" a line from David's psalms.

"Leave the Cananeans, please," Mary said quickly and drew away her hand from his.

"Leave them? Never." He leaped the wall and was gone.

Open-eyed, open-mouthed, Mary caressed the fingers he'd pressed. She replaced the waterpot on her head and stepped back into the street. Ancilla hobbled up beside Mary, her eyes shining with mischief. Mary leaned close to whisper in her sister's ear.

"You'll keep a secret?" At eight, Ancie had all the

power of a prophet in her look of contempt, that Mary would doubt her. "He wants to marry me." Ancilla stopped and stared at her sister.

"Why you?" she asked and took a step backward.

"I don't know, but Father will say no, and I can't disobey him." Mary stared in the direction Joseph had gone. "And I'm sure Father is looking for a husband for me. The only reason he hasn't said anything is because Mother needs me." They continued the walk to the well, Ancilla agonizingly slow.

"You could try *something*," she said finally.

Mary had no answer.

On the way home she chose to go by the Way of the Sandals Makers, a street three lanes away from their own lane and lined with booths selling every kind of leather product used in Galilee. The shops stretching down the tunnel of street all looked alike, with leather goods hanging so thick they hid the entrances. The soft, sweet odor engulfed them. Then they spied it, The House of Aaron, Leather. They walked by slowly but did not see Joseph and dared not ask.

In the months that followed, Mary looked for Joseph whenever they had time to go by way of Aaron's booth, and in those months, Mary found it difficult to smile, even harder to appear happy or to avoid Ancilla's questions. She worried through a litany of doubts: *He will never leave the Cananeans. Father won't give permission. I'll never see him again.*

Two years later Mary peered out the window, looking

into the night, thinking of Joseph. Behind her, Anna placed bed rugs around the fire hole while Eli leaned against the opposite wall beside a flickering oil lamp. He scratched marks on a potshard with a piece of charcoal, mouthing numbers as he added the figures. Ancilla mindlessly pushed the pestle against the grain for the morning's pottage.

"Four men to cut our barley," Eli muttered. "God has prospered us sixty-fold this harvest. He frowned. "Anna," he said, as if reminding her of something they had talked about.

Anna took a step away from the wall, with hands braced against the stones behind her. Ancilla slowed the grinder, the grating stone across the mortar the only sound besides their words.

"Daughter," her mother said, "before you sleep, we've something to say to you." Mary turned to face her mother. Anna spoke quickly as though to finish something she'd rehearsed. "You're a grown girl, and it's time you had a husband."

Challenge flickered in Eli's eyes, as he met his daughter's look. "I'll begin making inquiries in the synagogue to find some man in need of a wife," he said. His eyebrows met in a gray line across his forehead. Mary pursed her lips and prepared to hear the worst. "How many summers are you? Odd you haven't asked us about marrying before this."

"I must not marry yet." Mary hurried over the words. "Mother needs me." Anna gave Eli an apologetic look. "Ancilla can't carry all the water by herself. She can't even grind enough grain for one day." Mary looked to Anna. "Mother, you need me, don't you?"

Anna's already pale face seemed more sallow. She said nothing. Mary turned back to her father. Eli shrugged, near surrender, but he still looked truculent. Mary spoke with more assurance.

"Ancie could never do the work alone—for two, maybe three years."

He grunted noncommittally and began scratching more figures, as though by writing numbers he could cipher why his will was being questioned.

Mary's shoulders relaxed. She took a breath to speak again, but was interrupted.

"But I'll keep in mind a husband for you," he said. They are not so easily come by. I will wait a time longer."

Though Eli never mentioned anyone in particular after that, Mary knew he searched. It would be someone she did not want to marry, of that she was sure, and as the months went by, the silent dread grew stronger like bad weather bringing blight. Who would it be?

CHAPTER 8

Mary often felt like parchment tossed in the wind, buffeted between despair and, in spite of hearing no word from him, hoped that Joseph still did intend to marry her.

Six months after her father's dictum, she and Ancilla again walked home from the well by way of the Street of the Sandal Makers in the faltering hope that she might see Joseph. And God favored her. In the crowded street she recognized his dark head bent on weary shoulders. As they met, he moved toward her, but she drew back, afraid he did not remember the custom that they must not talk nor touch until betrothed. He spoke to Ancilla instead. "How are you little sister? Come, let us go to my uncle's."

Neither Aaron nor his wife Huldah were in the booth, but Joseph leaned over the counter and told Ancilla to choose a coin purse for herself. While she studied the tiny drawstring bags, he spoke under his breath to Mary, telling her that he was working as a stone cutter in Sepphoris and saving money for her brideprice. Her heart leaped. She glanced around, fervently hoping no one would see them and report it to her father.

On their way home Ancilla's frown matched her words. "Mary, why don't they find out whom *you* want to marry?" Mary gave a deep sigh.

"It's the custom, Ancie. Parents choose a mate who will produce strong children." Mary looked down at her sister. "They look into lineage and how well they feel a man and woman will work together."

"I think that is a very silly idea."

"It has worked for thousands of years."

"I suppose our parents were chosen to be married, and look what they produced. Me."

"Ancie, you're the best of us all." They laughed together until heads turned.

The sisters often walked the Street of the Sandal Makers after that and occasionally met Joseph. He and Mary would smile at each other—enjoying the fruit of forbidden conduct—speak a quick hello, always with Ancilla beside them. Sometimes he would look at her arms, with laughing eyes, and she would remember that day when he said he wanted her for his wife. Once she thought she heard him whisper, "I'm no longer a Cananean," but she could not be sure she had heard him rightly and hadn't dared ask.

On Sabbaths, Mary chose a seat near the lattice on the women's gallery and looked down upon the heads of the men below. Easily she identified Aaron's bald head and Joseph's black curls. On the way home, lest her father question her about the scriptures, she would pretend to listen to Ancilla explain them but Mary's thoughts were only of Joseph—and far away from priests and prophets.

A few weeks later, on the way from the well, the girls bravely decided to stop at Aaron's booth.

"There it is," Mary said.

The girls stepped to the front of the shop. A round face held up by four chins and twinkling dark eyes studied them.

"What will you have?" Aaron asked. Mary spoke just above a whisper.

"You are Joseph's uncle?" His chins wobbled.

"Ye…es. And you are the daughter of Eli. What brings you here?"

"Could you…" Mary's resolve failed. Ancilla jabbed her with an elbow. "Could you tell me—" she swallowed, her voice just above a whisper. "—is Joseph still a Cananean?"

Aaron bent his head near Mary's, she could smell the sandalwood perfume on his beard. He said, "No, he is not. He left them about a year ago. The move surprised me, as well as Clopas and Matthias. His brothers," he added, as he saw Mary's questioning look. "We talk of it often. He is not the revolutionary he once was." Aaron's eyes lost their twinkle and took on one of content, as though he joined Mary in her relief.

But now the little shop became busy, and a man smelling of camel rudely pushed the girls aside.

When Mary turned seventeen, her father came with the word she dreaded. Mary glanced at her mother, trying to read her face, then at Ancilla, who shrugged and grimaced. Mary dipped her bread in lentil stew and forced down three bites. *He's found a husband for me.*

Someone I won't like. I can tell. She chewed a fourth bite of bread and washed it down with watered wine.

Except for prayers, Eli did not speak. He wiped the inside of the pot with the last piece of bread and chewed slowly. When he finished, he stood against the wall, arms folded across his stomach.

Mary saw nothing in his face but she could sense a stiffness in his manner. *He's putting off telling me because he knows I won't like what he's going to say.*

Insects hummed, and in the evening stillness the bleating of lambs carried from the hills. Anna poured sand into the pot and scoured it, while Ancilla turned to her nightly task of grinding grain.

When Eli finally spoke, his voice was too loud for the room. "I talked with Pashur yesterday," he began. "His son, Malchus is ready for marriage and has asked for you, Mary."

"No! Not Malchus." Mary looked wildly at Ancilla, but she only ground more furiously, using all her strength to push the stone and send up a cloud of dust around her. Anna fingers gripped each other.

"Father," Mary whispered, "you must not make me marry him." The outside corners of Eli's eyebrows lifted.

"You say 'no' to me?"

"I say no to Malchus, Father." Mary took a breath. "He's—horrible. *A tax collector!*"

Anna intervened. "You'll be near Salome—and wealthy, Mary. He could choose from any woman in Nazareth or Kapher Nahum."

"Let him," Mary said.

"But he's chosen you," her mother said, glancing at Eli timidly. Ancilla straightened up.

"Jobab said he stomped a lamb to death." No one heeded her.

The air in the little room seemed charged with summer lightning.

"We'll wait a little longer for your mother's sake," Eli said finally, but his look promised nothing good. He sat down and began unlacing his sandals.

Mary dropped her head on her arms in the window hole, taking deep breaths of cool night air. Then she dove out the door and up the stairs to the roof. *Joseph, where are you?*

Ancilla lay down beside Mary and patted her shoulder. "Why Malchus? Why did they choose him?" Ancilla asked indignantly.

"I don't know. Those sweaty hands. That awful stringy hair." Words failed Mary.

At the well next day, shepherds and sheep jostling for a drink kept Mary and Ancilla waiting their turn. They thought of wild, unworkable plans while they filled the jug and goatskin bag: They would run away to Cousin Elisabeth in Juttah. Mary would throw herself down the well—Ancilla's suggestion. She would—.

Mary quickened her walk on the way home. They turned down the Street of the Sandal Makers. Ancilla hastened to keep up as Mary stepped to Aaron's booth. Ah, he was there.

"Can you give Joseph a message for me?" Mary asked.

"Yes, I'll see him tonight." He hesitated on seeing

the distress in her face. "What shall I tell him, daughter of Eli?"

"Tell him—," she thought wildly, "the girl in the mud needs him," *Oh, why did I say that?* Aaron blinked, but said he'd deliver the message.

That night Mary lay awake until sometime after the last jackal barked. She slept fitfully dreaming, waking every few minutes to wonder if Joseph would reply.

Just then something hit the shelter over her head with a tiny thud. Her eyes blinked open. She looked around in the dim light and saw a figure silhouetted against the stars. Someone was standing on the wall behind her house. *Joseph?* She sat up quickly, but careful not to waken her parents sleeping below her, and stepped to the edge of the roof.

"I got your message," Joseph whispered.

"Oh, Joseph…Father betrothed me—to Malchus."

"So soon?" was all he said for several moments. Her heart began to hammer. She heard someone turn over downstairs. Was her father awake?

"I'll come tomorrow at first star."

Mary started to speak, but Joseph had disappeared into the darkness.

Next day she went about her work, silent for fear she would reveal his visit.

That evening, just as they finished cleaning out the pot and stamped the last glowing twigs of the fire, there came a knock on the gate.

"What sapskull is out in the night air?" Eli growled, going outside to open the gate. Mary nearly dropped her basket of bread. Ancilla scrambled upright. Seldom or ever did visitors come after the first star. The women peered out the door.

It was Aaron, closely followed by Joseph. Eli started to shut the gate, stopped in time, and reluctantly beckoned them to enter. Eli gave Joseph and Aaron the two kisses of welcome as custom required, but coldly. He did not ask them inside the house nor give them the cup of wine. Joseph looked across the yard at Anna and Mary in the doorway, with just a twitch of an eyelid instead of a smile. Mary did not try to stop her smile. Then the women went inside, out of sight, but with hare's ears.

"Eli," Aaron began with a note of amusement, "you know my nephew, Joseph, son of Jacob of Cana. I come as the friend of the bridegroom to ask for the hand of your daughter, Mary."

"No daughter of mine will marry an enemy of God," Eli said, glaring at Joseph. He tightened his girdle. "What does he offer?" he said to Aaron.

"At this time, he has no brideprice, but he works as a mason in Sepphoris and saves his money toward what you require." Aaron's silky voice did nothing to smooth Eli's anger. Joseph stood quietly beside his uncle, his head held high, a regal pose to his shoulders.

"A Cananean, is he?" Eli sneered. "With nothing to show for his years." Joseph said nothing, letting the friend of the bridegroom speak for him. Eli continued with contempt in his voice. "So he has nothing to offer for her, no home, no brideprice."

Joseph forgot to let Aaron speak and answered more sharply than Eli was accustomed to hearing.

Anna and Ancilla drew breath, but Mary merely smiled at the words.

"Give me a year and I'll have all you ask. As to being an enemy of God, you know full well that I gave up being a Cananean a year ago."

Eli sniffed and flipped a hand over his shoulder as Joseph went on speaking.

"Why do you think I fought, if not for the throne? Your daughter will be queen yet, Eli, son of Matthat, son of Nathan." Joseph was of higher lineage than Eli, and Eli knew it.

"You'll not have her."

Joseph gave Eli a long slant-eyed look and walked out the courtyard without looking back. Aaron hurried after him, arms swinging.

Eli slammed the gate behind them. Mary stood white-faced and silent.

While Anna lighted the lamps and Ancilla helped her with the night's chores, Eli began beating Mary with words.

"Where did you meet this brigand? Where would he hear of you?"

"He helped me home when my ankle turned." Mary only spoke when required to answer, her shoulders straight and her determination undaunted.

On Eli raved, finishing with: "There's more to this than you let me know, but I'll tell you this: You'll not marry him—at least until he proves himself. Now to bed."

The girls crept up the stairs and slipped under the rugs. Mary prayed to God as all good Israelites had done since their return from being slaves in Babylon. *Lord God, hear me. I want to obey, but I cannot marry Malcus. I don't know why; I just know that I must marry Joseph. Help me, Lord God.*

At first her faith that Joseph would somehow convince her father to let her marry him was as firm as the mountains around her. But sometimes, in the following months when Joseph sent no word, that faith wavered. In the quiet of the nights she felt utterly alone—except for Ancilla. Ancilla was her comfort, her ally, her buttress.

"Don't worry, Mary. He'll come for you. Aaron said so."

"But will he come in time?"

CHAPTER 9

At the time of plowing, a year after Eli refused Joseph, Mary's father returned from the fields two hours earlier than usual.

"I delay no longer," he began. Mary sensed what was coming. "Malchus' father brings the brideprice tomorrow." A chill went down Mary's arms. "You are two years past the marrying age now, and we've heard nothing from that Cananean."

"But Father, he's not a Cananean! You know he no longer follows them!"

Anna stepped in quickly: "Your father has put this off long enough, Mary," she said kindly but firmly. "He'll take no more refusal." Mary closed her eyes tightly for a moment, biting back words. "He's honest in his dealings. And someone must collect King Herod's taxes."

"Mother, he's a bad man—in his heart. He will not be faithful."

"Marriage is never easy." Childhood discipline kept Mary silent until she felt she must speak. She swallowed to steady her voice:

"Don't—" Her voice broke. "—don't make me marry him." Now, Ancilla came to her defense.

"If Malchus will be so rich, why doesn't he choose someone from Kapher Nahum? Or someone who wants him, like Rachel?" She answered Mary's glance of appreciation with a tiny nod. But Eli said nothing.

"We'll discuss it no further," Anna said. "Your father has given you more than enough time."

Eli looked over his shoulder as he stooped to go out the door. "Tomorrow we settle on the brideprice," he said.

Anna drew a sigh from the depth of her sympathy, then looked at Ancilla. "It's time you girls went to the well," she said.

The shouts of shepherd boys echoed as they brought the flocks down for the night. Each herd followed obediently behind its shepherd, eager for water, lambs close beside their mothers. The black shapes of pine trees were silhouetted against a blaze of sunset on the hills to the west.

"You'll think of something, Mary, and whatever plan you spin, I'll help you." Ancilla limped away to join the girls in the shade of a gnarled olive.

"We'll go home by way of Aaron's leather shop," Mary said casually, ignoring Ancilla's eyes.

"It will be full of men returning from work. We can't go that way—this late." But the sharpness in Mary's look stopped the argument.

Mary scanned the faces of the men coming toward her. Then she saw him, head bent, shoulders drooping. A smile lighted his eyes when he saw her.

"Father betroths me to Malchus tomorrow," she whispered.

"I'll come," he said and passed on.

Mary glanced around quickly, hoping no one had seen them.

The lamps burned feebly from their shelves of protruding sandstone and broke the dusky interior into pools of light. Eli sat on a low stool stuffing lentil pottage into his mouth with fresh-baked bread cakes. Anna's eyes met Mary's with raised brows as the girls quickly washed, dropped to their knees, bowed their heads and asked God's blessing, then silently picked up bread to begin their meal. No one spoke.

When they finished, Eli rose.

"Mary," he began, but heard a banging on the gate.

It's Malchus. A shudder ran down Mary's back. *Or Joseph!* She took another breath.

The girls were ordered to the roof but watched over the low wall. Above them the first stars sparkled silver against an indigo sky. Eli unlocked the gate and flung it wide to welcome Malchus and his father. But it wasn't them. Aaron's rotund form pushed through, followed by that of his wife, Huldah, rosy as a ripe apricot and the same shape. Behind her came Joseph.

"Ah, friend Eli." Aaron rumbled, arms wide. Eli flinched when they in turn gave him the kiss of custom. Eli responded with a spurious courtesy.

"Peace be upon you," he muttered mechanically. Aaron's voice boomed in answer.

"I come again to speak for my nephew, Joseph. I come as friend of the bridegroom since his father Jacob sleeps with his ancestors. He again asks the hand of your daughter, Mary."

"Humph," Eli closed the gate and faced the men standing in the center of the courtyard. Anna stepped into the yard and beckoned to Huldah. They touched fingertips and went just inside the door. Joseph stood straight, his hands folded behind his back.

"What does he bring as a brideprice?" Eli gave Joseph a look of contempt.

"One hundred denarii," Aaron said, his voice smooth. "One-third of his year's wages." From a goatskin bag, Aaron counted the coins and held them in his hand, palm upward, letting them clink together just a bit. Then Aaron slipped them back into the bag.

Eli stopped his head just before it nodded. The two men faced each other across the firehole. Ridicule tingling his words, Eli turned from Aaron and spoke to Joseph.

"You are a man of only twenty-three winters. You have spent your manhood chasing rebellion." Eli's voice held triumph now. "Why should I give my daughter to you?"

Joseph took a half-step toward Eli and bent his head to speak eye to eye.

"I took the allegiance to Herod last year, as you well know. I've worked from dawn to dark and walked a half-day's journey. Slept on Aaron's roof that I might save denarii for a brideprice. I make you a fair offer." His voice rose. "I shall care for her like a queen of Israel, like the daughter of David that she is." Mary's heart swelled in pride.

"Malchus gives more," said Eli smugly.

Again Aaron slowly drew the money bag from the embroidered girdle that belted his robe and counted another hundred denarii. "I double the brideprice," he said.

Eli looked at the coins, calculating.

"Then it's settled," Aaron said. "Here's the dowry and the troth is plighted." He took parchment and charcoal from his girdle. "Let us sign the pledge."

"Girls, you may come down," Eli said.

Ancilla whispered, "God is good," as they descended the stairs. Mary closed her eyes in a silent amen, then looked only into Joseph's, saying all he wanted to hear with the look.

Joseph took Mary's hands, cold as the stones in a brook, and let one eyelid flutter as she knelt before him.

"Mary, daughter of Eli, before the God of our fathers, Abraham, Isaac, and Jacob, and before these people, I ask you to be my faithful wife, to care for the home that I shall make for us and our children—a home that shall stand firm throughout the ages—a testament before the God of Israel that we are man and wife." The warmth and strength of his hands sent a flush through her body. She could barely hear her own voice repeating the lines she and Salome had learned as girls.

"I, Mary, daughter of Eli and Anna, do accept you as my husband before the God of Israel and before Aaron, your uncle, as friend of the bridegroom, and before my parents, Eli, son of Matthat, and Anna, daughter of Heli. I do promise to serve you faithfully, as a daughter of Sarah, and love you with the love she bore for Abraham."

Joseph slipped a fine gold ring set with lapis lazuli onto her ring finger.

"Mary," he said, his words holding all he felt, "the blue of this stone stands for love. I place it on your left finger where the line runs straight to your heart. See by this ring thou art set apart for me, according to the law of Moses and of Israel."

Eli's shoulders relaxed. He looked up at Joseph and said the required words: "You shall be my son-in-law." He glanced at Anna, a look which expressed his relief that his daughter was safely betrothed, if only to Joseph. He turned to the bridegroom and shrugged.

"You may kiss her, but I say before you all, no good will come of this marriage and that you shall wait a year before you come together as man and wife, lest you again decide to free us from the yoke of Rome and set yourself up as king." Mary knew that her father could not keep himself from giving that final stab.

The pressure of Joseph's fingertips lifted Mary up. He kissed her on the right cheek and on the left, leaving her breathless.

"Mother," Mary said, her feet back firmly on the floor again, "Do we have anything for a betrothal feast?"

Anna looked desperate, but Huldah had brought her own special cakes of dates, figs, nuts and honey, made with fine flour. Anna brought a wine bag from its storage under the floor and with salt on buttered bread, they feasted the betrothal in the traditional manner.

Now Joseph and Mary were allowed to sit together on the bench under the olive tree. Their fingers entwined, they smiled into each others' eyes, remembering the times they'd talked secretly.

"I must save money again to repay Aaron and find a house for us, a house of our own before the wedding day, though you know we are officially married now." Joseph pressed her hand to his cheek. Shyly she laid her head against his shoulder.

"A year will seem forever," she said and was silent a moment, then added, "as long as a lifetime with Malchus."

Joseph took her hands in his and studied her face. Finally he said, his eyes full of laughter, "And now I have you in place of the Cananeans." Somehow the idea seemed to amuse Joseph. Mary saw no humor in it.

He said more seriously, "I believe God meant us to meet and to marry. He has some purpose for our lives." Mary did not answer. Her only thoughts at the moment was the feel of strength and safety his arms gave her as he held her close against his heart.

Eli nodded to them from the doorway. She felt Joseph's arm tighten around her. He spoke without the trace of a smile but she felt him laughing inside at their private joke.

"I must say goodbye until we chance to meet again—perhaps in the Street of the Sandal Makers."

Mary nodded, feeling suddenly reticent. She wound her fingers through his. The look between them said all they could not speak.

Half of Mary went with Joseph when Aaron trumpeted, "We must go; dawn comes early."

"Worry not, Mother of Israel." Joseph took Anna's

frail hands in his strong ones. Anna shook her head.

"I named her well, Mary, obstinate. Remember that."

Joseph's voice softened. "I'll love her as Jacob loved Rachel." He said his goodbyes, then strode across the courtyard after Aaron, with Huldah waddling after. Joseph and Aaron gave Eli the kisses of farewell, which he returned, and the final handshakes. Eli's parting "Go in peace" held a note of relief.

A year, thought Mary. *So many things can happen.*

CHAPTER 10

The moon rose over the eastern hills while Mary lived her life again in thoughts. She watched stars pricking the darkness and thought of God, the God who created each one and could name them. "You are a great God, El Shaddai," she whispered to the sky. Ancilla's crooked hip touched her side. Jackals ceased their barking and one owl hooted to another. Sleep captured her.

Mary knew not how much later it was that fear crushed her against the mat. She tried to lift her hand to push it away and could not. Her body shook. Someone was with her—a presence. Alien, frightening. Prickles of fear mouse-footed across the top of her head.

She strained to see into the darkness. The parapet stood dimly outlined against the stars. Moonlight reflected on the poles holding up the roof of the shelter. No breeze stirred the leaves, no night sounds—only the hammering of her heart.

Suddenly a figure blocked the stars.

A cry lodged in her throat.

"BE NOT AFRAID, MARY," said a man's voice, melodious and serene, seeming to fill the sky. He towered above her. Except for his great height, he could have been any man from Nazareth, for he was dressed in an ordinary tunic with a wide girdle. Her eyes grew great with understanding: this was an angel.

"Who are you?" Mary forced the words from a dry throat. "Why are you—," she swallowed, "—here?"

The voice held the softness of dawn and the power of thunder when he said, "BE HAPPY, MARY." A shiver ran up her backbone. "DON'T BE AFRAID." The angel held out his hands—palms up, showing peace, as though he'd come to bestow a gift.

Mary slowly raised her hand to hold her throat. She forced the words: "Not I."

With physical effort, she sat up to stare into his face. The angel stepped closer. A warm feeling enveloped her. All fear disappeared and a quietness and peace which must have existed before God formed the world took its place. She felt as though she and the angel were the only beings in the universe.

"GOD IS HERE, NOW. HE HAS CHOSEN YOU ABOVE ALL THE WOMEN IN ISRAEL." The angel spoke slowly, letting each word make itself clear to Mary.

"YOU WILL CONCEIVE AND BEAR A SON, AND YOU SHALL CALL HIS NAME JESUS, SAVIOR. HE WILL BE GREAT AND WILL BE CALLED GOD'S SON. HE WILL RULE OVER ISRAEL FOREVER."

"But I...have not yet gone to my husband," she said. The angel moved closer.

"HE WILL BE THE FATHER OF THIS CHILD," he said gently. "THE HOLY SPIRIT WILL COME UPON YOU." With each word Mary felt a greater peace. "THE POWER OF GOD WILL COVER OVER YOU." Mary held her breath. "GOD CHOOSES WHOMEVER HE WILL." In a more determined voice, the angel said. "ELISABETH IS IN HER SIXTH MONTH. NOTHING IS IMPOSSIBLE WITH GOD."

She looked into the angel's face and knew with perfect certainty that every word he said would come to pass. She closed her eyes. A sensation of floating and a peace filled her such as she would never know again until she saw God face to face.

"Let everything happen just as you have said," her words barely a whisper, she waited for him to speak, but he said nothing. Suddenly, there was only darkness and glimmering stars where he had stood a moment before.

She lay back, savoring each word the angel had spoken. *God has chosen me for great honor? What honor can he mean? My son? He must have meant Joseph's son, but he said God would be the father. I do not understand. Why did he choose me? But he said God chooses whomever he pleases, like Elisabeth to have a son. And my son will be king!*

She lay awake until the hoopoo birds' monotonous "poo poo" lulled her to sleep as the first pink light of dawn touched the eastern mountains. She slept with no dreams, and never knew when the Spirit came upon her. She never knew.

CHAPTER 11

Shepherd boys woke Mary, calling to their flocks in the street below. Ewes bleated to their lambs and the dainty tap of hoof beats echoed off the walls. Ancilla stirred beside her. Every word the angel had spoken came back as if chiseled in marble. Mary knew she had not dreamed. She, Mary of Nazareth, would bear the king who would free Israel.

Ancestors of her son paraded before her: Rahab the harlot, Ruth the foreigner, Bathsheba wife after murder—and herself. God chooses whomsoever He will. She touched her fingertips together.

Though it was barely dawn, a persistent rapping on the gatepost stopped her reverie. Eli came out the door.

"Do people think this is an inn, coming at the fourth watch?" He rubbed fingers through his sparse hair as he crossed the courtyard. "Who knocks?" he growled.

"Misheal," said a gravelly voice, "nephew of Elisabeth and cousin of Anna." Mary's mother hurried across the yard to the gate.

"It's my cousin from Judea. You've heard me speak of him," Anna said, her voice high with excitement. Eli unlocked the gate and opened it barely enough to let a figure slip inside. He gripped the man's hand in a hardy shake.

"Misheal, cousin, what brings you at this hour?" he cried and exchanged the kisses of greeting with his guest, a man wearing a cloak so old its bottom fringed four inches up.

"Ah, Anna," Misheal tossed uncombed hair. He took her hands in his gnarled ones. "It's good to see you." His grin showed missing teeth.

"Such a long time." She noticed his skin, the color of desert varnish, his eyes serious.

"Aunt Elisabeth sends her love." He leaned his staff against the wall and entered the house. "How have you been, Eli? Your crops good? Your flock increasing?" Mishael asked.

Anna told him there'd soon be warm goat's milk and bread. Mary dipped water into the stone bowl from the storage urn and then blew upon the coals in the firehole. Eli reached a towel from its peg and bent to his task of foot washing, while Misheal leaned back against the wall and let Eli minister to his calloused feet. Ancilla limped down the stairs and went around the house to the goat.

"What brings you today?" Anna asked as she broke cheese into pieces. "You seldom leave the wilderness." Misheal removed thorns from the fringe on his tunic and did not reply. Her brow wrinkled. "Is it Zacharias?" Misheal shook his head.

"I have much to tell you, but it's good news. It can wait." Mary could not hide her smile and bent her head to put more thorns on the fire. *I have something to tell, too, and it cannot wait.*

The family broke their fast with Eli reading one of David's longest psalms and praying even longer. When his eyes were closed, Ancilla openly looked at the wedding chest. Mary glanced at Misheal and saw a twinkle in his eyes. Eli finally finished with "Amen." Each person washed hands again and was ready to hear their visitor.

"You'll never believe it." Misheal let the secret out between the gaps in his teeth, as though spitting melon seeds. "Elisabeth is to have a child. In her sixth month already. Elisabeth! Seventy years old."

Anna raised both hands over her head. "Hallelujah! How could it happen?" she said, smiling more broadly than she had for months.

Mary's face glowed. *And I already knew.*

Eli frowned, hunched his shoulders and turned down the corners of his mouth. "You're jesting," he said. Misheal's shaggy eyebrows drew together.

"How did this come about? How did you hear?" Anna interrupted.

"A deaf-dumb boy in their village brings messages to my cave." Misheal squinted his eyes. "It's a strange story, Anna. Zacharias was taking his turn at his priestly duty in the Holy Place, lighting the incense..."

It was Eli's turn to interrupt. "He must be past eighty years. Is he still able to take his place?" A nod told him yes and to listen further.

"The Angel Gabriel came and told him that Elisabeth would have a son."

An eerie silence filled the room. Mary's smile vanished. Last night: *The Angel Gabriel?*

"An angel!" Anna said.

"That's who Zacharias said it was, and I'll not dispute the word of that old priest. Hasn't uttered a word since."

"Lost his power to speak?" Eli asked, "or won't?"

"Elisabeth says God shut his mouth because he doubted the angel's words."

Eli took a sip of water. "I don't recall that happening in the books of history, someone seeing an angel in the Temple." Misheal straightened his shoulders and looked at Anna.

"Elisabeth sent me to ask your Mary to help her."

Anna reached for a woolen bag. "Mary—you must go to her."

A quiver of excitement brought a smile to Mary's face, but it quickly died. *See Elisabeth again—but leave Joseph.*

"When do you leave?" Eli asked Misheal.

"As soon as Mary is ready." He picked up his stick as though to leave on the instant.

"So soon?" Mary's fingers pressed her chin bone.

But I must tell Joseph the angel's message. She listened again to Misheal.

"The roads are not safe except with caravans, full of Roman soldiers and bandits. A group of trading Syrians leaves this afternoon, and we'll join it." He left with Eli to inspect his crops.

Mary went to the peg where her clothes hung and began taking them down, while Anna admonished her.

"Stay close to him, Mary. Stay close. Rough people follow caravans."

No time to tell them of the angel's visit. Mary hurriedly rolled a tunic around her sandals and put on heavy walking shoes. *If Elisabeth keeps her secret, then so can I—until I return.*

While Anna wrapped a cheese in linen and placed it with a bundle of bread, she explained to Mary that Misheal had been a member of the holy community at Qumran, a sect of the Sadducees or the Essenes, she did not know which, who guarded the laws that would govern Israel when the Messiah came, and that they thought themselves more pure than the Pharisees.

Mary only half listened, wondering about Elisabeth.

"But he disputed their teachings and was expelled," Anna continued. "Now he lives somewhere in the wilderness, and studies the scriptures for himself." Mary thought about the rough man who would be with her on the long journey and decided she was not afraid. "Zacharias thinks he is a very wise man. Cousin Misheal spends his time in prayer and preparation for the coming of the Messiah."

"The Messiah will take the throne of David," Ancilla proudly displayed her knowledge. "How long will Mary be gone?"

"A few months, I would say," said Anna, adding dried olives to the pack. "Till the Festival of Trumpets when someone from here will be in Jerusalem."

"Months!" Mary lowered her voice and said, "Yes, I suppose it will be that long."

"You will need to return to prepare for your wedding, Mary," Anna said, brightening.

But Mary turned away.

I wish I knew when I will bear God's son. Perhaps I have conceived already. Mary smiled serenely feeling great peace. *What a great celebration my wedding will be.* She carried her head like a queen.

Now her mother lifted the lid of the chest holding the wedding garments. It had not been opened since Salome's wedding seven years earlier. Again they marveled at the beauty of the embroidery, the rich sheen of the pearls, the fine texture of the veil.

Ancilla ran her fingers through the coins and sighed. "You'll look so beautiful, Mary."

Mary only smiled and did not answer. Her mind was elsewhere.

"Remember, Mary," Anna said, "when I am gone this dress is Salome's to keep for future generations. It is not yours; it must always go to the oldest daughter."

"Come, try it on," said Ancilla.

Mary shook out the folds of the gown, the same color as her lapis ring, and held it up to herself, while her mother went on talking about Salome and her three grandchildren.

"Bring me the mirror, Ancie." Mary looked into the wavy reflection on the polished brass and saw a small round face framed with auburn hair, straight and shining. Gray eyes stared back at her under arched brows. But then the wonder of the angel's message overcame her and she set the mirror down, turned to her mother and reached out her arms.

"Mary! What is it?"

"I—" she began. "I want Father to return soon!" Mary finished lamely and stepped into the courtyard.

"She is upset because she is leaving us, Ancie. Ask her to come try on the veil." Ancilla followed Mary to the back of the house, where she found her with her arms around the goat.

"Come back, Mary. We won't have time to try your veil on."

Mary sighed and rose to follow.

Anna lovingly folded the garments back into the chest while the girls went out on the hills to pick fire weeds and thorns.

But what about Joseph? I must tell him of the angel!

"Ancie, tell Joseph where I am."

In the streets, heads turned to stare at Mary, walking with a man whose dress declared him to be a hermit. *I do not care what people think.*

In the village square they joined the hubbub of the caravan. About fifty men busied themselves heaping camels with merchandise. Men, women, and children squatted in the dust, wiped away sweat, and waited for the caravan to move. Fifteen camels swung into line behind the lead donkey. The people fell into step, three or four abreast, with Misheal and Mary the last in line. More camels followed behind them, especially a nasty-tempered one which spat accurately at his driver's tunic when goaded to rise and pulled back his lips to expose stained brown teeth. He wore the same haughty expression as his driver.

They trudged steadily, resting for a few minutes every second hour, down into the lush Valley of the Kishon towards the grain fields of Samaria and straight toward Jerusalem, by the shortest route. At last they came to Capercotnei, where the caravan would turn southeast the next morning, down the coast road to Egypt.

That evening Mary mixed with other women as they prepared food over their small fires, but she could not speak to them because they were Syrians. One or two smiled at her with snaggled brown teeth, and she returned the courtesy.

The village lay nestled in olive groves at the base of an abutment that rose several hundred feet to the plain of Samaria above. A black basalt wall surrounded the village, and the five roads joining there were filled with people. To the west lay the ruins of the old town of Megiddo.

Misheal and Mary joined another caravan and went south, up through Samaria toward Judea and Juttah. They walked for two days through fields ready for spring harvest, past villages, but never speaking to any Samaritan—anathema to Jews because they did not worship in the Temple.

Mary hummed a melody from sheer joy, because she would bear God's son, and—was it only three days ago—she'd been betrothed to her Joseph. Oh, God was good!

On the third day as they passed Jerusalem, Mary touched Misheal's arm.

"May I ask you—" She searched for words. "—about the Messiah?" He looked surprised. "You study the scriptures and wait for his coming. When? When is he coming?" The holy man paused on the roadway and looked long at the girl.

"I do not know for certain, but—soon. Only two prophecies are yet to be fulfilled—although many do not agree with my thinking. Why do you ask?"

Mary did not answer him.

"Come," Misheal said and plied his staff again. "We've a day's journey yet."

Juttah looked just as it had when she first saw it eleven years before, dusty crooked streets, a jumble of houses. Nothing out of the ordinary would ever happen in this drowsy village. Here even the chickens scratched more languidly than in other villages. But it was here Mary was to help elderly Elisabeth prepare for the birth of a child.

"You have walked well. Been a real pilgrim." said Misheal and led her down twisting, narrow alleys to stop before Zacharias' gate. In her excitement she stepped ahead of Misheal and knocked, her heart beating faster. Misheal knocked again with his staff. The fragrance of sweet myrtle lay heavy in the spring air and doves murmured in the fig tree.

I can tell Elisabeth. I can tell her.

CHAPTER 12

Elisabeth flung the gate open, thin gray hair flying. "You're here; I'm so glad you came, Mary." She looked at Misheal. "Thank you for bringing her."

"I was just a little girl when I last saw you!" cried Mary. Then both women laughed and hugged each other again.

Mary saw Elisabeth's sparkling eyes, saw a handprint of flour on each hip that had not been dusted off, probably not seen by tired eyes.

Zacharias came slowly across the yard. His silver-white hair and beard, his regal walk—everything about him awed Mary until she remembered his kindness to her as a child. His lips moved, then he turned to Elisabeth.

"He welcomes you, Mary, wants me to thank you, Misheal, for bringing her," Elisabeth said. She patted Zacharias' spindly arm. "It is hard for us both."

"I'll not stay," Misheal answered. "Been gone too long. Times are moving, Zacharias. Be prepared." He shook his hand, bobbed his head to the women and was gone.

Once inside, Mary saw the house was just as she

remembered it. Zacharias with stately dignity returned to his cushion on the platform, picked up a scroll and began to read.

While Elisabeth washed Mary's feet, she kept up a steady flow of questions about Anna and Eli and beamed when Mary told her how God had betrothed her to Joseph. Behind the talk, Mary wondered how to ask Elisabeth the thing she wanted most to know—about the angel who had spoken to Zacharias.

Outside the sun blazed down on the little village surrounded by its groves of olive and fig trees. Above the cooing of the doves, a lark trilled. As Mary sipped a mug of cool water, she told Elisabeth of Salome and Zebedee's growing fishing fleet and their two girls, a boy named James but called Thunder James because he was so boisterous, and of another baby on the way.

"Now, please explain why you called me," Mary said. "Misheal was so close-mouthed. He only told us you'd have a child in three months."

Elisabeth's laugh carved deep lines around her eyes. "Oh, Mary. It's such a story." Her laughter died and she spoke with awe. "Zacharias was lighting the incense in the Holy Place," she began. "It had never fallen his lot to do this before in the fifty years he's been a priest. You remember how much he wished to?" Mary nodded. Elisabeth's voice was now almost a whisper. "Suddenly the Angel Gabriel appeared—" Mary leaned closer, her lips apart. "and told him we would have a baby. That's all," she said, and busily began forming a bread loaf.

Mary looked at Zacharias, then asked Elisabeth, "How do you know it was Gabriel?" Elisabeth's hands stopped. She looked toward Zacharias.

"The angel said he was."

Zacharias laid down the scroll and nodded his head. Mary waited for him to speak, then remembered.

"He doubted. That's why he can't speak a word. We pass written messages," Elisabeth smiled. "After fifty years married, I usually know what he's trying to say." The old lady busied herself slicing cucumbers.

"The angel said that he came from the very presence of God. Said that we would have a son. A son who is going to turn our people back to righteousness." Elisabeth's look was now serious. "A son!" She went back to her cucumbers.

"I knew," said Mary, almost whispering the words. Elisabeth laid the knife down carefully, her head bowed. Mary leaned forward as if far out over a ledge to feel the wind and said: "Elisabeth—I *knew.*"

Elisabeth raised her head to look at Mary. Zacharias rose slowly and stepped down from the platform and to stand beside her. Mary forced herself to look at him.

"An…an angel told me you were to have a son," she said almost fearfully.

Zacharias looked intently into Mary's eyes.

"There's more. I have something more to tell you."

Again, the lark warbled high in the sky until its song was lost. A gentle breeze ruffled the leaves on the fig tree outside, harbinger of coming evening.

"I was not going to tell anyone," Mary began, "but I feel I must." She stood a little straighter, speaking directly to Zacharias because he'd seen God's messenger also. "The angel told me that I, too, will bear a child."

The old couple stood as Adam and Eve might have, waiting for God to speak.

"The angel told me he will be *king*. His father is...God himself."

Frantically, Zacharias motioned Elisabeth to bring parchment and a charcoal. He wrote feverishly. Mary watched the feeble fingers write.

"Blasphemy," he had written. Mary drew back.

Zacharias wrote again and handed it to Mary.

"You fulfill Isaiah's prophecy. *I* believe you; others will not. Tell only Joseph." The old man wiped his forehead with gnarled fingers and sighed.

Mary felt a coldness in her heart.

Elisabeth lifted Mary's palms between her own.

"You are the most blessed of all women!" Elisabeth's voice rose in ecstasy. "How wonderful the mother of My Lord should come to me! You are blessed of God, my child—and you *believed*." Mary bowed her head. "Does your mother know?" Elisabeth asked in her normal voice.

"No, not yet."

"God so wills," said Elisabeth.

Zacharias sat rigidly on a stool, watching the women.

"How did you know," Mary said to Elisabeth, "that I carry the Son of God?"

"Because the moment you told me, my own baby leaped within me.

Elisabeth knelt before Mary, and Mary dropped to her knees facing the fragile figure. Zacharias knelt with them. He laid his hand upon Mary's head in blessing.

They could not hear his words, but read on his lips the words peace and safety.

Safety? Why safety?

Now Mary rose, speaking as if the Spirit of God moved through her, her hands spread above her head, palms open, her eyes closed:

"I praise the Lord and my spirit rejoices in God my Savior," she began, looking up.

Elisabeth and Zacharias pulled back amazed.

"He knew I was not a great person but chose me, and from now on all generations will call me blessed above all women. He has done great things for me. His name is holy. He is merciful to those who fear him, from generation to generation. He does mighty deeds, scattering the proud. He brings down rulers from thrones and lifts up the humble." Mary continued to look upward.

Zacharias' white head bobbed as he recognized centuries-old scriptures in Isaiah and the Psalms and saw the fruit of his teaching. Elisabeth's face mirrored the joy on Mary's.

"He gives food to the poor," Mary's melodious voice went on, "and sends the rich away hungry. He helps Israel. He was merciful to Abraham and to his descendants forever, just as He promised."

Slowly she lowered her hands and knelt with the old couple again as if unaware of all that she had just said.

Several moments passed. The two women then rose and embraced simply. Zacharias picked up the scroll of Isaiah he had been reading and rolled it rapidly to the text he was looking for. At Zacharias' trembling finger on the parchment Mary now read:

"Therefore the Lord himself shall
give you a sign; Behold a virgin
shall conceive, and bear a son,
and shall call his name Immanuel."

Some time passed in silence. Mary wiped a tear.

"Well," Elisabeth said at last and picked up her knife, "if we are to eat, I'd best finish." The women worked busily, each keeping her own counsel. Mary felt as tired as though she'd worked all day in the field. The rustle of a parchment scroll turning, turning, and the snap of the fire were the only sounds. Rich smells of pottage and warm baking bread filled the room.

CHAPTER 13

The next three months moved swiftly. At the well each evening, when neighbors asked where Elisabeth was, Mary said they shouldn't expect an old lady like her to carry her own water, and that Elisabeth's stomach was growing, that she felt sickly.

"A tumor," said a portly old woman.

"Maybe a baby," said Mary, but the women only laughed.

One afternoon Mary ground grain and Elisabeth rested on a cushion, feeling more frail each day as her pregnancy advanced. "Mary," she said, "listen to me." She took the girl's arm with surprising strength. "You *must* tell your parents that you are with child, as soon as you reach home."

"I would have—"

"Have you thought how they will feel?" Mary started to answer. Now Elisabeth spoke firmly. "Why didn't you tell them before you left home?"

"There wasn't much time—I just couldn't seem to talk about it. But I'll tell them. They'll be so happy. What parents wouldn't be?" Mary paused midway in a thrust of the stone as Elisabeth shook her gray head, speaking softly now.

"I'm not so sure...not so sure. I am a married woman. You are a virgin."

Mary pushed the grinding stone away and sighed, not quite understanding all Elisabeth meant. Zacharias sat studying his scrolls, rich treasures in any home. He beckoned Mary to him and pointed to a portion. She read aloud: "Bethlehem Ephratha, from you One will go forth for Me to be ruler of Israel." The old priest grabbed another scroll and rolled it to another portion. Mary read from Daniel: "Out of Egypt I called My son."

"It is confusing," Elisabeth said, "First he comes from Bethlehem, then Egypt, and you're from Nazareth."

Zacharias showed them other portions which spoke of a powerful king, others of a suffering Messiah, a lamb led to the slaughter, a king who would judge all nations with a rod of iron and others of a man so gentle he wouldn't step on a reed.

"The Messiah? Is my son to be the Messiah?" asked Mary and waited impatiently for the old man to scribble his answer.

"Difficult to understand," Mary read.

"Well, what we cannot understand," Elisabeth said flatly, "we must take on faith and wait for God to make it plain."

But Mary could not put the thoughts aside so easily. She pondered the messages as she lay on her pallet at night and decided the Messiah and the king were too different people. Gabriel's prophecy seemed clear: "He will be called the Son of the Most High and the Lord God will give Him the throne of His father David; and his kingdom will have no end."

She thought of Joseph and the rapture he and her parents would show when she told them. And Aaron and Huldah, those dear people.

Elisabeth's time came one morning when the air was spicy with the fragrance of grapes, but Zacharias was gone with his shepherds. The fragile old lady walked the floor, wincing as each cramp tightened. Mary ran to bring the midwife.

She beat on the woman's door and spoke without preliminary. "Come quickly. Elisabeth is bringing forth a child."

The craggy woman's eyes grew wide, but she automatically reached for her bag and started out the door.

"Elisabeth! *Wife of Zacharias!*"

"Oh, yes, yes, do come. I'll explain as we go. Believe me."

While they hurried through the lanes, Mary told her that Elisabeth was bearing a special child, one sent from God. Like Samuel of old. The woman only muttered that she was bent on a fool's errand.

Four hours later she burst from the house bellowing the news that she had delivered a miracle.

Inside Mary handed the tiny wailing bundle to its mother. It was a boy. They looked at each other, wreathed in smiles. Elisabeth closed her eyes to rest. Zacharias returned and knelt in prayer beside his son.

Zacharias' courtyard soon filled with people. A woman carrying a baby on each arm shouted angrily, "Why didn't you tell us earlier?" Mary at the door, smiled and told them gently that she had kept the secret because Elisabeth was afraid no one would believe she was with child. Another woman cried, "Well, who *would* believed it?"

A woman with a twinkle in her eye reminded the others. "Well, the girl *did* tell us."

The village women spoke quietly to each other as they gathered, ashamed of the times they'd mocked Elisabeth for being barren. One by one they went in to honor the miracle.

On the eighth day, as it would happen, Mary's brother-in-law Zebedee came by on his way home from Egypt.

"A baby! Yours?" Zebedee's voice woke the child, who protested as loudly.

On Naming Day, men from Juttah packed the house and women filled the courtyard, come to share in the ceremony of circumcision and naming. It was a fine excuse to see the miracle child again. Men laughed and joked, slapped Zacharias on the shoulders, and spoke loudly to him as though his ears were shut as well as his mouth. In his hand he held the stone knife for the circumcision. He lifted his head proudly beside Elisabeth. Neither tried to hide their smiles.

"Who'd have thought it of you, my friend. At your age." A bent stick of a man shook a finger at him, playfully. The men laughed again. Zacharias stopped smiling and gave them a stony look.

*

Zebedee's teeth gleamed through a well-trimmed black beard as he led the talk. "Here's another Zacharias to take your place as priest, eh, cousin?" His voice shrank the room and stopped all other talk.

But Elisabeth said firmly, "His name will be John."

Men frowned.

"You can't call him *John*. You have no kin called John," said one.

Zebedee clamped his huge hand on Zacharias' frail shoulder. "Zacharias?" But Elisabeth handed her husband a piece of parchment and a charcoal. He wrote four letters: J O H N. And this man struck dumb by the angel Gabriel spoke loud and clear. "His name is John."

Everyone gasped. Zacharias repeated it quietly, as if afraid of his own voice. People drew together, fearful and uncomprehending. The women in the courtyard heard Zacharias speaking and murmured together.

Elisabeth lifted her head proudly. Mary knelt in prayer behind them. A shaft of light came through the window, giving her a kind of halo.

Now Zacharias' voice was that of a prophet, compelling, with quiet power: "It's just as the angel said. 'Many shall be glad at his birth. He will turn many back to God. He will prepare a people for the Lord.'" At this, he turned his intense gaze at Mary. "Through this girl." No one spoke now.

Tears ran down Mary's cheeks. The women gave her wondrous looks, but feared to question.

Before the friends left, each man touched the tiny boy in Elisabeth's arms. Soon everyone had gone out to tell of the miracle throughout little Juttah and up into the hill country surrounding it. All was quiet in the house of Zacharias and Elisabeth.

Elisabeth looked down at the sleeping child. "He's my Touchon John, my *Special* John."

Zebedee turned to Mary. "You must come back with me; you've been gone three months. Eli and Anna will want to hear about this birth from you. Elisabeth will not lack for help now." Mary glanced at Elisabeth.

"Yes, you must return." Elisabeth nodded, but gave Mary a double-edged look. "With the news." Zacharias seemed to be seeing something far away.

"Goodbye, Mary," he said, "Remember we are here if you should need us."

CHAPTER 14

As she and Zebedee left Juttah with his camel train, Mary let her thoughts drift to what she would say when she reached home. A skylark trilled its melody in the blue above her. The fields were a carpet of summer flowers, silvery thistle, yellow iris, blue ox-tongue. In the fields men worked in the vineyards, tending vines. When she looked back at Juttah, before they topped the last hill, she saw an ominous gray thundercloud lying over the village. The wind was from the northeast with the smell of rain, but the storm would go south and not touch them.

Mary's heart ached with the beauty and with the anticipation of telling Joseph. She rubbed the lapis stone and remembered the love in his eyes when he told her that it led straight to her heart. She bore the promised Messiah all Israel waited for. Everyone would exalt her.

The day Zebedee and Mary arrived in Nazareth was as beautiful as any she remembered. The camels plodded on while she watched a huge crimson ball of sun drop through golden clouds toward the Great Sea beyond Mt. Carmel.

Ancilla answered their knock. "Mary!" she screamed. "Zebedee!" and hugged Mary so hard she nearly cracked her sister's ribs.

Eli and Anna rushed out now, Anna to embrace Mary twice, Eli to shake Zebedee's hand. Her son-in-law slipped a silver box into Anna's hand. "A little gift, Mother, to keep your needles in," he said.

"What of Elisabeth, Mary?" Anna asked, bringing cool mugs of water.

"She has a boy, John." Anna frowned.

"I remember no John in Zacharias' family."

Eli hung the towel after drying Zebedee's feet. "What of the old priest's not speaking?"

Zebedee answered, "He regained his voice as soon as he said the boy should be named John. Proved he believed God—finally."

Eli shook his head. "To think God should choose him. I wonder what he has in mind for the boy—the priesthood, I suppose." Eli was now more interested in Zebedee's fishing business than in the miracle baby. He kept him talking long after the girls climbed the stairs to sleep.

Why should I tell him about Gabriel's message to me? He only thinks of crops and shekels, thought Mary with a trace of bitterness. *But*, she brightened, *he will care about the king—or that I bear the Messiah. Tomorrow I will tell them. Tomorrow, but first...*

Lying where she had lain three months before, Mary asked Ancilla about Joseph.

"How is he? You told him?"

"Yes, Mary, I told him." Ancilla grinned. "I went

112

right up to him in the street and told him, very quietly of course, that you had to go to Juttah to help Elisabeth."

"Right in the street?" Mary turned on her side to look at her sister. "You didn't."

"I did. Because I'm crippled, I do all kinds of things that others can't do." Ancilla's smug smile told Mary she enjoyed breaking customs—and getting by with it.

"He said to let him—or Aaron—know as soon as you were back."

Ancilla studied Mary in the starlight. "You're different somehow," she said.

Although Mary was exhausted, sleep would not come. She peered into the darkness. In memory, she saw the heavenly being again, majestic against the starlight, and knew, now, that it was the great Angel Gabriel. The same thrill tingled her shoulders.

When Mary awoke, Zebedee was gone. Eli too—out to supervise harvest of the first ripe grapes. Mary waited until her father returned.

Shadows filled the corners of the room when the evening meal was finished. The familiar stones, smoke twisting upward from the lamps, all were soothing and familiar. Eli rose and rubbed his shoulders against the wall to relieve an itch, his eyes closed. Ancilla jabbed a needle through leather, mending a wineskin, while Anna sat on a stool twisting wool around a spindle. Mary swallowed and began.

"Mother—Father—I have something to tell you."

Eli opened his eyes but went on scratching. Anna tipped her head sideways to look up at Mary, her fingers at the spindle never pausing. Ancilla dropped the wineskin

113

on her lap, her lips parted. Her mother said: "Well?"

"The angel Gabriel," Mary began, "brought me a message, too." She held her breath and looked at each one. They could have been made of clay. "I'm to bear a son," said Mary quickly, "whose father is—is—God." She let out all her breath to quiet her beating heart.

But something was wrong. Neither her mother's or father's face showed they had heard a word she said, although Ancilla's face glowed.

"My baby will be born about the time of the Festival of Lights," she added, as if this would explain it all.

The skin pulled tight across Anna's teeth. Her right hand extended like a Roman statue. "You're *what?* You are *what?*" she repeated, her voice as thin as new ice.

Ancilla moved to stand beside Mary. Eli tightened his girdle. The look on his face killed joy completely.

Mary hurriedly repeated the whole story. "I asked how this could be since I hadn't gone to my husband, but he said nothing is impossible with God." She glanced at them wildly. Wrong, something was terribly wrong. Mary took another breath: "I'm to have a baby and I am not to be afraid."

Silence.

A living coldness permeated. Mary saw her parents' faces harden. Even Ancilla's glow had long ago faded.

"My child—" Mary started, but choked on the words.

Anna stood up and carefully hung the wool and spindle on a peg. It was a long time before she turned back to face her daughter. She said in a voice as flat as worked stone, "I don't believe you."

Her father's face had turned white, now a dull red mottled his features. He lowered his head like a dangerous bull. "You are with child?" he asked. Mary's chin quivered.

"The Angel Gabriel..." But she never got to finish. Her father grabbed her by the shoulders and shook her like a dog shakes a rat.

"What have you done? Expect me to believe? Take me for a *fool?*" Dimly Mary heard Ancilla shouting for him to stop. Anna stood, hands clenched at her sides.

Eli let Mary go so suddenly that she stumbled to the floor. Ancilla tried to help, but Mary was faster and calmly rose to her feet. Nor did she weep.

"Fulfill a prophecy," snorted her father, his nostrils pinched. He spat to one side. A long moment passed in which no one dared move or speak—including Eli.

At last he said evenly, "You know the law. You'll go before the leader of the synagogue. You'll be cast out. You know your sin. It's fornication."

Anna covered her eyes with her hands. "Eli, no! They will stone her!" Ancilla cried out at their words. Mary's resolve began to shake. But Ancilla now looked her father squarely in the face.

"They can't stone her. Only Rome can decree such a death. There's no magistrate in Nazareth."

Eli pulled at his hair and beard. "The shame. The shame!" he cried.

Mary felt her mother's coldness, her father's misery. *El Shaddai*, she prayed, *help them both to see.* But God did not answer her prayer. She would have to answer Eli herself and comfort him if he would let her. Then she would see about her mother.

She moved toward her father to tell him of the scriptures Zacharias found. He listened but did not respond. Anna took up the wool again and began her work, ignoring Mary completely. Ancilla wiped her eyes.

Five minutes later, Eli shot out the door to bring Joseph. *Joseph!* But she wanted to tell him herself! Mary crept outside to sit on the bench under the olive tree and swallowed rising sobs.

"Here." Ancilla held out a kerchief.

"I'm not crying!" Mary said. "Why don't they believe me?"

"I believe every word you said. You'd never do anything wicked."

"But why doesn't the angel come and tell them?" Mary brushed hair from her face with both hands. "Joseph will believe me." But her throat felt brittle.

Eli and Joseph hurried into the courtyard. Eli walked directly into the house, speaking to Joseph over his shoulder.

"She's your responsibility now." Ancilla ran into the house behind her father, leaving Mary alone with her betrothed.

He strode across the courtyard and knelt before Mary.

Mary reached out her hands and looked into his eyes—eyes full of pain.

"What's the matter?" he asked with such tenderness she almost sobbed.

"Joseph!" gray eyes full of tears looked into his, "a wonderful thing—has happened to me. But my parents won't believe me."

"I'll believe you."

"I wanted to tell you before I left for Juttah, but there wasn't time."

"Tell me what?" He took her hands in his.

A little breeze trembled the branches of the olive and a nightjar cried.

"The night before I left," she began, "an angel came to me."

Joseph dropped her hands, rubbed fingers across his brow, looking bewildered.

"The Angel Gabriel—" He pulled back from her a little. She went on bravely. "He told me I was to—bear a child. A child who will be king."

Joseph's face lighted.

"My son a king," said Joseph. "Well!" He shook his head. "This is marvelous news!"

"I am already past three months with child, Joseph," Mary replied almost coldly. "God's child." There was an awful silence. Joseph's mouth twisted with pain.

"What have you done, Mary? What have you done?" He stood quickly. "I must think what to do," he said and ran from the yard, leaving Mary alone under the olive tree.

Cold as death, Mary watched the moon slide behind scudding clouds.

Alone, alone, alone, the breeze whispered.

Ancilla came around the corner and knelt before Mary. "Come inside," she coaxed, pulling Mary to her feet. "You're shivering."

"I do not know what Joseph will do with you," her father said hoarsely, "but you are no longer welcome

here." Ancilla and his wife nearly drowned him out with
their cries. Mary's hand tightened on Ancilla's arm, but
she did not let her father see how his words wounded
her. She turned to go, but Anna stopped her.

"Eli, you cannot mean that," she said, an unusual fire
in her eyes. "We can send her to Salome or to Elisabeth
until it is over."

"No!" he insisted, keeping his eyes lowered. "She
will take the punishment synagogue leaders decide she
deserves. She has broken the law—"

"The law, the law—" cried Anna, exasperated, flinging her hand out. "This is your *daughter*, Eli!"

"—Broken the law—and must pay the price. We will
talk about it no more."

"At least she will sleep the night here," Anna said in
a tone that even Eli did not dispute. "But tomorrow…"
he did not finish his threat.

CHAPTER 15

Mary lay thinking, praying, staring unseeing into the diamond-pricked sky. *Now I don't ever have Joseph.* She rubbed her lapis ring and wept quietly into her pillow until there were no more tears. *Oh, Great and Mighty God, you know I tell the truth. Mighty God, help me—and your son.* The jarring cry of the nighthawk came and a whir of wings sailed past the shelter. *Like King David, I will rest and not be afraid—but oh, it will be so hard.* Mary wept, and although God took away her fear, she could not sleep.

Mary was still awake when morning light let her see the parapet around the roof. Warblers welcomed the morning. The scent of fresh-cut hay drifted across the village. Then Mary thought she heard her name being called very faintly. She drew on her tunic and tiptoed downstairs to the gate.

"Joseph?" she whispered.

"Open the gate." Mary eased it open and Joseph wrapped her into his arms. She dared not speak. Whatever he might say, at least she had this moment of warmth.

"Come," he whispered and led her a few steps down the empty street. "My poor Mary," he said stroking her hair. "I'm so sorry. Forgive me."

She laid her head against his shoulder.

"I was going to divorce you," he hurried on, "hide you away quietly." She lifted her head, her eyes flashing alarm. "But last night the angel came to me, too." The street whirled around Mary, stone walls, trees, Joseph's face, like a water reflection stirred by a dropped pebble. Joseph tilted Mary's face up, his fingers gentle on her chin. "He said the baby is God's. That I should have believed you. I'm truly sorry."

Mary looked out towards the rosy dawn and said out loud, "You did not forget me." They walked to the gate. She held fast to his fingers.

"Now, away," he said quickly, as they paused. "I'll come for you this evening. We'll not have a public wedding. Your father would never allow it."

Mary started, but only for the briefest moment. Joseph was right—it was true. No wedding. Poor Mother. Poor Ancilla. She heard her mother slap the bedrugs as she rolled them up.

"They're awake, Joseph. I must go in."

"Tell him I'm coming for you tonight. That I do not require him to return the brideprice." Their lips met in a lingering kiss. Mary did not smile as he hurried away.

The air was frozen as the family broke fast, no one speaking so much as a good morning. Anna set out curds and bread, but only Eli ate.

"Father," Mary finally said, "Joseph is coming for me

this evening. He will not require that you give back the brideprice." Her father said nothing, nor did he look at her. Soon he went off to supervise the vineyard.

Anna clamped her lips shut and moved her spinning outside under the olive tree as though her daughter were not at home.

"I will go with Joseph tonight," Mary whispered to Ancilla as she collected all she owned. "It will be my wedding."

Ancilla's confusion filled the room. "But there isn't time to invite the guests or prepare the gifts—or feast!" Her disappointment hurt Mary deeply. Ancilla had looked forward to this wedding as her own, knowing she herself would never be a bride. Mary held her sister close as Ancilla wept.

After a silent evening meal Eli and Anna went into the courtyard. Ancilla and Mary opened the chest, the scent of lavender filled the room. Mary slipped the dress over her head, lifting her shoulders to support the weight. *Some great, great, great-grandmother wove this linen and dyed it lapis-blue. Each bride since has added embroidery or sewn jewels on the bodice, but I can add nothing but heartache.* Mary ran her fingers across six rows of pearls around the neck. Ancilla fastened the scarlet belt, embroidered with pomegranates, stitched with threads of gold. Mary fitted the scarlet headdress over her hair.

"You look like a queen, more beautiful than Salome." Ancilla did not smile, but gave Mary a long look. "Do you think Mother will let you wear it?" That thought hadn't entered Mary's mind. A hot spark of anger struck.

"I'm a true virgin bride, and I *will* wear the wedding garments." She lifted her head proudly, making the coins on the headdress jingle. "You come with me, Ancie," she said softly, "as my bridesmaid." Ancilla beamed. "You can bring the clothes back home with you afterwards. Because they refused to believe me, I'll be denied all that which is due me as a bride, but I *will* go dressed like one."

Joseph, Aaron and Huldah stepped inside the gate. Torches in their hands threw dancing shadows on the walls. Eli and Anna gave them the kisses of greeting reluctantly and stood aside to let Joseph pass.

Joseph looked the king he should have been, tall, regal in the crimson tunic of his ancestors, decorated with golden braid and bound with a leather girdle studded with garnets and emeralds. Opals shimmered on his shoes.

Aaron spoke first. "I come as friend of the bridegroom again to lead the procession as Joseph takes his bride." He did not smile, but looked toward the door. Mary paused in the doorway. Joseph's eyes caught fire as she walked across the courtyard and knelt before him. He lifted her up and led her to her father.

"Eli," he began, "I have come to take my bride as my wife. I will make no excuses except that I love your Mary. God has chosen her for my wife. I will not insist that you return the brideprice."

"Your wife has told me as much," Eli replied curtly.

Mary picked up the bundle that contained all she could count her own. Joseph tucked it under his arm and led her to the gate. Eli said nothing, only walked behind the house. Anna looked at Mary, eyes full of tears. Mary blinked back her own and took Ancilla's hand. Together they stepped to Joseph's side.

Huldah pressed Anna's hand, but Anna just looked at the ground. Then Aaron and Huldah held their torches high and fell into step behind Joseph, Mary and Ancilla. Aaron's words rolled off his tongue as they departed, "I'll bring Ancilla back as soon as they are settled," he said, his face grim.

"Goodbye," Mary said in a whisper, all she could manage. Aaron gave the gate a push with an elbow and let it slam behind him.

No more the rosy dreams of everyone rejoicing because she bore the coming king. She and Joseph would keep the secret hidden from all the world until God told them to reveal it. Her baby would be Joseph's to all the world. Only Ancilla knew. And Elisabeth. And Zacharias. And Aaron and Huldah, if Joseph had told them. Mary didn't know.

Mary began the song sung by all bridal processions on the way to their new home. Ancilla joined in, raising her voice above the rest. Neighbors, Sarah and Ezra, joined them. Others on the streets fell in step according to custom, whispering questions about the absence of her parents, but turned back when they realized they would receive no gifts and that no feast would follow. Gossip would thrive on the morrow, but Mary held her head proudly and even had courage to smile. The song faded at the edge of the village.

"Joseph, where are we going?" she asked, looking around puzzled, for she saw no houses.

"There," Joseph said as they passed the well. He pointed up to the hill beyond. "See that shepherd's hut? No one is using it now. It's small with no courtyard, but it has a grinding stone."

Ancilla looked shocked, but smiled when she saw Mary's face. Huldah said with an embarrassed laugh. "It was all we could find at the moment."

Joseph took Mary's arm more firmly in his. "It is only for now." His eyes took on their usual twinkle. "We'll live in a palace someday." Aaron nudged Huldah as if to say it wouldn't surprise him if they did.

A black nanny goat, tied to a bush beside the hut, stood up on her hind feet and bleated a welcome of sorts. They stepped inside the door and saw evidence of Huldah's loving work. The place shone clean in the torchlight. Joseph's bedrugs lay on the stone ledge above the dirt floor. A sack of grain, a basket of bread and figs and a jar of water waited by the door.

Huldah and Ancilla went inside to help Mary take off the wedding garments. Huldah untangled a coin from Mary's hair while she talked.

"The place is clean, that I'll say, for I came this afternoon and scrubbed it myself."

Mary enfolded Huldah with loving arms. "You and Aaron are so kind. I will always remember this little hut." Huldah sensed the girl's troubled heart and put a torch to a wick in a bowl of oil. Mary embraced her sister.

"We'll meet each evening at the well, Ancie. I'll come early before the shepherds and the others."

Ancilla said, "Mother and Father will get over it. You'll see," as she hugged her sister tightly.

With good-bye embraces, Aaron, Huldah and Ancilla started down the path toward Nazareth.

Joseph and Mary sat on the stone bench before the tiny hut and watched them down the hill until they were lost in shadows. A few lights flickered in the village.

"God will take care of us," Mary said a few moments later. She failed to notice that Joseph did not confirm her words.

He stared toward the Great Sea where Mt. Carmel stood a black lump against a bank of crimson clouds beyond the Valley of the Kishon.

CHAPTER 16

Four months passed with only a few visitors to Joseph's hut, Aaron and Huldah, and twice Deborah, Mary's childhood friend. Each evening Mary had met Ancilla at the well, but now, in the cold of winter, her sister did not come as often.

One winter morning Mary watched green and orange chaffinches shoot flashes of color against the somber clouds heavy with rain and listened to them calling, "Tsip, tsip, tsip. Go, go, go." She watched Joseph climb the path and ran to meet him as swiftly as her swollen body allowed, ignoring the baby's kicking. They walked toward their hut, their fingers entwined.

"Report's true. Men must go to the village their families came from. To register," he added. "Rome has a new legate over all the east. Quirinius. He wants no one missed in the census for a new tax."

"Can I come, too?" she asked, but he shook his head.

"No. Women don't have to go and roads may not be safe." They walked slowly up the hill, pausing to give her time to catch her breath.

"I've thought it all through," she said, hurrying her words to stop his protest. "There are three or four weeks before the baby will come. Plenty of time." But she had forgotten Zacharias' prophecy.

"No, Mary."

"But I feel well and I can easily walk to Bethlehem. I did it before, Joseph." He was losing.

"You don't want him to be born on the road, do you?"

"We'll just walk more slowly. You don't mind, do you? There'll be so many people...we won't be alone."

Despite her brave words, she knew they would be alone. Few in Nazareth talked to them publicly. Joseph had no idea how isolated they had become. But she knew. Mary saw all the averted glances, felt it when few would speak to her. Out of her careful control, her sense of rejection broke through suddenly.

"I can't stay here if you're gone. You don't notice because you're not here all day, but I don't see anyone. I'll be so lonely."

They touched their fingertips to the mazuzah and stooped to enter their hut. Mary looked into her husband's eyes, his face a battlefield of indecision. She joined ranks with his desire to have her come. Joseph smiled down at her and flapped his hands. She knew that she could go. He murmured into her hair.

"All right, we'll go together." She reached up to kiss him.

The sky still promised rain, but they decided to leave as soon as they were ready. Mary put the wooden kneading bowl and dried fruit and cheese in Joseph's pack, pushed her feet into her heavy walking shoes and tied her cloak around her neck. Joseph hoisted up the pack and rolled sleeping mats onto his shoulders. They started for Bethlehem.

On the road south through Nazareth they left the goat with Huldah and then knocked on Eli's gate. Ancilla opened it. Mary had hoped she might see her mother, but it was not to be.

"Mary!" Ancilla cried. Quickly she stepped into the street and shut the gate behind her. "Where are you going?" she whispered, fear clouding her eyes.

"To the census in Bethlehem."

"But Mary—" The girl looked at her sister's protruding middle. "You can't walk all that way."

"I can and I will," Mary said, "We'll be back in less than two weeks."

"And I will stay here," Ancilla said wistfully.

Mary hesitated. Was she wrong to go? No. Something stronger than her own reason told her she must.

Mary kissed her sister. "Tell Mother and Father I miss them." It hurt to be home again and not to see them.

The couple joined hundreds of men returning to their birth places. Only a few women journeyed with them. In spite of resentment toward Rome, people turned the journey into a holiday. They laughed and sang—sometimes David's psalms and sometimes the popular songs of the day. Joseph and Mary occasionally joined the singing when they found themselves at the tag end of a group, but for the most part, they walked alone among the people.

They started down the escarpment into the Valley of

the Kishon River and the Plain of Esdraelon. The air was crisp, almost cold, and so clear they could see the Great Sea shining to the west beyond Mt. Carmel. Below them the Valley spread left and right, a checkerboard of fields already planted and waiting the spring rains. Tiny villages dotted the valley. To the east, Mt. Tabor blocked the view, but across the valley, a half-day's walk, rose the misty hills of Samaria.

As they passed the village of Capercotnai, Mary pressed close to Joseph.

"Did you notice those men who pulled aside to let us pass, rather than walk with us? And they've been neighbors all my life."

Joseph looked away. His voice held a touch of rare bitterness. "But they don't know what we know, Mary." He squeezed her hand. They walked on in silence.

"Joseph," Mary said a half-hour later, old memories catching at her heart. "I'm afraid of Herod."

"Look," he said, waving his hand behind him at the line of people and towards those ahead. "We're just two among thousands. Two Galileans who hardly count as citizens. We're no threat." But Mary was not convinced.

"I bear the king who will *replace* King Herod," Mary whispered, "Joseph, Herod has killed his own sons."

"Have no fear. God will protect him."

They walked on several hours toward Sychar under a sky threatening rain. Around them newly planted fields waited to burst into green.

"It's too bad my brothers refused to register," Joseph said as they trudged down the next dusty hill. "We could have walked with them." Mary moved more and more slowly, not speaking of the growing ache in the small of her back.

"Joseph, aren't your brothers in danger?" she asked a little out of breath as they climbed another hill. "Won't Herod find out. Won't he punish them? Kill them, even?"

"They're hiding up in Galilee," he said quietly. "They're careful. Herod doesn't consider common Galileans a threat."

"He considers your leader Ezekias one, and he's hidden up north." She held her back with one hand.

"Something wrong? Tired?" Joseph asked, but Mary waved it off.

She struggled on, determined not to lag behind nor to let Joseph see how tired she felt, but he guessed and paused often to rest. Men's reproachful looks asked why he hadn't left her at home.

The third day, with an east wind chilling them, they plodded on. Mary could not know Joseph's thoughts, but hers were about the birth of her baby. She determined to deliver him back in Galilee, far from Herod. She knew now she should not have come.

That night the clouds brought rain. Mary and Joseph stayed snug under an overhang of rock near Sychar. Here in the south a stubble of green covered plowed fields. The afternoon of the fourth day they passed Jerusalem, sulking under a canopy of clouds, but even in the gloom, the Temple shone on its hill.

Hundreds of the people turned towards it, but Mary and Joseph pressed on.

"We'll come back for the baby's redemption," Joseph promised, "but not until the weather is better."

Bethlehem lay only two hours away. Like the approach of an unseen menace the ache in her back increased with each step, and with each step, the soles of her feet hurt more. The baby turned and kicked as though he, too, could hardly wait to reach Bethlehem.

Heavy clouds threatened rain again. Dark came early and dulled the huge yellow sandstone walls of the caravansary looming ahead of them just outside Bethlehem. They passed temporary shelters of brush thrown up by the Romans to house the hundreds swarming into the village.

"Stay tight behind me while I elbow us through this crowd." Joseph said to her. "The crowd is blocking the entrance to this inn." Mary clutched the back of Joseph's cloak and followed.

"I hope there's room," she panted.

Men jostled against them. Mary looked up at the dingy sandstone blocks that made a massive front to the caravansary, more like a fort than an inn. They stepped up to the gate and stopped, unable to see inside. The baby kicked and turned over. The guard with an empty socket for a left eye, held a knotted staff across the archway.

"We wish a room," Joseph said briskly. He held out his fist. Mary knew it concealed a denarius.

"Rooms only for those who can pay double." The guard stared rudely at Mary's stomach. He waved his staff at open spaces around the courtyard. "Try the stable.

Price is one denarius." The gateman looked over their heads at the crowd of people pressing up behind them. "Next!" he roared.

Joseph looked down at Mary, then reluctantly gave the man the coin.

The gateman pulled aside his staff just enough to let them pass through the gate. "No room! he shouted to those outside.

Mary and Joseph reached the safety of the platform close by the gate in a cacophony of donkeys braying, camels spitting fountains of foam, goats bleating and oxen bellowing. Now a trumpet announced curfew from the city gate.

The stable stretched the full length of the inn. It was merely a raised stone platform covered by a roof, separated into cubicles with reed walls dobbed with mud. A stone trough on the edge of the platform provided a manger for donkeys, goats and an occasional ox, all tied to posts before it. Around the other three sides of the courtyard small doorways opened into rooms. A porch on the second floor gave entrance to other rooms reserved for the wealthy.

They had the last open compartment in the entire inn. It faced a well in the center of the courtyard with a large drinking trough. The area was crowded with women shouting in five languages at animals crowding in for water. Men haggled over charges for fodder. Lost children cried for mothers.

"Oh, Joseph, it's dreadful!"

"We'll get no sleep in here!" he sighed as he lifted Mary onto the stone floor. "But I suppose we must be thankful." He banged the packs onto the space and stretched his shoulders.

"God saved this space just for us," Mary said as she unpacked bedmats. They sat upon them and Joseph wiped her feet with olive oil.

"I don't think I could have walked another minute." She divided what was left of their cheese, but kept enough dry bread for morning. Over the hullabaloo in the courtyard, they thanked God for their food and ate it as though it were their last meal.

Later he said, "I must go inside Bethlehem to register, but you will be safe here."

"Oh, no. I want to go with you." Mary looked out across the yard, filled with strangers. "Why can't I go?"

"Because women are not required. Only men will be there." His eyes smiled.

In spite of voices in the next partition, the baby's thumping and the throbbing in her back, she fell asleep immediately.

The inn's motley inhabitants settled down for the night, children quieted, animals dozed. Finally the courtyard cleared. Stars looked down on the sleeping village and on the hills surrounding Bethlehem, on shepherds guarding flocks of sheep.

But Mary had slept not more than an hour when a commotion at the gate awakened her. She raised up on one elbow.

"What's that?" she whispered, but Joseph quickly pulled her down.

"It's soldiers," he said in a low voice. "Just be still." He appeared to be asleep almost at once, but Mary lifted her head and watched, her heart pounding, just as it did that day a soldier had kicked her mother, for the men were dressed just the same. She sat up with her cloak covering all of her except her eyes and saw eight or nine soldiers erect their tents beside the well.

They spoke with what she thought was a Judean accent. *They aren't Roman. Must be Herod's.*

"Place looks quiet enough," one said, "A mix from all over the country."

"Doesn't matter," said another. "If we want to keep our heads, we'll see no disturbance starts."

The enormous leader barked, "Quiet!" The men crawled inside their tents, all but one, who sat on a stool at the flap of the tent, his gaze moving down the row of cubicles on the stable and across each door on both levels of the inn. No voice challenged the soldiers.

Sleep finally caught her.

Water dripping in their faces wakened them. Moving their rugs to a dry spot in the tiny cubicle, they broke fast on cold bread and water while other travelers began the day, some preparing to move on, and others obviously settling in for a stay. Those with camels packed and moved out through the gate.

The soldiers came out of their tents. All talking ceased for a moment, and then resumed more quietly. People hurried from the well, giving the soldiers full use of the water. Mary pulled her cloak over her head to partially cover her face.

Joseph secured his money in his girdle. He pushed three sheep away from their manger.

"I want to be there before everyone else," he said.

"When will you be back?" she asked, with a glance at a soldier drawing water.

"By noon, I would think." Mary bowed her head.

"Those soldiers are looking right at me." She pulled her cloak farther over her face. Joseph reassured her.

"They're looking at everyone. They're Herod's guards, but they don't know who you are. Just stay quiet." Joseph jumped off the manger.

Mary leaned her back against the rough stones where she could watch the movement in the courtyard. Herod's soldiers cast as much gloom on the crowd as did the steady drip of rain. Every hour one of them circled the courtyard, and each time it seemed he stared right at her. She waited for Joseph all morning.

He did not return.

Rain came down steadily.

After what seemed hours, in the next cubicle, some woman began shouting. "Idiot! Son of a toothless Amorite! Don't return until it's done." A paunchy young man splashed through the puddle in front of Mary and stumbled out the gate.

Now here came the woman, heaving herself up on Mary's stable. Mary drew back in horror at the hennaed hair, lips heavy with a greasy red paste, a red carnelian stone in her right nostril and dark eyes thickly lined in kohl. Out of a tunic slashed to the waist peeped bulging breasts, like two melons. The woman came straight at her with a big red smile.

"Hello there," she said and climbed onto the platform. "My son Stephanus is an idiot."

"Shalom, peace," was all Mary could think to say, and it sounded false even to her ears. She stared like a bird hypnotized by a snake, but the woman only laughed.

"I shouldn't be talking to such as you, but I get lonesome." A sadness checked her smile. "My name is Sherah, from Magdala." She twisted an emerald ring the size of a grape.

Mary moved aside. She couldn't ask her to leave. "Sit here where it's not leaking."

The harlot lowered her bulk onto the rug and said, "Where's your man?"

"Registering." Mary glanced at the soldier strutting by.

"Don't fear that soldier," Sherah said and barked a laugh at him. He quickly moved on.

Mary couldn't help liking Sherah. And she felt safer with the woman there.

"We've been here two sabbaths," she now said to Mary. "The proper official still hasn't come."

"Two sabbaths!" Mary pressed both hands to her stomach.

"Don't you fret. There's a midwife here."

The puddles grew deeper. The wind picked up. People hurried by with shoulders hunched, heads bent against the blowing rain. The guard's commander did not move from the door of his tent.

The early darkness stole in before Joseph returned. They might be there many days.

*

For the next three weeks, Joseph went each day to the market place, only to return dispirited. Their supply of money dwindled to a few denarii, and still their turn to register did not come. The baby moved lower. Mary's back ached more each day.

Sherah continued to vilify her son Stephanus, who returned with Joseph daily. During the days she sat with Mary, brought cheese, carried water. Under the woman's paint, Mary found a real person she began to enjoy. Sherah never spoke of her own life, and Mary told her only a little about hers. Neither woman asked questions. It seemed to be a gentle pact between them.

"Sherah," Mary said one dreary afternoon, "why do those soldiers continually stare at me?"

"Well, our spaces are directly in front of them, and," Sherah quickly hid a whimsical smile, "perhaps they think they know me."

Sherah gave Joseph a large rug which he fastened over the entrance. Mary breathed easier when soldiers could no longer look at her, and although they kept guard, they bothered no one.

Rain kept a chill in the air and nights grew cold. Each day she trudged around the courtyard, holding fast to Sherah's arm.

Late one afternoon, Joseph, returned and leaped up on the platform.

"At last!" he cried. "We signed today!" His hearty laugh turned the soldier's head toward their space.

Mary smiled, the first real happiness he'd seen in her face for many days.

"We leave tomorrow," Joseph said, "that is—can you?"

"Oh, we've got days and days," she said, if a little uncertainly, "although Sherah thinks it may be soon." Mary put an eye to the slit between the curtain and the wall. "I wish we could leave tonight."

"The sky is clearing. Tomorrow should be sunny. Besides, you'll want a night's rest before we start." Joseph began packing their belongings. "We'll start at daybreak."

CHAPTER 17

The night turned clear and cold with no wind. Stars winked through the black spaces around the door hanging. Mary turned from side to side, heavy and stiff, and finally slept.

A sharp wrench of pain jerked her awake. A moan escaped. Teeth chattering, shivers shaking her body, she sat up slowly. The baby did not seem to be moving, but her abdomen tightened. She poked Joseph in the ribs. He shot upright.

"What is it?"

"It's time. I think it's time. Get Sherah."

"Sherah showed me where a midwife lives—outside the walls. I'll fetch her," Joseph burst from the curtained platform.

What am I doing in Bethlehem, with no one but a harlot to help me? Nothing for my baby, not even bands to wrap him in? Mary would have wept if she hadn't been so frightened. Sherah hoisted herself up on the platform.

"No need to fret," she said, her voice calming Mary's fears.

"I've nothing with me, no winding bands." Mary shivered again.

"Here are my funeral binding strips." Sharah set a bundle beside Mary. "I always carry them with me," she said in a matter-of-fact voice. Mary fought back tears. She would not cry. But she didn't want her baby bound in funeral strips, but all she could do was use what God provided.

Sherah brushed thanks away as she would a fly. When Joseph returned with the midwife, she let herself off the platform and settled in next door. Joseph walked the courtyard.

In the hour that followed, while Mary underwent wave after wave of pain, the plump, kindly midwife kept up a steady flow of talk, telling Mary of life in Bethlehem, where she had delivered hundreds of babies. She had brought the pottery birthing bowl, just wide enough to fit between Mary's feet.

"What a baby wants to come into this world for is more than I can fathom," the woman said, quietly massaging Mary's back.

"But there's a reason—" Mary murmured. She received only a questioning look. Spasms came one after another in the coming hours, and the woman knew just what to do. Mary determined not to cry out and she did not.

"You squat now." Mary heaved into the awkward position over the bowl. "Let me put another rug around your shoulders. This little fellow is coming quickly. Just breathe deeply. That's right—. Push hard now. Take little breaths. It's coming!" Mary pressed down mightily and gasped as the midwife caught the baby. It let out a strong, healthy cry. The woman helped Mary to lie down and placed the baby on her stomach, then took the afterbirth. "You did just fine. As easy as this birth was, you can have dozens." Mary smiled and said she didn't know if God wanted her to.

The woman stuck her head outside the curtain. "You can come in now." Joseph climbed back up, carefully drawing the curtain tightly behind him.

He knelt beside the baby and looked long into the pinched little face. He smiled the tender smile Mary remembered from their first meeting.

"How little—and red," he said, "but he's beautiful," he added quickly.

"It's a boy," the midwife said, cutting the cord and tying it.

"We knew it," said Joseph.

The midwife looked at Mary, her eyebrows pyramids of perplexity, then back at Joseph and shook her head.

Joseph kneeled beside Mary and pushed the hair from her wet forehead. The midwife rubbed the baby's body firmly with salt and washed it off with cold water, while the baby howled his protest. Then she took Sherah's yards of funeral strips and wound them tightly around him. The midwife left soon after, and Mary and Joseph were alone with her baby.

Lights danced in Joseph's eyes. "We do find ourselves in strange circumstances, don't we?" Mary could see no reason for amusement.

In the fitful shadows of the oil lamp Joseph took the baby's tiny first finger between his calloused ones.

"You don't amount to much, do you," he said quietly. "For a King."

"He's beautiful." Mary said and held him closer.

He eased down beside his wife and placed his hand over hers, the one that cradled her baby.

In the tent, the red glow of a lamp outlined a soldier speaking into the ear of his commander.

Rough voices woke Mary.

"There's no savior here," she heard the gateman growl.

"Joseph," Mary whispered, shaking him. "Joseph! Listen. They are looking for a newborn baby." Mary's throat tightened.

"Give him to me." Joseph pulled the bundle from Mary's arms, threw a cloak over his tunic, and stepped outside before her outstretched arm could stop him.

Peering through a hole in the curtain, she saw Joseph push a sheep and two goats away from the manger and lay the baby in the straw. Now he spoke quietly to the gateman, then came back and stood beside the sleeping child.

Mary's heart raced. She looked out a crack in the curtain to the soldiers' tents. The guard stared at Joseph, a sword across his knees. A group of men entered the gate. Heavy feet shuffled up to the manger. She saw a dozen shepherds of all ages kneel before it, and listened to an old man speak in a rough hill dialect.

"We just seen a miracle."

"We was sitting 'round the fire," said another in a low voice filled with awe. He turned his head to look back over his shoulder to the east. "And right there was an angel." His voice hushed and others nodded. "It loomed up out of nowhere." He looked slowly up into the starlight.

"There he stood right in front of us," another said, throwing his arms wide. "Then the whole sky flared with light, so bright we're nigh blinded." He turned to Joseph. "Didn't you see it?" The shepherds stretched necks to watch the baby.

They're worshiping your son, Father God. Mary rejoiced even as her heart pounded.

Joseph pulled back the curtain. "Here is the baby's mother. This is a special child sent from God." Mary knelt on the manger above them, wondering what had brought them.

The gateman joined them. Other heads peeped out of cubicles. Stephanus and one or two men joined the gateman. Only the shepherds spoke.

The soldier's hands tightened on his sword.

"We sat there shaking," another shepherd went on, "afeard to speak. Then the angel spoke, right out loud." The men behind pressed closer. "It said 'Fear not, I bring good news.' He told us to go find our Savior. It said—find the Savior. Said that he'd be a baby wrapped in swaddling cloths and lying in a manger." He gestured down dramatically at Mary's child, then bowed his head to the ground. "Just like the angel said."

Mary heard several indrawn breaths. She glanced at the soldier. Joseph smoothed the straw around the baby. Others joined the men with the shepherds.

Now a lad could keep still no longer. "I knew this

place had mangers," he said, "so we came here first. We ran all the way." He looked at the old shepherd, who nodded his white-thatched head. "And we've found him!"

Another man, with a lion skin hanging over one shoulder, took up the story. "Then the sky filled with strange creatures like nothing seen on this earth before," he said in a resounding voice. "Singing, they were, praises to God, and blessing us with peace." Mary gave Joseph a frantic look and nodded toward Herod's guard.

This soldier stood erect as another joined him. Mary's heart hammered in her ears. She cried a warning, but too late, Joseph didn't hear it. He was standing beside the manger holding the baby up for all to see. Calloused hands touched the baby's wrappings as softly as feathers.

Then they all began to shout at once: "Hallelujah! Hallelujah! We've found the Savior." More people tumbled from stables.

Joseph raised his hand for silence.

The soldier jerked his sword.

"Something about a Savior of Israel," they heard him say to his commander.

"There's no savior but Herod!" said the officer, his face mottled red. He advanced, calling his soldiers. A *sisst* from the gateman turned all heads. Like shadows everyone disappeared into cubicles, and the shepherds slipped out the gate. The gateman slammed it behind them. Outside came their distinct cry: "The Messiah! The Messiah is here."

*

Mary settled the curtain behind him as Joseph climbed with the infant onto the platform. She quickly hid the baby against her body under the bedrug.

"Where's that baby?" roared the soldier. He strode across the courtyard and pulled open the curtain. The couple laid still as death, praying the baby wouldn't cry. The man looked long, then stepped to Sherah's opening.

She said with a voice of contempt, "Do you want Herod to hear of a disturbance over a baby?" The soldier slammed his spear against the ground.

"You were there. I saw you. Who is that child? Is he a child of the royal line?" Sherah stared him down.

"Royal? Born in a stable?" She reached out plump fingers and snapped them on the soldier's armplate. "Now," and she winked, "tell King Herod that his old friend Sherah sends her greetings." The soldier considered her, turned on his heel, and was next heard saying that it was a mistake. Just shepherds looking for a baby they thought was the Messiah.

Mary looked at her son in the starlight. What if the shepherds had said *King?* The tiny boy opened one eye and yawned. He opened the other eye and looked at his mother for the first time. She hugged him to her more tightly.

Herod shall not have you!

She laid down the challenge but knew it was feeble against the strength of the King. Tomorrow, tomorrow they would leave for home.

CHAPTER 18

When Mary awoke, Joseph was gone, but Sherah sat beside her. She helped Mary put the baby to nurse. The smoky smell of campfires told them people were rising to break their fasts.

"Here, have a sip of water," Sherah said. Mary released the baby and sat up as her friend held a cup to her lips. "I've warmed the last of your cheese on a stick and brought you fresh goat milk." With a grateful sigh, Mary took the food.

"Sherah, what would we have done without you?"

"Eat; you'll need your strength." The cheese, hot and spicy soft, warmed Mary as she listened to Sherah. "Joseph and Stephanus are gone to find a donkey for you." Color left Mary's face at the words. The floodtide of last night came back to her. Sherah took Mary's shoulder firmly. "I heard the shepherds last night—" Her voice trailed off. "Is this little mite the promised Messiah?"

"Yes…yes," was all that Mary could say. With a deep breath, she added, "Please tell no one. No one."

Sherah patted the baby's back, swaying with him as women do. "That the Almighty would allow me—. You must go from here. The shepherds were at the gate again this morning."

"Do the soldiers know?" Mary put on her cloak and hid the baby inside.

"You must leave quickly." Sherah busied herself with putting things in a pack. "Joseph says he'll take you to Elisabeth."

He returned with a,"Good, you're ready. Thanks to Sherah, we have a donkey for you to ride." Mary hugged her, but she said not to mash the baby.

Joseph pulled back the curtain and stepped off the platform, promising never to forget Sherah, and helped Mary mount the donkey.

Sherah nodded toward the soldiers and then toward the gate. She lifted her plump, majestic figure and walked toward the soldiers' tents, moving her hands just enough to let the jewels on her fingers catch the light. Every eye in the courtyard was upon her.

Even the gateman did not see Mary and Joseph go.

Without looking back they hurried the donkey south through the village. At every corner, voices buzzed with the miracle the shepherds had blazed all over the village.

Joseph talked of what he'd planned. "We will be safe with Zacharias 'til Naming Day and his redemption. Then we'll go straight home to Nazareth."

"I'll be so proud to show him to Mother and Father. Surely when they see him, they'll forgive us." Joseph fingered the auburn fuzz on the baby's head when Mary took him from the sling.

"His hair shows a mite of red, like yours," he teased.

The baby opened his mouth like a little fish and began to cry.

"I'm holding a *king*," Mary said and tickled the baby's chin. "What a long time before men will kneel before you again. And you'll fulfill the message to the shepherds, too, for you will save Israel from Rome."

Mary looked up to the hills where sheep dotted the pastures, and hugged her baby tighter. They moved on through the rolling hills toward Juttah.

Elisabeth welcomed them with beaming face and out-stretched arms as Mary introduced Joseph.

Zacharias greeted Joseph with sincere kisses of greeting and they talked on the platform while the women said all the things which mothers say, praising and complaining with great pride, comparing their baby boys.

Later they sat visiting around the fire, holding the babies while Zacharias quoted the Prophet Micah, who said the Messiah would be born in Bethlehem.

He gazed fondly at his son who was cooing and jumping against Mary's restraining arms. He shook his head over Mary's baby.

Zacharias turned to Joseph. "You are a kind man, a good man to take Mary."

"In a dream an angel told me to," Joseph replied. Zacharias' look said he understood.

Elisabeth said in wonder, "All three of you saw angels. I never saw an angel, but I have John. That is good enough for me." The women put the babies to sleep in a cradle.

On the eighth day Joseph circumcised the child with a stone knife as Moses' law required.

"What will you name him, Mary," Elisabeth asked.

"I name you Jesus—Savior," said Joseph. "The angel of God told us."

"And Emmanuel, as Gabriel told me," Mary said, her eyes shining, "God with us."

"Yes, Mary, Jesus Emmanuel," Joseph said solemnly, placing his hand over the baby's head in blessing. Zacharias raised his hands to heaven.

They would stay in Juttah three more sabbaths until they could leave for the Temple—and then safety in Nazareth. But surely there was safety in God's Temple.

CHAPTER 19

Clouds threatened the day they left and a cold, blustery wind from the eastern desert seemed trying to blow Judea into the Great Sea. Mary tucked Jesus into his sling against her heart and pulled her cloak tightly around him. Joseph hoisted up the packs to the donkey's back and started for Bethlehem, where they would return the donkey and stay the night.

At dawn they hunched their shoulders and plowed through the wind toward the Jerusalem, the City of Peace. As they topped the last hill, pine and cypress on each side of the roadway bent before the wind. They paused to look down upon the city, and Mary pulled her cloak more tightly around the baby.

"It looks so different." Mary shouted. "Today it looks —foreboding." Joseph did not respond.

Massive walls dwarfed the buildings, except for the great Temple, rising phoenix-like from past destructions. Trees on the Mount of Olives to the east bowed before the wind's onslaught. In the Hinnon Valley directly below them the acrid odors of refuse fires and smoke caught at their nostrils. Black clouds boiled above them. Mary tucked Jesus more securely into his sling and pulled her cloak even tighter. *I'll keep you hidden, except for when we stand before the altar.*

As they dropped down into the Hinnon Valley, the gusts slackened. They rested on a slab of stone under a gnarled olive tree and looked across at the Temple—its roof glowing white and gold against the glowering clouds—and at the gray mass of the Antonia Fortress. Jesus struggled and began to cry. While she put him to her breast, Joseph contemplated the city.

"To stand right there and see the altar." Mary smiled as she spoke. "I'll never forget this day."

"It may not impress you as much as you think, Mary. If you're fearful, you needn't go—I can leave the offerings for you."

"No, no! Of course I want to go!"

As she put Jesus back into his sling, she kissed his cheek. "We must go, Little One," she whispered to him, and faced into the wind again, but there it was not as strong. To her it seemed full of demons, moaning on the hilltops, warning Herod that she was bringing the rival king.

"Come," said Joseph, "there's nothing to fear. It's not God's plan that His son die—surely not!" A sudden gust shook them.

Mary and Joseph followed others on the crooked trail to the valley bottom. There more people joined them, following the path beside the eastern wall. Above them loomed the gray stone blocks Nehemiah had used to repair Jerusalem four hundred years before.

They flowed with the crowd through the narrow

stone archway of the Fountain Gate and into the old City of David and edged their way through the great throng packing the narrow lanes leading to the Temple.

A blare of trumpets resounded across the city. Joseph turned his head. An echoing trumpet pealed from a tower behind them. A long shrill note followed another short one. "It's the Levites," he said to her. "They've begun the Psalm. The altar is open."

"Hurry, Joseph. Hurry." Mary pushed ahead, pulling at his cloak.

From ancient cobblestones they stepped onto a street of white marble where twenty men could walk abreast. It led straight to a mountain of steps made of the same marble and these led to the doorway of an arched tunnel. People climbed the steps, bent double against the wind funneling up from the Kidron Valley on their right. Joseph took Mary's arm as they hunched their way up the steps toward the tunnel opening. Jesus wriggled inside Mary's cloak.

Inside the tunnel the roar of the wind ceased abruptly. Pitch-wood torches flickered on the walls. They stepped into the swarming mass of people in the Court of the Gentiles.

In awe they looked up, up, up at four rows of columns of snowy marble, each pillar carved from a single block and twice as high as the city walls. Mary clutched Joseph's sleeve. "Don't lose me," but her eyes glowed.

"Hang on, then," he said. Mary noticed worry lines around his eyes and looked more carefully around her.

The court was a mosaic of swirling color on acres of

variegated marble pavement. Multitudes milled between vendors' booths. Merchants hawked wares. Barbarian tongues clacked. Cattle, sheep, goats and birds, all meant for sacrifice, made a cacophony, causing the baby to cry. Mary hushed him, patting his back with one hand and holding Joseph's cloak with the other. At a variety of tables with signs above them, bland-faced bankers changed coins into the shekel of the Temple.

"We must change our money, then return here to buy the lamb for your sacrifice." Joseph steered Mary through the crowd toward the table with a sign Galilee above it. A wizened man behind the table looked Joseph up and down as though examining some strange insect. Joseph piled the required denarii on the table to exchange for the shekel of the Temple. A gold-ringed hand swooped them up and dumped them on the scale. He muttered, "Ignorant Galilean," and thrust out his hand for more. Joseph looked at Mary, frowned, shrugged and dug into the pocket in his sleeve. He piled a few more coins on the scale, then a few more. At last the man pushed five Temple shekels toward Joseph and turned to the next customer.

"He cheated!"

"Is there enough for my lamb—and the turtledove?"

"No, we must make do with birds—as the law allows those in poverty. We've almost nothing for food on the way home."

Mary waited while he strode to a booth with bird cages holding doves and pigeons. Joseph returned, head bent, holding two turtledoves by their feet and bumped into a richly dressed young Pharisee. "Fool!" snarled the man as he shook his robe to free it of contamination with a common man. Joseph clenched a fist behind the man's back, but Mary pulled on her husband's sleeve.

They wove their way through hurrying people to the four-foot wall where there were signs in three languages, warning non-Jews that crossing it meant death.

From the bedlam of the Court of the Gentiles, they climbed fourteen marble steps to the Chel. This pavement separated the Court of the Gentiles and the next one, the Court of the Women. Farther than that no women could go, except on the day of their purification. Mary held Jesus up to see the marble and gold, the maze of small rooms, the mass of Jews milling about.

"Look, Little One," she said. "Look at Your Temple. See the wrongdoing here?" Joseph frowned.

She glanced up at the gray stone of the Antonia Fortress looming above them and the old stab of fear came again, although these soldiers were Roman.

Joseph threaded his way between the people— haughty Jews from Jerusalem, humble country people, proselytes wearing Babylonian tunics and flowing desert robes. "Look! Romans," he said, pointing them out to Mary.

"Romans. Here! Do they worship our God?"

"Many do," he answered. Mary stared at the men, sincere in their immaculately folded togas. A farmer struggled by carrying a lamb and another pulled a bulging-eyed ox toward the Altar of Sacrifice. Priests and Levites hurried about their business. Scribes and lawyers elbowed through, their arms loaded with parchments. White-robed Pharisees stood aside so they would not be defiled and critically eyed the worshippers, seeking to catch them in some deviation of the Law. Occasionally a woman walked toward the Court of the Women or one passed them carrying a basket of goods, taking a shortcut through the Temple. Mary and Joseph moved into the Court of the Women with its marble, gold, silver and bronze decorations. Thirteen silver trumpet-shaped devices awaited offerings as substitutes for sacrifices, or for gifts to God. Friends called greetings and busy merchants hurried across it to save time. Worshippers carried sacrifices.

"Much is done here that Moses never thought of—just as that Pharisee dropping in coins of silver and golden talents for everyone to see. I'd work twenty years for that much. Come."

They stopped at the bottom of a flow of steps on the east side, leading to a gateway flanked by massive bronze doors, elaborately carved, now open to the Altar of Sacrifice. Joseph took Jesus in his arms and gave Mary the birds by their feet. As they climbed the steps, the wind again whipped at their clothing. Mary's heart beat against her chest. *Now I'm going to see it. See the curtain.*

Two pillars loomed into the sky beyond the altar, guarding the Holy Place. Before them to the left, the fifteen-foot Altar of Sacrifice awaited their offerings.

"Look, Jesus!" Mary said.

While Mary and Joseph stood in quietness of soul, priests slaughtered, skinned the animals and laid them on the fire, as Moses' Law required. The wind howled above their heads and whipped the white breeches, coats and bonnets of the priests, walking up and down the ramp of the altar, splashing the blood, laying the animals on the fire. The odors of smoke, incense and burning fat assailed them.

Mary's breath came in little pants. *Is God watching us? Does he see you, Jesus?*

The sound of a priest's shuffling steps and the murmur of prayers and psalms were lost in the wail of the wind. Ripples chased each other across the huge brass laver of water where the priests washed.

Mary looked at the heavy multi-twined Babylonian curtain that hid the Holy Place. *I wish I could see beyond it to where Zacharias stood.* Joseph bent his head to speak in her ear.

"That's where Zacharias entered. It's death to go beyond the second curtain where God dwells in the Most Holy Place." Mary looked at Jesus. The baby stared up at the fire on the altar and began to wail.

"Here's where your Father lives!" Mary said aloud. A priest turned for a moment and stared at her, but Jesus continued to cry. Joseph shushed and patted him to no avail.

Another priest, rheumy-eyed and almost as old as Zacharias, stopped before them. Joseph handed the crying Jesus to him and drew the five shekels from his girdle and handed them to the priest. The baby stared into the old face and screamed louder. With Jesus in the crook of an arm, the man raised the other hand over their heads and said two benedictions in a sing-song quavering voice, the first in gratitude for a firstborn son, the other in rejoicing for his redemption. He handed Jesus back to Joseph and the child quieted.

Mary wanted to remember this scene forever and stared openly. For her sin offering, she gave the priest one turtledove. Its eyes looked dumbly at her, and Mary's were as sorrowful as the bird's. Carefully, she laid her hand upon the head to transfer her sin to it. The priest expertly wrung its neck from its body. Blood flowed into a golden bowl. He walked to the southwest side of the altar and tossed some of the blood below a red line, then poured the rest against the base and laid the bird on a table for the priests.

The old man returned and took the other turtledove from Mary, rung its neck, caught the blood and dashed it against the altar below the line. He removed the sinew of the thigh, the entrails, the feathers and wings, and salted the whole bird. Then slowly he joined other priests ascending the ramp and laid the bird upon the fire. Mary watched the flame leap. *My sins are gone, but the poor birds—the poor birds.* It was over. The priest tramped down the ramp, ignoring them, and turned to the person waiting in line behind them.

Mary took Jesus from Joseph, sighed and looked back once more as he guided her down the steps. A mighty gust of wind shrieked across the Temple Mount. The hourly trumpets sounded weakly, muted by the gale.

As they neared the bottom of the steps and the mass of people below, a feeble figure with flowing white hair and tattered prayer shawl ran up to them on spidery legs.

"Give me the child that I may bless him," he shouted in a surprisingly strong voice.

Mary cried out, "Joseph! Who is he? A prophet?" and backed away.

160

"Yes," Joseph said in a strangled voice.

Around them the crowd thickened. Reluctantly, Mary handed her baby to the insistent old man. He climbed two steps and held Jesus out to the crowd on trembling arms, then looked up into the sullen sky.

Don't drop him. Don't drop him. Mary's heart cried to the feeble old man. Joseph reached out, instinctively ready to catch the baby should the prophet lose his hold. The voice rose in a high wail.

"Oh Lord! My eyes have seen your Salvation, before all these peoples, a Light for revelation to the Gentiles, a Glory to Israel!"

People surged tighter. Mary tried to focus her thoughts upon the old man's words. Jesus smiled and waved his arms.

A man in the crowd roared, "What else, Simeon? Tell us, Old Prophet."

Joseph's arm around her steadied Mary, while he looked for a way to escape once he had Jesus, saw none and held her tighter.

Every voice hushed. Heads leaned forward to listen as Simeon spoke to Jesus.

"May God bless you and keep you safe. May you be His delight. May He make known His paths to you and fill you with joy in His presence." The crowd murmured hallelujahs. Mary wanted to grab her baby from those gnarled hands, but did not. The prophet cried again. "Behold! This child will cause the fall and rising of many in Israel and is appointed a sign which will be spoken against." The people stood hypnotized. Mary's heart hammered harder.

The old man wheeled around and looked directly into her eyes. He spoke to her soul, his voice too loud for his body.

"A sword will go through your own soul, also—that the thoughts of many hearts may be revealed." He handed the baby back to Mary, turned abruptly and went away wailing, "Thank you, Oh Lord! Now I can depart this life!" He was swallowed by the buzzing crowd.

Joseph shook his head in disbelief, seized Mary's arm and hurried her out the Court of the Women, across the turmoil on the Chel toward the north gate. Mary did not even take time to hide Jesus under her cloak. Now they were crossing the Court of the Gentiles. Above them loomed the Fortress, menacing, barring escape. Mary felt the eyes of Roman soldiers. They had seen the commotion in the Court of the Women and watched Joseph and Mary.

"Hurry, Mary!" Joseph glanced at the soldiers on its balcony. "They've heard the commotion but can't come into the Temple. Hurry."

Trumpets blared their warning again, reminding Jerusalem of the Kingdom of God, of divine Providence, of the final judgment, and that the time had come for the noon sacrifice.

Before they'd pushed halfway across the Court, they were stopped by a woman old as time; she must be the one Zacharias had told them about and said anyone who'd ever been in the Temple could recognize the prophetess, Anna. Frail as a bent reed, she spent all her days and nights in the Temple courts praying and fasting—waiting for the coming of the Messiah. They stood hemmed in before her.

"It's the old prophetess, Anna," said Joseph.

The wizened woman's eyes glistened from sunken brown hollows. The strength of her shout astonished them. She threw her arms in the air, grabbed her forehead, white hair flying, and bent double, then threw back her head, waved her arms again and shouted. "Here's the Messiah. The Deliverer is here! All you who are looking for deliverance," the old voice cracked. "Come! Come! Come see! I've lived to see the Deliverer!"

Soldiers high above them put hands to swords. The crowd parted.

Joseph grabbed Mary and ducked past Anna.

The wind slammed against them as they raced through the city, and out the Damascus Gate in the outer wall to disappear among travelers headed north.

CHAPTER 20

The effervescence of a baby's first laugh woke Mary. She dragged herself up from hours of sleep on Aaron's couch to see Ancilla dancing Jesus on her lap and Huldah busily pounding almonds for pastries. Aaron and Joseph sat in a corner watching the baby's performance.

Ancilla rubbed her nose against the baby's, making him laugh again. He stared into her face and cooed with all the wisdom babies know and, somehow, forget when they learn to talk.

Mary watched her sister with the baby, then jumped up to hug her fiercely.

"How's Mother...Father?" Ancilla set the baby on her crooked hip and looked at him. Mary knew she was sorting her words. Finally Ancilla spoke.

"They've missed you," she said simply.

"Do you think they'll want to see us?" Mary looked at Joseph now.

"I—think they will wish to see the baby," said her sister and her eyes filled with tears. "They just don't understand."

Mary's lips trembled. Joseph scratched his fingers through his hair. Aaron heaved his bulk up with the excuse of minding the shop, but he didn't leave the room. Huldah and Joseph looked at Mary, then back at Ancilla. She lumbered up to Joseph and spoke defiantly.

"I'm going to take him to them."

"Ancie, you can't. He's too heavy." Mary tried to take the baby from her.

"I won't drop him. He'll fit right here where I carry the water jug."

"No, Ancilla. Joseph?"

"I'll take him," he said and laid Jesus against his shoulder. Mary instinctively reached for him, then let her arms fall at her sides.

"Your parents have a right to see him," Joseph said, and she knew he was right. Joseph and Ancilla stepped out into the sunlight, leaving Mary to mourn.

Joseph returned more quickly than expected.

"Well, what did the old miser say?" Aaron asked, his voice edged with reproach. Joseph smiled a little, for Mary's sake.

"I didn't see them. I waited outside. Ancilla told me your mother held him." Joseph took a date cake and turned it in his fingers without eating it. Then he set it down again.

And my father? Mary wanted to ask, but she knew the answer.

As if reading her thoughts, Aaron said: "Eli will put the law above all else—every time." They knew what he meant.

Through a haze Mary heard him tell Joseph they could stay with them until he found work. She did not understand the import when Aaron said building in Sepphoris was over.

Weeks passed without Joseph finding anything to do. One night as they lay side by side in the shelter on Aaron's roof and a gentle rain pattered over their heads, Joseph put into words what Mary had feared for weeks.

"I believe we should leave Nazareth. It's too hard avoiding your parents."

"But Ancilla—?"

"We'll go where we must," he said gently but firmly. Not as impulsive as her husband, she had to take time to think things through. She tucked Jesus deeper inside his cradle and pondered.

Joseph could find employment wherever Herod was building because he knew stone work, and there were many places: Tiberius or Paneus in Galilee, the port of Caesarea, a whole new town—Sebaste in Samaria, Jerusalem.

"None of those," Joseph said. "We'll go somewhere Herod will never expect to find us. We'll go to Juttah!

Joseph and Mary lived in a hut at the end of Zacharias' field in Juttah. Jesus Immanuel grew into a robust two-year-old. Mary and he walked across the field each day to visit Elisabeth and her boisterous son John, and on into the village for water and food. A smile that lit Jesus' whole face caused strangers to smile in return, and he wanted to stop and greet everyone he met.

Joseph surprised Mary when he began making harps, a skill he'd learned from his father. She did not know he was a carpenter as well as a stonemason. The harps and lyres found a ready market in surrounding villages.

"Tonight I won't be home until well after dark," Joseph said one afternoon in late autumn. "I must deliver a harp to a man in Hebron."

"Clear to Hebron this late in the day?" But Joseph only kissed Mary and left soon after.

Without him the house yawned empty, and Mary let Jesus help her light three clay lamps and watch shadows dance on the walls. She idly sewed a rent in a tunic and watched her son pile scraps of wood until they fell, then repile them again. After a cold meal of bread and goat cheese, Jesus sat on his mother's lap, and she told him a story about David and the lion.

When she finished, she sat for a few moments lost in thought. Starlight threw silver on the window parchment. Somewhere in the distance a dog barked.

After an hour, Mary lifted her head to catch unfamiliar sounds outside, then footsteps and a beating on the heavy oak door. Cautiously she put her hand on the bar. "Joseph?"

A gruff voice in Greek with an accent not of Judea said, "We seek the King of the Jews."

Flesh bumps rose on Mary's arms. Herod! Mary held Jesus' hand tightly.

"Why do you come to this house?"

"We saw his star in the east and were led here. We mean no harm," the voice replied.

"Open the door," Jesus said and reached up toward the bar, unafraid.

Mary opened it just a crack and saw an arm covered in rich crimson brocade and a sinewy hand reaching toward her.

"Good mother," said a mellow voice, "We come in peace."

Mary pulled the door wide and caught her breath as twelve men knelt before her and Jesus, their faces touching the ground. Silk robes. Jewels. An entrancing odor—was it incense? Camels richly saddled.

"Who...who are you?"

"Jewish Magi," the leader said, "From the south, from Susa in Elam, come to worship the king."

They prostrated themselves before Jesus, who squatted down and bent his head to touch his knees. They repeated their obeisance. The leader, still upon his knees, looked up at Mary. His saffron skin stretched tight across high cheekbones in the flickering light, his eyes lost in shadow under a snowy turban on which emeralds sparkled in a strange sheeny light.

Mary beckoned the men to come inside and six of them entered to arrange themselves cross-legged on the floor, filling the little room. The light from the oil-lamps reflected off gold and silver stitching. The curious scent followed them. A man in black brocade swung down a pack. Mary filled a stone mug with wine, and each man drew deeply from it, passing it on to the next. When they had finished, she sat before them with Jesus on her lap. Sharp-featured men with intelligent eyes inspected the boy. Jesus beamed at each man, as he did to stranger and friend alike. "Shalom," he said. The men ducked their heads, then looked at their leader.

"Many years we searched the skies for the star which would tell us of this king's birth," the leader said. "Two years ago a strange star arose." Turbaned heads bobbed in assent. "Our most noted wisemen studied it. It was the Star of the Messiah." Mary listened so intently her ears rang. "We came to Jerusalem to worship him," the man continued, and Mary caught her breath. "King Herod knew nothing of it." A sharp fierce pain stabbed Mary's heart. All color drained from her face.

"You met with Herod? He *knows* you come here?"

"He understands that we are searching. We would not be surprised if he has spies out, but his wise men are not so wise. It took them three days to search their parchments. The whole town is in a frenzy, thinking the Messiah has come—but his coming is not as they expected." There was a chuckle from one of the men.

"Finally, they determined that the Messiah was to be born in Bethlehem," their leader continued. "King Herod—I like not that man," he added with a scowl. "—told us to search for him, then let him know where he was found, that he might worship him, also."

In the silence, a nightjar called and Mary flinched.

"When we left the palace, we knew not where to look. But their prophecy said the child was to be born in Bethlehem, so we started south. And there was the star again," he waved a silk arm toward the window, "which we had seen two years ago."

Now another man leaned forward, white brows protruding over piercing black eyes. "It lay in the constellation of Pisces—Jupiter, Mars and Saturn together. We were overjoyed to see it again and it seemed to beckon us." The old man reached forward as though still following. "It led us here."

A star pointing to our house. Joseph, come back! Hurry!

The man in black brocade drew three objects from his pack. Slowly, deliberately, he unwrapped each one. From a pouch, he pulled two small bags, which he lifted with difficulty. From these bags he spread an array of gold: small bars, intricate chains, coins. He laid it all at Jesus' feet.

"From Elam, from treasures collected for you, O King, we bring you pure gold, symbol of your perfection."

Next the man unwound a parcel from a covering of camel's skin to reveal an ivory box the size of his hand, carved with prancing lions. He laid it beside the gold. Jesus seized the box. At last Mary recognized the odor.

"Here we give you frankincense, symbol of the beauty and loveliness of your life." Again the men bowed to the floor. Jesus rubbed his fingers along the outline of a lion.

The Magi next unwound another object, this one from gossamer green silk. Between his fingers he held up an alabaster bottle, so delicately carved as to be almost transparent. Jesus took it, his mother's hand hovered over fingers. Then she took it from him.

"This, oh King, is myrrh, a reminder of the precious sweetness of your death." Mary's head shot up, but before she could protest, she heard more voices outside.

The door opened. Joseph stood outlined in the same strange light that flooded the room.

"Father, look!" cried Jesus, climbing down from

Mary's lap. "Look at it." He held the box with lions up to Joseph. All the men had risen to their feet. Their leader spoke to Joseph.

"We greet you in the name of the Magi of Arabia. We have come to worship the King of the Jews." He gestured toward Mary. "His mother will tell you all, but now we must go quickly, for we have been warned in a dream that we must return by a different route. May all the gods and Elohim, the Great God of Israel, care for you and for this son until he sits upon the throne of his father David."

Too bewildered to speak, Joseph lifted Jesus in his arms. The magi each bowed to kiss Jesus' feet as they filed quickly from the room. "Peace be on you. Peace be on you."

Shadows of the twelve strange men moved across the field and disappeared into the forest. Together Mary and Joseph watched them go. And there was the great star to the west, just about to drop behind the hills.

"Look, Joseph!" Mary pointed. "Come, I will tell you all they said!" Joseph lingered to watch the tremendous star, then followed her inside with Jesus.

When she had finished telling him, he rubbed his chin. "It was not meant that I be here," he said, "but I wish I had been." Except for the gifts and the illusive scent of incense, it could all have been imagined.

"It confirms the promises, doesn't it, Joseph? He will be king. And Herod knows it."

CHAPTER 21

Joseph threw off the bedrugs and sat straight up as though prodded with a goad. With shaking hands, he finally struck a spark to the light with the flint.

"Get up! We've got to hide," he whispered.

Mary threw off her covering. "Why? Herod?"

"I've had another dream!"

"What this time?" As she scrambled clumsily to her feet, her hand instinctively reached for Jesus on his mat, then drew back before waking him.

Joseph took a pack from its peg on the wall. "This is for food."

Their whispers did not awaken Jesus. Mary asked about the dream again, but Joseph was busy pulling the rock from the wall and taking out the treasures. She began fitting whatever came to hand into the pack.

"I knew it. I knew it when those men said they'd talked to Herod. I knew it."

Mary yanked a knot to tie a small sack of ground barley. Joseph jammed his feet into leather boots and pulled the laces tight while he talked. "An angel came again— not Gabriel—" he glanced at Mary, his voice lowered, "—a greater one, I think. He said take Jesus and flee, and stay gone until he tells me to return." He took their cloaks off a peg.

Now Jesus awoke and kicked off his rug. He whimpered and was told to hush as Mary tied on his shoes and pulled a tunic over his head. Joseph dropped down beside them.

"Mary,—he said Herod is going to destroy—" He looked at Jesus. Mary covered her face with her hands.

"I knew it. I knew it." She hugged Jesus to her, swaying back and forth.

"Hurry, Mary. He said we must.'"

"But where to?" Mary asked as Joseph tied the lace on a bag of coins.

"Pack everything we can carry on our backs," was all he said.

She rolled the gold and the carved box inside tunics and laid the bundle on a rug. The alabaster bottle she wound tightly in the green silk, slipped a leather string through a knot, and tied it around her neck. I'm not going to chance losing this." Jesus just watched his parents.

"The dream said to go to Egypt," Joseph said. The bread mixing bowl she'd lifted clattered from her hands.

"So far!"

"Herod will never think to look for us there. We'll go to Alexandria." Mary stood dumbfounded, then slowly bent to pick up Jesus.

The brightest star in Pegasus blinked over the village and sleeping fields as they hurried to knock softly on Zacharias' gate.

Zebedee opened it. His presence did not surprise them; he was on another delivery to Egypt. They slipped inside the house, telling him and the bewildered old couple about Joseph's dream.

Zebedee looked thoughtful, then said crisply, "Zacharias, John may be in danger, too. Take him to Misheal. Hide with him in the wilderness." Elisabeth's hands flew to her cheeks, then out to touch John's tousled head. "John's a miracle child,' Zebedee said, frowning."but why is Herod after your Jesus?" The women looked at each other, at Zacharias. After an uncomfortable pause, Joseph answered.

"Zeb, we can't tell you. Not now; just believe that God has told us to flee." Mary knew Zebedee's rough ways hid a keen mind and a true devotion to God, and was not surprised when he nodded.

"Where are you going?" he asked Joseph.

"To Egypt," said Joseph, beckoning Mary to the door.

"Egypt?" said Elisabeth and Zacharias together.

"I'm on my way there now," Zebedee said, accepting their decision without question. "Taking a caravan." He pulled on his beard a moment then looked at Joseph, "Start for Raphia. I'll catch you on the road tomorrow."

Joseph hurried Mary and Jesus into the night.

Hours later they trudged through the tawny hills of lower Judea, ever alert for bandits. Mary saw no beauty in plowed fields or in the green tinge of newly planted grain. She felt as though the sun were pointing her out in a glare of light. Every few minutes they looked back for a cloud of dust on the horizon that might be the camel train—or Herod's soldiers. At last they saw the shapes of twelve camels, heavily laden with barrels of fish strapped to their sides and their humps piled high with woolen cloth. The caravan came closer and stopped beside them in a jangle of bells and creaking saddles. Zebedee, leading the caravan, stepped from a white donkey.

"Are you looking for a ride south?" he asked in a ringing voice, and Mary knew he did it to make his cameleers think that they were strangers. Six men, one on every other camel, waited impatiently. One man muttered to let them walk, spitting into the dust. With no show of friendliness the last man, a young one, urged his camel to the front.

"Who have we here?' he asked. Keen eyes which would miss nothing searched the couple. Zebedee explained in a low, quick voice that they were kinsmen, and to Joseph, said that this young man was his partner, Andrew.

"Pretend they are strangers," Zebedee mouthed to Andrew. Then, his voice rose to its usual rock-cracking level. "There's room for you both." Quickly he rearranged packs and put Mary upon an old camel, while Andrew forced a spitting one to kneel for Joseph. He used the goad and the caravan moved on.

Mary hung on to Jesus with one hand, the camel's noose with the other, sure they would be thrown onto the sand. Her thoughts jangled along with the brassy ring of camel bells—pondering—starting with Gabriel and back around to this flight. *Why? When he's God's own son?* Then it rained, a heavy spring torrent, which chilled her. She sheltered Jesus under her cloak. Afterward the sun came out quickly and the odor of steaming camel hair almost turned Mary's stomach.

After three hours they stopped at an oasis and the men forced the camels to kneel. Zebedee helped Mary off her animal to rest in the shade of an olive tree which had probably shaded Moses it was so old and gnarled. Joseph and Mary sat with Zebedee, apart from the others, eating date cakes and drinking water like camels after a desert crossing. Jesus ran to talk with the camel drovers.

"All right, now. Tell me everything," Zebedee said.

Mary gave Joseph a questioning look, remembering Zebedee's kindness to her when a child, and without speaking they agreed. *We must trust someone.* And so in a few words Joseph told his brother-in-law of the Magi's visit to worship Jesus—that the boy was the looked-for Messiah. Zebedee watched the boy.

"This is a great secret," he said quietly, "I will keep it." He folded his hands across his heart. "I will keep it."

"Not even Salome," Mary warned. Zebedee flopped his hands over his shoulders, shut his eyes and shook his head.

The second evening they stopped early at a dirty, little inn at Raphia near the Great Sea. Zebedee secured rooms for them in a caravansary. His drovers and Andrew would stay with the camels and goods. Just before Joseph and Mary lay down to sleep, he knocked on their door.

"I've bad news from Bethlehem," he whispered.

Mary's heart stopped. Zebedee gripped Joseph's shoulders. "Herod…," Zebedee fought to control his voice, "—has strangled every boy two years of age and under." A low sound came from deep in Mary's throat. She swallowed bile. "In Bethlehem, and in every village around," he added. Joseph grabbed Mary with one strong arm and beat his other fist against his heart. Dry sobs tore Mary's throat as she began to wail and sway.

"Will they find us here," she moaned, her hands pressed against her eyes.

But Zebedee said, "No. We're well ahead of them."

Then the three huddled on the floor together, leaning on each others' shoulders, sobbing, swaying. Mary's head jerked up.

"John?" she murmured. "Zeb, he's two."

"Hidden. They left right after you."

An hour later, when initial shock was becoming deeper sorrow, Zebedee silently rose and left.

"Joseph, we must flee. Now."

"No, we must wait for the caravan to leave tomorrow. We are hidden with it."

Mary lay down upon the bed beside Jesus and cradled her son in her arms, smoothing his hair, feeling his warmth, and ached—ached for all those mothers.

Joseph spoke quietly, lying down beside her. "Jesus is God's own son. He'll be safe."

But Mary, hollow-eyed, did not answer him. She could hear a thousand mothers grieving for a thousand infant boys as they were strangled.

CHAPTER 22

On the caravan plodded toward Egypt. Sweat trickled down Mary's back. A breeze from the sea
instead of cooling only stirred the humid air and brought
clouds of insects. Whenever she turned to look back at
Joseph, his camel spit at her. As they moved south along
the sweltering coast, she pulled her hood and Jesus' out
farther to screen them from Egypt's sun god.

Jesus held the saddle horn, shouted to the camel, trying to mimic the shouts of the cameleers. Occasionally
he threw back his hood and turned to look up at his
mother, a tiny line wrinkling the smoothness of his brow
under auburn curls.

Mary could talk with no one, not even Joseph, and
ignored his attempts to draw her out. He spent evenings
with Andrew. She knew Joseph was hurt and that he was
grieving as much as she, but she could not talk about it—
knew she could make no one understand her emptiness.
At the back of her mind was the nagging thought that
this was God's will for His child, for his safety. But the
upheaval of all that was familiar and the horror—she
needed time to heal.

*

They moved down the coast into the desert, ever-watchful for robber bands and Herod's soldiers. In mid-afternoon they met another caravan coming back from Memphis, led by a Jew from Caesarea, a man known to Zebedee. The two spoke alone, then Zebedee walked back and talked quietly to Joseph. The caravans started again. The man nodded to Joseph as he passed.

When they were but a cloud of dust, Joseph rode up beside Mary. "Zeb told him to get word to Ancilla that we are safe in Egypt. He can be trusted." Mary lips parted in a semblance of a smile, her first in days.

The journey's miseries increased. Each time Joseph's camel came close it bit Mary's and he'd jump sideways to bite back, forcing her to grab Jesus and the saddle horn. Black flies and fleas attacked voraciously. The boy wiggled and cried as she rubbed him and herself with her own mixture of rue, rosemary, basil and wormwood oil. Still they were a mass of welts.

At night Mary, Joseph and Jesus slept in the only tent, while the men stretched out on the sand beside their camels. The desert cold worked its way down to her bones. Wind flapped the goatskin tent and kept her awake. Besides the fears she knew, the unknown pressed: spiders? serpents? lions? brigands? All were possible. Jackals and wild dogs woke her just as she'd get to sleep. Because she received so little sleep at night she dozed during the day, lulled by the swaying of the camel, her arm fastened around Jesus.

Day followed scorching day like the parched sand dunes they crossed. An oppressive sorrow filled her, which she did not try to dispel. The camel ahead—her focus—and Jesus' hot little body were her only security. Each step led them forward to an unknown city where they would be strangers without work, without family— no one but their God and His child—for she knew not how long.

Mary no longer heard even the camel bells; she heard only her thoughts, plodding one after another: *That old prophet in the Temple said a sword would pierce my heart. The stab of pain I felt when I heard we must flee? And Jesus' death? When? Not before he's king!* She held her son a little tighter as they moved on toward Alexandria in Egypt. Jesus turned to give her a puzzled look, but she only wiped his face with her sleeve. She rubbed on more oil to vanquish flies attacking their eyes, nose, mouth. Hour after hour, Mary watched the sand swirling around the hooves of the camel ahead, her thoughts tumbling like wind-blown thistles. The odors of camel hair, fish, and sweat had become too familiar to notice. She longed for enough water to wash away the filth.

Then, from the top of a dune, Egypt spread before them like a dirty rug—and just down the declivity stood six soldiers. She pulled the resisting boy inside her cloak.

The sight of leather cuirass, iron helmets and drawn short swords sent Mary's heart pounding. But they were only customs guards. Zebedee cleared the caravan, showing a parchments with a seal, and on they moved.

Two weeks after they had left Juttah they finally saw a strip of green on the horizon where the delta of the Nile wormed its way through the monotonous yellow ocher.

Zebedee signaled the caravan to stop, and Joseph

and Mary rode up beside him, followed by Andrew on the last camel.

Zebedee looked apologetic. "Those border guards said the Nile's flooded so we can't ford at Pelusium. We'll have to go down to Memphis and up the west side."

"That'll take us a week longer," Andrew said. Joseph looked behind toward Israel, but Mary looked down at Jesus.

With sagging resignation, the camel train fell into line again.

Their last night before they reached the rich grain fields of Goshen, they camped beside a sparkling oasis. She dipped gourds of water and washed both herself and Jesus. Stately date palms towered above them as Mary automatically ground grain, kneaded bread and cut date cakes, handing Zebedee and Joseph their food without speaking. She ate only a bite of cheese.

After everyone was finished, she walked to a nearby sand dune, where a cool breeze caressed her face. The descending desert night matched the black in Mary's heart. She sat hugging her knees, thanking God for His protection thus far, and looking back toward home, thinking of mothers with empty arms. She felt as dark as the coming desert night.

"Come, Mary." Now Zebedee crouched beside her. For a moment she thought he might shake her as her father would have done, but he did not. "We live in a wicked world, Mary; God saw fit to spare *your* child. You must let Joseph share this with you." Mary looked beyond the tents and saw Joseph and Andrew, black silhouettes against an orange sun. A deep sigh came from her inner being.

"Send him to me," she said.

Mary rose to meet him.

"I'm sorry—," she faltered looking up into his eyes.

"Oh, Mary, you've been so far away." It made her chin quiver.

That night, the wind rattling their goatskin shelter, she responded to his love and then slept through the night, held close in his arms.

The next day at Pelusium, they moved south toward Heliopolis and Memphis. Like spring at home, newly sprouting grain greened the plateau of Goshen. People in brightly-colored tunics tied up above their knees worked the plows, seeming friendly.

Zebedee pointed out the tips of three great pyramids. Another time her heart would have leaped at the thought of them, but not now. Beyond lay the road to Alexandria, her only hope of safety.

The caravan stopped on the bank of the Nile across from Memphis, the sun blistering white-washed buildings. Once off the camel, Jesus ran to the river bank with Mary clutching his tunic. He caught a little frog. They stood in the shade of a royal palm while the camels were led on board a barge and tied to posts. Jesus stroked the fat little frog in his hand, then let it go free. With a soft breeze fanning her skirt, Mary finally felt cool. The great river rolled past, carrying the brown treasure of upper Egypt, dotted with boats, their white, pigeon-wing sails billowing before them. Boatmen with blue garments tucked up between the legs hawked their services in noisy competition.

Once on deck, Jesus climbed to a bale of wool at the edge of the boat. Mary stood beside him, clutching his tunic. The barge skimmed its way across the river. On the opposite shore they mounted the camels again and to the monotonous, brassy rattle of camel bells, skirted the city, following the west bank northward toward Alexandria.

On the third day out of Memphis Zebedee rode his donkey up beside Mary and told her to keep her eyes open for a lighthouse.

"Pharos?" Joseph asked and shaded his eyes.

"Yes. The greatest sight ever, four times higher than our Temple. One of the wonders of the world."

An hour later they saw it, rising toward heaven, but no light burned in it now, nor had for many years. *My son,* thought Mary, *will be a light for people.* She shaded her eyes and pointed the lighthouse out to Jesus. *You'll be safe here, but I won't be happy. How can I be, so far from home?*

She rode on, tired and lonely into a strange city, its streets crowded with dark people in flowing robes and speaking a babble of Greek in a dialect Joseph and Mary could not understand. She wondered if ever again she would see the beloved hills of Galilee.

At the eastern edge of the city, Zebedee put Andrew in charge and sent the caravan on to the warehouse by the dock. He flapped a brass knocker at one door among several in a stone wall. After a few minutes a dark, wizened old man opened the door and bowed deeply before him. Zebedee led Joseph and Mary down a corridor lined with marble columns and closed doors, to step into the atrium. Mary shook her head in disbelief. The area was filled with short palms and exotic flowers she could not identify. In the center a fountain bubbled from a bronze lotus flower. Golden carp swam lazily among water weeds. Jesus immediately lay on his stomach and tried to catch them, but they darted through his hands. Mary and Joseph sat down with Zebedee on wicker stools beside the fountain.

"This is my home," said Zebedee. "I bought it for investment and a place for my caravans to stay. I insist you make it your home as long as need be." Mary stared about her, fascinated.

Joseph shook his head. "You are most kind, Zeb, but we could not do that."

"These servants keep it for me and they'll serve this little king," he said, smiling as he lifted Jesus to his shoulders to take them through the house, showing rooms with Roman beds, a dining room for twenty people with an upright table and ebony chairs.

"But I insist on paying you," said Joseph, pausing to confront his brother-in-law, but Zebedee said no.

The next day, Zebedee showed them the city. Joseph hoisted Jesus to his shoulders. They entered Canopic Street, two hundred feet wide and stretching as far as they could see, lined with buildings so magnificent that the Temple in Jerusalem looked commonplace in comparison. Mary felt small and lost as they craned their necks to see the massive columns of rose marble lining both sides of the street. Crowds hurried by them, ignoring the city's magnificence. Jesus stared around him, but only spoke when he saw a man leading a monkey, dressed in a loincloth and a turban.

"Look. Look. Is that a boy?" His parents shushed him, but Jesus watched the animal as long as he could see him.

"Herod will never find us here," Joseph said, switching Jesus to the other shoulder.

"You haven't begun to see it's wonders," Zebedee laughed his thunderous enjoyment at their naive wonder. "Come, I have much to show you."

Mary stared at palaces, villas and at the Mouseion, the library holding every book ever written, except for a few thousand Caesar burned when he took the city, Zebedee explained.

"Even our own Testament is here—translated into Greek—not that it's read by *these* Jews." Mary noted the contempt in his voice. He pointed out Jews on the streets, whom she and Joseph couldn't distinguish from other Alexandrians.

They turned right onto the marble street leading to the lighthouse, then left to the quay, where a cool breeze refreshed them.

Zebedee stopped beside a black stone warehouse on the edge of the harbor. Naked slaves moved barrels of fish, mountains of cotton, casks of fine wine from around Lake Mareotis—merchandise from all the known world. They chanted a strange rhythm which made Mary feel foreign and afraid. She looked away quickly toward the sea where Pharos' lighthouse rose four hundred feet into the sky. Atop, the god Poseidon ruled the city and below him the harbor sparkled, an aquamarine jewel, set off by the white stone battlements of the causeway which separated the bay from the Great Sea. Beyond the causeway, deeper waters shone cobalt and azure. But Mary turned her head to the east. *And over there is home.*

She held Jesus' hand at the edge of the quay, lined with triremes and looked into the water where slabs of marble glimmered like opals among the swaying seaweeds. Tied to marble posts, the boats creaked and rocked, their sails folded like the wings of resting gulls.

"I'll be a sailor," Jesus said, looking seriously at his mother. Mary smiled at him and stood quietly, sensing the beauty, trying to let it fill the empty place in her heart. She took her son's hand and let him feel the motion of the boat as waves lapped against the shore.

"Come, we've more to see," said Zebedee," slapping Joseph on the back. They returned past temples and palaces. The tomb of Alexander the Great did not interest them, though he lay in a coffin filled with honey to preserve him. Instead they entered a synagogue richly ornamented with golden chairs and lamps. They heard the Chazzan ask a blessing from Augustus Caesar. Mary and Joseph exchanged bewildered glances.

Outside again, Joseph took Zebedee's arm.

"Did I hear that right, Zeb? This African Greek is hard to follow, but it sounded like he was asking for Caesar's blessing!"

Zebedee spat contempt. "The Jews here are no better than these heathen. No better than our people who were here in Egypt two thousand years ago, slaves to Pharaoh. Now they're slaves to luxury."

"Then we won't worship with them," said Joseph and strode ahead purposefully.

"You are wise," said Mary, with a last look at the synagogue. She contrasted it to the simplicity of Nazareth and was not pleased. "We will not have Jesus learn from them," she added and took Jesus more firmly by the hand.

Men dressed in silk robes ambled out of the synagogue to hail rich carts drawn by slaves.

An Ethiopian slave, tall as a giant and holding a cheetah on a leash, strode behind a woman dressed in a sheath of gossamer linen so transparent that her pink body shone through the cloth. Mary quickly turned Jesus' head to look at buildings, rising like mountains behind the columns, and wished she could have turned Joseph's also. Better the mud-brick houses of Nazareth than the splendors of Alexandria!

Joseph and Mary watched Zebedee's caravan until it disappeared in the crowded street at dawn the next day. With heavy hearts, they went into the house filled with treasures.

CHAPTER 23

Mary found a friend in the servants' daughter, Cleo, a girl of fourteen. Her friendliness rubbed away the ache of loneliness. She took Mary to the marketplace and taught her how to select foods, how to recognize meats forbidden by Moses' Law—lizard, zebra, crustacea, and strange foods from the jungles of Upper Egypt. Some would bring hallucinations, she had explained. "Why would anyone want them?" Mary asked in wide-eyed wonder.

"Oh," laughed Cleo, "Alexandrians like that sort of thing."

At night Mary and Joseph lay listening to the wind in the palms. They joked about their rise from a shepherd's hut to a mansion, many servants and a fountain, from a mat on the floor to an ebony bed with fine linen sheets.

"I did promised you a palace," he said, his eyes twinkling. Mary smiled, then glanced across the room to where Jesus slept, thinking again of those mothers whose arms were empty and whose hearts were broken. Those thoughts curdled her happiness.

"We don't deserve it," she said abruptly. Joseph did not answer immediately.

"Be grateful, Mary," he said at last, 'for Jesus' sake. If you can, be content."

But Mary grew more restless day by day. She was not used to being served and had she not had Cleo, would have sunk into melancholy again.

Joseph searched for work as a mason or as a carpenter, but without success.

"All hiring is done through guilds," he complained. "No outside person is allowed to join, but I'll keep looking. In the meantime God has blessed us with the magi's gold."

Their money rapidly disappeared. Joseph sold the gold chains and chipped off more gold from the bricks, a bit every week, and finally, when only a thumb-sized piece remained and the casket of frankincense had been sold, he began to give up hope of supporting his family here. Mary told the head servant that they must be very careful with their purchases now. No doubt Zebedee would have insisted on supplying their needs, but they would never ask. God would take care of His son. In the meantime Joseph would go back to making harps.

He fashioned the first one and polished the wood until it gleamed with a life of its own, carefully strung the catgut and plucked the strings. "There must be women who can afford harps," Joseph said, "but if I do not find someone soon, I will have to sell the alabaster bottle."

"No." Mary touched the vial hanging on its silk cord around her neck. "Someone will buy the harp quickly," she said with more confidence than she felt.

"Maybe the woman who owned the cheetah?" Joseph teased. Mary looked quickly at him. "I'm jesting!" he cried. "I'll see if rich Jewish women might wish to learn to play the harp." Owning one of Joseph's harps soon became a fetish and Joseph could not keep up with the orders.

But the family waited impatiently six months for news from Israel and were grieved when the caravan finally came. Andrew, brought sad news. Zacharias, Elisabeth and John had escaped to the wilderness, but the horror of slaughter had been more than the old priest's heart could stand. He lay buried somewhere near Misheal's cave. His death brought back to Mary the horror of the slaughter. She would miss him. Joseph accepted Zacharias' death philosophically. He'd experienced death more often than Mary.

It was part of life, he told her.

Two years after coming to Egypt, Mary found herself pregnant again. On this day she wiped perspiration from her face as she pulled rosy threads through pink linen for a new night garment. Her seventh month sat lightly upon her, but she did wish for the cool breezes of Galilee. Soft winds soughed in the palm branches overhead and helped wipe away the heat of an Egyptian spring. Joseph concentrated on polishing the ebony to a lustrous shine, while Jesus helped by rubbing his piece with a leather rag.

Camel bells and someone clattering the great knocker stopped everything. Zebedee? Andrew? All flew through the house. Joseph unbolted the door. It was Andrew and fifteen men on camels.

"Herod's dead!" he shouted, even before the required greeting. "Herod's dead!"

"Elohim be praised!" Joseph cried.

Mary raised her arms toward heaven. "We can go home." She grabbed Jesus and twirled around and around to the boy's surprise. "Home, Jesus, we can go home!.

"Can we ride a camel?" asked Jesus. Joseph looked from him to the camels and said they'd see.

Andrew introduced Joseph and Mary to a man some ten years beyond boyhood, his brother Cephas. He was more broad-chested than Andrew, with umber colored, laughing eyes.

"Herod died of worms," Cephas shouted. "Isn't that something?" Andrew gave Mary an apologetic look.

"Pardon him, Mary. Always speaks before he thinks," he said stepping back to his lead donkey and picking up the reins.

"We'll prepare a feast," Joseph said. "We'll celebrate when you get back."

When they were gone, Mary and Cleo threw shawls over their heads to brave the midday sun. Mary ran in spite of her bulk. She felt like dancing, leaping, shouting, conduct inexcusable in a very pregnant matron. Her heart beat a rhythm with her feet: *We're going home! We're going home!*

Cleo caught her enthusiasm as they picked out a joint of beef, eaten only on great occasions, melons, oranges, strange fruits brought down the Nile, and Chalybonium wine from Damascus. On an impulse

Mary bought peacock feathers to decorate the table, and she paid three beggar boys a drachma each to carry home the purchases.

"This is a great night, my son," said his mother, letting him help light the candles.

Andrew came with all fifteen of his men. They had stopped to bathe in one of the hundreds of public baths in Alexandria and now relaxed around the table, sitting upright on Egyptian chairs. A cool breeze blew from the atrium and fluttered gauzy blue curtains at the windows of the dining area.

Mary wore her richest gown of lavender linen, ungirdled, in bright contrast to the men's somber gray wool. She swept her hair back in a silver net.

"Every man in Israel has been lighting a fire," said Cephas, as he sat down beside the boy. Jesus smiled and asked him why.

"To spread the news of Herod's death across the land from one end to the next," he replied. The young man looked across at Joseph and grinned. "Rome thought it was one of our festivals. Herod's men didn't know whom to take orders from, so no orders were given to stop the fires. The whole country looked ablaze."

Cleo, her mother and father entered the room carrying huge trays of sizzling lamb roasted over the fire, dripping mint sauce, and beef mounded high with onions. A basket of hot bread turned all thoughts to the feast before them. While they ate, Andrew told what he knew of the family.

"Your mother wasn't well the last time Salome visited home. Some trouble with her heart. Zeb said you should return with us if you wish to see her." Mary glanced at Joseph and her look said, Can we?

"Andrew," asked Joseph. "What's going on in Galilee? What about Ezekias and Judas, and the others?" The excitement dulled. Mary sensed trouble.

"Jesus, it is time for your bed." She took his hand to go, but first he had to say goodnight to every man, stopping at each chair and saying a word or two. Mary sat on the balcony near Jesus' bed but where she could hear the men. They would talk more freely without her there.

"Have you heard anything of my brothers?" Joseph was saying. Andrew began somberly. "They are fine, as far as I know." Joseph, the former Cananean, asked who ruled now Herod was dead, and Andrew explained that all Herod's sons were in Rome, each trying to be made king. Mary buried her head in her hands. *Fighting over my son's throne.*

Joseph pounded his fist on the table. "It's time King David's own sons rule again. Why didn't Clopas—?" He bowed his head and muttered softly. "I know why. What can we do against the power of almighty Rome?" Andrew nodded his agreement and went on.

"And what of Ezekias?" Joseph asked after a moment.

"As you've guessed," Andrew answered, "That leader took this opportunity to start a revolution wherever he could, especially in Sepphoris and all over Galilee."

"Sepphoris!" Joseph shouted. "Nazareth? The family?"

Mary leaned forward, holding her breath.

"They're safe," said Andrew. "No fighting there, but Archaelaus' last act before he left was declare that 2,000 rebels should be punished by crucifixion."

No one spoke. Then Cephas lifted a wine glass so delicate Mary feared it would crack in his hands. He shouted like a victorious soldier.

"Joseph, I lift a toast to Ezekias and to your brothers. To those bold men who would free our land for God!"

All raised glasses except Joseph. The men looked at him with questions in their eyes, but did not comment.

"Joseph," Andrew's laugh echoed around the room, "you know those bands are too smart for Archaelaus. They'll stir up all the trouble they can and disappear into the mountains. No need to fear for them if that's the reason you didn't raise your glass."

No, he didn't raise his glass because he knows only Jesus can free Israel.

Again Cleo filled the glasses with the blood-red wine and the men lifted them with a shout. "To freedom!" Joseph joined them.

But on the balcony Mary whispered, "To peace. Yes, peace. El Shaddai, bring peace to my son's kingdom."

"You're coming with us, Joseph?" Andrew's question knit the wandering skeins of Mary's thoughts.

"I must think on it," Joseph replied. But Mary knew he would not go until God gave him word to return.

Once again God spoke to Joseph in a dream. They were to go to Askelon by ship.

CHAPTER 24

Contrary winds whipped the boat like a bit of driftwood through the troubled seas to Israel. She feared she would lose the baby two months early, but Jesus seemed to love the roll of the waves, the whine and slap of the sail. Mary tried not to think of the three banks of slaves below, each chained to his oar. Fighting seasickness with every breath, Mary tied Jesus to her wrist and shivered on a mat behind a pile of ebony logs. When needed Jesus helped her to the side of the ship to vomit. Joseph was with the other men.

First they would go to Nazareth to see her mother— and her father. Surely her mother would live until they got there, would be willing to see her after all this time. To keep the worry at bay, Mary tried to focus her thoughts on Elisabeth and could almost feel her cool fingers and see the parchment of her aged skin. By now, with Herod dead, Elisabeth would be in Juttah with John. Mary crawled to the side of the ship again as the trireme lifted up on another crest and plummeted into a trough. Icy water drenched her and Jesus.

The fourth day they docked against the rocky quay at Ashkelon, and Joseph hired a porter to carry their packs to the inn. Mary dragged herself after them and collapsed on a straw mattress, while Joseph took Jesus and went into the courtyard to glean the latest news. She slept and awoke hours later with Jesus sleeping beside her, to see Joseph on his knees in prayer.

"What?" Mary asked, sitting on the edge of the bed.

"I wish I were a heathen, Mary. I would take revenge on my enemies with no trouble to my conscience."

"Oh, no, Joseph. That isn't like you. What's happened?"

"Archaelaus promised amnesty to those who rebelled against his father when he died. Then he had them all stabbed." Mary shuddered, her face ashen. Joseph sat down beside her, his eyes closed.

"Stabbed them," he said wearily. "In the Temple as they prayed." Mary covered her face with her hands and rocked back and forth. A feeling of intense cold came over her.

"And now the Cananeans are warring with the Herodians and with their Roman soldiers. It's anarchy. We don't dare go anywhere in Judea." Mary took her hands from her face, startled.

"Not see Elisabeth?" She felt his arm tighten around her.

"A child of Jesus's age," he finally said, "—one born in Bethlehem—will be suspect. Young Herod's spies are everywhere." Mary's eyes glanced at Jesus, then at the window.

"Where will we go?" she asked, her voice tight in her

throat. Joseph closed his eyes and did not answer. Jesus rolled over and sighed.

In the morning a brilliant sun swept the courtyard of shadows. The caravans had gone. Mary washed linens at the well while Jesus played with two little boys nearby.

"Father's back." He ran across the courtyard to Joseph, who hoisted the boy onto his shoulder and nodded at Mary to return to their room.

"What have you learned?" she asked, afraid of his answer. Joseph slumped on the edge of the bed, his head between his hands.

"We must go back to Nazareth. God spoke to me last night."

"*Nazareth*, But you said—!"

"God told me to go there! Would you disobey?" He looked with angry eyes, then pleading ones, and she spoke no further.

They plodded up the Way of Maris toward Samaria, by fields where men pulled flax. The familiar sight of sheep at pasture lifted Mary's heart a bit. She pointed them and familiar flowers out to Jesus and taught him their names. He picked a blood-red poppy and handed it to her. She thanked him and stuck it in her girdle, delighting him, but Joseph frowned and hurried them along.

Later that day, Mary's steps slowed as heat scorched them.

They ate a lunch under an acacia tree and Mary rested her back against it. She said wearily, "Zacharias said that the Messiah would be called a Nazarene."

"So he did. Maybe he'll be safer there." But the grim lines around Joseph's mouth kept Mary from saying any more. She knew he feared for his brothers and the troubles in Galilee.

Mary's worries were of her mother as she trudged on, wondering if the nagging pains in her back meant she would not reach home before the baby came—two months early, no Sherah and no midwife.

The fifth day they stood on the south brow of the Valley of the Kishon and looked across to the familiar hills of Galilee, half-hidden in hazy sunshine. Joseph stood behind his wife, his hands on her shoulders. Jesus looked across the valley and then at his mother.

"Is that home?"

"Yes, my darling, that's home. We'll soon be there." But the look she gave Joseph was one of anguish.

"Good years are ahead," Joseph said, glancing at her stomach. "We'll raise our sons there," he added quietly and gazed with misty eyes toward Galilee, "It's a land worth dying for." For the first time, Mary understood something of the urge he'd felt as a Cananean.

The road led to the brow of an escarpment. Below lay Capercotnei, hidden in olive groves at the base. Had it only been four years since they were there? From the village, roads branched four ways. One led straight north to Galilee. Joseph pointed to the bluff they'd climb to reach Nazareth. *All that way!* thought Mary.

"Joseph, what is that I hear, like wailing?" Both paused to listen, as did others walking with them.

"Must be some grand funeral," said Joseph and urged them forward down the twisting lane of the bluff.

The road soon emerged from a thick grove of myrtle trees, where it made a sharp bend and led some thousand paces straight to the gates of the village.

Joseph saw them first, six dying men sagging on wooden crosses, bodies ghastly gray, purple welts striping their bodies. And blood—much blood. Before he could turn her, Mary saw them too, saw a sea of people filling the street and beyond them a flash of sunlight reflecting off a spear drawn back by a soldier. A needle of pain shot through her heart. She grabbed Jesus and hid his face against her. He struggled loose.

"We must go past! There's no other road!" Joseph cried as they pushed through the crowd, held back from the crosses by a band of Syrian soldiers. A man slumped dead on a cross. "Ezekias! God in heaven. *No.*"

Joseph half-carried her with Jesus hanging on her skirt to the side of the road behind a low wall away from the appalling scene. Women ranted and wailed. Men cursed and tore their beards.

A hand grabbed Joseph's shoulder and turned him from the sight. "Brother! Look not!"

"Matthias!" cried Joseph.

Jesus stood tall to see, but Joseph pushed him down where he could not view the crosses. The scene swirled around Mary as she leaned against Joseph, gasping for breath, the world turning slowly around and around while she fought dizziness. As Matthias led them inside the walls of the village, Mary held tightly to Joseph and to Jesus.

In some way, Mary felt bound to those men on the crosses. She listened dully to Matthias talking to Joseph and realized he was speaking about Joseph's brother, Clopas. He was telling Joseph that Clopas was dead—had died fighting in Sepphoris. But he spoke so low that she could not hear it all. Joseph bowed his head, wiped his eyes and looked at his older brother.

"Come," said Matthias. He led them through the streets of Capercotnei toward the Nazareth road. Joseph hurried Mary and Jesus along. "I led the capture of Rome's arsenal myself," Matthias said proudly, "burned every building." His voice trailed off as though he'd have added something and thought better of it.

"Sepphoris!" Joseph drew back. "Burned? The buildings I made. Ezekias dead. Clopas dead." He shook his head slowly.

Jesus listened round-eyed, his hand holding tightly to Mary's. He hadn't seen the crosses. Or had he? The boy sensed some horror. That was clear. Joseph looked back, then turned abruptly toward Mary.

"Are you well enough to go?" Joseph supported her with one arm and led Jesus. He did not look back as Matthias returned to his crucified leader.

Ahead of them, across the Vale of Esdraelon, they could see where Nazareth lay hidden in its bowl of hills. The sun reflected harshly off the rock bluff at its edge. Mary prayed silently for strength as she put one foot ahead of the other.

CHAPTER 25

"I can't go any farther—I can't—" said Mary, bending, one hand on her stomach.

"We're almost there." Joseph helped her forward. "There's Uncle Aaron's house just ahead."

Huldah took charge, giving them cold pomegranate juice, washing feet, and telling Mary not to worry; there was plenty of time for the midwife to get there. Ancilla came quickly, her eyes bright, brown hair flying as soon as Aaron took her the message. A young woman now, matured through pain. The sisters held each other, then turned to Huldah, who ordered the men from the house, sending Aaron for a midwife.

Mary gave Joseph not the promised son, but twin girls instead, identical replicas of himself with dark hair and large brown eyes. With a baby bundle in each arm, Mary lay content upon her mat with Jesus sitting beside her holding a finger of a baby. Only then did Ancilla tell her the sad news. Anna had died six days before they arrived, of heart trouble, as expected.

Elisabeth, also, was gone, buried in the wilderness where she had escaped with Touchon John to Misheal. The hermit had sent word to Zebedee that he would keep the boy and raise him safely. All in Nazareth already knew of Ezekias and Clopas—and the burning of Sepphoris.

Mary wept. And wept. For her mother, for Elisabeth, for all the sadness in the world. And these two little babes, too early into the world. Huldah would care for them and her. Blessed Huldah.

But Ancilla was the medicine she needed to regain her strength, and she came daily to visit her sister. The loving care of the family drove away the nightmare of those crosses, or perhaps, just buried it deeply in her soul, like a demon ready to pounce.

Joseph grieved for the loss of his brother Clopas. Now, his only family, beside Matthias, was his Uncle Aaron and his three nephews. But he had Mary and two girls of his own—Helen and Julia they would be named—and Jesus.

The house Joseph found for them stood only a short distance from Mary's old home, making it easy for Ancilla to visit, which she did every day or two.

Mary's life was busy in the next four years— with a home and children, but her heart felt hollow as a gourd with her mother gone—and a father who would not speak to her.

Mary had now given Joseph two sons, Joses and James—and Mary rejoiced with Ancillla for God gave her a son, also. It had happened soon after they returned to Nazareth. Matthias had rescued a boy from a burning building in the raid on Sepphoris, a tall blond boy of five, with a thatch of hair the color of broom. Matthias had named him Chuza and wanted him for his own son. When Matthias' wife refused to have him, Ancilla took the boy. Never had she been so happy, never had her face shone with such peace.

At the time of the Feast of Tabernacles, when they'd been in Nazareth five years, Ancilla came to help Mary prepare food. All the kin were coming to Nazareth for the feast, the families of Salome and Matthias, and Clopas's widow Rebecca with her three boys from Gabara.

Mary wiped sweat from her temple with the back of her hand, leaving a gritty trail of barley dust, and rose from the grinding stone to help Ancilla crack almonds in the courtyard. Under the olive tree the chubby twins played with wooden dolls carved by Joseph. Joses lay napping on a mat and baby James slept in his cradle.

The village dozed at noon, with no sound but the never-ceasing zinging of a locust, the crack of almond shells and an occasional hushed remark by one of the sisters, when suddenly the unlocked gate swung open to admit their sister Salome.

"So soon?" Mary gave Salome the kiss of welcome. "We didn't expect you for hours. Come, sit in the shade." In a dress of fine blue linen embroidered in silver, Salome might have been a princess visiting the poor.

"I'm so glad you've come, sister," Ancilla said and knelt to wash her feet.

"Oh, how hot it is." Salome bent to kiss Ancilla. The twins quietly stared at her. She smiled sweetly. "What pretty little girls." They hung their heads and said nothing.

Ancilla hung the towel on a peg. "Where are your girls?" she asked.

"Oh, they're with friends at home. Didn't want to walk clear up here," Salome said breezily. "Zebedee's in Caesarea, so he won't be here, either, and the boys are cutting branches for the booths with your boys. We met them as we came." She turned to the twins, "Would you two like to watch for them at the corner of the street?" The little girls, with a nod from Mary, scampered out the gate.

"This may be the only time we have to be alone," Salome said firmly, "and I want to speak to both of you."

Mary could feel the little stone of resentment she'd felt since a child whenever Salome 'wanted to talk.' She didn't relish a quarrel on a holiday and sighed.

As she fanned herself, Salome looked around her, at the beaten earth at her feet, the firehole with no brick oven, at the one-story house, its shelter on top, and then looked Mary up and down.

"Mary, how do you ever manage with five children in this meager house?" She waved it all away with the fan.

"The same way our mother managed," Mary said crisply.

"Well. It just isn't necessary. And you, Ancie, I'm sure Father could afford a servant. If he'd had help before, Mother wouldn't be dead now. He's probably killing you just like he did Mother, and whatever possessed you to take on that child for Matthias?"

"It was her choice," Mary cut in and set a wooden bowl down on the bench with a thump. Salome never came closer to making Mary angry than when she spoke against their sister. "Ancilla," Mary said with narrowed eyes, "was ashamed to have no children of her own, as any of us would be." Ancilla pursed her lips and noisily dumped almonds from a sack into the wooden bowl. "Can you deny her one small boy?"

"I suppose not," Salome turned to helping Ancilla crack nuts, "but she could have raised one of yours."

"Or yours," said Mary.

Salome changed the subject. "How is Joseph doing now, Mary?"

"Joseph is making furniture," Mary replied. "We're happy here, Salome, and well content. I have Ancilla and sometimes Sarah comes to help."

The mention of Sarah reminded them both of that day—the day their mother would have died and Ancilla with her, if it were not for that dear neighbor.

The children returned from the hills with branches to make booths in the courtyards and on the roofs representing the time the Hebrews escaped from Egypt—and woke Joses and James.

Later in the day came Rebecca and her three boys from Gabara, a half-day's journey to the north. After Clopas died she had refused to leave her village and the Cananeans had shared the stolen riches from Sepphoris with her. Everyone loved Rebecca, a kind soul who never criticized and could always be found quietly helping, always with a cheery word.

She told her sisters-in-law of the Cananeans. "The men are not fighting now, waiting to see what Rome will do next. But my boys are determined to take their father's place as soon as they are grown."

Mary wondered how Rebecca could be so cheerful— as a widow, her family always in danger. She looked over at Ancilla, who was struggling to rise. If Ancilla could have walked, Mary knew, she would have been a Cananean, too, at least have acted as a spy, for she would listen to not one word of reproach toward Matthias' activities.

The Festival of Booths lasted a week, and Mary could only breath a sigh of relief when all were gone. She could go back to caring only for her family—and to watching Jesus grow toward manhood—and to the time when God might put him on his throne.

In the meantime? In the meantime she would do whatever God asked of her. What would it be—another Alexandria—or just living day by day until that time?

CHAPTER 26

"Mary," Joseph said one night three years later as they lay preparing for sleep, "I am a happy man. Putting aside the great honor of raising God's son, you've given me two sons—and two girls for you. Shouldn't any man be happy." Mary patted his hand as they lay on their straw mattress. "Two sons: Joses, who's my image, and—" here he laughed softly, "James, who's the very image of your father."

"Preserve us." Mary said vehemently. She remembered the violent storm that raged when James was born and wondered if that was the reason for his contentious nature, even now as a little boy. Or was he indeed simply another Eli? She fervently hoped not. So much sorrow, so much sorrow because of a stubborn, unforgiving spirit.

"But I'm most proud of Jesus," Joseph went on. "Brightest boy in the school, according to the Chazzan—except for Chuza. I'm glad they are such good friends. Jesus will need a friend." Mary dismissed a prickle of fear.

"Joseph, don't forget the girls. Only eight, but they are learning so quickly—all those things which they must know in only a few years before they marry—so much to do."

"I know, my Mary. I know how hard you work, and I

could almost wish at times that we were back in our palace in Egypt."

"Never!" said Mary and with a deep breath prepared to rest, safely in Joseph's arms, here in Nazareth.

One morning in late fall, with nature decked out in frosty diamonds, Jobab, Eli's head shepherd, knocked on Joseph's gate and stooped to enter the house. "I've come for Jesus," he said with a snaggle-toothed smile. "Your father needs another shepherd up in the hills. We'll be back at barley harvest." Mary frowned.

"May I, Father?" asked Jesus. "I'm old enough."

Joseph frowned too, but on a nod from Mary, he said: "You may go."

Joseph took the boy's bony shoulders in his hands. "Learn from the shepherds. You owe them a debt." His glance at Mary brought back the memory of the night Jesus was born. The boy looked puzzled but joyfully began to gather what he knew shepherds needed, his heaviest cloak and sturdy boots.

At twelve, Jesus had learned all that the local Chazzan and Joseph could teach him from the scriptures and was ready to be taught in other ways than books. He could have no better teacher than this old shepherd and nature itself.

Mary smiled, but inside her heart was torn. *I'll miss him so. And I think my father will miss his visits, too.*

"I will learn all that I can." Jesus gave his mother a hesitant smile. "I have wanted to do this for ever so long. Thank you for letting me go."

"Your words please me." said Joseph and took

Jesus's hand for an adult shake. Jobab said to Mary:

"I'll see he comes to no harm." He reached for his shepherd's staff. "I'll return for Jesus as soon as I've seen the flock is ready to move." They listened to his staff marking each step as he crossed the courtyard. Then everyone became busy. Jesus went about putting away his childish treasures.

"And do not meddle with them," he warned Joses. "Here, you can have the horse I carved." Although Joses had wanted the horse ever since its inception, he took it grudgingly. Jesus shrugged and went outside for some purpose of his own.

Mary knew he would not return from the hills for four or five months, until the barley was harvested and the sheep came down to feed on the stubble. Joseph sensed her mood.

"He must learn to live in this world. He cannot always be at his studies. He's not to be a rabbi, you remember."

"No, a king," she said. She filled Jesus' pack with bread and dates and rolled his cloak around it.

No, he is to be a king and there's never a day goes by but what I think about it. She reached for another dried date cake and stuffed it in a tunic pocket as a surprise. "But I'll miss him so."

When Jobab returned, Jesus reluctantly let his mother hug him goodbye for he now thought himself a man. He did not look back and so did not see her tears. She sighed the deep sigh a mother gives when her first born leaves.

*

The next morning the family sat in the house silently breaking their fast around the fire hole in the house. Joses frowned and tore a piece of bread with his teeth. "Jesus'll be lonely," he said between bites. "I do not want Jesus' horse. I want to go with Jobab and be a shepherd. He doesn't know about sheep like I do. I've helped Grandfather lots of times. I'm five years old; Some boys go when they're seven." His mother frowned and hugged him against her side.

"You must wait a few years," she said gently. Joseph ran his fingers though his son's black curls.

"Then you can become a chief shepherd," he said. But Joses still looked stubborn.

Mary missed Jesus more than she would admit in the following months. She prayed daily, asking God to keep her son safe from wild animals, from wickedness and trouble from the older boys. But why did she have to pray? Wouldn't God keep him safe without her prayers?

One thing she continually pondered: when should they tell Jesus about his birth? How much should they tell him? She pushed Zacharias' prophecies and Ezekias' death to the back of her mind. She would not think of them. But she must tell him that he was not Joseph's son. Her heart ached just thinking of it.

She whispered to Joseph one night when the children were asleep. "Does he realize whose son he is?"

"No." The flame in one lamp flickered. Mary raised up on her elbow.

"You think he's like other boys, but he's *not*. He

never causes any trouble. Never disobeys. He's kind. Ancilla tells me even Father doesn't find anything to criticize."

"But we'll raise him as an ordinary boy," said her husband. "He must grow up learning to live in this world. We don't want Herod Antipas to hear of some remarkable child, do we? He is as ruthless to keep his throne as was his father."

"But we must tell him soon," Mary said and laid back against her pillow, "before someone in Nazareth tells him that his birth did not measure nine months. I often see Sarah look at him with questions in her eyes. I'm sure Mother told her of my sin, but she will never ask. There are others, though. What of Malchus' father? Remember our shameful wedding?" She lay back down and Joseph tightened his arms around her.

"We'll tell him when we go to Jerusalem next Passover, when he becomes a Son of the Commandment," he said. Mary didn't sleep for many hours.

Unusually hot weather brought on the barley harvest weeks early. One afternoon while men worked in the fields, Jesus burst into the quiet of Mary's afternoon.

"Mother," he cried, "I'm back!" She rose to greet him, surprised.

"You've grown over my head!" she said happily and hugged him. He did not resist.

Joses and James welcome him too, James with hugs around the knees, Joses with questions about the sheep. He put a sheep carved by him from a oak burl into each sister's hand. Julia and Helen shyly thanked him.

Mary lifted a hot loaf from the firehole and spread it with warm butter. She took down the jar of grape molasses, kept for festivals, and smothered it thickly on the hot bread.

"I fixed a sheep's leg," Jesus said, chewing eagerly. "After that I was the doctor for all the crippled sheep, and Jobab said I cared for the sheep better than any boy he ever had." Yes, he had learned a great deal. Yes, the older boys had treated him well. Yes, he'd been hungry and cold sometimes. That was part of being a shepherd. Then he said, "Are we going to Passover?"

"We usually do." Mary went about preparing the evening meal.

"Will I see my cousins?" She knew he meant Clopas' and Zebedee's boys, and Touchon John in particular. She told him he'd probably see them all, but not to count too much on seeing Touchon John. Jesus looked dismayed.

She hated to douse the eager flame in his eyes, but how could anyone say if Misheal and John would come. Since Elisabeth and Zacharias had died, Misheal kept Touchon John safe somewhere in the Wilderness of Judea. No one ever knew when Misheal might appear. Once or twice in the last few years they had seen them at Passover, a hermit in his wild dress, holding by the hand a growing replica of himself. There seemed to be a great love between them. The family did not fear for the boy, and Misheal knew that God had given this special child into his care. In the times when they appeared, Jesus and John had formed a firm friendship, one started when they were toddlers in Juttah.

*

Every Israelite went to Jerusalem for Passover, except those too old or too crippled to walk for three days or those needed to tend children and animals at home. Joseph decided they would start a few hours before the others—to talk with Jesus.

From the ledge south of Nazareth they could see a silver streak of the Great Sea to the west. The top of Mt. Carmel turned from muted gray to rosy pink. Fog hid the Valley of Esdraelon. The tops of Mt. Tabor and the higher hills rode like silent ships on a sea of mist. Joseph slowed his walk and Mary dropped back a step. The boy looked up from the path.

"Your twelfth birthday is behind you," Joseph began, "and you are to become a man." Jesus glanced sideways at Joseph. "A man must know his mind, Jesus. He must know what he will do with his life, what God wills for him." Jesus nodded. "Your mother and I have some things to tell you which will seem strange. Indeed, we do not understand them ourselves." Jesus frowned and stopped walking. All stepped to the side of the road. Jesus looked steadily at Joseph, a frown between his brows. "But first, I must go back before you were born and tell you of a message an angel brought for your mother and me."

Jesus looked at his mother, who smiled just slightly, then back at Joseph, his expression one of disbelief mixed with awe. He said nothing. "Yes," said Joseph, "a message which God sent though the angel Gabriel to both of us." A puzzled frown creased Jesus' brow.

"The Angel *Gabriel?*"

As Joseph talked the fog drifted away below, showing a misty patchwork of fields ready for harvest. The breeze off the Great Sea rippled the grass as they all sat down together on a large rock. Mary's heart hammered against her ribs as Joseph spoke to Jesus, telling him the whole story—that he was God's son and his birth a miracle from Jehovah. Jesus looked up into the blue of heaven and did not speak for several minutes.

Then he looked at his mother for a very long time. At that moment, Mary's heart was so full she could not speak, only look deep into her son's eyes, willing him to understand and accept the message.

"How can God, who is a spirit—?" he began.

"I do not know myself," was all she said. Finally Mary found strength to speak without her voice breaking. "It was not an easy time for us," she said very quietly. "The people of Nazareth did not understand." Jesus' eyes never left his mother's face. "Gabriel told Joseph to take you as his son, and he did it willingly." Jesus turned to look at Joseph and finally smiled.

"So—you are not my father," he said. "My father is—" Now he stood up and walked away from them across the grass to the brow of the hill and looked out over the Valley. His back was to them. Mary saw her son, a boy trying to understand that which was beyond the human mind to fathom. In a few minutes he returned. He nodded to them to continue the journey, as if in that little time he'd added ten years to his age.

It took his mother's breath away.

CHAPTER 27

A t Esdraelon the family joined the procession: Zebedee, Salome and their children, Andrew and Cephas and their wives, too. Jesus, a boy again, climbed rocks and wrestled with his five cousins and Chuza, bragging as they outdid each other.

Mary joined the singing, smiling up at Joseph as he added his "Selah's, so be it," between verses. She thought back to that lonely walk she and Joseph had taken to Bethlehem—no noisy children underfoot, no shy lovers, no songs started by someone ahead and passed back with each new voice adding volume. Today, just as Jews had done for centuries to prepare for the Passover, they walked on roads recently repaired, crossed newly-made bridges, saw graves glistening with fresh whitewash in each cemetery, warning pilgrims not to touch lest they be defiled and prohibited from the Passover Feast. Ahead lay Jerusalem's grim stone walls.

Straggling back six miles to Bethel, the procession came into Jerusalem from the north. The family entered through the Herod Gate and turned left to Zebedee's house near the new north wall close to the Fish Gate. Although Mary had stayed at Zebedee's several times, she never looked at it without comparing it to his house in Alexandria.

This house stood two stories high, surrounded by a wall of pink limestone. The upper story was divided into eight sleeping rooms, the lower floor into a large meeting room, a kitchen, and Zebedee's office. A tiled courtyard lay the length of the house, on which stood stone benches and several blossoming pomegranate trees. Zebedee's reed chair reigned in the middle of the courtyard, facing the gate, replete with back and arm rests and a crimson cushion. Good enough for Tiberius, Zebedee would say with a laugh, and no one sat in the chair if he were present. High standing bronze lampstands illuminated the courtyard at night.

In this week of the Passover, Salome, Mary and Rebecca gave up trying to keep their own children separate from dozens of others. They just cooked great pots of lentils, baked enough bread for Solomon's army and chopped raw vegetables until knives dulled. It all disappeared as though they fed the Leviathan.

And this year Misheal brought Touchon John.

Touchon and Jesus fell upon each other, laughing, punching with man-sized muscles. They said little, but soon went off by themselves in the courtyard.

Zebedee would lead the Passover Feast that portrayed the escape from God's curses upon Egypt. He would scrupulously follow each order as prescribed by Moses' law. While the women cleaned the house of leaven and prepared for the feast, the men went to the temple to offer the sacrificial lamb before sunset.

They returned with the feast lamb, quickly slaughtered according to the Law. The feast required joyousness and celebration, and that the oldest man and the children search the house for any bit of leavened bread. The fragrance of the lamb roasting on a spit over an open fire drew the children to watch and lick their lips.

Jesus stayed close to Touchon John. Mary watched them and saw Misheal's eye upon them, also. Mary wondered if he knew who Jesus really was. Probably so, since he prepared for the coming Messiah.

The rich odor of roasted lamb permeated the house as the women laid the feast on the table inside the large main room and arranged the cushions around it, representing their rest from being slaves in Egypt. On a snowy linen cloth Salome placed hot unleavened bread, bitter herbs of chervil and coriander, parsley, salt water, lettuce, beets, succory, the Charoseth—a mixture of raisins, dates and vinegar—and in the center of the feast the lamb, to remind them of the shed blood which saved them from the Death Angel, who slew every first-born of men and beasts in all of Egypt.

The women now inspected each child's face and rubbed offending spots clean with moistened fingertips. When friendly arguments had ceased about who should sit by whom, the feast began. They followed the tradition, eating each item at the proper time, asking the required questions. Zebedee's son John, as the youngest boy, must answer the questions.

"Why is this night different from all other nights?" Zebedee asked in the hush, and John answered the centuries-old response that this night they ate only unleavened bread.

"Why on this night only, do we eat bitter herbs?"

"Why do we dip our vegetables two times?"

"Why on this night do we recline to eat?"

And John answered correctly that when they were slaves and God brought them out with a mighty hand and in such hurry that they could not leaven their bread, that the herbs reminded them of their bitterness in Egypt and Babylon. Jesus nodded his head at each right answer.

Lastly, they dipped their vegetables in salt water to remind them of the tears shed in bondage, and into the Charoseth as a reminder of the sweetness of freedom. And so the feast and the ceremony went on, until it was ended with singing of the Hallel. All raised their voices, but Jesus' high tenor sang out above them all:

"You are my God, and I will praise you;

You are my God, and I will exalt you:

Praise the LORD, for He is good;

His love endures forever."

The feast ended with a shout: "Next year in the rebuilt Jerusalem!"

The moon was dipping behind the western hills before the children stumbled to their sleeping mats, but as Jesus passed his parents, he paused to say something that stunned them both.

"Now I understand," he said with a little twisted smile. "I am the Lamb."

CHAPTER 28

Joseph led Mary and Jesus through streets so narrow he could reach across them, through crowds already filling the city, crowds intent on parting from their hard-earned money just to prove they'd been to Jerusalem. Mary wanted to take her son's hand but knew she must not. On this day he'd go through the ceremony to become a man, a Son of the Commandment. She carried two loaves of bread made of fine flour and oil and a cruse of wine needed for the meal offerings.

They entered the Temple's North Gate into the Court of the Gentiles.

"Jesus," Mary said, "it was here the old prophetess frightened us so. Right here where Roman soldiers could hear her. 'Look,' she cried, 'the deliverer of Israel is here.'" Jesus looked up to the balcony of the Antonia Fortress and to the soldiers staring down at them.

"Yes," Joseph answered the boy's unspoken question, "*They* were there and almost frightened your mother to death."

Mary stared about her at the same confusion as twelve years before—sharp-eyed merchants, people making the Temple a thoroughfare—and also devout

Jews come to worship God from all over the known world. Chuza had told Jesus of this last year when he became a Son of the Commandment. They watched the confusion, listened to the bawling of cattle and the shouts of the merchants. "How does one worship in such noise?" Jesus waved his arms angrily at the bedlam around them. But before Joseph could answer, trumpets blared.

Near them a farmer drove six bullocks through the animal gate from the northeast. Suddenly, one of the bullocks smelled blood. Its tail rose stiff behind it like a pump handle. It bolted across the Court, bellowing terror, trampling stalls, baskets of doves, scattering people. Mary leaped behind a partition. Joseph flung his arms to turn the animal, but when the bullock saw Jesus, it immediately stopped. The farmer, with a look more startled than his bullock's, drove it peaceably into the animal pens. Mary and Joseph just looked at Jesus. He shrugged. None of them, including himself, knew how he'd done it.

A gentle breeze carried the odor of hot dung, the bouquet of frankincense, and the aroma of roasting meat. The business of the Temple went on: boys frantically delivering doves and pigeons; goats and sheep looking dumbly at masters, birds hanging mute, helplessly tied by their feet with cords around merchants' necks—and money changers—always money changers—behind rickety tables, eyes avid with expectation.

Mary knew Jesus felt the importance of the day, the fifteenth of Nisan, a holy sabbath. For the first time, he'd offer the family sacrifices as a Son of the

Commandment: a female goat for the sins of his family, a male lamb as the burnt offering showing their complete surrender to God, and a peace offering of another male lamb.

They stopped at a pen of sheep. Jesus picked up a lamb and felt along its bones for solid flesh.

"Look the animals over, Father. We don't want ones with runny noses. See if they are clean, so we know they're healthy. A sacrificial lamb must be perfect."

Mary stood aside and watched Jesus and Joseph select two male lambs and a black female goat, which looked at Jesus with mournful eyes. Joseph laid out the required coins. She wondered how much they were being cheated this time.

In the court below the altar, the sun shot flashes of light from the golden covering of the Holy Place above their heads. Joseph carried the two lambs, one under each arm, with the loaves stuck in his girdle. Jesus tucked the cruse of oil in his girdle and stroked the head of the goat in his arms. They climbed the twelve steps. Mary stood on the bottom step below them.

Twenty men forced the bronze doors open, and Joseph and Jesus entered, the first to bring their offerings. Mary could no longer see them. She would never again stand at the place of sacrifice, but she would never forget.

A few moments later, coming back down the steps, Jesus smiled wistfully. Mary put out a hand to stop them when they reached her.

"Here is where we stood when Simeon prophesied about you," she said. Jesus stopped walking so suddenly that a Pharisee bumped against him.

"What did he say?" asked Jesus with urgency, ignoring the Pharisee, who wiped his sleeve where it had touched Jesus and hurried on, muttering some epithet. Joseph told him Simeon's words, of how he had held him and gave praises for seeing God's salvation. Jesus looked behind him back up at the altar, then toward the place where masses of animals waited to be sacrificed.

Mary wondered what Jesus was thinking. Did he really believe he was the Lamb of Isaiah's prophecies. She doubted it.

Early the next morning, the family started for home, singing and shouting. The men walked ahead, the children in the middle of the cavalcade, and the women following to make sure none were lost. By the time the parade crossed the new part of Jerusalem and out the Damascus Gate, the procession strung out a thousand paces. This time they would take the road down to Jericho and up along the Jordan, and divide to go their separate ways at Scythopolis. At sundown, they camped on a grassy meadow beside the Jordan River. But where was Jesus?

"I thought he was with Salome's boys," said Mary.

"Well, he's not, nor with Rebecca's boys either." They scanned the crowd. "I'm sure he's among the family, but I'll look." Joseph left quickly—but an hour later returned alone.

"In the morning we'll go back and get him," he said.

Neither slept for hours, Mary imagining every horror that could happen to a boy.

At dawn Joseph shook Mary's shoulder. "Come," he whispered. "Don't wake anyone." Light glowed in the

east and sparkled the dew on sleeping bodies as they tiptoed away, their long shadows leading them. At noon,
they knocked on Zebedee's gate in Jerusalem to ask if
Jesus were there. He was not. All afternoon they combed
the city and the Temple and did not find him.
Reluctantly they went back to Zebedee's house for the
night.

The second day, at the first blare of Temple trumpets, they again searched the Temple courtyards. Where
could they find one boy among thousands? That second
evening they sat in Zebedee's courtyard, spirits entirely
drained. "Perhaps he's a prisoner," Mary said flatly, a bitter note to her voice.

"Matthias and the other Cananeans weren't arrested,
with all their talk," Joseph pointed out, "so they wouldn't
arrest an unknown, quiet boy like Jesus. Come, we'll
look in the Temple one more time, first thing tomorrow
morning. We'll find him." Mary shook her head.

When the Temple trumpets blew at sunrise, they
hurried along the Street of the Fort beside the Antonia,
straight through the first gate into the Temple. Already
the north court was filling. Mary gripped Joseph's cloak
as they elbowed their way through the people, eyes
straining to catch sight of their lost boy.

Hours later they walked wearily back and forth
through the packed bodies, the smells, the noise. Mary
brushed tears with her sleeve. Joseph kept a firm hold on
her arm, giving her hope to keep looking, though he
walked more slowly, his eyes automatically scanning the
crowd. Then they noticed a doorway to the level below
the Court, leading to one of the priest's rooms.

"Mary," he said suddenly pointing to the steps. "We didn't look there. Come."

They hurried down a stair to a small room packed with dozens of men who were listening intently to five or six rabbis speaking with someone they could not see. A tug on Mary's sleeve turned her head. "Misheal!" she cried.

"Come," he said and led them to the front of the room. Directly before the rabbis sat Jesus and Touchon John.

"Oh, no," mouthed Joseph.

"But God says..." Jesus argued. Mary cried out, unable to help herself, and Jesus turned his head. Without a change in his voice, he told the rabbis he would talk with them again another day. He touched Touchon John's arm and they rose.

One of the rabbis shouted at Joseph, veins pulsing in his throat. "Galilean! Is this your son? Take him away!" The anger in his voice moved Joseph forward.

But someone in the crowd called out, "Where are your answers, Rabbi?"

At the top of the stairs Joseph pulled Jesus aside.

"Child," he said sternly. "We have been looking for your for three days."

"Why did you do this to us?" his mother scolded.

"I'm sorry," he said, and his concerned look softened his mother's heart. "I did not think—and Misheal was with us—but those men, those rabbis were wrong." He turned to Touchon.

"Those men," Touchon said looking at Misheal, "did

not know the laws of Moses." Mary looked exasperated, but Joseph just grimaced. Now Jesus looked into Joseph's face.

His eyes puzzled, Jesus said, "You knew I must be about my Father's business."

They thanked Misheal for his care of Jesus and parted.

Not another word was said until they halted to rest a mile or so out of the city.

"What was it you talked about?" Joseph then asked. Jesus pulled on his lower lip. Then he spoke, his brow furrowed.

"I asked them," he said, "about the passage in Isaiah, the one that says the Messiah will be killed. They became furious and answered me from the writings of the scribes—but *not* from the scriptures." He appealed to his mother now. "I want the answer," he said, looking for a moment at a black cloud to the east that promised a storm. A sudden cold wind whipped their cloaks. "Does the Messiah die," he asked, "or does he establish his eternal kingdom?" The cloud moved closer.

"I do not know," she answered.

She looked at her son with sympathy. She had pondered those same questions ever since Simeon the prophet spoke of his death.

The storm moved swiftly across Mt. Olivet, the wind driving sheets of rain before it.

CHAPTER 29

Ancilla surprised the whole village of Nazareth one Sabbath when she showed her baby at the synagogue. It had all happened the afternoon before.

Matthias had pushed open the gate carrying a baby girl and handed her to Mary. "My wife died giving birth," he had said, his face mournful. "I want Ancilla to raise her. If she will—like she did my Chuza."

"Of course," Ancilla answered, taking the bundle. "Of course, I'll keep her. I'll call her Joanna, which means God is gracious. "I've wanted another—and now I have a *baby.*" It all seemed so simple.

Before Mary slept, nestled in Joseph's arms, she made a confession. "I have something to tell you. I'm to have another child this spring."

Mary gave Joseph another boy at the time of the first barley harvest. They called him Jude, a husky boy with brown hair and dreamy eyes like Joseph's.

It did not really surprise the town when a year later Eli agreed that Ancilla should marry Matthias, on condition he leave the Cananeans. Galilee was quiet—for now. He agreed to work Eli's fields and herds and inherit them when Eli was no more. Mary, Julia and Helen, now twelve, began planning like generals ready for war. Mary determined Ancilla's wedding would be the best Nazareth had ever seen, and it was.

Although Eli never changed in his attitude toward Mary, he did allow her children to visit him. The boys helped in his fields and with the flocks, especially Joses. But Mary he would not forgive. She had broken the law and disgraced him. She must pay the penalty.

Mary had long ago forgiven *him*. He simply did not understand, nor want to. She also knew how important keeping God's laws was to him, even those interpretations added by the scribes for a thousand years.

In the four years since they had found Jesus in the temple, they never again talked to him about his Father: something in his eyes told them not to ask. He studied more diligently than ever— privately with the Chazzan, since he had finished the village school. He did not say what they talked about, nor did he share his inner thoughts with his parents. Mary's heart ached for him at times, when he seemed so alone within himself.

The year before, Matthias had sent Chuza to Jerusalem to study in an academy that trained young men to become clerks for local government posts. Once when Mary was not supposed to be listening, she had heard Matthias confide to Joseph that a post would give them someone in the government to report on Herod Anitipas' activities. Chuza stood a half head taller than

Joseph, his hair still that sunshine yellow which had attracted Matthias when he rescued him in Sepphoris.

Mary watched Jesus grow into manhood and waited for the day he'd take the kingdom. Hadn't Gabriel promised?

Jesus and Joseph studied scriptures together each evening, worrying their minds over prophecies and laws. Joseph, like most people in Galilee, did not conform to all the ordinances required in the many books which interpreted the laws of Moses. Joseph, well-taught by his father, let Jesus think freely for himself. Mary listened and remembered that Joseph had been a Cananean, those men who thought to bring back the truth of the scriptures.

Joseph made a comfortable living in a shop a few lanes away making furniture for the magnificent homes of rich Romans and Greeks in Sepphoris and, later, to rich Jewish publicans like Malchus in Kapher Nahum. The carpentry shop kept them both busy. Mary often stopped to watch them on her way to the well.

"I'm sending him to obtain orders," Joseph said, laughter in his eyes. "He has a way with him." Jesus' laughed indulgently.

"Father says it's because I can look right into their souls."

"You do have a way of doing that, Jesus," his mother said, "whether you are looking with friendliness or when you are not so happy with them."

"I like people, Mother, good and bad." Jesus carefully chiseled away a chip of wood, then looked back at her with a smile that made her catch her breath. Who was this son of hers, after all?

Joseph finished cutting a board and laid down his saw. "I could not do without him." He picked up a wooden plane. "However, I think I will bring Joses in to help me; I cannot keep up with this man." He gave Jesus a friendly thump.

Jesus looked at his mother and said gently, "I'll be home to share a meal tonight, but tomorrow I'm off to Gabara. I'll look in on Aunt Rebecca and the boys." He went back to his work.

Mary went out into the Galilean afternoon. She loved the walk just before sunset, a time alone, to think her own thoughts and watch the flashes of color as hoopoos darted beside the path. The pungent odor of dust and ripening grapes were as familiar as life. She walked the streets where she had once looked for Joseph as a girl, frightened that she'd be given to a man she could not abide. God had been so good to her.

She stood by the well and looked across to the shepherd hut where she and Joseph had first lived, at the brown hills, at the ridge of cypress on the crest of the nearest one. She listened to the shepherd boys calling to their sheep and the animals' bleating response, and let it bring back memories. The stony path to Cana hadn't changed. The village behind her looked, she supposed, the same as it had looked for a thousand years.

I've lived in a shepherd's hut and a mansion, she thought as she started home with the water jar on her head. *Will I always be here—even when Jesus is king? Will I be left behind?*

Mary held three-year-old Jude on her lap and peered between the cedar lattice work on the women's gallery of the synagogue, waiting for the service to begin. Behind her the twins, now fifteen, whispered with their friends. Mary looked down at her Jesus seated on the bench in the middle of the synagogue. Joseph, his hair thinning at the back, sat between Joses, now twelve, and ten-year-old James. How different those boys were! Jesus was slight of frame, average of height, with the muscles of a man. His hands folded on his lap were large for his size, rough-skinned, but gentle enough to set a broken wing or hold a baby. Joses resembled her grandmother, slight and fair-skinned. James grew more like Eli with each day. Jude, wiggling on her lap, would look like Joseph. Her girls had Ancilla's optimistic attitude toward life.

A blast on a ram's horn brought Mary's attention back to the usual order of the synagogue. The Chazzan sat importantly on the platform, rose to cross it and select a scroll for the morning's study. Another man of the city took it from him and read at the time appointed for study, and then explained the meaning.

When Jesus was nineteen, just when Mary thought she was beyond child bearing, she surprised the family, and herself, with another set of twins, Elishaba and Simon, a sturdy little girl and a delicate, sensitive boy who resembled James in looks but not in temperament. She fulfilled the role of a mother of Israel for Joseph, with seven children, the perfect number in God's symbolism. And Jesus.

Already Mary's twin girls were betrothed to farmers' sons, good young men, whom they loved and would marry in two years. *There's not one child I could do without.*

233

A harvest of blessings. She whirled her spindle, while the wind whispered in the olive leaves above her. Fleecy clouds drifted by on their way to the desert. Another day they would gather, darken and pour their anger on the land, but today all was peaceful.

Jesus came in and sat down beside her. He rocked the twin's cradle. James strode through the gate and walked straight to Jesus.

"I learned something today," he said, challenging his brother like a dog presenting a bone. "I learned that when the Messiah comes, God will open the Torah and each of us will get our reward."

Jesus gave James his full attention. Mary went on spinning but listened with sinking heart. They were at it again. Jesus asked seriously, "What will that reward be?"

"We didn't talk about that," he said. James looked crestfallen, then brightened, "but it will happen when the Messiah comes."

Jesus smiled at his brother. "If you cannot find it in the scriptures, are you sure it is true?"

James stood straighter. "I will ask the Chazzan tomorrow." His face was a bit flushed. "He speaks for God when he teaches us."

Jesus stood up. "Ask him tomorrow what our rewards and punishments will be. Ask him who will receive which. Ask him—," he said and his eyes glittered for a moment, "—ask him if Matthias' Chuza, a slave from no one knows where, will receive a reward."

James ran across the courtyard. "I already know that answer. Chuza cannot inherit. It's against the Law. He is not a true Israelite."

James slammed the gate behind him and Mary sighed.

Next evening all the family except James sat in the courtyard watching a dust devil whirl. It rattled the branches, tore leaves from the olive tree. James burst upon the family, scowling and went directly to face Jesus.

"The Chazzan said those who keep the law won't be punished," he announced.

"Can you keep the law perfectly, James?" asked Jesus.

"Enduring misery cancels punishment," said James with finality, as a parent to a child. He climbed up on the bench and jumped vainly to capture a whipping branch. "There are two schools of thought. Shammai's and the great teacher Hillel." Then James caught the branch and snapped it in his fingers.

"But what does God say, James?" asked Jesus. He did not answer, and Joseph said they had better send James to study in Jerusalem.

Joses frowned. "And I suppose I'll be left to do the work here. And the shop will never be mine because I'm not the first born." He looked defiantly at Jesus.

"Your time will come, Joses," Jesus said and sighed. "Great responsibility goes with the birthright".

One morning during the olive harvest, hot already, Matthias rushed inside the house. "Your father is dying. Unable to rise from his mat." Mary stood very still looking into Matthias' face, a stone pestle dripping olive oil unheeded in her hand.

"I don't want him to go without forgiving me." She laid the pestle carefully on the olives in the mortar. "I'm going to him whether he wants me or not."

CHAPTER 30

She placed a cloth over the beaten olives in the stone bowl while she spoke to the children.

"James, go to the shop and tell your father to prepare a bier. Jude, stand by the gate and listen for Ancilla's wail. Girls, get the winding bands from the chests." The memory of Sherah flitted through her mind. *Like her, I now have them with me always.*

Mary hurried through the few lanes to her old home. Ancilla sat on the floor beside her father, bathing his face. She glanced up at Mary and shook her head, fighting tears with firm lips. Mary sat on his other side. In spite of the heat, Eli's frame shook.

"Father, can you hear me?" Mary asked, her face near his ear.

Eli's knuckles turned white as he clutched the bedrug more firmly, but he did not answer.

"It's Mary." She took his free hand in hers and felt the cold of his fingers. "I've come for your forgiveness, Father." He tried to turn from her, but she held him fast. "You do not know it all. There was no sin." He shuddered and pulled his hand free. "Forgive me, for *your* sake." Mary held his bony shoulder, felt him convulse. Ancilla looked frantically at Mary.

"Father, don't go yet." Mary cried.

Eli gasped, took another breath, then lay still. His daughters watched the life drain from his eyes. Ancilla was crying openly, but Mary, dry-eyed, closed her father's.

"She's howling," cried Jude and ran inside to his sisters. "Can we go?"

"No," Julia said, "but we'll all join the procession to the grave when it goes by."

While Joseph prepared the funeral bier, Matthew summoned the mourners and brought spices for anointing. Keening neighbors joined the mournful piping of flutes as neighbors brought supposed comfort to the family. Two women pushed Ancilla and Mary aside and began to wash the body, tears streaming down their faces. Mary handed them the roll of linens and sat down beside Ancilla. She did not cry.

Soon Jesus came into the room. "I've hired the funeral orator and six singers. They'll bring the psalms and the old songs he would remember. We want this funeral to be all that it should be. Grandfather was always so concerned about the proper thing."

"Yes, always *that*," Mary said under her breath.

His daughters sat with their backs to Eli with the prescribed one-inch tear in their tunics. No food was eaten. Mary's ears rang with the never-ceasing whine of the flutes. Still she did not weep.

Sarah, withered with age, pinched Mary's shoulder

with bony fingers and said with scorn, "Have you no feeling for your father? He will see you do not weep and think you don't grieve for him!"

Mary looked at Sarah, at the others who knew her so well and knew Eli even better. Yes, she would weep, but not for Eli and his unforgiving spirit. She would weep for all he had lost, the years they could have shared together. She would weep for him, but not for herself. She cried then, for an hour. *At least I'll keep the traditions, act as though I mourn. He'd want that.*

As the sun dipped behind the western mountains, Joseph and Matthias led the funeral procession out of Nazareth, followed by his daughters and grandsons, then neighbors. It stopped at the family tomb. Nostrils pinched against the smell of decay and a hint of spices. The flaming torches threw shadows as Matthias and Joseph laid Eli's body on a shelf carved from the rock. Jesus stood beside his mother in the cramped space.

Mary traced the carvings on the ossuary box containing her mother's bones. Suddenly her whole body began to shake convulsively. She tried to move and could not. Jesus steadied her.

"I feel death itself upon my soul," she said.

"I know. I know." Jesus replied.

Following the month of mourning for their grandfather, Mary's twin girls, Helen and Julia, were married in simple ceremonies that their farmer husbands could afford. They were brothers and their mother would be kind to her girls; they would be happy.

After the wedding Joseph and Mary told Ancilla and

Matthias their plans: they were moving to Kapher Nahum.

On the day they left Nazareth, Jesus and Joses carried Simon and Elishaba on their backs. James, Jude and Mary each led a donkey so loaded that only the ears and hooves showed. They would meet Joseph in Kapher Nahum, where he'd gone ahead to find a house and a shop.

"You'll be back," old Sarah said, as she clung to Ancilla with one hand and shook a finger at Mary. "The soil of one's birth draws its own. You'll be back." But Mary knew she was wrong. Kapher Nahum, then Jerusalem and Jesus' throne. No more of sleepy Nazareth.

Bushes waved scarlet and golden leaves as the family followed the road down to the sea. Lake Genessaret sparkled like a blue jewel in a dun-colored setting.

The mountains threw shadows across their path as they reached the gates of Kapher Nahum. The tax collector's booth barred their way, making sure duties were collected on any merchandise entering or leaving the city. A portentous man turned from counting money to face them.

"Mary!" cried Malchus "How long has it been? Twenty years?" Here was her old enemy swollen with age and importance, his cheeks etched with tiny red lines, hair and beard thinning—and with the same leering eyes, his smile shining with a golden, false tooth. Mary accepted his profuse greeting. He gave her the same false smile she had hated as a girl.

"You're as beautiful as ever. And such a fine family."

"How is Rachel?" Mary interrupted, asking questions sweetly as though she didn't know and hadn't heard all the gossip about Malchus all the years. "How many children do you have?"

"Rachel? Fine. She has done me proud with nine sons and five daughters." Jesus now stepped up and declared they only carried their own possessions, nothing for sale. Malchus narrowed his eyes at Jesus, then waved them toward the gate of the city. Jesus moved the family quickly away.

Joseph met them just beyond the gate. His teeth gleamed white against his black beard as a grin split his face. He took a smiling child on each arm. "Come," he said, "I'll take you to your new home. He led them down a straight street toward the sea, lined with houses three times as large as theirs in Nazareth.

The final street to the left was a wall of black basalt buildings on one side and the open shore of Lake Gennesaret on the other. They could look beyond fishing boats, across to bare hills on the eastern shore. Halfway down the street, Joseph stepped to a high, carved door. Mary didn't try to hide her exasperation.

"Welcome, Queen Bathsheba." Now Mary looked incredulous, her mouth a bit open. The family entered a wide hall running the length of the house. They paused to adjust their eyes to the dimness and caught a glimpse of sky above an open courtyard at the end of the hall.

With a flourish, Joseph opened doors to each side of where they stood. The pungent smell of cedar and newly-sawn wood caught their breath. "Our carpenter's shop. Grand as Caesar's, eh, Joses?" said Joseph. They explored the rest of the house.

"Of course, it's smaller than the one in Alexandria," Joseph said in mock apology.

She poked him a little with her elbow and then finally smiled, "But it's ours."

In the courtyard she slipped her sandals off and walked across smooth black stones, cool on her aching feet. No more beaten earth floors! Her heart lifted in spite of her weariness. Water bubbled from a fountain into a tiny pool, and red rosebushes clung to the wall. Both a pomegranate and an almond tree hung heavy with fruit.

She trailed the others as they crowded back into the hall to the first door on her right. She stopped, her head leaning a bit forward, as she looked at lapis-blue walls and a ceiling not of mud but of stucco, and painted to look like gold. Jesus walked over to a raised hearth.

"Look, Mother, you won't have to bend to a firehole again. Matthias must make one of these for Ancilla."

"I cannot believe it," she said, turning suddenly to Joseph. He looked from Jesus to Joses.

"We have opportunity here," he said and told them that Kapher Nahum was a center for trade in North Galilee.

Joses interrupted, "And it's on the main route carrying these things south even to Jerusalem. Look at Uncle Zeb, how rich he is."

"Is rich what you want to be?" Jesus asked and looked around the room, then at his mother. "And you, Mother, what do you want here in Kapher Nahum?"

Mary looked directly at Jesus for a moment before she answered.

"I want God's will," she answered and her look said it was a foolish question. Jesus studied the ceiling and rubbed his hand down a carving of ivy and pomegranates on the door frame.

"I'm happy Mother will have this lovely home, but I'd be just as happy sleeping under a mustard tree. How about you, Jude?" The small boy took his brother's hand and nodded.

"Let's go look at the sea, Jesus. Let's go see the fish."

Mary studied the room: the hearth, wooden stools, and cushions, the smooth walls and golden ceiling.

"As Father would say," Mary said grimly, "'may God do and more so' to anyone who mars this room."

The years in Kapher Nahum drifted by like clouds, unnumbered and unnoticed. The shop prospered with Joseph, Jesus and Joses working each day from dawn to dusk. James enrolled in the Academy of Shammai in Jerusalem, and they saw little of him except when they went there for Passover. Simon and Elishaba grew into sturdy children and entered the synagogue school with Salome's grandchildren, for now Roman rule insisted girls be educated, too. Once or twice a year Mary visited Ancilla and Joanna, now almost grown. She also visited Julia and Helen and her grandchildren. Sometimes they came to Kapher Nahum—but never Ancilla.

"Mother," Jesus said one rainy afternoon. "I'm going to Judea. I will not return soon."

"Why now?" Mary frowned.

"I'm going to find Touchon John."

"Can Father do without you?" Instinctively the mother found reasons why her son should not go.

"I want to talk with him while Misheal still lives. He knows the writing of the Essenes who expect the Messiah soon. I must know what those writings say."

The next morning, with a fog chilling the bones, Mary stood in the doorway giving Jesus a final goodbye. Her heart felt the dull pain she often felt when he was gone. Like any mother, she kept a mental account of the health and whereabouts of each child, but the tie that held her and Jesus bound as tightly as ivy.

"Greet Misheal for us. And Jesus—" she paused and pressed her lips together for a moment. "Jesus—stop at the graves of Zacharias and Elisabeth—for me."

"Yes, I will do that. Do not worry—I will come to no danger." He smiled the smile that always melted her heart. Where did it come from—his Father?

Although James was gone and the arguments over lessons no longer drove Mary to take valerian teas, a problem of greater importance simmered below the surface. She sensed Joses' resentment toward Jesus growing. Joseph thought it the normal antagonism of brothers, but Mary knew it went far deeper.

It exploded one evening with Joses brooding in a corner, picking bones from the fish and jamming bread into his mouth. With a sudden jerk, he tossed his knife onto the hearth and turned to Joseph. "I'll stand it no longer," he said with a defiant look at his father. "I'm going back to Nazareth." He stood up with his thumbs stuck in his girdle, his face angry as thunder clouds on the sea. "Jesus takes credit for the work I do." Mary's fist flew to her mouth, but Joseph calmly put down his fish and waited for Joses to continue. "You know I'm a better carpenter. He goes all over delivering my work and taking the credit for it."

"All right, Joses," Joseph said calmly and went back to eating, "what is the real reason for your anger?" Joses bent his head and did not speak. Finally he looked up.

"I'll work all my life, and the shop will be his when you die."

"Joses!" Mary said. Joseph answered slowly.

"You need not worry. Jesus is oldest and has the birthright, but God will reward you justly for the work you do, my son." He said nothing for a moment. "Do not let this fester in your mind—and besides, you know it is not true—that he takes your credit. Think on it."

In spite of Salome's sumptuous house, most evenings found the young men sitting in Joseph's atrium with Zebedee's John expounding on the wonders of the world outside of Galilee, news he gleaned on regular trips delivering fish to Jerusalem. And tonight Jesus was with them, having returned from visiting Touchon John. John brought a report which struck fire.

"Caesar Tiberias," John roared, "has deposed the high priest." Jesus' question was almost as loud.

"He's what?"

The men all spoke at once, until Thunder James, Zebedee's oldest son, shouted above them all. "He can't do that."

"We actually have two high priests," John went on in the awed hush that followed. "He made old Annas the priest in charge of spiritual matters and Annas' son-in-law, Caiaphas, the priest in charge of matters concerning the government."

Jesus's mouth twisted in a quizzical look. "I wonder how our James likes living with two high priests? Did you see him last trip?" John's laugh rang out over the murmuring of the others.

"He's raging about like an ox with a goad pick in his shoulder. He's studying every book in Jerusalem, proving it can't be done—two high priests." John laughed again, but the men grew sober as they thought it over.

"This is only the beginning," Jesus said quietly and looked at his mother.

CHAPTER 31

Mary sat beside the fountain sewing a tunic for Elishaba and thinking over the ten years she had lived in Kapher Nahum. It seems such a long time and yet the time had gone so swiftly. All her children were grown except the last twins. The boys worked with Joseph and Helen and Julia were married and living in Nazareth. Ancilla's Joanna almost ready to marry. Chuza ready for a wife, as well as Joses and Jesus. She and Joseph knew tongues would wag when Jesus didn't marry before he reached thirty years. They had faced harder times; this would work out, too. All in God's time, Joseph would say, all in God's time.

Now in early spring, Mary and Ancilla sat in Eli's old house. Her frame was more twisted and pain lines etched her eyes. They sipped hot comfrey tea spiced with cinnamon and huddled before the hearth, warming their bones while they waited for a spring shower to pass.

"Ancie, don't tell me you are fine because I can see that you are not."

"I'm just an old fig, slowly drying up, full of lines and gritty seeds, but I'll be here when *you're* gone." Her eyes lighted with the old mischief. "I'll admit it only to you, but I wear pain like my tunic. It's gets more difficult to move about, as you see. I sit most of the time in this lovely chair Matthias made me. My left leg is as stubborn as a fisherman's mule and won't do as I tell it. But a lame camel must run with the rest." A smile crinkled the lines around Ancilla's mouth. They treasured memories without words, then, as though they'd both been thinking the same, Mary spoke:

"I'll never forget how angry Father was and how you stood up for me—when they wanted me to marry Malchus."

"Do you ever see him?"

"Ancie," Mary hooted, "he's losing his teeth. His hair is gone except for a few wisps around his ears. He still leers like an idiot whenever he sees me, but I refuse to speak to him. Ancie, they have fourteen children. *Fourteen.*"

"How thankful you must be that Joseph rescued you."

"Every day," said Mary and took another sip of tea. "Every day. After a moment she said, "Ancie, where is Matthias' son Chuza now? Do you see him often?"

"I see Jesus more often. Chuza comes only about twice a year." Neither woman spoke for a moment. Then Ancilla said, "Isn't it odd, Mary, how we miss our children all the time, no matter how old they grow or where they are?" Mary didn't answer. Tears blurred Ancilla's sight.

Then, as she looked at her sister over the mug of hot tea, her eyes again filled with laughter.

"You'll never guess where Chuza is now." Mary

shrugged her shoulders. "He's working as a clerk in Herod's new palace in Jerusalem."

"Herod's!" Tea splashed from Mary's cup.

"Don't look so stricken. He has a high position. Is much trusted."

"Aren't you terrified for him?"

"No, Mary. Chuza knows just where Herod Antipas is at all times and what he's up to." Mary shook her head, unconvinced, her eyes reflecting the fear. "Besides that," Ancie continued, "Herod pays him as much in one moon as Matthias earns in a year." Ancilla refilled their cups.

Mary frowned. "Still, I don't like to think of him right in Herod's palace."

"It's not for long," Ancilla said. "He wants to be steward in the palace Herod is building in Cana."

"In Cana!" Mary's hand flew to her heart. "He'll hear of Jesus."

"Herod will never go there. He hates Galilee. And I must talk to you of something else." Ancilla paused and pushed her graying hair back behind her ears. "Matthias and I have worried where to find a wife for Chuza."

"I've thought of that, too." said Mary, sitting up straighter.

"Well—" Ancilla took a breath. "He's going to marry our Joanna."

"Joanna!" Mary drew back. "His sister!"

"She's no blood relation. He's been gone almost ever since she's been with me." Mary sat back in her chair and gave it thought.

"Yes, they will make a good pair."

Ancilla rose to stir the fire, then went to the window and studied the sky, noting the breaking clouds.

"Mary, you never mention Jesus' future." The light went from Mary's eyes, but Ancilla kept talking. "What is he now, twenty-five? What are his plans? Surely he tells you."

Mary stared into the flame on the hearth. "Ancie, I know no more than the night I stood here and listened to Father tell me to leave." Mary lowered her head. "I think about what the angel said and I try to understand how God can keep his promise—how Jesus can be king." She fingered the alabaster flask tied in its silk around her neck. A flash of sunlight brightened the window. Footsteps came across the courtyard.

"Here comes the king right now, I think," said Ancilla, her eyes blazing. "Why is he waiting? The country is ready."

Mary picked up her cloak and embraced her sister. "We must wait for God to tell us," she whispered.

"Mother of the King." Ancilla smoothed Mary's forehead with a finger.

And there he stood before them, the splash of light making an aura around him.

"Are you ready, Mother?" The women stood for a moment, hand in hand, then followed him into the courtyard, where blue sky reflected in puddles. He kissed his aunt goodbye.

"Tell Chuza I'm waiting for him to come to Cana."

"I will. God bless you." Jesus turned—hesitated— came back and kissed his aunt again, and left for Kapher Nahum with his mother.

*

In the fields men pushed plows through rocky soil and scattered seed. Jesus walked without speaking, deep in thought. Mary stole glances at him, thinking of her talk with Ancilla. She was reluctant to ask, but she had waited so long to know.

"Jesus," she said at last, laying a hand on his sleeve, "are you afraid of what God may give you to do—or can't you tell me?"

"It is not that I cannot tell you. It's that I do not know myself." Mary stopped walking and Jesus did, too. He looked up into the heavens. "I do ask Him, but I receive no answer." His eyes held puzzlement and a little pain.

Nor do I, thought Mary.

They walked on down the Valley of the Doves toward Magdala. As though no time had passed, Jesus went on speaking.

"I see so many things to make right that I don't know where to start." Mary did not interrupt, since he spoke of these things so seldom. "Will my Father expect me to do miracles like Elijah? Or save my people like my namesake Joshua? Or something more humble, like Ezekiel with his rotten figs?" A whimsical smile lighted his eyes.

"Jesus," Mary made a decision without asking Joseph. "There are things we did not tell you." Her son stopped still and looked expectantly into her eyes. Mary clasped her fingers tightly and took a breath. "Gabriel told me you would be *king.*" Jesus nodded.

"I had seen that in the scriptures but was not sure that it meant me."

"The angel told me that you would sit on King David's throne. That your kingdom will be eternal."

Jesus moved forward so rapidly that Mary had to hurry to keep up. "But that is not what Isaiah says. He says that I will die."

Mary's heart gave one hard thump. She knew this, too. Wasn't Jerusalem noted for killing its prophets? But her son wasn't a prophet. He would be a king, a different matter.

That walk with Jesus was one of the most precious moments in Mary's life, along with what happened when they reached Magdala.

The sun dropped behind the hills to their backs and turned the clouds to apricot above a sea of liquid gold. Near the village several men hurried by them to reach an inn while there were still rooms open. One fat merchant walked just behind Jesus and Mary. Huts straggled along the road, lived in by lepers and others not allowed in the village. One hovel made of rushes and mud leaned drunkenly at the road's edge. A girl sat beside it holding a ball of clear quartz crystal in her lap. In spite of her filthy rags, she was the most beautiful girl Mary had ever seen. Black curls hanging to her waist framed the perfect oval of her face. Dark brows and eyes and a straight nose above full lips gave her a classic beauty. Creamy skin shone through the dirt on her face where tears had washed a rivulet through the filth. Mary guessed her to be no more than twelve.

The girl's expression changed to one of cunning when she saw the man beside them. In a voice like a whining saw, she called, "Come! "I'll tell your fortune! Come! I'll tell you where there's wealth for you, dangers to avoid! Come!" She laid the crystal aside, and jumped up to clutch the man's robe. He leaped away.

"She speaks fortunes through demons!" he shouted. Off he hustled, cloak flapping.

Others stepped aside and hastened on until Jesus and Mary were left alone with the strange girl. Now she looked at Jesus and uttered a high-pitched shriek, her eyes full of black hatred.

"I know you!" the girl's voice made the hairs on Mary's arms rise. She backed away, pulling at Jesus, but he stood straight, his fists clenched at his sides as though meeting an enemy.

The girl gripped his left hand and pried open his palm. He looked up quickly toward the sky then into the girl's eyes, while her voice took on an eerie whine.

"You are a holy man. Honor—power—great crowds. You will sit—" Suddenly she screamed, *"Leave me alone! You are the Christ,"* and fell backward, writhing in a fit. A few people coming up behind them scurried past, glancing furtively at Jesus.

He stooped beside the girl, laying his hand on her damp brow and spoke with an authority Mary had never heard before.

"BE GONE!"

Then he took both the girl's hands. "Hush!" he said sternly. She began to sob, no longer a demon-infested, ageless fortune teller, but a frightened child who had just awakened from a nightmare.

Mary stood frozen. A sentient feeling quivered her

arms, as if touched by something from another world. *He simply spoke and the demons left her. They knew him.*

Now from the hut came a feeble, piteous cry. Again it came. Mary looked inside the door. When her eyes adjusted, she saw an old woman lying on a mat. Flies fed on suppurating sores on her hands and face. The woman's chest heaved with each labored breath. Suffering eyes stared at Mary. She knew this woman. "Sherah, oh, not this!" Mary fell to her knees beside her.

"Mary—is it you?" Puffy fingers squeezed Mary's hand and did not let go.

Now Jesus and the girl blocked the light in the doorway. A moment later he knelt beside the mat. The girl cowered in a corner.

"This woman helped us in Bethlehem," Mary said,"when you were born. I've told you about her."

"The vial of myrrh—you have it?" he asked as he looked at the woman.

Mary unwound the wrapping on the alabaster bottle. Jesus took the vial, soaked a bit of cloth, and carefully dabbed each sore.

"Girl—" he said, motioning to her. She crawled to him.

"See the size of the drop I'm putting on her tongue? Do this each hour. It will ease her pain." He handed her the alabaster bottle. Mary watched it leave his fingers and closed her eyes. *Jesus'…never really mine.*

Sherah was attempting to speak, and Mary put her head close to her warty face. "—named after you— granddaughter." Sherah reached for the girl's hand.

"This—Mary—Bethlehem, mother of—" she could say no more.

Mary looked again at the wretched girl whose eyes never left Jesus' face.

Light was quickly fading and the evening wind began its moan across the sea.

Mary turned to the girl. "Where is your father?" she asked. Mary of Magdala looked at her with no sign of the slyness which had marked her face before.

"In prison," she said matter-of-factly. Jesus rose and spoke to her.

"You understand how to give these drops to your grandmother?" She nodded. "When she is gone, sell this. Go to the rabbi and pay the sacrifice necessary to declare you clean. He will accept you." Jesus spoke more quietly. "The money will allow you to bury your grandmother and keep you until you find work."

Mary of Magdala looked doubtful, but Mary of Kapher Nahum tucked a bedrug around Sherah and gently withdrew her hand from the dying woman's.

"Bless you," whispered Sherah.

Jesus and Mary found the synagogue in gathering twilight. She waited while he went inside, and when he returned, they set off swiftly in a race with darkness on the road north toward home.

This is what she had expected of her son. Mary glanced at him with new confidence. Now he would move toward the throne.

CHAPTER 32

"John's preaching—to thousands of people!" Zebedee was speaking as Mary entered the shop a month later, "and baptizing!" His thatch of white hair fairly bristled as his hands told the story, too.

Mary sat down suddenly on a pile of cedar logs, her legs no longer holding her up. Her ears seemed to ring with Zebedee's words. He now spoke to her. "John's pronouncing judgment, Mary. Telling people to repent and be baptized because the Kingdom is at hand!"

Mary gripped a log to stop her trembling.

"Multitudes are going to hear him. They think he's a prophet, maybe Elijah come to life. He's down by the Jordan near Bethabara, putting the fear of Almighty God into people." Zebedee laughed loudly. "He's even got Pharisees and scribes all worked up. The wind's bringing heat right off the desert down into that hole, but still they're coming from all over anyway: Qumran, Jericho, all over Judea. But most from Jerusalem."

Joseph looked up from his sawing. "Jerusalem!" There was a silence then, until Mary finally spoke, her face so alive it seemed to glow.

"The time has come. Jesus' time," she said.

"Well, I don't know about that," Zebedee shrugged his shoulders, "but Touchon John's certainly stirring things up, still wearing that camel hair tunic he's worn for fifteen years. He won't touch a bite of food except dried carob pods and wild honey."

Joseph laughed heartily. "Just like Misheal," he said. "Fruit doesn't drop far from the tree. Too bad he didn't live to see this." Mary went inside and returned with cool mugs of water.

"What's Touchon John saying?" Joseph was asking.

"He says he's a voice crying in the wilderness. Tells them the Lord is coming: prepare to meet him! Shouts that the Salvation of God is coming to establish his kingdom."

Mary set the mugs down and stood tall in front of the men. She raised her arms, fists clenched, and cried: "Now! Now, Jesus will take the kingdom!" Joseph frowned at her.

Zebedee drank half the water at a gulp, staring at her over the rim, then—hesitating a little—continued, keeping one eye on Mary.

"John shouts, 'Repent! Repent! Repent!'" Zebedee waved an arm wildly again. "People *run* headlong into the river to be baptized, so they can be ready to meet the King—even Pharisees."

Joseph crossed the room to take Mary's hand.

"I cannot believe Pharisees," he finally said.

"Believe it or not," Zebedee shrugged. "Sadducees, Pharisees, scribes, Essenes, common people, and those lawyers of the scriptures they call 'the Jews.' Touchon's calling them names that aren't so pretty. Named them a brood of vipers and asking what makes them think they can escape judgement."

Mary clapped her hands. "This is why he was born."

"Who? Touchon?" Zebedee's brow wrinkled. Excitement made Mary young again.

"Him, too," she said, "but I mean Jesus."

"Naturally," said Joseph, "people are only thinking of how to *escape* this judgement."

Zebedee took another swallow of water. "He's telling them to share with the poor. Give away half of what they have." Mary frowned. "He's telling the publicans to repent." Zebedee laughed again, "to quit cheating. Soldiers…"

"Soldiers?" Mary took a step toward Zebedee.

"Soldiers to quit being ruthless. Be satisfied with their wages."

"And the people from Jerusalem, Zebedee?" asked Joseph, staring out the door at the sea. "What do they think of Touchon John?" Zebedee's voice dropped to a murmur.

"They're saying he's the Messiah."

Mary opened her mouth but shut it again without speaking.

"I haven't forgotten what you told me thirty years ago," said Zebedee standing up and lowering his voice. "When people ask John if he's the Messiah, he says 'no,' someone greater is coming—so great he's not worthy to tie his sandals—but nobody believes him." Zebedee stepped close to Joseph and lowered his voice to a whisper. "Is he talking of Jesus?" Mary and Joseph looked at one another, remembering when they confided in Zebedee on the way to Egypt.

"Yes," said Joseph, "he's speaking of Jesus, but John may not know it." Zebedee shook his head.

When he had gone, Joseph held Mary's hands to stop their shaking. She looked up at him, eyes shining, a smile trembling around her mouth. "The kingdom, Joseph!" But the smile quickly disappeared as she thought about what Zebedee had said.

Touchon John's wild pronouncements disturbed Mary more than she liked to say. He'd bring trouble on himself if he kept condemning powerful religious leaders. *Odd that he should draw such attention to himself now, when he's lived a hermit all these years. He must have been born for this reason, born a miracle like my Jesus. No wonder they are drawn so close to each other.*

She went about preparing the evening meal, but her mind was far from fried fish and barley bread.

Morning found everyone gone in different directions except Mary, Joseph, and Jesus. She was watching the men building a cabinet, when Jesus spoke to Joseph.

"Last spring John told me the time had come to proclaim the coming of the Messiah." He picked up a hammer and a peg.

Joseph pursed his lips, then said, "Does John know that you are the Messiah?" Jesus fitted the peg in its place and tapped it twice before he answered.

"He suspects."

"You must tell him," Mary said.

"No, Mother. I have no word from God to do that, but the time has come to let you know what God *has* told me." Mary's lips trembled.

"What..." she could say no more.

Her son stood quietly, his hands holding the hammer lightly. "I am to prepare myself through prayer and study of the scriptures, and to wait." There was silence.

"That's all?" said Joseph. "Wait for what?" But Jesus did not answer this directly.

"Touchon and I both feel the nation is not ready. That's why he is preaching repentance."

Mary sat down, one hand across her eyes, then with a shake of her head, marched back into the hearth room. Joseph picked up a saw. Jesus carefully tapped the peg again. His answer had been entirely unsatisfactory.

The next four years seemed longer than all those that had gone before. Joseph and Mary did not discuss Jesus in front of anyone, but often their eyes met, saying without words: "When? When will he take his kingdom?"

Joseph's hair was streaked with gray. Mary went about more serenely than before, and although white ones hid among her copper hair, her walk still had a spring in it.

Much happened in those years. Joses married Drucilla, the daughter of a wood merchant in Chorazin. She was a quiet, helpful girl and Mary cuddled grandsons, Joachin, Josiah and Jacob. And there was another marriage: Elishaba to a farmer in Nazareth, near her twin sisters. Joseph stopped tongues wagging about why Jesus did not marry by telling them he needed more time to prepare himself as a teacher of the law. Ancilla sent word that now Chuza lived in Herod's palace in Cana, a half day's walk away. That news did not please Mary.

As though the world were setting its stage, in Jerusalem came changes also: in the twelfth year of the reign of Tiberius was appointed a procurator of Judea, one Pontius Pilate.

John came with the news and found the family at the evening meal.

"Joseph!" he raved, throwing his arms to embrace the world. "You were a Cananean. Something must be done." No one spoke, waiting with one breath, shoulders tense. "That Pontius Pilate has less sense than our babies; can you imagine? He marched his soldiers right into Jerusalem bearing their standards with the head of Tiberius emblazoned on them. The city erupted, as you can imagine."

Now everyone talked at once in a babble of unbelief. They silenced when John raised his hand.

"Jerusalem's blood ran in the gutters, until even Pilate realized he'd made a mistake and withdrew them to Caesarea."

"And," said Jesus.

"The people are raving. They'll bow to no god who is a man! Pilate doesn't even try to understand the people he rules."

Joseph narrowed his eyes. "A dangerous man. Dangerous."

Mary sat on the hearth sorting horse beans and Joseph worked a thong through a sandal hole. Joses entered followed by a smiling wife, holding a baby in her arms and with two children hiding behind her skirts. Mary raised her eyebrows. Joses should be about his work. Joses crossed the room in two strides to kneel before Joseph, his voice quivering with excitement.

"Never, Father, never will you believe what Jesus has done for me." Joseph had just a twitch of a smile as he listened. "He asked me to go with him out along the shore. We spoke of the shop." Color rose in his cheeks and he glanced at his wife. Drucilla stood quietly smiling at Joses as he went on. "He—he gave me the birthright," Joses said. "It will mean he does not inherit. Can he do that, Father?"

"Yes," Joseph smiled and Mary's eyes gleamed.

"But will it be legal?"

"Yes, my son," said Joseph. "I told you to trust. Jesus was just waiting for the right time. Come, Joses, you'd better be about the business of the shop. We have orders."

Mary picked up a goatskin, filled it with milk and began sloshing it back and forth, back and forth, churning butter. When she felt the curds rattle, she drained the whey and pressed the butter. Then, a pot of beans settled over the fire, she eased herself to her knees before the hearth to pray. To the east the evening star signaled all good people to be in their houses.

As the family sat down to beans, fresh fenugreek with olive oil and garlic, barley bread with new butter, and small crusts of toasted bread spread with crushed almonds and honey, in came Jesus.

"A feast day?" he asked as he pulled his robe over his head and laid it on a chest. He washed and smoothed his hair with both hands. Mary handed him a plate of food.

"Joses tells us," she said, "that you've given him the

birthright. We're celebrating." Jesus smeared beans on the bread and ate a bite of it before he spoke. Simon and Jude listened so intently that the flames on the hearth seemed noisy. Joseph reached for another helping of greens.

"Well, Jesus, what are your plans now?" Joseph asked, as if it were a normal question. But it was not.

Jesus looked at Mary, then at each of his brothers in turn, then back at Joseph. "I'm going to Touchon John in the morning." Mary and Joseph leaned forward slightly, catching every word. "I don't know how long I'll be gone, but Chuza's wedding is in fifty days, and I'll be back in time for that. John's baptizing down at Pella, and that's only a day's walk." Mary rose to stand behind him, her hands lying lightly on his shoulders. "I'm going," he said up to her, "because Touchon John has a message for me." He gave his mother a significant look.

I'll have to wait all that time to hear John's message—if I'm told. Mary sighed and began clearing the table.

Chuza had been steward of Herod's palace in Cana for five years. The wedding would be the greatest celebration ever held in northern Galilee, since people would come from miles around to see inside Herod's palace—and to feast. And only fifty days to prepare. Because Ancilla could do so little, the planning of the wedding fell to Mary and Salome. Chuza's servants would do the work, but the supervision must be theirs. This they could do for Ancilla.

Jesus left for the Jordan and it began to rain, then

turned cold, leaving a thin glaze of ice on the cobble-stones. The next morning a cart laden with heavy oak logs arrived. Joses and Joseph went to the shop to help unload them. A sudden thump and a muffled cry from Joseph brought everyone running. A massive log lay across his foot.

"Don't move!" cried Joses. He and the cart driver lifted the log and heaved it aside. Joseph bent over his foot and rocked with pain. Mary ran to her store of herbs for comfrey, made a plaster and bound Joseph's ankle.

The foot healed slowly and as the wedding approached, Joseph told Mary to go without him. "Tell Matthias I'm sorry. You'll see that everything goes as it should. Ancie won't have to worry. Nothing will go wrong with you in charge."

If only that had been true.

CHAPTER 33

On the day of the wedding lazy clouds drifted toward Syria, playing tag with their shadows on the hillsides below. All the family from Kapher Nahum except Joseph, Drucilla, and the children were on their way. Neither Zebedee's sons, his partners nor Jesus had returned from seeing Touchon John. The family could only hope that they would be in Nazareth when they got there. Finally Mary would learn of Touchon's message to Jesus.

The family reached Cana before noon. The palace lay before them more splendid than the one Mary had seen in Jerusalem on her first trip to Elisabeth's. White marble buildings rose three stories with so much glass the whole building seemed transparent. Terraced gardens and fountains sparkled with rainbows in the sun.

In spite of knowing that Herod Antipas would not be there, Mary's heart fluttered as they were led to the right door by a servant. Chuza proudly showed them inside. The entrance hall seemed a maze of clay water jars. Along one wall, stone amphora, some as tall as a woman, gave off the spicy scent of wine. *At least we will not be embarrassed by running out of wine,* thought Mary.

Three grand dining halls five times the size of her hearth room would hold the hundreds invited to each feast. The family marveled at the wealth, gold leaf everywhere, gilded chairs, and tapestry lounges. Already linen cloths hid tables laden with food, with servants scurrying about preparing more.

After refreshments of cold water and melons dipped in wine, Chuza led them all down the Way of Cana to Nazareth to bring back his bride. He would lead Joanna and his parents and all the invited guests from Nazareth, bestowing the gifts of the bridegroom. James was waiting for them, in his immaculate Pharisee robes. But Jesus and the others had not yet come.

The sun dropped toward the hills to the west before one of the grandchildren leaped the wall shouting that Jesus was coming, plus the cousins and several men they did not know. As the men entered Eli's old courtyard, Mary stared at her son in dismay. He was skin and bones. She saw a new expression in his eyes, too, and felt a new quietness in his spirit. But there'd be no opportunity to talk with him until after the feasts. She watched him with a mother's concern.

The family squeezed into Eli's old courtyard. Joanna, looking as beautiful as Salome, came from the house and took Jesus' hand. Smiling with his old radiance, he led her to Chuza, who looked like a prince in Matthias' wedding garment. Jesus joined their hands. Her nephews helped Ancilla onto the chair and hoisted the poles to their shoulders. Everyone burst into song as they started for Cana.

The procession grew as they moved northward. With

a wail of flutes and the throb of drums, their cavalcade entered the palace. A sweet smell of burning oil from hundreds of lamps perfumed the night air. The crowds from Cana pressed into the dining room behind the procession. Three days and nights of feasting began.

Before everyone retired for the night, Jesus paused beside his mother. "I'll be by the highest fountain as soon as you can get away."

He waited on a marble bench, watching the water rise and fall in its circle of rosy marble. The first stars appeared. Mary arrived and gave him a handful of figs she'd brought from the banquet table. "You're just bones." He ignored this and set the figs aside.

"Mother," he said, his eyes serious. "I want you to know before anyone else." Her heart began to hammer against her ribs. Mary tried to smile, but something in his face smothered it. "God has spoken." He wrapped his warm hands around her icy ones. A strength passed to her.

"Touchon John publicly declared that I am the Lamb of God."

"At last!" Mary's eyes glowed.

"I insisted that he baptize me, though he didn't want to—and when he did, the Spirit of God came upon me." A warmth lit his eyes, too. "My father spoke out loud to me."

The garden and fountain whirled slowly, around and around in rainbows of light. Mary gripped his hands to keep from floating away. She whispered, "What words did He say?" and waited for the fulfillment of Gabriel's promises.

"That I am his Son. That He is pleased with me."

Disappointment again. Nothing about being king. Then she experienced a new sensation, the uneasy feeling that he knew her every thought. Jesus put his arm around her waist. He looked troubled, as though from some deep hurt.

"I have been tested, but I won—I used the scriptures as my weapon." Mary dared not ask how. She only knew that he had paid dearly. She traced his gaunt cheekbone with a finger.

"Mother—" he began. She felt the depth of his words, knew what they would cost and dropped her hand into his, where they lay folded in his lap. "Believe what I say. You know that I will always do just as God tells me. But it may not be what you expect." Mary could scarcely hear her own voice.

"Didn't He tell you," she swallowed, "that you'll be king?"

"I am." His confidence drove away the dark shadows she sensed in him. She felt as though light filled her.

He knows he's the king. Now nothing can stop him.

"Come," she said, rising. "Let's tell the family." But he held her from going.

"No, this isn't the time. Many things must happen first. Tell no one a word of what I've said." His look of authority stopped her protest. With bowed head, she walked silently beside him back to the palace.

The middle of the third day, as Mary sat at the end of a banquet table watching the feasting, Chuza's head steward slipped up beside her and said, "We're out of wine."

That cannot be! her shocked expression said. "Let me find Chuza." But no Chuza. She followed the steward into the hallway, where servants were drawing the last grainy dregs from each amphora.

"There's none in the marketplace, either," said the man. "There's not a drop anywhere in Cana." He looked as desperate as if Herod himself were demanding wine.

Jesus walked in just then and paused at the confusion. His mother marched up to him.

"Look at that. Wine's gone and there's none in the market. We cannot let Chuza be disgraced by running out of wine. There must be some rich man in Cana who has a store hidden."

Jesus threw up his hands and the expression on his face said, What do you expect me to do? But Mary ignored this and said impatiently, "If Joseph were here, he'd find some. Since he isn't, *you* must." She turned to the servants. "Do whatever he tells you to." With that she returned to her place at the table and looked at Ancilla and Matthias at its head, at Salome fanning herself with an ostrich plume unaware the wedding feast was going to end in social disaster. Mary watched the glasses empty, the wine disappear.

At that moment came a slave with a glass carafe of clear wine as red as rubies and set it beside her. He poured some into a rabbi's glass, and the man sipped.

Then he shouted, "Matthias! Wherever did you get this wine? It's better than our pomegranate. It must be from Herod's own storehouse!" A general laugh followed as the new wine touched everyone's lips.

Mary slipped away to find Jesus. She had only asked

for his help a few minutes ago: Where did he find that wine? In the hallway fifty excited servants buzzed, some licking fingers dipped into spilled wine. Jesus stood among them, resignation sagging his shoulders. Mary felt at fault but couldn't find her offense.

"Please, my friends," pleaded Jesus, his hands held out in supplication, his voice strained, "tell no one what you have seen today!"

No one listened. They ran about repeating the story with all the embellishments a story gains in retelling. This man from Kapher Nahum has turned water into wine. They'd seen him do it with their own eyes. They'd filled the water jars themselves just as he told them to, and when they poured it out—it was fine, red wine! A miracle! Like Elisha! Mary turned startled eyes on her son.

The shouting stopped as each person looked at Jesus. With sudden silence, they went about their work, casting furtive glances at him. Mary's fingers flew to her temple and into her hair. The head steward touched her arm.

"What did your son do? How did he make water into wine?" Mary could only shake her head, her eyes as startled as his. He tiptoed away, muttering, "A miracle. A miracle."

Like smoke before a wind, the story spread to guests and family as they sat feasting.

"The Messiah!" shouted someone.

"The Lamb of God," cried those who'd been with Touchon John.

"To the King!" shouted Judas and raised his glass.

Musicians grabbed harps, timbrels, flutes, and everyone began a rousing song of celebration. Young girls left the table to dance and twirl. The feast ended with a great roar from everyone.

"Jesus! Jesus! The King! The King! The King!"

But the king was not there, nor could he be found.

"Wait," Chuza commanded when the guests had gone and before the family dispersed. His voice held the authority of Herod's steward. "Let's understand this. I want to know where Jesus found that wine. I don't believe for a minute that he turned common water into wine. Where's this so-called miracle worker of ours?" Chuza sent every servant to scour the palace gardens in search of Jesus.

Matthias spoke in the quiet that followed. "Remember in whose house this feast is held. Herod's."

The talk stilled, the family horrified, now fully realizing the danger to Chuza. He looked around the table at his cousins who'd raised the toasts, at his parents, at his bride Joanna and lastly at Mary.

"I just don't know!" she said quietly, and shook her head. Mothers went from the room to put children to bed, leaving only the men, the three sisters and Joanna.

The servants returned without Jesus. One servant did not return at all. "Probably on his way to Herod," sneered Judas. Chuza dismissed the servants to their sleep and sat down beside Ancilla. Weariness lay in purple shadows around her eyes, but those eyes shone brightly. With a nod to Joses to see that the door was closed and no one listening, Chuza turned to Zebedee as the oldest member of the family, and Zebedee now took charge.

"Let's start at the beginning, Mary," he said, turning to

273

her as did all the heads in the room. She did not speak for a moment, choosing each word carefully, wishing Joseph were there to share this.

She began, "The things I'm going to say will seem a fantasy, but they are true." Then Zebedee stepped around to Mary, took her arm and lifted her from her chair.

"God chose our own Mary," he boomed. "Tell them, Mary."

The silence became a living presence. Before Mary could speak, Ancilla hoisted herself up and threw both arms in the air.

"Jesus is *God's* son, not Joseph's! I've waited thirty-odd years to say that." She sat down in triumph. Stunned silence followed. Mary's heart was so full she could find no words, nor could she have uttered them. She looked around the room, proudly daring anyone to argue. Her nephew, Thunder James, broke the moment.

"*That's* what Touchon John said. Touchon called him the Son of God, and some of us believed him." He looked at others who'd been with them at the Jordan.

Then all talked at once: Those who had been Cananeans— Matthias, Clopas' sons, and Judas—planning strategy; Chuza, Zebedee, and Mary's James talking government; the women chattering about Mary.

"And Herod?" asked someone.

The specter of the king entered the room and stilled the talk. Shivers raced up and down Mary's spine. Soon everyone was looking toward Chuza and whispering among themselves. One way or another, Herod would learn of this. Jesus was in mortal danger.

CHAPTER 34

Those bound for Kapher Nahum left at dawn the
next morning, at different times and by different
roads. Mary and her four sons went back the way they
had come, through Magdala. Part-way Jesus joined
them. He walked into the middle of the group and said
nothing for awhile, looking ahead to the sea shimmering
in the distance. Then they began talking about the wedding and the weather, until finally Simon asked the
question in each mind.

"Jesus, how did you do it? How did you turn water
into wine?"

"I spoke to the water," Jesus said, a wry look on his
face. Mary smiled, remembering his power with Mary of
Magdala, but his brothers frowned. "I know you want
more answer than that, but it is all I can give you for
now." He looked at each expectant face, a little longer at
his mother. Then to all of them he said, "I know it will
be hard for you—but now you must realize who I am."

In the pregnant silence that followed, a flock of gulls
flew overhead with their discordant cries. Jude and Joses
looked up, then back at Jesus. They waited for more.

"Yes," said Joses. "One day you are just our brother,

and the next you are— Who are you?" Mary now helped her children understand that which was beyond them all—and almost beyond her as well.

"Jesus is the Messiah!" She shrugged and looked at him for help, but he did not speak. "We must do all that we can to help him. Whatever it may be," she added lamely. *Why doesn't he explain?*

They walked on, passed other people, and when alone again, Simon asked another question. "Are you going to be King?" Jesus stopped walking, glanced into the sky and answered.

"I already am." His voice told them that he would not explain further, but James spoke up sharply, saying he just couldn't see his brother as the Messiah. Jude said cryptically he didn't think Jesus ever would be a *king*, but if he ever was he hoped he'd see the roads were improved. Joses said that he wanted nothing, only to stay in Kapher Nahum with his wife and work in the shop.

When Jesus asked Simon what he wanted from him as king, Simon replied that he really didn't know. He would wait and see.

"Mother?" Jesus said, "What do you expect?"

"I want to see you on David's throne—as God promised," Mary said and stepped ahead faster.

Finally Jesus answered the questions they had not asked. "My kingdom will be the Kingdom of Heaven, not an earthly one. Keep that in mind, Mother." He reached an arm around her for a moment. No one asked him anything further, but Mary kept glancing at Jesus, her forehead as wrinkled as the contorted hills beside them.

*

At home, Jesus talked with Joseph alone. Mary never knew what he told him, and Joseph never spoke of it.

A week later the family left for Passover on a cold, windy morning. In spite of Joseph's limp, they took the King's highway along the Jordan in hopes of seeing Touchon John. But John had disappeared.

They talked of many things and finally of that uppermost in their minds, but Jesus' brothers seemed not to have understood what he had told them about his kingdom. Mary and Joseph listened to the brothers.

"Where will you attack first, Jesus?" Simon asked, "to take over the kingdom?" Jesus shook his head, but Jude leaped in.

"Yes, will it be the Antonia?" He pointed rapidly with both hands. "Or Herod's palace?"

Jesus sighed. "You haven't understood," he said.

"Better win the Sadducees and Essenes first!" James said with authority. "Without them on your side, you'll never rule."

Jesus dismissed the idea with a flap of his hand and waited to speak until everyone was looking at him. "None of you understand." He glanced at his mother, including her in the statement. "I'm going to start at the Temple."

"The Temple!" Brother looked at brother as though Jesus had lost his mind. Joseph laughed out loud, and Mary gave him a reproachful look. But Joseph laughed again. James smiled self-righteously. Jesus started to speak to him, then closed his lips. The new authority in his voice stopped the conversation. "I will start in the Temple."

They panted up the torturous trail from Jericho and

rounded the shoulder of Olivet Mountain just as the setting sun shot gold from the roof of the Holy Place. One by one they dropped to their knees before Jerusalem. The somber Antonia fortress seemed to devour the light and stood cold and menacing beside the Temple.

"It's like Heaven and Hades," Simon said, rising with the rest of the family.

"There's not as much difference as you think," Jesus said. Joseph added an amen, but his brothers looked shocked.

"Say no such thing about our Temple," growled James.

"You know yourself, James, if you'll admit it, that there's prejudice and hatred, politics and corruption in the priesthood, and hypocrisy in the leadership." James twitched his shoulders.

"It is true," he said somewhat reluctantly, "well, perhaps in the Sadducees, but not among the Pharisees. You're mistaken." He left them outside the east wall to enter by another gate.

"He will have to learn for himself," Joseph said. "Youth sees black and white." He rubbed his chin. "We learn with age."

Outside the north wall thousands of sheep, goats, oxen, and heifers milled about in pens, waiting their fate, bawling, kicking dust and dung. The family hurried to enter the Fish Gate before it closed for the night. They would all stay in Zebedee's house, where they always stayed at Passover.

The next day the men went to the Temple to select

the lambs, while the women cleaned the house for the Pascal feast.

"Mother!" Simon's shout brought women and servants rushing to the entrance. Joseph limped in behind him, both panting for breath.

"What's gone wrong?" cried Mary.

"Jesus has cleaned out the Temple," Simon caught his breath.

"He's *what?*" Mary looked wildly at Joseph. Laughing and panting, he sat down and rubbed his foot. "Simon?"

"Jesus took a whip," Simon threw his arms wide. "Threw the money all over." He took a breath. "I never saw anyone so angry in my life." Mary looked helplessly from her husband to her son. Joses and Jude ran in, followed by Zebedee. Joseph threw back his head and laughed and laughed again. At this, Zebedee added his howl to Joseph's. Mary threw them a bitter look and covered her eyes with her hands.

Joseph sobered and said, "I'll start at the beginning. Jesus was angry with the money changers. I've always been angry about them, but Jesus *did* something."

Jude slapped his knee and rocked back and forth with howls of glee. "It was in the Court of the Gentiles," he took over for his father, "with everyone watching. Jesus suddenly grabs a leather rope off a stall, kicks the stall down, and yells at them to quit making his Father's house a market place. Money was rolling all over. Men trying to scoop it up. Pharisees shouting for the guards."

Mary's heart pounded, her eyes intent on Joseph.

He couldn't have done those things. Not my Jesus. He's doomed his chances. "What about the soldiers?" she shouted above the laughter.

"The soldiers were laughing, too," said Simon, grinning. She could see no reason for the mirth.

"What happened to Jesus?" Mary waved her hand as though it held a whip. "What happened to Jesus?"

Joseph stopped smiling. "I stayed right beside him, Mary. He had a power about him which put the fear of God in everyone. He kept shouting, 'Take these things out. Quit robbing my people.'"

"And where is he now?" Mary asked coldly, but did not receive an answer.

"He said," finished Zebedee, "to tell you that he won't be here for Passover. I think he's gone to find Touchon."

Joseph turned back to Mary. "Strange," he said, "no one asked Jesus *why* he was desecrating the Temple. They just screamed at him, asking by whose authority he did it."

"And what did he say?" Mary asked flatly. Joseph answered her, serious now.

"He said, 'Destroy this temple, and in three day's I'll build it up.' The Pharisees turned purple. Herod's been building it for forty years, and Jesus' answer didn't make sense. I guess they thought he was a lunatic. Then Jesus just walked out."

Over the Passover days, the story was told and retold by everyone who'd been there. But where was her son? He'd never missed a Passover since he was twelve.

Before they left for home, Joseph found news of Jesus. "He said to tell you, Mary, he's going to be here in Judea for a few months. Teaching. He'll be back in Galilee later."

"Teaching?" Mary tossed her hands to both sides. "Teaching what?" But Joseph only gave his wife a rueful smile and shrugged.

"Something about preparing people to receive the Kingdom," he said.

At the turning on Mt. Olivet, Mary looked back at the maze of streets. Her son was there—teaching. She would have liked to have shaken him.

A gentle autumn breeze filled the courtyard with the pungent odor of ripe grapes. Shadows of almond leaves fluttered across the writings of Isaiah where Joseph sat reading the parchment aloud to the family.

They'd heard Jesus was back in Galilee and doing miracles, greater than Elijah's, but he'd not come home. A Roman official from Kapher Nahum had gone to see him in Cana and asked Jesus to come heal his slave. Jesus had told him to go home, the boy was well already. The town had buzzed with that miracle. The family hoped Jude would see Jesus on his travels for Zebedee, and while they were talking about it, the door slammed. In rushed Jude, just home.

"Jesus is back in Galilee. He almost got killed in Nazareth." As from the bottom of a well, his words drummed in Mary's ears. *Killed. Killed. Killed.* Jude slumped on a bench in the atrium while the family surrounded him.

"Jesus is dead?" Joses grabbed Jude's arm.

281

"No, he's all right, I guess." Jude raised his hand in defense. "He's back in Galilee because of Touchon John."

A babble of voices all asked, "What about Touchon?"

"First," Jude went on, "Herod had John thrown into prison a month ago."

"Why?" all asked in unison.

"He condemned Herod for marrying his brother's wife. Condemned them publicly. Said they'd committed sin."

"But Jesus?" Mary whispered.

Jude didn't answer her but went on. "Touchon said that anyone who doesn't obey Jesus will have God's wrath on him. Herod won't like that." The same Stygian blackness consumed Mary which she'd felt when she saw Ezekias on the cross. "At least Jesus had sense enough to get out of Judea," she heard Jude faintly. "After all the things he did in Jerusalem, he's been received up here in Galilee like he was Elijah—except in Nazareth."

"Go on about Nazareth, Jude," Joseph said as he sat down and crossed his legs.

"Well, I was there when Jesus came back. Everyone in town crowded into the synagogue to see him, even Ancilla. They asked him to read the scriptures. He read from Isaiah, but stopped before he was supposed to, and just sat down."

"Before he explained them?" Joseph looked from Jude to Joses, his eyebrows making a black U.

"He said he'd fulfilled them," Jude said lamely.

"He didn't! He didn't say *that!*" Joses exploded.

Mary said nothing, but her hand pressed harder against her heart.

"At first," Jude said, "everyone was kind of spellbound. Then as he talked more, they got riled up. Kept muttering, 'Isn't this just Joseph's son? The carpenter?' As though that proved he didn't know anything!" Jude paused while the family waited. He pressed a fist against his teeth and then spoke quietly.

"If only he'd stopped there! But you know Jesus. He just kept talking in that soft voice of his. Then Jesus thundered so loud everyone jumped: 'No man's a prophet in his own village.'" Jude stretched his arms in unconscious imitation of his brother. "'I know what you're thinking,' Jesus said. You are saying 'Physician, heal yourself!'" Jude looked from one face to another. "Jesus' voice filled the whole room like the sound of an earthquake!" Jude paused again, his voice low. "But it was strange—he really wasn't speaking very loud." Jude seemed to be seeing it all again from a distance. Impatience frowned on each forehead. If Jude would only get on with it.

"But that was more than the men would stand. The men—you know them all—pushed and shoved Jesus out of the synagogue."

Her face white marble, Mary thought it through. *I can see him deliberately making people angry like he used to do with James—to make them think. Only now, now he is endangering his own life.*

Each person leaned closer to hear more. "The twins' husbands and I—we tried to stop them. Those old neighbors just hurled curses and dragged him toward the cliff."

A sob came from deep in Mary's throat. Joseph's fists clenched.

"Ancilla came limping behind, screaming. We tried to get through to him." Jude looked down at his hands. "I've got a few skinned knuckles to prove I tried. I was almost as mad at him for starting it as I was at the men for trying to kill him. Just as they began to hurl him over the edge—"

An end-of-the-world roaring pounded in Mary's ears. Jude went on, as though still enthralled.

"They got him right to the edge of the cliff—" Mary closed her eyes, seeing that steep drop. "I can't explain what happened next. With their last shove—Jesus simply turned and walked back through the crowd. We all stood there, kind of paralyzed. Everybody. I never saw him again."

The family sat as transfixed as the Nazarenes.

And suddenly, Jesus was with them and laughed out loud.

"You look like a room full of statues. Will you get me some water, sister? I'm thirsty." Mary only looked at her son. Looked and looked, carving into her memory the sight of him.

Jude leaped up and grabbed Jesus, pounding his back, then stepped back as he remembered Nazareth. Joseph looked deeply into Jesus' eyes and went for a washing towel.

"Why so serious, Mother?" Jesus asked. He gave her a twisted grin. "I'm preaching the Kingdom. I'm going all over Galilee telling everyone 'The Kingdom of God is near.' Isn't that what you wanted?"

Mary went into Jesus' arms and began to shake, too overwhelmed to make a sound.

What will he do next? Nothing safe, of that I'm sure.

CHAPTER 35

In the synagogue the next Sabbath in Kapher Nahum, Jesus rolled the scroll several turns beyond the text he'd been handed by Jairus, the leader of the synagogue. Like the tolling of a clear bell, his rich strong voice now broke the silence: "The Spirit of the Lord is upon me; because of this he has anointed me."

"No, no. He's reading the same text as he did in Nazareth," Mary whispered to Drucilla.

"—to proclaim deliverance to the captives, to bring sight to the blind—"

Suddenly a man leaped up, shrieking, "Let us alone! Let us alone! What are you doing, Jesus of Nazareth?" His hands clawed the air, his mouth contorted. "Have you come to destroy us? I know who you are! The Holy One of God!"

An audible breath as from one man came from the men below the platform. For a moment no one moved. Then Jairus sprang down and grappled with the man. What Jesus did next struck terror into every heart. He said with majesty:

"BE QUIET. COME OUT OF HIM."

The man's eyes bulged and he fell sideways, knocking

over a bench, his muscles jerking convulsively. Then he rose to his feet, panting as though exhausted, and kneeled before Jesus.

As evening shadows filled the hearth room that evening, Simon turned from looking out the window. "Something's going on at Cephas'," he said. "People are running. Let's go see."

At Cephas' door, the family watched people trying to crowd inside, jostling aside those trying to leave.

"What's happening?" Joseph asked a neighbor who came rushing from the house.

"Your son healed Cephas' mother-in-law of a deadly fever."

It seemed as though everyone in Kapher Nahum who was sick, lame or blind pushed inside Cephas' house. Many came out in tears, praising Jesus.

Jesus went home with his family and Joseph barred the door before anyone could put a toe inside.

Mary slept fitfully, hearing again the demon's scream. *Why does he forbid them to say he is God's son. Shouldn't everyone know?*

At breaking of fast, Jesus was gone. His brothers found him up in the hills praying and returned to tell Mary.

"What's he saying?" Mary asked.

"Oh, that he's got to preach the Glad News to other cities now."

This time Mary understood and sighed with relief. He hadn't been sent to earth to be a physician to every person who came to him; he'd die of fatigue. He was right to press on.

*

A month later, Joses brought news which did not encourage his mother. Jesus was doing miracles everywhere, casting out demons and unbelievable healings, but Joses told her reluctantly that he thought that people only followed him for the excitement and for what they could get—free food and healing.

"But he does talk about the kingdom, doesn't he?" Mary stopped her furious scouring of an iron pot. Joses turned as he started for the carpentry shop.

"He says it's coming, but doesn't say anything about becoming its king."

Next time he's home, I'll ask him if I may go with him, thought Mary. *I want to be part of all he does—once he really starts for the throne and quits this foolish traveling here in Galilee. I must be part of it.* She thought of her childish dreams of standing beside him as a queen. No more. Now she saw her role. She must be with him to help, to protect him. *I'll ask next time he comes.*

When the latter rains slowed and Passover again lay only weeks away, Jesus and his followers returned. Mary, seeing the tired lines under his eyes, chided him for not taking care of himself. She insisted he stay home long enough to rest and gain back his lost weight.

"I'm well," he said, but Mary knew differently. He seemed discouraged and hollow-eyed.

"My son," Mary began and groped for the right words, "let me travel with you...be part of all you do...hear all you say."

"No, Mother."

"But I would only be there to see you eat and care for

your clothes...and..." She saw rejection in his eyes.

"No, Mother. You mean well, but it is not God's plan that you be with me." He did not explain and no balm could salve the hurt his words gave Mary.

Jesus again taught in the synagogue on the next Sabbath, this time without incident. James was visiting from Jerusalem and pointed out Pharisees he knew, wondering what they were doing in Kapher Nahum.

"Probably spying for Caiaphas—or for Herod." He did not know the terror that remark stirred in his mother.

Fists pounded on the door that evening. A burly man with a twisted leg burst in, impelled by the crowd behind him. The family sprang to stop them. Mary's cry was lost in the tumult. People filled the hallway, spilled into the hearth room until there was no room to breathe. Mary jabbed her elbows into ribs and thrust through the crowd. She could hear Jesus speaking in the middle of the room but could not see him. Bodies crushed against her, shoving her rudely. She heard her best pot clatter to the hearth.

More people crowded through the door, and there was Jude. His powerful hands circled the waist of a man with a weeping ulcer and plucked him off a stool as easily as though he'd been a wooden statue. He set him on the floor and with a quick grab stood his mother on the stool where she could see.

Demons screamed. People wept and tore their clothing, beseeching Jesus to heal them—heal them, then they shouted praises. Some scribes and Pharisees jostled in with broad phylacteries on their foreheads and scowls on their faces. They squinted their eyes at this prophet.

"Why are *they* here?" Mary fumed. "Why is anyone here? Look what they're doing, Jude, standing on my cushions." Someone broke a stool. "Why isn't Jesus in Nazareth healing Ancilla?" Never had Mary been so angry. Blood pounded in her ears.

Suddenly the noise lessened just a bit. Feet tramped on the roof. Mary turned a startled look at Jude. Someone was pounding the roof. Dust and bits of plaster, golden flakes, drifted down. An iron stake jabbed a hole. Someone tore off the tiles, one by one.

"Stop them! Stop them!" Mary's shouts went unheard. More tiles disappeared. She saw stars through the hole. Something in a rug was being lowered into the room. People pressed back to make space. Jude craned his neck.

"It's a man," Jude cried into Mary's ear. "It's Caleb! He's been paralyzed since he fell from the rocks when we were boys. Listen."

Jesus' voice rose clear in the center of the tumult.

"Take courage, Caleb. Your sins are forgiven."

Mary took a deep breath. Men on the roof stared down through the hole. A distinguished-looking Pharisee pushed through to stand beside Jesus. Jesus looked directly at the Pharisee, who narrowed his ferret eyes.

"Why are you questioning?" Jesus voice rose. "Why do you think evil? Which is easier? To say 'your sins are forgiven,' or 'pick up your bed and walk?'" Then Jesus' voice seemed to shake the house. "To show you I have the authority to do both, I say, PICK UP YOUR BED AND WALK."

Every voice hushed. Caleb grabbed the mat, and the crowd parted as if split by lightning to let him dart through. Jude ran after him.

As though their leaving were a signal, the people hurried out, pushing and shoving, awed and muttering until the ravished room stood empty except for the family. A bit of plaster cascaded to the floor from the gaping hole in the roof, followed by a shower of dust.

"Well, now I've seen it all," said Mary, her voice shrill. "Just look at my house." Joseph and Drucilla began straightening stools. Jesus looked ruefully at the hole above his head and grimaced, half-way between a frown and a grin.

"And my ceiling," cried Mary to him. "My beautiful ceiling. What are you trying to do? You've made those Pharisees angry. They'll go back to Jerusalem and make trouble for you. What are you trying to do? Destroy every chance you have?"

But Jesus bent to pick up tiles and did not answer her. Joseph tried to assuage her anger. "He's just doing as God wills, Mary," he said, as he screwed a leg back into a stool.

"I don't think God told him to tear my house down."

"Mother," said Jesus and took her hand. "Isn't it more important that Jude's friend walk again?"

"Tell him, Joseph!" She turned to her husband. "Make him see. He's killing himself helping people. They're using him—selfishly."

"We must let him obey God in his own way," Joseph said firmly.

"And fulfill the prophecies," Jesus said. "You know

the Messiah must fulfill them all." No one said a word as he went on. "I must keep teaching here in Galilee and bring good news to the afflicted, encourage the broken-hearted, proclaim liberty to the captives—all the things Isaiah prophesied. You know I must do these things first, Mother. You know I must."

Mary frowned. She refused to think of any other prophecies.

"Was it prophesied to wreck my house," she finally asked but now she said it without anger. And when Jesus said he didn't think so—but he'd have James check the scriptures, Mary's lips twitched.

"They want to put him in prison—like Touchon John." Mary's voice broke as she brought Joseph the latest news of Jesus. Joseph laid down his piece of wood and took her in his arms. She rested her head on his chest, letting the tears spill.

"Now, Mary—," he said, but she interrupted him.

"Touchon John won't ever be free."

Outside, a cart clattered by, disturbing the heat waves in the street. Someone cursed mules in Syrian.

"Mary," Joseph said and held her away from him to look into her eyes, "Jesus knows what he's doing. He's picked twelve men to be his companions. Men he can trust, mostly kin, actually, and friends. Some women, too."

"Who?" *Why, when he wouldn't let me go?*

"Joanna for one; Chuza can't go with him, but he's giving all the money possible and keeping his ears open to know what Herod's up to. By the way, John tells me

Herod has called Chuza back to serve him in his palace in Jerusalem. Jesus knows what he's doing," he said again and picked up the board.

That evening Mary and Joseph stood in the doorway looking out over the sea at the coming darkness, listening to waves lap the shore. Later as Mary pushed the grinding stone across barley for the next day's bread, Jesus appeared beside her.

"I've slipped away for a little while," he said. "I'll be home whenever I'm near and can come without being followed." He kneeled and put an arm around her. A smile lighted her face.

"I must go to Nain tomorrow. I'd like you to go along, if you don't mind walking so far. It's more than a day's journey. Mary said nothing for a moment, but pushed the grinding stone thoughtfully. Then she wiped her hands and looked at him.

"Yes, I'll go."

"We'll leave at dawn," he said.

He wants me to go with him, but why this time?

CHAPTER 36

Mary joined Jesus just as sunrise touched the clouds across Gennesaret. At the edge of town, his men fell in step, along with twenty or thirty others, some from Kapher Nahum and some unknown to Mary. She had hoped to be alone with her son, but by the time they'd walked an hour at least a hundred people were following, begging to be healed of everything from leprosy to nosebleeds.

Someone with a strong voice, back down the line, started a psalm of praise and everyone joined the refrain clapping hands to the rhythm. "Oh, give thanks unto the Lord. For He is good. For He is good."

Intent on scorching the world, the sun circled the sky. Blue ox tongue and galbanum grew waist high, green bay and myrtle sweetened the air, and red-crested bee-eaters darted after insects, while above the voices, locusts droned. Mary walked just behind Jesus' chosen men and listened to them talk. *Why is he teaching these things that so disturb everyone? No one would be upset if he talked about setting up Israel's kingdom.* Mary decided Jesus' purposes could not be fathomed. Just when she thought she understood, he did the unexpected.

The second evening, just outside the village of Nain, a funeral procession barred the way. Above the cacophony of mourning, a woman shrieked. She was about Mary's age with ashes matting her hair and tears streaking the soot on her face.

"My son! My only son!" echoed from hill to hill in the evening air. Jesus walked up to her and took her hand.

Mary's heart went strongly to this woman, and she moved with Jesus through the crowd to stand beside her.

"Don't weep," Jesus said. Then he stretched his hand toward the funeral basket. John grabbed his arm, but recoiled as though scalded when Jesus raised the lid on the basket.

"Young man," Jesus said sternly to the corpse, "get up."

Mourners stopped their wail on a breath. Men carrying the basket let it down with a thump. The dead youth sat up and shook his head. Eyes bulging, he looked around him. "You were about to bury me!" He looked frantically at his mother. The woman stood as stone, then slowly realizing what Jesus had done, with a great wail, clasped her son to her heart.

The next morning at dawn, Mary and Jesus turned back toward Kapher Nahum, taking a shorter route than the way they'd come. Still crowds came out in every town shouting and straining to see the miracle worker. By evening Jesus and his followers reached Magdala on the same road Jesus and Mary had taken when they had seen Sherah five years before. The hut was gone and market stalls lined the roadway where the demons screamed at Jesus through Sherah's granddaughter, Mary of Magdala. Mary never thought of that time without sadness. She supposed the girl had followed her grandmother's way of life and left Magdala years ago.

While Jesus, Mary and his men sat eating the evening meal with other travelers camped in the city, a tall, hawk-nosed Pharisee cleaved the crowd and looked down at Jesus.

"Rabbi," he said with the hauteur of a Babylonian king, "I have heard great things about you. Dine at my house this night." He looked over Jesus' men as though selecting a joint of meat. "You may bring whomever you wish." He turned on his heel and cut through the crowd. A low muttering followed his wake, like a warning the sea gives before a storm.

"Simon, the Pharisee," a man spat, "thinks himself the high priest." Jesus lifted Mary up by her fingertips and spoke to Cephas.

"I am taking my mother with me this evening. Camp here, and I will join you at daybreak for the return to Kapher Nahum."

Why me instead of one of his men? Mary knew a woman would not be welcome at Simon's feast, but would he refuse Jesus? Mary was learning that to follow her son meant being prepared to break every rule of tradition.

A servant met them at the gate and led them directly through the entrance hall and into a high-ceilinged dining room set in Roman fashion. The servant looked at her as though she were an odd kind of beetle and placed her at the foot of the table where she could look up toward Jesus and Simon lying at its head. Both male and female slaves moved about, filling wine glasses and bringing in platters of food.

A pock-faced woman whom Mary had not noticed among the servants, stopped at Jesus' feet. Without a word she stooped and began to wipe them with her deeply hennaed hair. Mary saw she was weeping quietly, but so copiously that some of her tears dropped on Jesus's feet. He took no notice but went on speaking with his host.

The woman pulled an object from her bodice and began unwinding green silk. Mary stiffened. An alabaster bottle glowed with the soft luster Mary had loved. The vial of myrrh? The woman pulled the stopper and poured the myrrh on Jesus's feet, its spicy fragrance filling the room. She stroked the oil into his callused feet. With tears flowing silently down her wrinkled cheeks, she now bent and kissed those feet.

Simon barked a command that straightened every slave. The woman fled to stand at Mary's feet. Jesus frowned at Simon and asked him if he'd seen how the woman had done for him—all the things which Simon had not done: washed his feet, given him a kiss. In spite of the hatred burning in Simon's eyes, Jesus continued with a story about a moneylender who had two debtors, one who owed much and the other little. The diners stopped eating.

"If he forgave them both," Jesus went on condemning his host, "which man will love him more?" Then the guests murmured and caught each other's eyes.

"I suppose the one who owed the most," Simon mumbled.

"You've judged rightly," said Jesus and looked him straight in the eyes. "You saw that woman. *Her* sins are forgiven because she loved much." Jesus continued to stare at the haughty Pharisee until he looked away. "He to whom little is forgiven loves but little," Jesus finished.

He looked again at the woman. "Your sins are forgiven." Mary turned to her but she disappeared through a curtain. Mary rose to follow her down a hall and into a bedroom done in ornate wood and piled high with blue and purple cushions. A single lamp, burning on an ivory table, revealed a beautiful woman standing beside it, richly dressed in a flowing green gown. Black hair framed the perfect oval of her face.

"Sherah's Mary?" Mary folded the woman in her arms. "Oh, I've wondered so often." Sherah's granddaughter called softly to the woman with the alabaster bottle. The woman knelt before Mary and without a word handed her the Wisemen's flask, rewound in its green binding. Mary held it tenderly, remembering all the years she had worn it.

Then the Magdalene told Mary how she'd become first the servant and then the wife of Simon the Pharisee and of a cold, unloving marriage. She had seen this woman standing in a slave auction in the market and known, that but for Jesus's help, she would have been the same. Mary Magdalene took the woman's hand and drew her to stand before Mary.

"I bought her and when Jesus came through Magdala some months ago, he cast evil spirits from her, just as he did me."

Mary thought of the sly child outside Sherah's hut

and of how Jesus had cast the demons from her, leaving her the peaceful, beautiful woman she now was.

"I don't care if Simon beats me or divorces me tonight," Mary Magdalene said, "but I had to give back the precious myrrh—so little to repay what Jesus did for me."

Mary handed the vial to Mary of Magdala. "You keep it," she said. "It was given to Jesus for this time."

To Mary's surprise, the two women joined them the next morning, and the Magdalene told Mary that Simon the Pharisee had handed her a bill of divorcement.

"I'm free," she said with a look of gratitude at Jesus. "We will serve him as long as we live." Mary of Magdala stepped into her new life with her hand in her slave's.

Mary pondered the events of the last two days. Yes, going with Jesus would be exciting. But she would not ask to join him. She felt a restraint—a faint notion that he really did not want her with him. She was not sure she could bear to be with him—feel his suffering—be always confused about his purposes. *What was his purpose?*

The crowd that day was more curious than praising. They muttered together. This man who forgave sins— was he a god, or a blasphemer? A blasphemer, said his enemies, and the punishment was death.

Oh, Almighty God, keep your promise. You are faithful. I will trust you, but—oh, Father God, keep our son safe.

At the beginning of grape harvest, when the air was pungent with the fragrance and workers frantically picked swollen fruit, Jude flung himself onto a bench beside the fountain where Joseph sat polishing a table leg.

"It's hotter than old Neb's furnace out there!" Jude said and stuck his toes in the pool. "Heard what Jesus is up to now?"

Mary stepped into the courtyard as he asked the question, and Joseph paused in his polishing, worry lines plowing furrows in his brow. "What?" he asked.

"Better sit down, Mother," Jude said. "I don't know how to say this more gently, but—people are saying Jesus is insane."

"Insane!" Mary sat down abruptly. "Who's saying it?"

"I hear it everywhere I go." Jude selected an orange, peeled it and separated it section by section, giving each part intent concentration. "It's not true, of course, but Jesus gets *himself* into trouble." He ate slowly. "It's embarrassing for me." Mary nodded her head.

Joseph's voice did not soothe Mary. "No more a lunatic than I am," he said. Jude sat erect now.

"Well, he acts like one. People say he doesn't eat—or sleep. They say he goes on the strength of the devil." Mary swallowed, bracing herself for more.

"Troublemakers," said Joseph and slapped the leather cloth across his palm.

"What are people to think," Jude said, thrusting out his jaw, "unless he *is* controlled by demons?" Mary paced the courtyard, her fingers massaging the top of her head, pulling at her hair. Joseph took her arm as she passed.

"He must eat and sleep sometime," he said and added, somewhat as an afterthought, "Perhaps, as God's son, he doesn't need to." Mary looked at Joseph for several moments.

"Joseph," she said at last, throwing her head back as if a decision had been made. "We'll have to go see him." Joseph drew back. "We can't let people think he's insane. He'll be an outcast, treated worse than a leper. We must do something." She looked at Jude. "Go find Simon!"

Joseph stopped her as she started away. "I don't think it is wise to go, Mary." She could not believe what she was hearing.

"You aren't going? Don't you care? Joseph, he'll obey you. We have to save him."

"You go, Mary. I will not. I won't interfere in what Jesus is doing."

"If you won't talk to him, I'll take the boys." A mother's love struggled against God's will. In this battle Joseph would not help her.

With her shawl shielding her face from the heat, Mary and her sons hurried through Kapher Nahum to the northeast, past acres of wilting gardens, heat waves dancing before them. Leaves on fig trees and vineyards hung dusty and lifeless. Jude tramped ahead.

"It won't do any good," he said over his shoulder. "He won't come home." But Joses disagreed.

"He'll listen to Mother," Joses said and steered Mary toward Chorazin, just over the rise of the hill. She said nothing, but with the look of an Alexander she marched toward the battle of wills.

They panted their way through deserted streets to a house where everyone in town overflowed into the street. When they tried to force their way through, elbows pushed them back. A slave whose shoulders reached above other people's heads, apparently the steward of the house, loomed over them.

"You can't get in," he said in a voice like iron wheels on cobblestones and glowered at them.

Joses spoke firmly. "I'm the prophet's brother, Joses, son of Joseph of Kapher Nahum. These are my brothers and my mother. We must get through." The huge man gazed down on them, one by one.

"Wait here," he said and elbowed his way through the crowd. Sweat trickled down the middle of Mary's back. She heard Jesus' voice but distinguished no words.

The steward returned. "He refuses to see you."

"Refuses!" Mary said. Strangers turned to stare at her. Mary's face flushed, then paled.

"What did he say?" Joses' voice trimmed the edge of anger. The steward hesitated and looked embarrassed.

"He said—," he cleared his throat, "—who is my mother, and who are my brothers?" He flicked his hand at the crowd behind him. "My mother and my brothers are these who are hearing the Word of God and doing it. Whoever does the will of my Father in heaven is my brother and my sister and my mother." The man quickly turned to listen to Jesus.

For a moment the family stood in stunned silence. Then Jude said he'd told them as much. Mary's look silenced him.

An old hag lying by the wall pointed a crooked finger at Mary and cackled, "Heh, heh, heh. Heh, heh, heh."

An aged man with rheumy eyes and a raspy voice suddenly snarled. "The *Messiah* has no mother. No brothers, neither! You're impostors, that's what you are. Just want favors."

Sweat on Mary's back turned cold. No one could know the wound Jesus' words had given her. No one. Joses and Jude gently turned Mary toward home, but Simon stayed to listen.

In the evening, Joseph and Mary stood at the door as darkness shrouded the sea, a gentle breeze blowing away the heat of the day. She leaned her head on his shoulder, weeping.

"He's out of our hands now, Mary," Joseph said, his arm about her.

"He rejected me—publicly." Not since Herod's slaughter had she felt such desolation. "My own son? He said, 'Who is my mother?'" Joseph's words brought no comfort.

Sleep escaped that night. Like twigs caught in a whirlpool, memories went around and around and around. Outside the waves of Gennesaret lapped the shore and an eastern breeze stirred the leaves. She turned from side to side, hearing again the words: Who is my mother? She who does my will. *I am, I am doing Your will. I'm trying...*

A blast of wind hit the house with such force the stone walls shook and tiles rattled off the roof. Everyone leaped from bed and stood shivering in the doorway. Window skins tore. Stools clattered about the courtyard.

The wind shrieked and screamed. For an hour they listened to the sea moan and crash against the shore. The wind howled through the house, slamming doors, tossing pots about, whipping leaves and branches from the almond and pomegranate.

And then it stopped on a breath. Not a leaf stirred.

"Jesus is at it again," Joses said ruefully, but everyone told him of course not.

"I just hope they're not out in Zeb's boat," Joseph said with a tinge of worry.

CHAPTER 37

Three weeks later Simon came home to tell the family that they *had* been on the lake.

"I never want to be in that kind of storm again. Jesus was sleeping like a dead man in the bottom of the boat—'til we woke him up to save us all. He gave us a kind of disgusted look—," Simon hunched his shoulders and groped for words. "He...he told the storm to stop. Joses, will you believe that?" His brother shrugged and said nothing would surprise him anymore.

Mary smiled triumphantly. Simon scooped a seed from a pomegranate with a fingernail and snapped it into his mouth. "He's teaching about the kingdom, too."

Mary's smile spread. The others started to go about their work, when Simon shot another arrow.

"But he said an odd thing. He said that some people will understand what he says and some won't be allowed to." Mary's smile vanished and Simon became more serious. "Jesus says the kingdom's a mystery. He compared it to a wheat field and a mustard seed, and I don't know what all. It was beyond me." He shrugged and scooped another piece of pomegranate, "I guess I'm not one of the chosen ones."

"Nor I." said Mary, remembering Chorazin. "Nor are any of us." Simon added that they could ask him themselves: Jesus was coming home.

He came—acting the same as ever—as though he hadn't grieved his mother and exposed her to public shame. When she asked him directly why he'd done that, he said that they must have realized that he couldn't quit teaching to come out and talk with them. But Mary's anguish burst from her.

"Why did you deny us?" she cried.

"Couldn't you see?" Jesus moved to embrace her, but she bent down suddenly to the hearth fire. He kneeled and put an arm around her shoulders. "Remember what I said in Chorazin?"

"Could I forget?" Mary stirred the fire furiously. Jesus raised her up and gently turned her to face him.

"Mother, *are* you hearing me? Following me? I don't mean travelling with me. I mean believing what I'm saying—understanding?"

Mary turned away. "Yes, I'm hearing and watching you and like not what I see." She faced him squarely. "Jesus, what are you doing? Is this really what God is telling you to do? To put your life in danger?"

"I am in no danger until my time is come," he said so confidently that she was shocked.

Before she could speak—and she wasn't sure any words would come—Joseph entered the room. He greeted Jesus and then gave Mary the news that there was to be a banquet that night at Levi's house, the tax collector who was now one of Jesus's followers, and he was invited. Mary threw both hands over her head and began

preparing a meal. It was beyond her—her son and husband eating with publicans—with the likes of Malchus.
Her reproachful look moved them quickly from the
room.

The first three stars had peeked over the wall, when
a bang on the door brought Joses to unbar it.

"James."

Not James! Mary pressed both hands to her forehead.
Not James, not tonight of all nights with Jesus at a publican's.

Without preamble James stormed up and down the
room like a Roman senator bent on convincing Caesar.
That familiar stab of pain shot through Mary's heart and
it wasn't because she was near fifty. She had felt it too
often—that stab that Simeon had warned her of in the
Temple.

"Mother, where's Jesus?" James asked, "I've run all
the way from Jerusalem to warn him."

"He's with Joseph at a banquet at Levi's house."
Mary braced herself. James jerked back his head as
though struck with a spear.

"A publican's! Did I hear you correctly? That's just
why I came. Spies are everywhere, from every sect;
they're mingling with the crowds, trying to trap Jesus—
so they can *kill* him."

"No!" Mary jabbed a fist into the pit of her stomach.
She sat down heavily. The rest of the family questioned
and talked and talked and talked. Intrigues. Threats of
death. On and on it went.

Joseph and Jesus returned to have James harangue his
brother with the need for caution. "You'll say something.

I know you. You always ask for trouble, and I'll be in the middle of it. I only came to warn you, but you won't listen. Can't you realize they are trying to kill you?"

"They cannot until my time is come," said Jesus complacently, "And now I'm tired and am going to sleep."

"Oh!" James now looked with apology at Jesus. "I forgot; I've news of Touchon John. He's still in Herod's prison with no hope of escape or pardon."

With that the rest of family retired, but not to sleep, thinking of Touchon John, raised in the wilderness, now locked up in a filthy, dark prison.

After breaking fast and saying prayers, Jesus left for the seashore and James made ready to go. "I've come on a fool's errand." He snorted like a restless horse. "Whatever you do, Mother, don't let him come to Jerusalem." He turned on his heel and started back toward the City of Peace.

Mary might have known that Jesus would do exactly what he was warned not to do. She should have known.

Weeks later a sudden rain shower lashed the windows and beat against the stones. The family sat around the hearth soaking up the heat. A pounding on the door sent Mary hurrying through the hall to open it to a strange woman. She was tall, rain running down her face, gray hair straggling from under a cloak, and with a huge grin on her face.

"Ancilla!"

Mary broke into tears. All the others heard her shout and came running, chattering, marveling. Ancilla danced

Mary up and down the hall to the music of Joseph's laughter.

"I'm dancing, Mary. See, dancing!"

Joses took her sodden cloak and brought her to a chair near the fire. The grandchildren stared at her while Mary explained that this was their Great Aunt Ancilla, from Nazareth.

"The one who can't walk?" asked Joachin.

"Yes, darling, Aunt Ancilla who couldn't walk well." Mary hugged her sister again. "But now she can. Now she can."

While Mary prepared a mug of hot comfrey tea, Joseph put Ancilla's sandals to dry on the hearth and placed a cushion beside him. Drucilla smiled at Ancilla and told her how happy she was to meet her, after hearing of her so often. Then she and the children sat quietly in a corner, listening.

"You must have been with Jesus," Joseph said, patting a cushion beside him, but Ancilla would not sit. She went from Joses to Mary, over to Joseph, back to the hearth.

"To think I'm here. Here with you, Mary. It's his greatest miracle."

Joseph's grin showed white teeth. "Tell us."

"Jesus stopped on his way back from Jerusalem," Ancilla said. "He usually does, to let Matthias and me know what's going on."

"Well, that's more than he does for his own family," Mary said under her breath. Ancilla glanced at her.

Joseph picked up a chair rung and his polishing leather and worked, quietly watching them both.

"Go on," he said.

311

"It was like this," Ancilla continued. "I was huddled over the fire on a day like this. The pain was especially bad in this old leg." She gave her left leg a slap and laughed a long laugh that reminded Mary of wild flowers blowing in the wind.

Mary could see it all, her old home, feel the wind whipping through the open window hole, see Ancilla sitting trapped there while the world went on without her, lonely and in pain, and felt as though she were there as she listened to her sister.

"With no warning," Ancilla was saying. "Jesus came through the door."

"What plots are you hatching now, Aunt?" he had asked and had reached his toes to the fire. Mary could see it as though she had been there.

"Oh, I'm sitting here planning a whole campaign for the Cananeans," Ancilla had said, "You know how much I'd like to be with them or with you, nephew. How I'd love to hear you teaching, see you healing."

"Well, why don't you?" he said. "I think it's about time you went with me to keep things going right."

"Do not mock me, Jesus," I said.

"I would never do that. I mean every word. Here put your hands in mine."

He had taken her fingers in his and began to pull Ancilla up slowly. Mary saw it in her mind's eye, could see Jesus holding her sister's gnarled hands.

"Mary! Are you listening?" Ancilla shouted.

Mary jerked.

"Oh, yes, I am seeing it so vividly. Go on."

"I felt a tingle throughout my whole body. I can't

explain it. Maybe like being carried on a ball of lightning. There was no pain; I just stood taller and taller, and my left leg grew straight and as long as my other. Then he let go of my hands, and I stood there, tall and even. And no pain." She turned to hug Mary again. "And I started to laugh. I don't suppose that's what I should have done—to the Son of God." She looked guiltily at Joseph, who grinned back at her. "Then Jesus started laughing, too, and we both just stood there and laughed and every time we stopped, we started all over again. Matthias came in just then and he began to laugh, too. While Jesus and Matthias just stood there watching me, I grabbed a jar and headed straight for the well. Oh, Mary, you should have seen the faces on the women when they saw me. You should have seen them." Anger with Jesus drew lines around Mary's eyes.

"Why did he wait so long?" she said through narrow lips.

"Why? I don't know. It must have been the right time in God's purpose." Ancilla shrugged. "Does it matter? I'm healed, and I'm going with him everywhere he goes."

Drucilla now rose and began to prepare the mid-day meal of bread and cheese, but Joseph told her to bring out the best wine and date cakes like Huldah used to make. There must be a celebration. Ancilla went on talking.

"I've been with Jesus ever since, going from one village to another." She turned to speak directly to Joseph.

"You should never have quit the Cananeans. The kingdom's coming. Clopas didn't die in vain, nor Ezekias. Jesus is going to bring in the kingdom." She turned to her sister, "And you'll be queen, Mary."

313

Mary turned away quickly so that Ancilla would not see her face. *I cannot tell her Jesus does not want me with him.*

Ancilla coaxed Joses' little boys to come to her and put Jacob on her lap.

"You're missing so much, Mary! You should be with him everywhere he goes. Then you'd know what he's doing."

"There's never a minute I'm not with him in my thoughts." Mary would say no more.

Ancilla looked at Joseph, but he only shook his head. Plainly he did not fathom Mary, either. "Perhaps God wants attention only on his son, so his mother won't be worshipped," he said.

Ancilla waited a few moments before speaking. "We're going to the other side of Gennesaret. Come with us, Mary." Ancilla put an arm around Mary's waist. "Come with us."

"He doesn't want me."

Talk as Ancilla would, Mary refused, even when Ancilla told her Jesus was sending his disciples to every village, saying that the kingdom was coming. Ancilla hopped up on the hearth, flung out her arms and spoke in her best imitation of a king's herald.

"The Kingdom is at Hand."

But Mary's gloom could not be broken.

"I only hope I live long enough to see it." she said with no humor.

"It won't be long," Ancilla said, stepping from the hearth. "There's thousands who'd jump into the sea if he said to. When he declares himself king, the people will rise up and give him the crown. Matthias and I have studied the scriptures. It's coming, Mary. Don't miss it; come with us."

Mary shook her head. "You do not understand."

CHAPTER 38

Just before sunrise, Jesus and Matthias entered the house so silently that the family did not know they were there until they heard a low voice in the hearth room telling Drucilla not to bake, in memory of Touchon John. Jesus spoke quietly, but Mary saw a great sorrow in his eyes.

"Touchon John is dead—beheaded," Jesus said. Gray grief deadened faces. "Herod Antipas gave in to the wiles of Herodias and her daughter Salome." Tears ran down Jesus' cheeks. "He put John's head—" his voice broke. "—on a platter—and gave it to Salome."

With one breath, the women began the death wail, comforting each other as only they knew how. Joses and Joseph drew sleeves across their eyes.

Then Jesus said, "No more wailing. We do not know what Herod may do next, so it's better if the news travels slowly. We do not want riots and more persecution."

By the next day, the news had reached Kapher Nahum. Then came Jesus' chosen men, the last two, Judas of Kerioth, a sly-eyed man and Jesus' cousin Simon, the Cananean, arriving in the evening.

Next morning, Jesus and his men were gone just

after dawn. Matthias waited as Ancilla and Mary took fresh baked loaves from the oven and packed them with fig cakes in linen.

As Ancilla prepared to leave, she asked, unspoken, the question Mary expected.

"I suppose I could come," Mary answered, "this once. If you'll promise that Jesus won't see me, that no one will know I'm his mother."

Ancilla laughed her usual bark of merriment. "How will anyone know? There's usually thousands, but he expects to be alone today, with just his men."

Matthias spoke: "They've taken boats across to that mountain beyond Bethsaida. Gone early to pray. Hopefully the crowds will not know where he is."

"Yes, come, Mary," Ancilla said placing the food in her pocket. "My bones tell me you should go."

"I thought your bones were healed, Ancie," said Mary as she changed into heavy shoes for the seven-mile walk. She felt a lightness of heart for the first time in months.

As Matthias led the women around the northern curve of Lake Gennesaret, they looked south at the sweep of sapphire sea, the ocher hills surrounding it, and at the black dots of villages along the shore. At Bethsaida, many people joined them, and much running back and forth and low muttering brought more until there were thousands.

By noon they reached the appointed hillside and saw Jesus sitting on a rock and speaking to a multitude. The three joined the crowd sitting among flowers on a grassy hillside and listened to his every word while eating their lunch. The air was clear, without a cloud and his voice carried to the farthest person, effortlessly on his part. Children played at the edge of the crowd, laughing and racing about.

The sun was hidden behind the hills to the west above Kapher Nahum before some child cried out that he was hungry.

Mary watched Jesus call his men to him and whisper something. Thunder James' voice could have been heard across the sea when he bellowed, "Why don't you send them home?"

Jesus spoke to him, but Mary couldn't hear what he said. Then Jesus turned to the crowd and asked in his calm voice. "Does anyone have any food to share?"

None offered any until a small boy said something to Andrew and he led the boy to Jesus. Mary strained forward and could only watch open-mouthed as Jesus began breaking two little buns and five fishes into pieces and giving them to his men to distribute to the people.

"Pass these out and pick up the left-overs," he said loudly enough for all to hear.

Quietly the people took bites of each, as the men passed among them, only to return to Jesus for more.

"There must be five thousand men here," whispered Mary, "plus women and children."

Finally Matthias brought them two minuscule bites. As Mary chewed them she felt as stuffed as though at a feast. "It is hard to believe," she said, but she began to see why people followed him—for his unusual teaching—and for food and healing.

319

The chant began with the women, a quiet murmur, was caught by the men and became a thunderous shout. "Our King. Our King. Our King."

But with a voice of such authority that no one argued, Jesus dismissed them. Obediently they rose, as if from a trance, and started for their villages.

When all were gone, Jesus joined the others at the shore. He smiled at Mary, saying with his eyes, Now are you believing?

He told them to take the boats back to Kapher Nahum; he was going up the mountain to pray. Ancilla and Mary watched him walk wearily away, then followed the men into the boats. Mary hadn't been on the water since her return from Egypt. She'd sworn never to go again after that dreadful trip home through the storm.

Reluctantly she squeezed into the bottom of a boat, already holding Ancilla, Matthias, and five of Jesus's men. She held tightly to the side as she seated herself in the bottom beside Judas. Cephas and Andrew pushed out into the sea. Darkness came quickly and soon they could not even see the flickering lights from villages nor the other boat, although voices drifted across the water. The air felt warm and the odors of dust and ripening grain joined with the gentle lap of the water to lull Mary to sleep. Later a cold breeze touched her arms. She awoke to an angry sea and clutched the side of the boat.

"We've not made much progress, Mary," Andrew said kindly. "The wind's contrary tonight. We often get these sudden blows off Mt. Hermon. But we will make it safely." He bent to the oars.

Muscles bulged. Everyone in the ship sat tense and silent. They could hear the shouts of men in the other boat. Without warning a monstrous wave lifted their boat and slammed it into a trough between waves. And again. Mary's stomach churned.

Don't let me die, Lord God, not until I see him king. Her knuckles ached from gripping the side of the boat. Then Cephas spoke to Andrew.

"We can't fight these waves. Never saw such a storm."

"Just let it drift," Andrew answered. "All we can do. It's going to blow us back to the east shore."

The boat rocked and tossed. Mary prayed and shivered, wet to the skin. The roar of the wind tore all sounds away but the lashing of the waves and creaking boards. Ancilla held to the other side of the boat, but she seemed to have no fear. *How can she be so calm? Where are you, Jesus? But what could he do in this storm?* Mary held on more tightly.

"Look," shouted Cephas. A faint light was coming toward them across the water. All eyes strained into the darkness whenever the boat rose on a crest. The form neared the boat.

"It's a spirit." Judas choked the words. The men grabbed each other. Matthias put an arm around Ancilla and Mary. She didn't know if it were the rocking boat or if all three of them were trembling.

Then the spirit spoke. "Take courage. It is I AM. Do not fear."

"Lord, if it is You, tell me to come," Cephas called out. Mary had never heard such fervor in a voice.

"Come!" said Jesus.

Cephas leaped over the edge of the boat and took three strides. At the united gasp behind him, he looked at the water and began to sink.

"Lord, save me!"

Jesus took his hand and lifted him up and into the boat. "You of little faith," he said, "what made you doubt?" When Jesus stepped into the boat, Cephas dropped to his knees before him.

Immediately the sea was calm, no wind, no tossing waves.

"You *are* the Son of God," Cephas whispered.

"Pick up your oars, men," Jesus called through the darkness loudly enough for men in the other boat to hear. "Row quickly, men. It is I, and we must start for Jerusalem tomorrow."

No. Not Jerusalem.

All were gone. Mary glanced out the door at the sea, sparkling in morning sunlight, remembering what she had seen and heard, feeling again the hurt. He had not asked her to go with him. Others would be there caring for his needs, exalting with him when he took the kingdom.

But no, he never mentions the kingdom, never makes any effort to secure his crown. And a king doesn't sit all day on a hard stone telling stories to people who only want bread and fish. Tears ran unwiped down her cheeks.

He does not want me with him.

She would play her role. But what was it?

CHAPTER 39

Two months later Jesus returned safely. He and his family sat eating broiled fish and bread spread with fresh-churned butter. The talk was of the shop's orders, of the weather, of the children's daily adventures.

Footsteps pounded out in the hall and burst into the room.

"Simon!" Joseph rose. Mary stood paralyzed as Simon shouted to Jesus.

"You must leave at once. I've just come from Malchus." Jesus tore a crust of bread apart and spread it with butter.

"Why, Simon?" Jesus asked calmly.

Simon was beside himself. With a frantic look at his mother, he answered, "Because they're going to *kill* you, that's why!"

Mary took a breath that was almost a sob. Simon stormed about the room, his fists clenching and unclenching.

"If you don't care about yourself," he said, "you might give some thought to Mother!" He faced Joseph now. "I was waiting at Malchus' booth to pay duty. He was talking with a scribe from the Temple, who'd ridden all the way from Jerusalem. They couldn't see me," he said aside to his mother. "They wanted to know where they could find you, Jesus."

Ancilla put an arm around Mary. Jesus went on eating. Two bright spots on Mary's cheeks stood out harshly against her pale skin. Her eyes moved from Simon's face to Jesus.

"Jesus!" Simon raised his voice yet higher. "Listen! Every scribe and Pharisee now has the authority to kill you on sight."

The only sound was the music of the fountain in the courtyard.

Finally Jesus said, "My men and I will go up to Tyre." Ancilla stepped forward to go, too, but he told her no women this time. He wanted her to stay with Mary.

Jesus took Joseph in his arms and held him, releasing him with farewell kisses on each cheek. "I'll see you— soon." Jesus looked into Joseph's eyes, but it was as if he was telling him something different. Mary noted the exchange, but gave it no thought. She was busy fixing a packet of food. She allowed Jesus to embrace her, leaned against him for a moment, then pushed him away gently.

"Go," she whispered.

"Do not worry, Mother," he said quietly in return. "Have faith."

"I do, but be careful. Be careful."

Jesus turned to Joses and Simon. "Take care of Mother." His mouth was grim.

A week later Zebedee brought news from Jerusalem. Some rabble rouser, Barabbas by name, was stirring revolt. Emperor Tiberius expected Pilate to keep every-thing peaceful. Pilate, afraid he and his head might part company, issued an order to find Jesus. The family listened, fear battering their hearts.

"Where is Jesus?" breathed Zebedee hoarsely.

"Gone," they said and drew a breath of relief.

The men spoke politics now.

"The two high priests," Zebedee explained, "have convinced Pilate to put all the blame for the revolts in Judea on the Cananeans in Galilee. That way it's Herod's fault, not Pilate's. They need a scapegoat. Annas and Caiaphas work one end against the other in convincing them both of whatever they choose." Joseph looked worried.

"And?" he said to Zebedee.

"By blaming Jesus and the Galileans, he plucks two pigeons at once. He's rid of Jesus and placates Pilate. Meanwhile, in case there's trouble, Pilate's ordered troops to Galilee."

"To Galilee!" said everyone. Ancilla looked triumphantly at Matthias, saying unspoken that now the Cananeans would triumph.

Mary walked to the door and took a deep breath. Thunder rumbled continuously in the northwest. Lightning outlined boiling black clouds with flashes of pink. *Where is Jesus?* She took another breath of still, sultry air. *What are you doing with your son, Lord God? What are you doing?*

Leaders in every synagogue gave orders for men to go the Temple in Jerusalem and pray. Only God could save Galilee.

In the end only Simon went with Joseph. Although revolt simmered, there should be no danger to pilgrims walking in small groups, but that did not stop those at home from praying for them continuously. They prayed even harder for the safety of Jesus and Matthias, up north among the Phoenicians.

A week later a warm spring wind whispered in the leaves, promising the hot winds of summer. The children napped. The only sound was the gentle tapping of Joses' hammer as he eased a stubborn joint into a miter and the scratchy sound as Ancilla pulled a needle through leather.

Peace shattered like glass hitting granite.

Simon and James rushed in and knelt before Mary. Joseph was not with them. *Dead! Joseph is dead.* Instinctively she knew. That stab in her heart again. Greater than she'd ever felt.

James took her hands in his. "Mother," he began. Dully she heard her sons talking. "Father wanted to pray for Jesus right away, so he went directly to the Temple. Simon met me at Zeb's. We heard the trumpets blaring from the Antonia but didn't think what it might mean. We even heard the shouting."

Joses' arms held Drucilla. Ancilla stood ashen-faced.

"We got worried and then—"

"And then—" Simon tried to finish but the words couldn't come.

"Ran to the North Gate," finished James, "but soldiers wouldn't let us in. And then...we heard the screams," finished James.

Mary said nothing, just clenched James' hands, her face an old woman's.

"Pilate," said James, "was in Jerusalem. He thought the men in the Temple were Barabbas' followers. He saw his mistake and called off his butchers, but it was too late. Thousands died."

No one said a word, just waited, waited.

"We finally got inside the Temple," Simon said, his voice breaking, "and found Father." He bent his head on Mary's lap. "They'd speared him kneeling in prayer on the steps to the altar."

"What did you do with his body?" Mary asked dully, her mouth dry. Automatically she patted her son's back.

They told her they'd laid it in a tomb belonging to a friend of James, just outside the northeast wall. Others had been carried out by Temple servants and laid on piles to be burned in the Hinnon Valley.

Joses helped a wailing Drucilla to her room, while Ancilla went out the door with James and Simon to tell Salome and Zebedee. Mary had no tears. The dead do not cry.

The month of mourning passed with no memory for Mary. During that time, she had been a bulwark for the others, helping Drucilla with house duties. Joses, Jude and Simon carried on in the carpentry shop.

This day everyone was gone, even Drucilla and the children, and Mary could finally allow herself to grieve. It was hot and the door to the street stood open to catch the breeze off the sea. Mary sat on a cushion in the hearth room, her cheek pressed against the bricks. If birds sang, she didn't hear them. She cried until there were no tears left.

"Mary," said a man's voice in the hall. Her head jerked up; she knew that voice. The door was blocked by Malchus.

"Say welcome to an old friend," he said, waddling in.

Mary's temper blazed. Malchus in her house, uninvited, where he'd never come before. There he stood with lips parted in a twisted smile, grizzled beard hanging to his chest where sweat soiled his robe, his stomach pooching out above stick-like ankles, a few gray strands of greasy hair carefully combed over his bald pate.

"What do you want here?" Mary backed away.

Malchus came farther into the room, his arms held wide before him as though to embrace Mary.

"Joseph's death has been a terrible shock, no doubt," he said, his voice purring like a cat, "but now you must move on." He gave her the same look as that day at the festival and said as though bestowing a gift. "I've come to take you for my wife, Mary."

"Your wife!" Mary shrieked. "What of Rachel—your fourteen children?"

"Oh, Rachel, I'll give her a bill of divorcement."

Mary could not believe what she was hearing.

"Get out!" she said in an ominously flat voice.

"You realize," he said, the simper replaced with a calculated stare, "that I can ruin Joses." Now Mary felt cold dread. "I can charge him so much custom he'll be a debtor in a day. I can prevent his selling anywhere—can ruin Zebedee." He smiled again. "Now, what do you say?" He took one step towards her, pressed an arm around her waist, and bent his face as if to kiss her.

Mary raked his cheek with fingernails. He stumbled

backwards, blood oozing along the marks. Mary advanced with her hand raised high to claw again. But Malchus' head jerked up to look beyond her out a window. With a scream of horror, he tore out the door.

Shaking, Mary picked bits of flesh from her fingernails and washed her bloodied hands, then slumped to the floor.

Cool fingers touched her forehead. Jesus knelt beside her. He lifted her up and she leaned against him, sobbing.

"He won't return, ever. He saw me—as his judge," Jesus said, and Mary trembled herself, feeling her son's power. She looked up into his eyes and forced the words from tight lips.

"Joseph is dead! He's dead."

"I know." He helped her to a bench in the atrium. Mary did not let go of his hand. "Everything," he said softly, "is as it should be." But to Mary, nothing was as it should be, except that he was with her.

Above them a breeze swayed branches pregnant with tiny leaves about to burst. They talked for hours. Even when he said, "You'll see Joseph again, Mother. Sooner than you think," she only nodded and closed her eyes.

"I also must die, Mother. You know that now."

In her heart, she did know, but would not acknowledge it. The pain was too great.

"It's why I came," he added gently. She stared into his eyes.

"You came to die?"

He nodded yes.

*

Life went back to its routine. Mary told no one about Malchus or what Jesus had just told her. The family heard about Jesus regularly. Matthias and Ancilla and others were with him in Bethsaida, Dalmanutha, the Decapolis across the lake. He'd confronted Pharisees and Sadducees again, with more threats to his life.

He and his followers didn't return again till plowing time. The Feast of Tabernacles was near, and the family would leave soon for Jerusalem to partake in this most joyous feast, and to visit Joseph's grave.

Reveling in being together, they quietly finished the evening meal before the journey. Jesus' brothers urged him to go with them to Jerusalem. If he was going to take over the kingdom, they exhorted, he needed followers from Judea. But Jesus said no, he would not go to Jerusalem.

"Well, stay here in Galilee and get nowhere, then," said Simon. *"We're* going."

Wind-whipped skies had cleared summer's haze and promised autumn. At the northeast wall, they visited the tomb in which James and Simon had laid Joseph. Mary looked at the tomb. A presentiment sent a shiver, she knew not why. *Jesus said I would see you, Joseph, but the resurrection is so far away.*

Jesus came to Jerusalem after all, but not to Zebedee's house. Instead, he went to friends on the Mount of Olives. Matthias, Ancilla and his men were with him.

James, handsome in his white Pharisee robe, joined the family. As a clerk in the Sanhedrin, that body of spiritual leaders who ruled the Jews, he brought news of Jesus they could have learned no other way and, as usual, James complained about him.

"Jesus knows exactly what to say to get on the Great Council's wrong side. It puts me in an intolerable position." The fringe on his shawl shook with his agitation. "Of course, few know that he's my brother, and I don't tell them."

The brothers stood up, sat down, exclaimed and denounced Jesus.

Now James said piously. "He'd be arrested any moment in the Temple if the guards weren't such cowards. And he needs to be arrested—for his own protection," But now his mother faced him squarely, her voice high-pitched.

"You could believe he's going to be king!" her voice quieted, "or whatever God wills." She looked tenderly at James, the son she was so proud of. "But you're right, James. He must be careful. I just pray he won't get himself killed." As an afterthought, James finished the challenge to his mother.

"Come with me to the Temple tomorrow. See for yourself."

It was past noon before Mary and James found Jesus and his followers by the treasury in the Court of the Women. A dense crowd made way for James the Pharisee and his mother, until they stood only a few yards from Jesus and could hear his clear, strong voice. "You don't believe me now, but when I've been lifted up, then you'll understand that it was God who sent me." A shudder went through the crowd. "And He's here with me now."

"He's right," some muttered. "This Jesus is the Messiah. I believe him." But more muttered against him. Jesus went on without pausing.

"If you believe my words, you'll be free."

But at this someone shouted, "We be of Abraham's seed and were never in bondage to any man, so why are you saying we'll be free?"

"Your sin makes you Satan's slave," Jesus answered them calmly, but the muttering grew louder. "I know you are descendants of Abraham, but you want to kill me because God's word is not in you. If you were true Jews, you would recognize me." Then Jesus' voice rang out above it all. "YOU ARE OF YOUR FATHER THE DEVIL. Abraham saw my day and rejoiced."

The murmur grew to a roar. A voice boomed above the rest.

"You're not yet fifty years old, and you say you saw Abraham!"

Then Jesus' voice thundered above them all.

"BEFORE ABRAHAM WAS, I AM!" Only Mary understood.

A deadly silence followed. Then with herd instinct, every man picked up a rock to hurl it at the Messiah, screaming: "Blasphemy! Blasphemy! He makes himself equal with God."

James and Mary frantically fought their way through the crowd toward Jesus, dodging stones.

He was not there.

Nor could the rioters find him. He had disappeared before their eyes.

CHAPTER 40

"Jesus' miracles haven't changed Kapher Nahum one bit," Mary said to Drucilla, wielding a dust cloth like a scourge. "Just as I thought, those people went right back to their old ways," Mary took a swipe at an offending cobweb, "just as soon as 'the great prophet' no longer supplied bread and excitement." Drucilla asked in a soothing voice what she expected of people, but Mary went right on. "His enemies are everywhere, starlings dressed as doves in those white robes."

"I'm just back from Caesarea." Joses came with news that startled Drucilla and brought only a tiny smile to Mary's lips. "Malchus charged me no customs. He said I will not have to pay it ever again. Malchus. Why do you suppose?"

Mary turned her back upon him and said it had something to do with Jesus and asked if he'd heard where Jesus was now.

"Teaching in Perea across the Jordan and starting north toward Galilee."

Rain beat against the windows with the authority of

autumn. Matthias and Ancilla came with their daughter Joanna, shaking rain from their cloaks and hugging the children. All three looked well but tired.

While the men visited, the women busied themselves preparing food and listened to Ancilla tell them of Jesus.

"The crowds don't follow him as before," she said, picking up a bowl of onions and a knife. Mary swung an iron kettle of millet pottage onto the fire.

"Why not?" asked Mary. "What's he saying now?" Ancilla hesitated. "He said he will be killed—" She looked towards Mary through lowered eyelids and waited for a response. Drucilla gave a little cry, but Mary said nothing. That was nothing new. Ancilla finished in a flat voice, "and rise again the third day."

Mary gave Ancilla a long questioning look. *Rise again—like the boy in Nain*. Mary steadied her knee against the hearthstones, remembering his words to her: I have to die. But she hadn't really believed him and had pushed them to the back of her mind. An unsteady hand dropped a fish in the fire; she let it sizzle in the flame. Ancilla put the onions on the table.

"Mary, are you listening?" Ancilla asked. "Did you hear Joanna? That we won't die before we see him in his kingdom?" Mary's face lighted, her eyes sparkling. "He said we'd *see* him in his *kingdom*, Mary." At those words Mary jumped up to embrace her sister.

"Oh, yes, I'm listening; I'm just trying to believe it." They laughed together, Mary for the first time since Joseph had died. "I'll live to see it, Ancie. I'll live to see him on his throne."

*

Before the food was ready, Jesus came. They would make it a celebration. Mary added more fish to the grill. Drucilla stirred garlic into the pottage and gave Ancilla more onions to cut. Mary reached under a floor tile to bring out the last of the old wine.

After the feast was finished, all sat resting about the room listening for whatever Jesus might say. He held Joses' youngest boy, a toddler of three.

"Ancilla tells me, you're talking about your kingdom now," Mary said.

"I've told all of you over and over about my kingdom," he said, frowning. Each person looked away from his stare. "Your ears are closed. Some of you refuse to see."

Someone coughed. "No," escaped Ancilla's lips, but someone rapped on the door and in came Salome's family and the rest of Jesus' men, with the Magdalene and her slave. When all were seated, Salome waited for a pause in the talking.

"Jesus," Salome said, "we have an honest question, one we've wondered about ever since the wedding in Cana." Jesus reached out a hand, inviting her to continue. "When you come into your kingdom," Salome went on with syrup in her voice, "who will be the greatest?" The men looked sheepish, especially her sons, Thunder James and John. Jesus did not answer immediately, but sat twining the boy's auburn curls around his fingers.

"Listen, Aunt Salome," he began finally in the embarrassing silence, "Unless you become like this little child, you won't even get into my kingdom. You will have to humble yourself," he said with finality. The child put his arms around Jesus's neck. "The least among you shall be the greatest."

Salome sat rigid, her eyes smoldering, but Mary lowered her head to hide a smile. John changed the subject, and they talked loudly of other things. Jesus closed the conversation.

"Be at peace," he said, his eyes holding a depth they'd never seen before. "Forgive each other—as many times as you are offended. Love one another. Forgive," he said again and put the boy on Mary's lap. He turned to those going with him the next day. "Meet me at the southern gate at dawn."

Everyone left quickly, as though escaping a schoolroom.

A cool north wind blew rain against the windows with no indication it would quit for the rest of the winter. Simon spoke with his mother as she stirred the fire. He had decided to go with Jesus.

"Salome's coming with us, Mother. I think she wants to make sure her sons get the best positions in the kingdom. Why don't you come too?"

"No, I do not think he wants me with him." Mary turned her back to him and filled a pack with dried fig loaves. "—and my sons will take whatever position God wills."

Her thoughts were her own.

Simon returned four months later, just before Passover. Again it was raining, this time the soft, warm rain which insures good harvest. He came in wind-blown and muddy and sat on the hearth, picking a thorn from the sole of his sandal. Mary bustled about heating cheese on a stick.

"You'll be glad to hear he has good friends, Mother," Simon finally said. "Influential ones, Lazarus of Bethany and his two sisters, Mary and Martha. He stays with them whenever he's in Jerusalem." He paused and frowned. "He keeps saying things that don't make any sense to me."

Mary hit the side of the pot with a spoon to dislodge sticking pottage. "When do any of his sayings make sense? What is it this time?"

"Kapher Nahum is going to be cast into Hades, he says, because the people didn't accept him after all his miracles."

Mary shrugged. "It's what I've always thought."

"He says love your enemies, care for our neighbors as much as for ourselves. He says pray and don't be bashful about asking God for what we need."

Mary nodded her head after each item, as if counting beads. Simon threw the offending thorn into the fire. His face brightened.

"The Pharisees have finally declared he was the Son of David. That means they recognize him as a king."

"They did?" Mary's face smoothed, relieved. "Yes, it means that—and maybe they'll not try to kill him."

"I'm not so sure. Jesus called them a brood of vipers. He asked how they could say anything good when they were so full of evil." Simon slapped his thigh. "You should have seen them. They turned red and swelled up like bladders!" Simon looked at the floor between his feet. "He mentioned you." Mary went on stirring the pottage. Simon hesitated, looked at her, then back at the floor.

"Some woman in the crowd had yelled to him, 'Blessed is the woman who gave you birth and nurtured you!'" Mary's hand stopped stirring. "Jesus said—he said 'Not so.' Mary closed her eyes against the hurt. Simon squirmed, an angry glint in his eye now. "'No,' Jesus said, 'instead, blessed are those who are hearing the Word of God and keeping it.' That again."

Mary stared into space, remembering Chorazin. Simon got up and speared a piece of cheese on his knife point, stabbed a hunk of bread and toasted both over the fire. "Has the news of Lazarus reached here?" he asked.

"We've heard nothing but how Jesus raised him from the dead." Mary sat before Simon on a cushion. "It does not surprise me; remember I was with him when he raised that boy in Nain?" Mary rubbed her neck. "No, it does not surprise me—but to have done it in Jerusalem."

"Yes, Mother, I'm afraid it stirred up everyone from the Pharisees to the street orphans. Jesus has been in hiding ever since. I think they're beyond the Jordan where Herod has no authority. The Sadducees wanted to kill him—and Lazarus."

Mary could not keep back tears. She wiped her eyes.

"Mother," Simon put a strong arm around her, "he sent a message to you." Mary twitched her nose and gave a little shrug. "He said to tell you he's going to Passover and all the prophecies will be fulfilled."

She looked up, her eyes deep pools of dread. "Even the ones about being killed?" A shudder shook her and

Simon held her firmly until she was calm. She drew away from him and bent to the fire.

"God will not let him die. It breaks His promise. He will not die," said Simon and went toward the shop to talk with Joses.

When Simon had gone, Mary knelt against her bed, making herself face those things she had so long put to the back of her mind. *He's talking in parables. Pictures of the Kingdom. He'll not really die. Not my Jesus. God's own son. It's a parable—a parable.* She rose and prepared for sleep.

She did not try to understand what he meant about the third day. She lay quietly thinking it all over once again from Gabriel's visit, trying to face the reality. Suddenly she sat up.

Yes, now is the time for him to take the crown in Jerusalem. I must go there. I must be with him. Now I realize what he meant. All the attention must be upon him, none upon me. I need no praise.

A week later she and Simon left for the Passover. Jude and Joses' family would not go this year; too much to do in the shop, they said, nor would Zebedee, now too old for a three-day walk.

Zebedee's house in Jerusalem bulged with people, all joining in the excitement of preparing the sacrifices, cleaning the house of leaven, greeting old friends. None of Jesus' men were there, not even Thunder or John, and not Jesus. The family could not resist the infection of the season, although under the festivity, each person felt tension, as though a hidden storm were

approaching. Streets were a solid mass of people: worshippers, street vendors, priests and pharisees, thieves
and revolutionaries.

On the sabbath before the Passover, Mary grateful-
ly rested because she could not wholeheartedly join in
the joyousness of the season. Constant thoughts of
Jesus intruded. *Where is he? Will he dare to come? As king—
or be...* She could not think the word *crucified*. Instead
she forced herself to remember other Passovers, and
especially that one when they lost Jesus. Passovers just
like this time, except now Theusas, Salome's head
steward, and other servants did the work. Then there
had been children under foot. Now, now, those same
children grown and not even here with their families as
required for Passover. Thunder James and John,
Clopas' and Rebecca's sons, Chuza. And where were
Ancilla and Matthias right now, for that matter? And her
own Jesus? Where were they? Hiding from Herod? She
felt again the terror. So many gone to Paradise: her parents, Elisabeth, Zacharias, Misheal, Joseph. Her eyes
filmed.

She came out of her world of memories and looked
about her. Everyone must be resting. She would do the
same. Tomorrow would begin the preparation for the
Passover. She climbed the stairs and lay down upon a
Roman bed of ebony.

"He's coming!" Simon's shout snapped her awake.
"Thousands with him! As king! He's coming as king!"

"Where?"

"Coming down Mt. Olivet. Hurry."

Quickly she stuffed her feet into sandals. "What time is it?"

"It's about half-way to noon." She threw a shawl over her shoulders.

"Where's everyone," she asked as they ran through the courtyard.

"Gone with the crowd, I guess. Some were here when I ran upstairs to find you."

They dashed to the Fish Gate and out into a mob of people streaming toward the Kidron Valley. Women dragged children as rag dolls. Men elbowed their way through the surging crowd. Temple trumpets blared above the tumult. Dust eddied and swirled.

Simon leaped upon a wall. "He's almost here. Riding on a white donkey! Surrounded as far as I can see. They're packing the road all the way up Olivet. He's almost here." Simon jumped down. He and Mary rammed their way through a block of people until they stood facing the road.

And there was Jesus.

Shouting came in waves: HOS—ANN—AH! HOS—HOS—ANN—AH! "God save us today! Save us today!"

Men and boys slashed branches from palm trees and threw them to women below. Those near the road spread the branches before Jesus.

HOS—ANN—AH! HOS—ANN—AH! HOS—ANN—AH!

A brilliant sun in a cloudless sky watched the earth while the very rocks seemed to cry with the people, "Blessed is the King who comes in the name of the Lord! Peace in heaven! Glory in the highest. Hosannah to the Son of David, King of Israel!"

Mary didn't try to stop the salty tears that streamed down her face and dripped off her chin. She shouted herself hoarse, her voice lost in the tumult.

"My son, the King! He's my son!" *Oh, Joseph, if you were only here.* "Glory to God who kept his promise to me!"

His chosen men strode triumphantly behind him. Jesus rode calmly, looking ahead toward the temple on the hill above. His head high, he heard the acclaim, saw the homage, but said not a word. Riding slowly, steadily toward Jerusalem.

Then Mary received a shock. *He looks—infinitely sad. He doesn't want the throne!* She saw with a mother's compassion. But like a piece of thistledown, the thought drifted away as she stepped out beside him. Mary's throat was so tight she could not speak. He took her hand as she walked beside him, her head high. The mother of the king, daughter of a line of kings. The crowd roared approval.

At the Beautiful Gate on the east side of the Temple, Jesus squeezed her hand and left her, riding into the muffled uproar of the crowd within.

But Mary was on the outside.

CHAPTER 41

Members of the family came straggling back for hours, reluctant to leave the excitement of bringing back the king. Some had squeezed inside the Temple and had their stories to tell again and again. Before sunset came Matthias and Ancilla, but not Jesus or his men.

"Just like he said, Mother," reminded Simon, "that day we talked after the wedding. He said he'd start with the Pharisees. That's where the power is—with the Sanhedrin, according to James. That's probably why he's gone to the Temple."

But Simon was wrong.

They heard the clamor even outside the Temple walls. Inside it was deafening. Sheep and goats fled, upsetting worshippers. Wild-eyed oxen charged. Tables and booths lay drunkenly on their sides with money changers on their knees scrabbling coins.

"He's at it again, Mother. Jesus is here somewhere."

Mary found him sitting quietly on a step leading to the altar amid a swirling mass of crippled, blind, dumb, leprous, doddering bodies. Hundreds of children milled about chanting, "Hosannah to the Son of David.

Hosannah to the Son of David." She saw a chief priest butting his way through the mob, followed by the Temple Guard. Mary ran to Jesus and pulled on his arm.

"They're coming to arrest you!"

"Yes, Mother, I know." He looked up with a peaceful smile. "'Out of the mouth of babes I've perfected praise,'" he quoted. Mary threw up her hands in exasperation. But at the last moment, the priest whirled away to confer with a Pharisee.

"—can do nothing with this rabble here," she heard the man say.

Above the tumult, the temple trumpets pealed the hours. Guards strutted about, pretending force, watching Jesus with sidelong glances. The Messiah was not arrested.

All day his followers watched at a distance. Just before sunset his men left with Jesus, gliding safely out the Susa gate toward Bethany. Ancilla and Joanna went with them. Only Mary and Simon were left to return to Zebedee's.

"Surely tomorrow," said Simon. "What else is there for him to do?"

"Who can know?" Mary answered. "If Joseph were here he'd say to let Jesus do things in his own time and his own way." She smiled at her youngest son. "His ways are certainly not our ways, are they, or we'd be crowning him tomorrow."

But on the morrow, Tuesday, Jesus again taught in the Temple with his enemies sidling about, alert to trap him, and his listeners massed around him. Mary and Simon worked their way through the crowd until they were close. Jesus spoke quietly, yet his voice carried to the farthest person.

"The kingdom of heaven is like a tiny mustard seed," they heard him say, "that grows into so great a tree, the birds nest in its branches. The kingdom of heaven is like a tiny bit of leaven that raises three pecks of meal."

Simon leaned over to whisper in Mary's ear. "He's speaking mysteries. At least *I* don't know what he means. He must not want these people to know either."

"The kingdom of heaven is like a hidden treasure which a man will give all he has to own."

Again Simon whispered to Mary. "It would seem Jesus' kingdom is something to be desired, but not attained by everyone."

"You are right, and I am trying to understand it. Why can he not speak plainly?" She looked back at Jesus. He leaned forward and went on speaking.

"The kingdom is like the most costly pearl in the world, which a man will give all he has to own. It is also like a drag net that brings in all manner of fish; the good are kept, the bad destroyed.

"Do you understand all these things?" Jesus asked, and the people all said 'yes,' but Mary knew that they did not. She did not herself.

A tramp of feet and slam of spears on marble floors turned every head. A Sadducee with Temple guards behind him pointed a finger at Jesus, but a low growl from the people, like an angry sea, dissuaded the guards. Jesus began to speak again.

Then Jews, those lawyers who thought they knew

345

more about the scriptures than anyone, tried to trap him with questions about divorce, if it were legal to pay taxes to Caesar, and what was the greatest commandment. Jesus spoke directly to these enemies, almost asking for arrest. He turned the questions around, making them all look fools. And the people laughed. Mary did not.

"He's making matters worse," said Simon, "every time he opens his mouth. Dare we try to stop him?" he asked. Mary's look told him, no, it would accomplish nothing.

She stood by a pillar quietly watching her first-born son, seeing the way his hair grew from his forehead, the slope of his shoulders, the quiet hands folded in his lap, and her heart ached.

Finally his enemies left him and asked no more questions. He spoke with the common people a while longer and then went peacefully out the gate, Mary supposed back to Bethany. Jesus did not speak to her.

Wednesday, Mary and Simon went to the Temple again. They could not keep away. *If he is to die, I must be with him. But—it cannot be true, cannot be.*

This day he was not as peaceful as on the previous days. His enemies did not speak to him directly. Jesus seemed to be teaching his men, although he actually spoke to the religious leaders, those jackals always listening behind every column.

"Beware of those who follow rituals and have no love." His voice carried across the masses of people. "Beware you scribes and Pharisees. You blind guides. Hypocrites. You serpents, sons of vipers, how are you going to escape Hell?" Gleeful looks from worshippers.

Mary felt the naked hatred of his enemies as a living presence.

She dared not look at anyone. Simon held her elbow firmly. "He's *trying* to get himself arrested." Simon's body twitched. But no one came forward to take Jesus in charge.

Mary and Simon followed him as he walked throughout the Temple. Jesus met their eyes at times or lifted a hand a fraction, as though in blessing. He and his men walked out on Solomon's porch and he talked to some Greeks, in a different way than he had talked before, answering their questions clearly and directly.

"The time has come for me to be glorified," he said to the Greeks. "Wheat doesn't grow unless the seed dies, then it bears much fruit."

He's speaking of his death? Mary listened again, the stone in her heart growing heavier with each word he spoke.

"My soul has been so troubled," Jesus was saying, "I could wish to say save me from this hour. But no, I came for this." He looked up into the sky. Mary followed his gaze.

"Father, glorify Thy Name."

Would God answer him, as He'd spoken twice before? There was silence in heaven—for a moment.

Then. Some said it was thunder. But Mary heard the words.

"I HAVE BOTH GIVEN IT SPLENDOR AND HONOR AND WILL EXALT IT AGAIN."

Mary's glance met Jesus' eyes in secret understanding. The three of them were together.

In the sudden silence, Jesus shouted: "The condemnation of this world is come and the ruler of this world is cast out."

Simon leaned close to Mary's ear. "Do you suppose he means Herod or Tiberius?" he whispered. But Jesus was speaking further.

"And I, when I am lifted up from the earth, will draw all men to myself."

"He means when he is exalted as king. He cannot mean his death," Mary said, trying to comfort Simon and herself.

The eve before the Passover day began calmly enough. At mid-afternoon Matthias and Ancilla came. The women and servants prepared the meal, polishing glasses, baking unleavened bread. Matthias and Simon stopped by Mary, at a table where she chopped endive.

"Jesus has sent all his disciples to their homes, except for the chosen men," Matthias said. "He says he has some things which he must say to them alone. He's sent some men ahead to prepare their Passover meal. I don't know where. Come, Simon. We'll go select the lambs."

Later in the afternoon, Mary went upstairs to give herself up to self-pity. There was no sound but the whisper of the wind in the palm trees. Passover with only Simon and perhaps James with her. It should not be that way. Nothing was as it should be. Never had been since Jesus began teaching. She entered the bedroom and caressed a wooden bed post. Joseph's hands had made this, sawed and smoothed it. She clasped it in her arms, her cheek against the oak.

"Mother." Jesus stood beside her. She went into his arms in a life-holding grip until he gently released her. Mary sat upon the bed, while he pulled up a stool and faced her.

"My Men are preparing the place for my last supper with them," said Jesus. "I've come to tell you some things which I want you to know before tomorrow."

Tomorrow. Ah, she knew what was coming now.

"Tomorrow I give my life as a sacrifice for the sins of every man. I am the Lamb."

Mary's voice came from the great place in her heart where darkness still held a corner. "No—oo," she moaned. She had promised herself that when the time came, she would be strong, but the time was here and she could not be.

"You remember Gabriel's message about me?" Jesus asked. She nodded. "He told you I'd be an eternal king. And I will be, but just as I've said, it is not an earthly kingdom. It could have been, but Israel did not accept me."

"But last Sunday?"

"A few people, only, not the leaders. Israel does not want a reign of righteousness." And she knew what he said was true. His next words came reluctantly. "Tomorrow I will be rejected and give my life for a different kind of kingdom." She put up her right hand to stop him. He took the hand, holding it firmly by the wrist.

"I've waited so long," she said with down-turned mouth, "to see God's promises fulfilled. But not one has been kept."

"Mother," he said sternly, "listen to me." But she interrupted him.

"All I've dreamed of—all I hoped for you. Gone."

He turned Mary's palm upward. "Now listen. You *knew* all these years, you knew, but wouldn't hear what I was saying, what all the scriptures said. You were intentionally blind." She stiffened.

"But—I wanted the best for you. I—" He gently stopped her with a pressure on her wrist.

"Mother, listen and remember what I'm going to tell you. These things *must* happen. I will be arrested." Jesus drew a line across her palm with an index finger. Mary tried to pull her hand away, but he held it firmly.

"Scourged." He drew another line.

"I will die on a cross." Another line.

Again she tried to pull away, but he would not let her go.

"These things *must* happen." He redrew the lines across her palm. Then with the same look he'd given Joseph when he said goodbye, he said to his mother, "I will live again the third day." She looked deep into his eyes—then at her palm.

Like a tiny candle flame seen from a great distance, confidence flickered. His smile brought tears to Mary's eyes. She blinked them away.

"Remember Nazareth and Egypt, Mother? You were strong enough to bear those things—for my sake." And her look told him she could do it now.

A raven flew by the window, hoarsely crying. It seemed to carry all the darkness and terror in Mary's soul. She looked at her palm and saw the three lines as clearly as though he'd used a stylus. He gently folded her fingers over it and left as quietly as he had come.

The lamb for the Passover meal was slain and roasted and the family reclined around the low table.

Matthias blessed the candles and the cups and washed his hands. The ritual food was eaten in its turn, the watered wine drunk, the bitter herbs chewed. Bread and wine. Red wine poured into her cup, and she lifted it to her lips. The bread was broken.

CHAPTER 42

Mary pulled a woolen bedmat over her shoulders and watched scudding clouds hide a full moon, then saw it emerge again, a silver eye watching with her. A wind moaned in the branches outside the window.

Sandals clattered up the stairs and Simon burst into the room. "They've arrested him."

The spear pierced her heart. "Ancilla!" Blindly, she and her sister pushed feet into heavy-soled walking shoes and threw on cloaks. Simon hurried them through shadowed alleys and marbled streets.

Herod's bridge arched waxy white in the moonlight. The wind, blowing up from the valley below them, tried to tear Mary's cloak from her shoulders. They panted through the empty city, past ghostly buildings, twisted between deserted stalls, silent and threatening, the goods wrapped in great winding cloths like so many bodies. As they started up the steps on the western hill, the wind moaned between the rooftops and carried the acrid odor of refuse fires in the Hinnon Valley. With panting breaths, Simon told them that Temple guards had taken Jesus to Annas' mansion.

"To the high priest?" gasped Mary.

"Why him?" from Ancilla.

Outside the door of the priest's house, torches flared. A guard stopped them. Simon clutched the man's tunic at the throat.

"Where have they taken him?"

The man wrenched away and raised his spear. "To Caiaphas," he snarled.

They turned and ran.

Cephas bumped into them, sobbing uncontrollably. Simon caught him by a sleeve. "What hap—"

"I said I didn't know him—didn't even know him. Let go—." Cephas jerked from Simon's grip and fled. Mary watched him disappear into the night.

Another man. Moonlight exposed white Pharisee robes.

"James!" Mary cried.

James ranted for all the world to hear. "The Sanhedrin's been called. It's wrong, all wrong; it can't meet at night." He twisted his hands. "Annas knows better! He must have done it on purpose." Mary shook him, but James barely noticed, so wrapped was he in his indignation.

"What has happened to Jesus?" Mary voice demanded an answer.

"Judas betrayed him. Told them where Jesus was—for thirty pieces of silver; you can buy a slave for that." Then her Pharisee son whimpered in his mother's arms. Mary's heart thumped painfully.

"There never was any good in that family," Ancilla said, her every word acid.

*

They walked to the gate of the house of the other high priest. James snapped a remark to the guard and entered Caiaphas' palace. Before the door swung shut Mary had a glimpse of Jesus's back, his hands bound behind him.

Matthias stepped from the shadow of a wall. "There's nothing we can do until this false court is finished," he said and put his arms around both sisters. "We'll wait here and see what happens."

They waited an hour, watching men come and go. Finally two men went inside, hustled along by the prick of a guard's spear. Angry, indistinguishable words drifted from the windows. The wind moaned in the treetops and they pulled their cloaks tighter. Flickering torch lights on the wall reflected off the golden hair of a man running toward them.

"Where's Judas?" Chuza's hair stood up like yellow broom. Although a broad sword was strapped to his waist, he swung an oak club the size of his arm. "Where's Judas?"

"The last I saw him he was kissing Jesus," Simon spat the words.

"I saw him slink into the garden over there only minutes ago," Ancilla said and pointed the direction.

"I'll find him." Chuza plunged into the shrubbery. *Pity Judas*, thought Mary. They heard Chuza snarling at a guard.

A blanch-faced moon paled against the blue of dawn. More men hurried up the street obviously just roused, chief priests and scribes by their dress. Shortly after, the guards at the door jerked to attention. James stepped out a side door, stammering in his anger.

"Couldn't stop them—breaking every rule—not everyone here—didn't see Nicodemus—can't hold court today—Passover." He grabbed his robe in both hands and ripped it. "They never gave him a chance."

Now came Jesus down the steps between two guards. Dried blood matted his face. Blood pounded in Mary's temples. She took a step, reached out her hands. Jesus nodded slightly. Simon helped Mary across the cobbles, over an open drain and down more steps, following Jesus and the Council leaders.

The moon sank behind the palace towers. Jesus' family retraced the streets they'd hurried along an age before. "Not going to Pilate," James muttered. Mary was too numb to understand what he meant. Temple guards pushed Jesus through a door in Annas' house on the Temple Mount.

"I'll see what's happening." James' figure was lost among the gadfly scribes following in the wake of the Council.

The waiting began again. Above their heads the first rays of light turned the golden roof of the Temple to fire. Pink clouds drifted westward. The wind had died as though it, too, had lost the battle. Ancilla cocked her head and listened.

"No birds," was all she said. No welcome for this dawn. Not this one.

An eerie silence hung over the city. Priests hurried up the steps and disappeared inside the tunnel.

"Look at that," Simon pointed to a long line of non-descript men making their way toward them. They came in twos and threes, furtive, creeping silently into the Temple.

"Sewer rats," Simon said. "Old Annas has hired them for witnesses or I'm much mistaken." Mary just blinked at him, her face ten years older.

A door flung open. Caiaphas waddled out wearing his priestly blue robes. Flaming torches made the gems on the holy breastplate gleam. Jesus walked down the steps behind him, head bowed, hands still bound. His eyes lighted when he saw his family.

Mary caught a sob in her throat.

They followed behind the procession straight toward the Praetorium. The crowd grew as dawn peeped into the alleys that branched off everywhere from the paving. The family and the rabble tramped steadily toward Pilate's judgement hall.

James caught up with the family, sputtering with indignation. "It's completely illegal. All agreed on the verdict; that nullifies it—should let him go. Caiaphas asked him point blank if he was the Messiah, and Jesus said: I AM, so that finishes it for Jesus!" Now Mary fought sobs—and won. The others said nothing, just looked up to where Pilate would appear.

A sudden hush fell. Pilate stepped onto the platform in full view of everyone. He was a smaller man than Mary had expected, hair cut short in the Roman fashion, a white robe thrown carelessly about him instead of the meticulously folded toga.

James jeered, "He's in his common tunic. Too early for him to be up."

With guards' spears in his back, Jesus walked up the steps and stood before Pontius Pilate. Pilate, the man with the power of life and death, strutted to the front of the platform, obviously irritated, and looked down at Jesus' accusers.

"Well," he whined, "what accusations do you bring against this man? Hurry up."

"We would not have come if—"

"Oh, take him," Pilate said with a wave of his hand, "and judge him according to your own laws. Why bother me?" He turned his back.

A man shouted, "He's perverting the nation and forbidding to give tribute to Caesar. We aren't allowed to put him to death." Another voice shouted, "He's the Messiah—King of Israel!"

Pilate turned back with a flick of his robe and spoke low to Jesus for a few minutes, then stared contemptuously at the throng. "I find no fault in this man." He turned to go, but the mob below stamped and screamed. Someone shouted something about Galilee.

"Galilee!" Pilate yelped. "It's not my jurisdiction. Take this man to Herod." Pilate pivoted and left the platform.

Herod! All the horror from a lifetime of that name chilled Mary. She clutched Ancilla's hand. Matthias steadied her.

Jesus walked slowly down the steps, his eyes on his family. Mary bravely lifted her head and looked into his eyes, but her heart was breaking.

Simon gripped Mary's arm and hurried her through the crowd until they walked just behind Jesus and his guards. They climbed the steps of the western hill again and moved toward the Hasmonian Palace. The three towers gleamed in the morning sunlight. Fountains sparkled rainbows.

The gate clanged shut behind Jesus and his guards.

Long minutes passed.

Then a woman inside the garden with a shawl covering her face whispered to the guard. He nodded, opened the gate a crack, to let the woman out and then closed it after her. It was Chuza's wife, Joanna. She flew into Ancilla's arms and wept.

"Tell us what is happening," Ancilla said in a voice as firm as the mountain they stood upon.

"Mother," Joanna said between sobs, "they spit on him—ridiculed him. Herod's soldiers put a moldy, purple robe on him to make fun of him as the king. He just wanted to see him do some magic." Bitterly she added: "Herod's sending him back to Pilate.

A spasm crossed Mary's face. Her nails dug into her palms. As though the lines were there, she felt where Jesus had marked. *This must happen. I will be arrested.*

Jesus walked toward them, head up, his eyes as calm as when he spoke with children. He wore the tattered cloak royally. The guards pushed him down the street. Matthias stepped close and wiped spit from Jesus's face. Tears ran unchecked down Ancilla's cheeks, but Mary squared her shoulders and clamped her teeth.

Pilate was in his toga, now, chewing on his thumbnail.

In front of him, Jesus in his faded purple looked more regal than his judge. Splotches of red mottled Pilate's neck and face. He looked at the Israelites below him, as though watching loathsome insects.

"You Rulers and Priests, I found no fault in this man. Neither did Herod. What do you want me to do?" The crowd shouted, but no words were clear. "You have a custom to release one prisoner on your Passover Feast." Pilate's voice took on a whine. "I'll chastise this man and release him." An evil tide of protest rumbled through the crowd. Pilate conferred with an aide beside him, then turned back to the people. "Whom shall I release, Barabbas, the murderer, or Jesus, who is called Messiah? Shall I release the King of the Jews?"

The weak cries of "Messiah! Messiah! Messiah!" were drowned in the roar of "BARABBAS."

A frown furrowed Pilate's brow. He leaned over the edge of the platform. "What shall I do with Jesus called Messiah, whom you call King of the Jews?" There was a note of panic in his voice.

"CRUCIFY HIM!" roared the crowd. "CRUCIFY HIM!"

Pilate's voice cut through it flatly. Like the downswing of a Damascus sword. "So be it."

Guards led Jesus into the depth of the Praetorium to be scourged.

His family waited. Waited. Eternity could not be longer.

"They're bringing him back." Matthias turned Ancilla around. "Don't watch. Don't watch."

On the platform, Jesus stood quietly under the robe, his hands folded before him, a mock crown of twined jujube thorns upon his head. Blood flowed freely past his ear and dripped on the shabby velvet. A hand print across his cheek stood out starkly against the death pallor of his face. Jesus looked out across the people, serene when they would have him humiliated. His eyes found Mary's, and he lifted his hand, palm upward. She feebly raised hers, tears blurring him. *I will not let him see me cry.*

Simon clenched his fists, jaw thrust forward, but it was no use. His shoulders slumped.

Pilate took a step to the edge of the platform. The veins were visible in his neck as he shouted. "I'm bringing him back to you so that you can see he has no guilt. Behold the man!"

"Crucify him!"

The earth rolled on in God's inexorable plan.

Pilate and God's Son soon appeared on the stone slabs of the Pavement of Judgment. Pilate turned and spoke to Jesus. Then he looked down at the mob below him. His look silenced the crowd.

"*You* crucify him!"

Pilate sat down upon the chair of judgment and called for a bowl of water. The veins in his temples bulged purple. His nose pinched, he dipped his hands in water and rubbed them, repeated the process, and again. A slave handed him an immaculate white towel. It showed red stains when Pilate handed it back. He stepped to the edge of the platform.

"Behold your King." Pilate rubbed his hands.

*

Jesus was led away.

Simon caught Mary as she crumbled toward the pavement. She turned to look. Her son was gone.

CHAPTER 43

The family stood in a knot, hidden under the colonnades. Mary clutched Simon's hand, shivering uncontrollably and held tight in his arms. Ancilla blinked in red-eyed rage.

"Where will they take him?" she asked. Matthias swallowed before he answered.

"To Golgotha." Mary flinched. Matthias looked to Ancilla and his eyes said, "Shouldn't you take her home?"

But now James ran up, gasping for breath, dust covering his white robe up to the knees. "Here you are! I've been arguing with the Council to release him. They won't listen, not even to Nicodemus." He smashed his fist into his palm. "Everything they've done has broken the law. I'm done with them. Jesus was right." His eyes darted toward the empty judgment chair. "Where is he? Where's Jesus?"

The tramp of boots echoed through the Praetorium. Soldiers dragged Jesus into the street, his face ashen and streaked with blood, muscles twitching. Now he straightened, took another step, and faltered. James and Simon rushed toward him.

"Get back!" A burly soldier shoved the flat of his spear against them. Two other prisoners staggered behind Jesus, carrying beams across their shoulders. Blood drenched their tunics, leaving a map of stripes. Jesus' blood-soaked robe pasted itself against his shoulder blades. Mary moaned. Ancilla stood rigid.

"Here, pick up your beam," said a guard who might have slain a dozen men and enjoyed it. He pulled a beam as tall as Chuza from a pile and lifted it to the bloody shoulders. Jesus winced and staggered. Matthias thrust forward again, but a spear point forced him back.

The procession started. At its head a slave carried three *tituli* under his arm containing the names of the prisoners. The condemned staggered behind him. A few Pharisees followed to see the death sentence carried out, self-righteously determined, fulfilling God's great plan for mankind. Those who cried for his death followed after, a noticeably smaller crowd than before, and those who loved him walked last.

At a turn of the street, Jesus staggered and fell.

"Here, you, Cyrenian! The soldier poked a huge black man with the point of his spear. "Carry that!" he snapped. The man bent towards Jesus and with no more effort than it takes to pick up a thistle, lifted the beam onto his massive shoulders and helped Jesus totter to his feet. With a glance of gratitude at the Cyrenian, the Son of God struggled on.

"Let this man be remembered forever," Mary breathed and glanced toward heaven.

A crowd had gathered along the roadside—the curious off the streets, ordinary people, his enemies furtively following to see the last of it.

Simon muttered to James. "Why doesn't he stop them? He's the Son of God."

"I never did believe that," James said resentfully. His words were just another wound in Mary's heart. "I don't see any of his men. Where are Thunder and John, and Clopas' boys, and Cephas? Where are they, Matthias?" Mary wondered that, too.

"If you don't believe him, leave," his uncle said. "You think you know so much. Go home and study your psalms and prophets." James looked at his mother, reluctant to obey.

Mary said quietly, "James, if you cannot stand to see him die, then go. But you won't escape what he is doing."

James and Simon looked at her, undecided. Their eyes followed their brother, struggling up the steps beyond. With a look at each other, they slowed their steps, ducked their heads, and turned back.

The procession wound past whitewashed graves, hewn from the limestone on the bluff to their right. One prisoner cursed everything in heaven and earth, but the other said nothing. The Messiah stared straight ahead toward the hill of Golgotha, taking careful steps. Mary saw only the crown of thorns.

Six streets lay between the Praetorium and the place of crucifixion. They climbed the path around the south side of the bluff called the Skull, Golgotha, to the top where three poles rose starkly, awaiting their burden of the damned. Red poppies nodded before a soft breeze. Jesus and the two malefactors collapsed on the grass. A Roman soldier brought them a sedative in a flask, vinegar mixed with myrrh. The two robbers grabbed it, but Jesus refused.

A soldier with hair like Chuza's jerked the robe over Jesus' head and then stripped the bodies naked, exposing them to shame. Another laid the beams on the grass and stretched the victims upon them. Iron spikes tore through flesh on wrists and ankles.

Now came the Magdalene, her beautiful face awash with tears, her slave with her. They joined the others, wincing and sobbing with each thud of the hammer.

Three soldiers heaved the crosses upright, thumped them into holes. One soldier nailed a *titulus* above each robber's head: Dimas, Thief; Gestas, Thief. The sign above Jesus's head, written in Hebrew, Greek and Latin read:

JESUS OF NAZARETH, KING OF THE JEWS

Mary forced herself to look into Jesus's eyes. What she saw shocked her. His look was triumphant! She nodded once and kneeled before the king.

"Come, he won't want you to watch," Ancilla said and tried to lift her up.

But Mary pulled away, her face unreadable. They let her be.

Jesus's weight pushed against the nails in his heels. He tried to pull himself up to gather air enough to speak. He sank. Fought to raise himself again. Pressure sent fresh rivulets of blood from his wrists. Upward he strained again.

"Father," he said, lifting his body to gain a breath between each word, "forgive them. Know not what they do."

Mary stared into his face, her eyes never wavering. She did not look at the great purple welts covering the prisoners' backs or at the black flies beginning to settle into the ooze on their bloody shoulders, nor at the strips of flesh already turning death-gray. She did not see the square nails driven through tendons above their heels that held the feet securely against each side of the posts. She saw only her son's suffering face and his anguished eyes.

Hours dragged by. Now Ancilla raged, but Mary bowed her head, palms together, hearing again Jesus's words.

"We must forgive them, Ancilla," Mary said finally. "You'll understand someday that these things must happen." By stages, Ancilla's rage turned to unbroken weeping.

The sun blazed down unrelenting from a cloudless sky. Time seemed to stop, as though the universe waited for God's command.

Mary watched the soldiers casting lots for Jesus's robe, the robe she'd woven herself, without a seam. Suddenly rage overcame her. *They shall not sport when my son is dying.* She picked up a rock and pulled back her arm to hurl it at the soldier, but Matthias's great hand closed over hers and he tossed the rock aside. She slumped against him.

Father God, take him soon.

People passed, mocking, sneering.

"Save yourself, would you?"

"If you're the Son of God, come down from there!"

"If you're the Messiah, save yourself."

"And us," Gestas, the man on Jesus' left, sneered.

367

"Oh, ho! He said he trusted God. Let's see God deliver him."

Men spit on Jesus. A soldier leaned idly against the base of Dimas' cross. Another sitting cross-legged below Jesus, yelled up at him. "Yea, if you're the King of the Jews, prove it," and gave a guffaw that seemed a curse.

Dimas whispered, "We deserve to die—he's innocent." He took a breath. "Remember me—when you come—into—Kingdom!"

"You'll be—today—with me—in Paradise," said Jesus, lifting his whole body to speak each word. Blood flowed afresh.

Mary looked away over the rooftops to the Temple, where thousands waited with their lamb. *But the Lamb is here and I will not let him see me in despair.* She rose from her knees slowly and with dignity lifted her head and looked squarely into the eyes of each tormentor. They turned away.

Others came. John, then Rebecca and Salome. Chuza supporting Joanna came last. All fell to their knees on seeing Jesus.

Only Mary did not sob. She looked again at her palm.

They heard the trumpet and knew it was midday. Jesus lifted himself and took a breath. He looked from his mother to John: "Behold your mother. Take her home." Mary looked lingeringly at her son, the Messiah, the King. Believing now, she turned to John. He took her arm to move her down the path, but she suddenly resisted.

"He means Salome," she said firmly. "Salome is your mother."

"No, he means you. Come, Aunt Mary. He wants you to go."

"He wants us all to go," said Matthias, jerking his head at the others. "Quickly." They started down the path.

Everything was too still, some kind of weather coming. A black cloud rose behind Olivet. "Hurry!" They urged each other. "Look!"

Boiling clouds covered the sky by the time they reached the Gennath Gate. They raced through dark tunnels of streets, holding hands as the air thickened to a Stygian blackness.

"What's happening?" Ancilla for once was not in command.

"I don't know! Run!" Matthias pulled her along. The others stumbled after, John supporting Mary and his mother.

He pushed open the gate. They felt their way into the courtyard. Theusas held a candle—a bare pin-prick of light in the blackness.

"Must be an eclipse," cried John, his voice high in the thick darkness. Then the candle went out, as if air had been sucked from the courtyard.

"God has turned his back upon the world," Matthias cried. Mary gripped Ancilla's hand, ready for whatever might come. She waved her other hand before her face and could not see it. No air moved.

The city lay as dead—no trumpets, no voices, as though waiting for the end of the age.

For three hours the darkness was so thick no one moved. Occasionally they voiced their thoughts, but for the most part, quietly waited, hearts aching as they thought of Jesus, turning over scriptures in their minds to see if such a thing had ever happened before, wondering how long this waiting would last.

"But who will bury him?" It was Salome's voice. Somebody shushed her, but the Magdalene soothed her.

"When it's light again, we'll go back and stay with him," she said. Everyone knew what she meant—until it is over.

Objects began to take shape in Zebedee's courtyard. Windows caught light. The men ran to look out into the street. The women, all except Mary, busied themselves collecting winding cloths and spices. Mary sat upon the pavement. They glanced at her, thinking to leave her to her sorrow.

Mary felt it first. A slight tremor, then a thunder of noise that shattered the stone wall around the courtyard. The earth cracked, reeled. Shouts. Screams. Waves of earth as high as the knee rolled toward them. John ran back and covered Mary with his body. The roar of falling masonry, a great moaning rumble as the earth tore apart. Dust choked them.

And then it was over.

Mary could hear a neighbor's child wailing, shouts near, some far off. The roof of Zebedee's house had fallen into the second story on one side. Bricks littered the courtyard. The sun reigned from a swept heaven.

John helped Mary to her feet. "That was no ordinary earthquake, Mary." Shaken, the men stretched legs, found no broken bones and went to help neighbors.

In that half hour, the women pushed aside debris,

and talked nervously about the darkness. The earth-quake. Jesus. Should they go back? Perhaps he could be freed? The men thought the same thing.

"Let's go," said Salome. "Hurry. They'll never let him live past sundown," she said. "Maybe the earth-quake freed him. There's still hope."

"Mary?"

"No, I'm staying here."

"Not coming?" The others looked at her in conster-nation.

"He sent me home to wait for him. He'll come to me." They glanced at one another, at her, and went out shaking their heads.

Mary went about the rooms helping Theusas sweep glass, push benches into place.

Just before dark, Matthias returned alone. He hesi-tated in front of Mary, then knelt beside her. "Mary—he died. Just before the earthquake."

The Messiah's mother bowed her head, then looked into Matthias' eyes. Her face was peaceful, relieved, but her eyes were misty. "Yes," she said at last in a great sigh. She took a deep breath and did not at first expel it.

"A wealthy man asked Pilate for his body," Matthias said as John climbed over the rubble of the wall to join them. Mary looked at him expectantly. John, the only one of the twelve who really believed Jesus, did not answer her look.

Then came Jesus' disciples. And the women, Rebecca speaking for them all. "They laid him in a new tomb, Mary."

James burst in, a ragged victim of the quake.

"And you, James," charged Matthias. "Where were you? That friend of yours from the Council went to Pilate himself for permission to bury him."

"Nicodemus," said James.

Matthias went on. "He opened his own tomb and sent spices, a hundred weight of aloes."

Salome took Mary in her arms. "We saw where they laid him, right near the base of the hill," she said. Mary tightened her jaw. "Tomorrow is the Sabbath. We can't go tomorrow, but we'll go early Sunday and anoint his body."

"Now let us rest, even as he is resting." That was Ancilla, her anger gone.

Mary only looked down at her open palm where Jesus drew the last line, *I will live again the third day*, and nodded. "Yes, now let us rest."

But no one slept at all. Each time sleep came near, another violent tremor shook the house. Stones fell from walls long after the tremors stopped, always when least expected.

The next day, the Sabbath, the family rested as Moses' law required, rested as their minds slowly adjusted to all they had endured.

Hour by hour, Mary watched the moon move across the window, and waited for the dawn of the third day.

He said he would come today.

CHAPTER 44

Pearl gray light outlined Olivet. Mary slept soundly without a dream. A hand gently shaking her shoulder roused her.

"We're going to the tomb," Rebecca said softly. "We want you to go with us." But Mary shook her head.

"No. I'm staying here."

"But we're going to anoint him!"

"He won't be there."

Rebecca looked perplexed, but left her to hurry away.

Rising to look out an eastern window, Mary watched the women climb over what had been the wall and start up the street.

She felt something tug at her heart, something more compelling than her loneliness, something felt so strongly she could not resist. She dug toes into sandals and flung a cloak around her shoulders.

The moon rode the western hills and streets lay in deep shadow as she turned right at the cross street and zigzagged northeast, picking her way over the crumbled walls and fallen brick to the Lions Gate. Fog filled the Kidron Valley, fingering its way inside the city. In a world of mist, she turned again along the path among the tombs below the Temple walls.

The earthquake's destruction and the eerie light of pre-dawn confused her. She finally found the stone sealing the entrance to Joseph's tomb and sat beside it on a marble slab covering someone's grave. A monument rose stark beside her.

She felt the earth move. A roar. Rocks split. Mary's body was thrown against the pillar then flattened against the slab.

Then all noise stopped. Figures moved through the mist and dust. She looked at Joseph's tomb. The rock sealing the entrance had fallen from the door. A figure stood in the entrance.

"Joseph!"

He took her in his arms. He had body, substance. Life.

"Jesus is alive," she said, looking up into his dear, familiar face.

"I know. He came to Paradise as soon as he died. We're being resurrected with our bodies now."

Mary found no words, felt only joy.

"I must go, Mary."

"No…"

He was gone. Her arms held nothing.

Now the city came alive. Women wailing. Shouts. Dogs. Temple trumpets blasting. She turned and ran blindly into the mist, sobbing, straight into someone else.

"Mother," the figure said softly.

She clung to him. It was Jesus.

"I said I'd come," he said and smiled. She stepped back to look at him and noticed that he wore a simple robe, as some gardener might wear, his face full and healthy, his hair pulled back behind a band. Alive. Radiant with a joyous smile which she hadn't seen on him for many years. She took his hands in hers. A shiver of horror twitched her body, for holes gaped in both his wrists.

"Remember?" he said and turned her hand to look into her palm. She caressed his cheek with trembling fingers with the other hand.

"Yes, and I believed you," she said hardly above a whisper.

"You were brave—showed such courage. Forever after this all people will gain strength from what you did."

"It was your strength." Her face was radiant too.

He took his hands away. "There are others I must see. I must set up my kingdom. It's a kingdom in people's hearts, not what Israel has always expected. I need your help, Mother. I need you."

"*Me?*"

"Go home and tell my brothers. The years ahead will not be easy. Listen to my men, especially Cephas."

Mary's brows drew together in a frown, hurt in her eyes. "Will I ever see you again, my Jesus?"

He nodded and smiled. "I'm going to meet you all in Galilee in a few days. Go there and wait. Take the family with you."

He disappeared.

She felt the imprint of his hands, but hers were empty. Like the streamers of light peeking into the hidden corners of the Kidron Valley, a renewed faith lit Mary's soul. Then the sun broke over Olivet, burned the fog and drenched the devastated city in crimson.

"Mother, where have you been?" James demanded as she climbed through the broken gate. "You could have been killed." James the Pharisee stood before them in torn robe, filthy to the knees, fringe ripped and dragging at his heels, his phylactery lost.

Mary Magadalene ran to Mary, leaping over rocks.

"I've seen him. He's alive." She looked about. "Where are the others?"

"I don't know. They went to the tomb early."

James scoffed. "Won't do them any good. It's sealed and soldiers are guarding it."

And then the women came chattering like frightened sparrows about angels.

Footsteps pounded on the tiles. Cephas and John burst inside. "He's alive," they yelled together. "ALIVE!" James and Simon leaped up. Mary smiled just slightly. Fresh with confidence, she gave orders: "Prepare a meal, Theusas, just a porridge of barley. They'll all want something when they get here." Her quiet assurance stunned everyone except the Magdalene, who helped dust plaster off benches and set bowls and spoons.

Thunder James and Mary's James left for the Temple to find out what was happening there. Cephas suddenly gazed around the room and said in surprise: "Where's Judas?" Chuza lowered his spoon.

"He hung himself," he said quietly. Cephas stared into space, as if repudiated. The silence in the room was absolute.

When those who had gone to the Temple returned, James was shouting.

"The great veil of the Temple is torn from the top to bottom!" Wide-eyed terror registered in every face. "Anyone who wants to can walk right into the Holy of Holies, where God lives."

Thunder James stopped his pacing beside Mary. "Jesus has made a way for us into the presence of God," he said, his voice now barely above a whisper.

This news was too awful. The destruction from the earthquake was nothing compared to this shattering of all they held holy.

Two hours later, Mary and her family left for Galilee, too stunned to do anything but obey. Jesus had said he would meet them there.

CHAPTER 45

As they neared Bethel storm clouds came in from the sea. With heads bent against the wind, they pushed toward Sebaste, where they sheltered under the same rock overhang which had protected her and Joseph so many years before. By noon the next day, they descended the hill above Capercotnei and turned right toward Kapher Nahum.

Mary's family waited for Jesus, just waited, not seeming able to pick up their daily work, only speaking of those things which had happened to him. On Sunday, a week after he rose, Jesus appeared suddenly, sitting on the hearth stone. Everyone stood rigid, then relaxed when Jesus smiled. Matthias was first to speak as though the question had burned a long time.

"Why were our minds so clouded," he asked, "that we could not see who you were?"

Jesus tapped his fingertips and said with the same wry smile, "My Men's minds were too full of earthly things—a kingdom, food, relief from suffering." His eyes twinkled at Ancilla. "And you, Aunt, would have obstructed the Lord's great plan."

All lowered their eyes, remembering their private plans for him. Jesus explained much they needed to know and finished by saying, "I died as a sinless man to take the judgment for everyone on earth." He glanced at James to remind him of those long-gone arguments over judgment. "I'll meet with my Men tomorrow and see you all in Jerusalem in a few weeks.

He was gone.

As though from a trance they shook themselves, began to talk, to set about mundane tasks.

"We'll leave in the morning," Mary said "and meet the men at the foot of Mt. Tabor tomorrow night."

"Then Jerusalem." Ancilla's eyes held the old gleam. "And then Jerusalem"

"Yes, Jerusalem," Mary said. But why was her heart so heavy—her hands so cold?

They paused outside Bethany. Jerusalem spread below them—the golden Temple on its hill, palaces and huts, broken walls and arched gates.

"There's where he rode, down this way," Mary proudly explained to those who hadn't been there when Jesus died. She pointed to the road ahead. "That's where they acclaimed him king."

"And over there," Ancilla said, "below on that knob to the left is Golgotha where they slew him." Mary noted the bitterness in her voice.

"See the cemetery just under the wall?" Simon asked. That is where we buried Father." No one spoke for several minutes, reliving all that Jerusalem meant.

"And see," James thrust out an imperious arm.

"There's the Temple—still standing." He shook his head and mumbled to himself. "All so wrong. We were so wrong."

Nicodemus' limestone house rose three stories, with a sweep of marble steps leading up to bronze doors. A pool sat in three acres of gardens. As they waited at the door, Mary let the fragrance of lilies and damp grass take her back to the atrium in Alexandria. She looked up the hill to Herod Antipas' palace and watched the same fountains bubbling which she'd admired as a girl. Light caught hundreds of shattered windows.

Nicodemus welcomed them himself just inside the front doors. This leader of the Sanhedrin stood no taller than James. He wore a magnificent green robe over an ankle-length tunic of a lighter green silk. Mary admired gold embroidery down the front of the robe and around the sleeves. He gave James the kisses of welcome, and James introduced those Nicodemus did not know.

"I'm glad to see you all here." Nicodemus addressed them with a smile which emphasized the lines down each side of his mouth. "I must warn you to keep inside my gardens. Talk to no one outside the house. All those here are faithful followers of Jesus. With them you are safe."

Safe? From whom? Mary felt a quiver of fear. *Jesus was gone now, so what was there to fear?*

They joined the eleven apostles and the others waiting for Jesus.

Day after day they tarried, fear always with them, for

just up the hill was Herod holding the power of Rome and nearby, Annas and Caiaphas, wielding the power of Israel. They cowered under Nicodemus' protection, went in small groups to the Temple on sabbaths, mixing with crowds as they returned. Always they talked of the scriptures and studied scrolls. Now, everywhere in the books of history, in the Psalms and the Prophets they saw Jesus.

Forty days later, the hundred and twenty studied the prophet Joel. Sunlight flowed through windows, gilding faces.

Suddenly Jesus was among them, this resurrected Son of God.

"I have some things to tell you," Jesus said, seating himself on a bench. "A most important message. Not many days from now you will be baptized not with water but with power, when you receive the Holy Spirit."

"Lord," Simon the Cananean could restrain himself no longer, "is now when you'll restore the kingdom?"

"Oh, you with zeal for the kingdom of Israel. Don't you understand? Only my Father knows the time of the restoring…and the end of the ages. Haven't you learned yet that my kingdom is of the spirit?"

Jesus spoke softly, but it seemed as though the words pounded each heart. "You will receive zeal for my true kingdom. Wait for this power. You will go everywhere telling what you saw and heard, explaining the scriptures and baptizing. You will witness in Jerusalem, in Judea and Samaria and even to the remotest parts of the earth." Now his voice was gentle as soft rain. "But you will suffer and die for it."

"We are ready," shouted Peter. Jesus held up a hand.

"Yes, Peter, but wait. Wait for the Holy Spirit. "He rose. "Let us all walk to Bethany."

"Someone will recognize you," Thomas said, a frown creasing his forehead above protruding brows.

"No one can see me. And no one will bother any of you this day."

They followed him silently. At Bethany Jesus led them to a bare place at the top of a cliff. Not a leaf stirred. No birds sang.

Jesus looked up into heaven. He spread his arms, palms down in blessing. His body rose slowly, slowly, up, up, up until a drift of clouds hid him. A symphony of bird song burst from every tree.

Only then did his followers take a breath and with one great sigh keep looking upward.

A deep voice asked, "Why are you men of Galilee gaping into heaven?" All stared wide-eyed and fearful at two angels in blinding white garments.

"This same Jesus will come again in just the way you saw him go," one said. Before even Peter could speak, they disappeared.

The Feast of Pentecost dawned clear and warm a week later. The odor of harvest grain drifted through the window from fields to the west. Jesus' followers rose, rolled their bedmats and descended the stairs to break fast. Food and dishes put away, they talked aimlessly. What were they to do this feast day? No Temple worship. Perhaps a grand meal later from Nicodemus and more waiting.

"Hush." Peter's voice stopped all chatter. He tipped his head. "Hear that?" He moved to a window.

A rushing wind seemed to be advancing from all directions.

"There's not a leaf moving," John said looking over Peter's shoulder.

The rushing grew louder, stronger, filled the room. Terror pulled muscles tight on every face. The roar intensified. Caught each one in a vortex of rushing ecstatic sound, yet nothing moved, not so much as a hair. Mary's fear disappeared as the blast whirled around her. She felt a peace she hadn't known since Gabriel spoke with her. Perfect peace with man, with God, with herself.

Then came lustrous flames flickering over their heads, sending tingling down each spine.

Roar and flame vanished.

As from a trance, each person moved a hand, took a step, wiped tears.

"It's the baptism he promised," Thunder whispered. "The Comforter has come."

Now the room felt as though charged by lightning.

"We must tell everyone." Light flooded into the room when Peter pulled the door, opening a path of sunshine down the steps.

Cephas, now called Peter, and John led Jesus' Followers. Apostles and Followers scattered among those filling the street, talking, gripping shoulders, looking into eyes, speaking to each person they met. Each person understood in his own language. They nodded, spoke back, talked excitedly with others.

It went on all morning. Thousands came. And with them came the scoffers. People surged up Nicodemus' steps praising God—or mocking. "They are drunk on sweet wine. Drunk," said several.

Peter climbed to the steps to stand beside Mary. Thousands of people looked up at them, talking among themselves.

"You men of Jerusalem," Peter began, "and you from far away, these men are not drunk. It's early yet."

Those near him stopped speaking, then those farther away quieted as his voice boomed out over them.

"LISTEN! Listen to the Prophet Joel. He told of this. These are the last days."

Faces looked in wonder at one another, then back at this Galilean who spoke with such authority in their own languages.

"He said God would pour out his spirit in the end times—on both men *and* women. He prophesied that young men will have visions. Old men dream dreams. Both men *and* women whom he chooses will prophesy.

"But," Peter raised both arms, letting his tunic fall back to expose weathered fisherman arms, "are you wondering when the Messiah will return? LISTEN! There will be wonders in the sky." He looked into a cerulean sky, not a cloud showing. Thousands of eyes looked upward with him. "Signs here on earth, blood and fire and vapors. NO SUN." He pointed toward the orb just passing the zenith. "And the moon will turn to blood before that time comes."

Even the scoffers quieted.

With lowered voice, Peter the Rock, once called

Cephas a little stone, now thundered his message to the men of Israel, reminding them of Jesus' miracles, of how they'd unknowingly accomplished God's plan when they crucified him, of how God had raised him up alive. He reminded them of King David's words that the Messiah would rise again. His voice carried across the city.

"This Jesus is both LORD and CHRIST."

Eyes stared at Peter, glanced at the sun, at each other. A fearful shudder went through the throng. "What must we do? What must we do?"

"Repent," bellowed Peter. "Repent. Ask forgiveness for your sin. Be baptized in Jesus' name. You'll receive the Holy Spirit just as we have. You'll receive power and comfort."

With one movement most of the people surged toward Nicodemus' pool. "We believe. We believe. Baptize us."

The chosen twelve began baptizing—three thousand souls that day.

Mary looked back on it almost in disbelief. Never again did she feel the same power as the moment the Holy Spirit descended upon her.

What next? What next, Lord God? What great and mighty things will you do now, through those who believe in Your Son?

EPILOGUE

Rain beats against stone. Wind rattles the parchment on the tiny window where Mary huddles beside the hearth, a bedrug pulled close around her shrunken shoulders. She hears military boots tramping nearer. Blood pounds in her ears. She does not breathe.

The stamping halts. Spear handles clatter on stone. They are Herod's soldiers ferreting out any who follow Jesus—with orders to kill them—especially the mother of the despised Messiah.

They are gone now, on down the street. She imagines them peering into windows, courtyards, doors.

At last they have found me, even hidden here outside the walls. They will be back, and I am ready...or am I? My heart yearns to be with you, Jesus. It is so easy to say death is welcome until one faces it. But death is not welcome when it comes with blood like it did to... I will not think of them now.

Here I sit in Zebedee's reed chair. If a soldier looks in the window, he will see an old lady sleeping. He will not feel my heart plummeting like floodwater over rocks in the Jordan. He will not know who I am.

That it should come to this, when your kingdom started so gloriously that day of Pentecost. I remember that morning, the sun drinking dew from roses and lilies, sparkling on the pool. We first heard wind far across the city, that rushing mighty sound advancing. No leaf stirred. Terror bit deep. The Holy Spirit came with a roar that filled the room, wrapped me in a whirling vortex of joyous power, yet not one hair moved. And flame—something like it—rested on my head. Then both were gone, leaving a peace and joy such as I won't know again until I see you face to face. But, you know all this.

The power of that baptism drove your followers into the street to talk to everyone they met. It did not surprise me that Ancilla went charging into the crowd.. But me? You know I shy from strangers, but that day I found myself reaching out to those around me. I looked straight into their eyes, told them you'd come, been crucified and had risen again. My mind staggers after all these years. What a day! Three thousand added to your kingdom.

The peace fades from Mary's face. She rises to place more coals upon the fire, watches them glow. She mounds bread dough rising in a bowl and places it near hot stones. She leans back and pulls the bedrug closer. Her feet rest on the hearth, her toes pointed toward the flame. She closes her eyes a few moments.

A gust of wind drives smoke toward Mary. She coughs, wipes her eyes. She rises to peer through the parchment, sees no one and lifts the heavy oak bar from the door. Pulling it back a few inches, she breathes deeply. Wind slams it shut. She sits down with her memories to wait.

I remember only sunshine those first few years. Oh, the miracles your chosen men accomplished. They healed the dumb and palsied, brought sight and new strength. Demons ran screaming from them. Just Peter's shadow healed those it fell upon.

My Simon was always with them, but not my James. I know now—although it embarrassed me then—that God placed James as a clerk in the Great Council of the Sanhedrin.

Without him there, we would not have known what your enemies were doing.

I see Ancilla in the streets, the markets, in the Court of the Women, telling them of You and your resurrection, your death in place of theirs.

Knowing I was your mother, people knelt before me, touched me. But that was not what I wished. My ministry was prayer. Whenever I went anywhere I was careful to pull a cloak over my face. You know, my son, I didn't want glory as your mother. All praise must go to you.

But I am your mother, and a mother is never free from her children, always held to them by invisible cords that cannot be severed. They bind more tightly every day.

The top of Mary's head feels heavy today. She massages it with cold fingertips, adjusts her back and presses a hand against her heart. She wonders why it races so. She takes several deep breaths and leans back against Zebedee's chair.

Simon and I talked of it often—why you allowed us to suffer. Maybe those first great victories gave us courage to face the rest. And you send angels. Always angels, but I only saw them twice—Gabriel that night and the two when you ascended. I still see the amazed look on the faces of Peter and John when angels opened all the locks on Herod's jail and brought them both out. I see Peter pointing his finger in old Annas' face and telling him Jesus' followers would not stop speaking about You.

"Whom should we obey?" I hear him say, "God or you?" If Peter hadn't been surrounded by your followers, he'd have been killed that moment. Those were exciting days.

*

Mary places more charcoal on the fire, settles back in the chair and presses a hand against her heart.

You didn't answer our prayers the second time, the time all of your twelve were in prison while the Great Council debated what to do with them. We sisters stood right beside their meeting place. My James brought us word as we waited. Why did you let it happen, Jesus? I think I know. We were so content in Jerusalem, saw so many believe in You. The Holy City was not where you wanted us. You had said Judea, Samaria, the uttermost parts of the world—to others we knew not of.

I do not know what will happen to them in those far-off places, I only know the persecution your men endured in the City of Peace, especially that dreadful time that accursed Annas had them flogged. I see them dragging themselves toward us across the marble of Solomon's Porch, white-faced but praising God found them worthy to suffer for you. We helped them to Salome's, carefully removed outer tunics from those bloody backs, cut away torn flesh. I found only valerian tea to bathe the wounds, to wash the purple welts. I had nothing else until Nicodemus secretly brought wormwood and skullcap. You knew such floggings would never stop your apostles.

No persecution could stop me, either.

It started with Saul—that prideful hypocrite, fierce and full of hatred. Hate—I've always had trouble with that sin. The first Herod who crippled Ancilla, Antipas who cru… I still cannot say that word. Now Herod Agrippa, whose soldiers search for me. Except the Holy Spirit gives me grace, I cannot help hating them.

It was sleeting that day when Stephen faced Annas and

others of the Council and told them they killed God's son. Ancilla and I watched them drag him to the Hinnon Valley, that burial place for the unrighteous dead. We saw them stone him. But you know all this. How could you allow it, Jesus? Then Stephen looked up into those black clouds and cried that he saw you standing at God's right hand. I stared upward, too, but I didn't see you. Oh, how much I wanted to.

At the window, Mary notices the wind has lessened, but rain still lashes the house. More waiting. Waiting. Waiting for death.

It is past noon, but she cannot tell the time with clouds so dark. She toasts a piece of cheese over the coals and spreads it's melted goodness on a fresh baked bread loaf.

It would be no wonder if my heart were as feeble as Salome's—after all I've lived through. They saw a human heart does not break, but, oh, it bleeds, it bleeds.

Was it only a year ago Salome's Thunder James and I walked across Herod's marble bridge, taking our time, absorbing the early sun?

Thunder James and I. We keep our secret. We've let no one know that an old priest, and one of your followers, helped us inside the Temple—early before anyone was about. We entered the Holy Place in awe. I saw the place where Gabriel spoke to Zacharias. I don't know how we dared, but the curtain that divided mankind from God's dwelling was split in two. We barely stepped inside. I never asked him if he saw it too, but I did. A glow of light that faded as I looked. We hurried back to hiding, past praying priests. I do not regret it. But—

*

Thunder James and I crossed the bridge and stopped to listen as Herod Agrippa spoke. He said something I could not hear and waved his arms. Before anyone could protest, a guard knocked Thunder to the ground, forced his head against a block of marble. One great sword swipe rolled his head to my feet. I picked it up, smoothed back the black curls, looked into his sightless eyes.

Why, Jesus, why? I know you loved him.

Your followers lifted his body, but I bore his head. How could I tell his mother? I needed to say nothing. When Salome saw her son, she wiped blood from his cheek, as a mother will— and joined him in death. Perhaps hearts do break. We buried them in Joseph's tomb.

Agrippa saw how his death pleased the Jewish leaders, and our lives were forfeit from that day. It matters not. They cannot touch me until my time is come. Didn't you say that more than once?

Mary glances at the parchment, notices the darkness. She wonders why her sight is blurry and thinks it is evening. She feels a pressure in her head, pays no attention, thinking sad memories bring it. Just a few more. So few left.

Jesus, the most sorrowful day of my life was at your cross. The pain never leaves. The day Ancilla died was second. That ache is always with me as well.

I blame Agrippa.. He pressed upon the priests and even ordinary people to watch that no one desecrated the Temple. He gave authority to common men to kill any breaking one of those Temple rules.

Ancilla and I were in the Court of the Women. She saw a woman crippled as she had been and brought her to me through the crowd. We were standing on the bottom step below the altar. Ancilla told her she would heal her, make her straight. Doubt clouded the woman's face—and fear distorted mine. That stabbing pain in my heart again.

Ancilla took her hands firmly, looked deep into her eyes and shouted that she be healed in Your name. A woman healing in the Temple! The god Pandemonium ruled.

They dragged her out the Beautiful Gate, down the steep road, past the roots of David's City to the Hinnon Valley. I felt the spear pierce her back. Saw her fall. Herod's soldiers marched past me, back to God's Temple. Then Matthias charged toward her, flinging workers aside. I reached them just as he lifted her in his arms, her blood staining his tunic. A most joyous smile replaced Ancilla's old pain lines. She was with you in heaven.

Mary lets tears bathe her cheeks. She does not wipe them away. The rain has stopped. She wishes the soldiers would find her, so that it would all be over before James comes. She would spare him seeing her die.

Herod will be here soon, and I am ready. I must face them alone, except that you are with me as you said you would be. But I cannot take your hand. I am alone as I was that night when no one believed God was your father, as alone as that day when Joseph died.

What happens when we die? Will I see You, as Stephen did, as did Ancilla?

*

Mary hears the tramping boots. They pause outside her door. She rises, heart fails; she half falls into the chair. A spear rips the parchment. She lies motionless, eyes closed.

Shoulders batter the door. Rough voices demand entrance.

Blood pounds in Mary's ears. Her breath comes in gasps. She opens her eyes. She no longer sees the door, only darkness.

Shadowy figures rise from corners of the room, not the soldiers, but Joseph—Ancilla—her mother. The battering shakes the walls. Something explodes in her head. Mary slumps slowly to the floor. Phantom horses march by. Herod in his chariot. The sights and sounds from so many years ago mix with crashing spears.

Mary lies on the cold stones. Sounds fade. She hears no more.

The door rips from its lintel.

MARY STANDS BATHED IN AUREATE LIGHT.
GOD'S SON, JESUS, TAKES HER HAND.
"COME, MOTHER,
COME WITH ME TO THE FATHER."

GLOSSARY

Abba	- Father or Daddy
Amphora	- Tall two-handled jar
Chazzan	- Teacher in the synagogue
Chel	- Terrace around the inner wall of the Temple
Diaspora	- Jews dispersed into foreign lands
Essenes	- Religous sect on Dead Sea, awaiting coming of Messiah
Gehenna	- Popular expression for hell
Goad	- Pointed stick used to prod animals
Hallel	- Hallelujah psalms chanted at Passover Feast
Levites	- Descendants of Levi, set aside for service in Temple
Mazuzah	- Box by door containing scriptures to protect family
Nightjar	- night bird with a raucous cry
Parapet	- Low wall around flat roof of houses
Pharisees	- Religious sect which scrupulously obeyed religious law
Phylactery	- Amulet containing a piece of scripture for good luck
Rabbi	- Religious teacher
Sabbath	- Seventh day, Saturday, day of rest and worship
Sadducees	- Religions sect which did not believe in life after death
Selah	- "So be it"
Scourge	- Three-thonged leather whip with fragments of bone or metal
Shard	- Piece of broken pottery
Soreg	- Stone partition separating gentiles from inner Temple
Torah	- Hebrew canon of Law (the five books of Moses)
Valerian	- Strong herb used as a sedative

JEWISH MONTHS / FESTIVALS

Month	Season/Activity	Festival
Tishri	- September/October Ploughing	New Year/Trumpets (1st) Day of Atonement (10th) Tabernacles (15th-21st)
Marchesvan	- October/November Grain Planting	
Kisleve	- November/December	Dedication/Lights
Tebet	- December/January Spring growth	
Shebat	- January/February Winter figs	
Adar	- February/March Pulling flax	Purim (13th/14th)
Nisan	- March/April Barley harvest	Passover/Feast of Unleavened Bread (14th) Unleavened Bread (21st)
Iyyar	- April/May General harvest	(7 weeks)
Sivan	- May/June Vine tending	Pentecost
Tammuz	- June/July First ripe grapes	
Ab	- July/August Summer fruit	
Elul	- August/September Olive harvest	

MONEY IN NEW TESTAMENT TIMES

Jewish coins	-	lepton, small coin, one sixteenth of a denarius
Greek coins	-	gold talent, equal to two years laborer's wages
Roman coins	-	denarius, a laborer's day's wagers
	-	quadron, small coin, equal to twenty-four denarii

FOR FURTHER STUDY

SCRIPTURES WHERE MARY IS MENTIONED

Matthew	1:16-25
Matthew	2: 1-23
Matthew	12:46-50
Matthew	13:55-56
Mark	6: 3
Luke	1:26-80
Luke	2: 1-52
Luke	8:19-21
Luke	11:27-28
John	2: 1-12
John	19:25-27
The Book of Acts	

SCRIPTURES WHICH INVOLVE MARY

Isaiah	7:14
Acts	1-12

SCRIPTURES WHERE I HAVE PLACED MARY

Matthew	27:52-53
Luke	7:11-17
Luke	7:36-50
John	7: 2-10
Acts	1 - 12

To order additional copies of

Above All Women

please send $14.95*
plus $2.00 shipping and handling to:

Patricia Pfeiffer
The Parchments
P. O. Box 104
Otis Orchards, WA 99027-0104

or to order by phone,
have your credit card ready and call

1-800-917-BOOK

*Quantity Discounts are Available